Dancing Blind

Morgan Zeitler

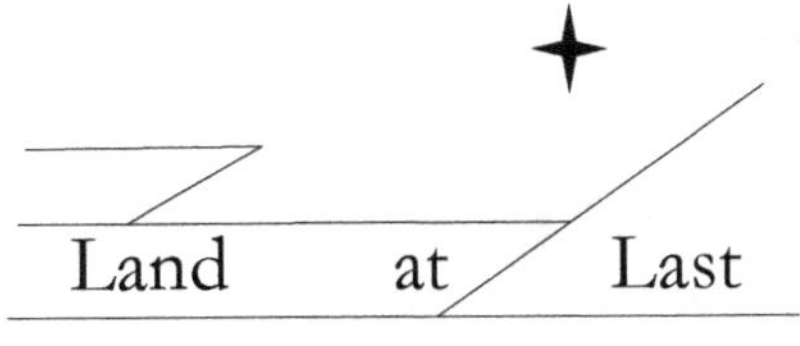

A Land at Last Book

Land at Last Publishing Company
15201 Seadrift Ave., Suite 98
Caspar, CA 95420, USA
www.landatlast.com

This is a work of fiction. All persons, places, incidents, things and entities named within are products of the author's imagination or are used fictitiously. Any resemblance to persons, living or dead, events, locales, things or entities is entirely coincidental.

Publishers Cataloguing-in-Publication Data
Zeitler, Morgan W., 1953—
Dancing Blind / Morgan Zeitler
322 Pages, 20 cm.
ISBN 9780997451603
1. Fiction, Literary 2. Fiction, Detective.
I. Zeitler, Morgan 1953— II. Title
PCN 2016909606

Cover art by Erica Fielder Studio, Mendocino, CA

Cover Design by Morgan Zeitler

Table of Contents

Acknowledgments

That this book approaches the one I envisioned is due largely to the advice of Deborah McCaskey and Robert Bovenschulte, who exhibited that rare measure of true friendship, in that they both cared enough to tell me the truth.

I also received invaluable advice from the cover artist, Erica Fielder, who gave freely of her experience with graphic design, layout, and use of color, all of which helped improve my book cover design enormously.

With special thanks to my wife, Carolyn, who yet harbors an unreasonable faith that someday she will be married to a successful author.

Will the people in Heaven be privileged to see the people in Hell—
—and what should their attitude be?

Saint Thomas Aquinas
(Allegedly)

CHAPTER I

ONE-WAY MIRROR

The old interview room was bigger, but there got to be too much clutter in Property and Evidence and the rooms were exchanged. Or the functions were. Little more than a closet, the tiny room's former self persisted—passively, stubbornly—asserting a mute and stark refusal to be so casually displaced. Six months later when Porter walked in there was that same mildewed cardboard odor not yet usurped by the sour reek of trapped sweat. The rest of the room's shortcomings had submerged into the familiar nearly enough to pass for acceptable until he was sitting on the other side of the laughably small table waiting for a response. Then he would notice, again, that no one had gotten around to painting over the stripes that shadowed where the shelves had been on the concrete walls, confronting him with a ladder print of gray horizons backed with beige. There was still the screw that once held the in-out log above a black crescent marking years of swinging clipboards. Curls of masking tape dangled orphaned corners of torn-down memos.

While there was no denying an unfortunate honesty about the room, the coarse nakedness of such an inept bureaucratic portrait made the idea of achieving real revelation in this setting seem as remote as intimacy; resolution impossible. At best, it was a poor rendering of regrettable liaisons long since departed. Packed away and carried out with the other boxes awaiting some final disposition that might never come, marked only for the shredder when and if it did. If perfection was ever imagined here, it was satisfied with paint-by-numbers commitment excused with policy gridlines and a check-box palette. What remained was even less, less than a waiting room, some ante-chamber of forfeit as forlorn as the paper clip on the floor there scuffed into a corner, exposing an abandoned and haphazard attempt to produce even a superficial depiction of integrity. Of order. And again he would wonder how he could forget that these things bothered him the minute he walked out. How the room that had remained unfinished for so many months could be overlooked again so easily, if never quite forgotten, because it was an annoyance renewed every time he found himself sitting there, steeping in the transparent expedience of it. That a room shrugged aside for so long because of its occasional use made the whole operation seem a complacent sham; the truth?—misplaced.

Of course his new partner, Joel Vega, was all for trading the two rooms, and the move was, in fact, Joel's idea. Joel was not much for cultivating ambience or waltzing with interview subjects. Increasing the sense of forced proximity was a way of upping the pressure on their guests that sat just fine with him. In a few more years Joel might learn that a larger, less threatening room had its uses, especially with virgin witnesses who might be unaware of information they could have rattling around in the white noise of their misapprehensions. The only way to tease it out was to get them to talk, and the bigger the room the more relaxed they would be, not realizing that a vaster emptiness exerted a subtle urgency of its own, and they would begin talking to fill that expanse. More room was an asset that could disarm a suspect. Could coax an unguarded admission or a conflicting statement. Space gave you options. Try an opening. Watch the reaction. Back off, slow down, cue a different overture if the plan going in did not work out. Take whatever time you needed because you had the room to wander.

Now the freedom to court a subject was reduced to simple extortion, served only confrontation; a shotgun wedding with the barest pretense of engagement. The new arrangement would minimize any opportunity to get real answers to some of the questions anyone else would have no right to ask. Not the whats, but the whys. The real whys. Why this person and not some other? People had a million ways to stray. Others had as many ways seemingly to be wronged. Each had a story. But there was a world of difference between hearing, *I did it for the money*, and, *I never had anything, so I always felt like a nobody. I want what others have.* Backgrounds that could incline someone toward victim as easily as offender. Either type of admission was unlikely to change the outcome, except for a reduced sentence here and there, but obtaining such disclosures had a way of coloring the proceedings with, if not redemption, at least a belated tint of humility, a blush of honor. It happened so rarely that the chances of witnessing such a fleeting touch of grace face to face in a tiny room were essentially nil. A confessional at least came with an expectation of trust and forgiveness, a shroud of anonymity. Joel had yet to learn that, but it would not be today. The room, the case itself, not to mention the ever-expanding caseload heaped on Senior Investigator Michael Porter's in-box, precluded it, unfortunately.

No, this interview was looking to be Joel's favorite, not Porter's. The criminal justice equivalent of a smash and grab. The prospect of being party to enlightening yet another unfortunate tripped up by human frailty was made more tedious by Porter's increasing conviction that the effort was doomed to be self-defeating under these cramped circumstances, like wetting your pants on a cold day for the momentary warmth. If the state could only impose its social norms via the blunt instrument of the power vested in the Porter-Vega puppet show, if their suspect's own crashing ineptitude in realizing even a penny from his nickel-and-dime enterprise was not embarrassing enough to send him on the straight and narrow, the two investigators could hardly kid themselves that they were helping anyone turn a corner, especially elbow to elbow in a room they could barely turn around in. Their subject would be back in a room just like this one in no time. The prospect was dispiriting and embarrassing, because to exploit a suspect's weaknesses for the barest nod of culpability was to acknowledge Porter's own, and the dull treadmill of his own circumstances. Which meant he and Joel could chew on this guy all morning, but there would never be an outcome of enough humanity, enough decency to imbue the proceedings with some degree of dignity. They might as well chew on their own neckties: colorful but flavorless wads of mastication with which to expedite a morning when Porter would not succumb to eating breakfast. At least in this regard he and Joel were after the same end for once.

Because, short or long, an interview in his current condition had another drawback. A growling stomach was sure to be a distraction for both Porter and their suspect, a grumbling giveaway that the investigator would prefer to be someplace other than such a grim room after fifteen years of police work, from which their guest might infer to his advantage that one of his interrogators still had a lot to learn, still had a long way to go, and not just until lunch. It could further suggest that he might succeed in being on his own way if he could draw out the proceedings long enough to outlast Porter's foodstuff deficiency. In that, their suspect would be mistaken. However sad his tale, however much Porter might regret the necessity, they would dispense with him faster than the first French fry in Porter's basket of crispy cod at the Wayfarer. No, the end of the line for the guy in the interview room might be unworthy of the state's expensive means, but his ride would soon be over for perhaps a year with good behavior, Porter and his partner would see to that, if only to retire a morning that was otherwise merely a shameful glimpse of tales people tell to disguise their failings. Then off to lunch, after which he could languish in the gloriously lukewarm soak of another box checked, and his latest success could be filed away in a cabinet stuffed with folders full of Porter's stock

in trade: paper-thin renditions of bumper-car entrepreneurs unlikely to self-invent governors for their throttles.

The freeway from Roseville was full of the brethren that
morning, all headed to the same end, just taking different off
ramps, and each one wanting to get there first. As if none of
them, including himself, had a destination beyond a crawl to an
imaginary checkered flag. Porter found himself sighing to the
windshield again.

It doesn't matter, folks. A cubicle is still a cubicle.

Porter knew where he was headed, but it did not help. Losing your way was not the way the boy scouts described it, as trav-
eling in circles, covering the same ground over and over hoping
to arrive at a different, happier locale. Lost was joining the same
stultifying funeral procession every day knowing exactly where
you were going to wind up. Would it be asking too much for a
little Dixieland jazz for an escort? Sacramento's radio stations
were not in the mood, apparently.

And then his chest hurt again. Center and, more disturbing, maybe a little to the left, but he was probably imagining
that. More likely a stuck vitamin pill gulped with day-old coffee for breakfast, or trying ten pushups when his daily regimen
was zero. But there was also this combination of near bursting and squeezing at the same time that seized his inhale half
way, choked it off. This won't do. Take it easy. Slow down. Just
breathe. Too much coffee and not enough exercise. He was going to work on that. Skip breakfast like this morning and cut
back on second-breakfast burritos from the roach coach. What
was he, a Pavlov dog to leap at the sound of cucaracha horns
tootling in the parking lot outside the office complex at ten every day? Tomorrow he would start bringing some self-respect
from home in a paper bag. The thing would take care of itself.
Nothing to see here. Move along.

Besides, the holiday spirit was upon the land. Porter could
tell by the wreath of pine boughs fronting the carnivorous grill

of a rubber-ducky yellow military menace filling his back window. In a hurry for Christmas like everything else, and Thanksgiving was still a week off. And all of this was reason enough for his funk, and none of it, and he knew it, which just made the trip seem interminable. But he was not ready to go through the whole file.

Porter told Joel he would fill him in on the walk, but only flipped through the folder for effect as he led the way down the narrow half-lit hallway, reciting from memory, omitting any speculation on what might contend beneath the unremarkable mendacity of the Hendricks' crime without a defensible reason for doing so, which Porter could not see at the moment. Joel would have only Porter's back and his matter-of-fact delivery to read as he brought up the rear. Truth was, Porter felt himself succumbing to a tendency to lump these cases by type, chagrined by his failed attempt to blot out the transcript of the interview he could see as clearly as if the clerks had already typed it up. Even without quotation marks to set off his statements, Mr. Hendricks' guilt would leap off the page as plainly as the stark facts of the life Porter was about to interrupt. Maybe if the recent bio was not in fact so mundane. Then he might not already have sketched the broad outlines of Mr. Hendricks' back story, a life he could guess as well as he knew his own. Likely the result of a youth squandered in a fantasy of heroic pretensions derailed by the first stumble that resulted in an abraded knee. Rather than attend to his setback and draw some value from the effort, Mr. Hendricks ignored his wound and let it fester until it scabbed over with capitulation and avoidance patterns that had a crippling effect, confining him to the playground of his first fall. He would be no match for the adult world street fight. For aspirations drenched in disappointments, much less actual blood. Porter could tell Mr. Hendricks a lot about that, as could the kid that bled out at Porter's feet, if he could. Each was about as unlikely. Certainly in that tiny room. That left discussing dust specks.

As expected, Mr. Hendricks was upside down and behind on his condo mortgage. Maxed out credit. He might as well have left a trail of runway lights to his doorstep which, unfortunately, left little reason, or at least official justification for picking through the understory; the one place that might better illuminate, might elevate the encounter for all involved. But Porter was hungry, and social worker was not his job, at least as long as he had a new partner barely on leash and a boss who even now was probably piling new case files on his desk. So which was worse, pretending this was not the second time in a week he had to hear how a car the owner could not afford got stolen out of his driveway and set on fire, with no compelling reason he could point to for taking time to unearth details that might set this story apart from the others and leave them all feeling like humans, or slogging through his own dreary routine with Joel? It was a brutal sort of efficient when Porter softened them up a bit and then Joel laid it out for them, leaning across the table with his wavy, collar-length eastside chop job and his cheesy little mustache—

You think we stupid, güey? Huh? You think you would be here if you weren't going *down*?—

A bit of a put-on since Joel, despite his common roots, had a law degree from Berkeley. Then Porter would stand and casually swing a thigh over the corner of the table to close the distance, ease his weight, exude a sigh to get the suspect's attention, and talk to his fingernails—

Look, son, it's obvious you didn't think this thing through. You're not alone. Everyone's feeling the pinch these days. People are losing their jobs, their homes. You must be under a lot of pressure. We can see that. Now it's time to do the right thing so you can put this behind you—

A one-size-fits-all cloak of human kindness to offer in exchange for his confession. But they would be in and out before the suspect knew what happened or, for that matter, before the two investigators knew what happened, what really happened. But that was not their concern. There was nothing to do but hand Joel the photo, along with his complicity.

You'll be happy to know this one's an in-and-out, Joel.

Joel was not having it.

A Chorro burrito says you don't roll him in under ten.

Joel would win either way on that bet, and Porter told him so, which made Joel laugh, which was as good an entrance as if they had planned it.

Mister Hendricks gave himself away with a little twitch when they burst into the room all flapping ties, slapping files, and scraping chairs. Then he settled back into the semi-slouch Porter had watched him practice through the one-way mirror. Skinny. Acne. Cheap haircut gone feral. Agitated equals guilt. Smart enough not to go flat out who cares banger-wannabe sprawl. Not smart enough to just sit up, fold his hands on the table and challenge them to put up or shut up. Been in here thirty-five minutes but not angry or asleep. Worried is why. And with good reason. He and Joel might as well be two muggers.

Mr. Hendricks was also at a tactical disadvantage in having to waste energy trying to decipher the disparity in styles presented by the Porter and Vega team. Joel was half a foot shorter, dusky, with a thick, low shelf of eyebrow and a knife ridge of nose that suggested innate physicality distilled through generations of nomads, perhaps Berber, but professed as Castilian on the pass of his thin lips and carved cheekbones. Despite his modest size, something about his lean frame was suggestive of violence barely suppressed, a man who would exact revenge for ordinary slights far out of proportion to the insult, perhaps sidling up to you months later in an alley with a child's baseball bat that could be both more easily secreted and employed with sudden and astounding dexterity. This volatile mixture was forced into dark blue or black Italian suits Joel could barely afford, cut short and tight so that his wrists and ankles were a little too much in evidence in the style favored by teens and reluctant adults. Joel's ensemble was completed with explosive movements and the intensity of his delivery.

Porter's style tended to brown-on-brown off the sale rack, a bit on the baggy side which afforded comfort, concealment of certain weighty disadvantages, and room for expansion, which seemed to be his latest trend. His tepid couture not only made sense for a sizable man with a family's expenses, but nicely complemented the washed out eyes that accused him in his morning-after mirror, the deflated jowls that were threatening to become his permanent dependents. It also helped to put him under a suspect's radar long enough for the setup, with Joel swinging by occasionally to kick the cage. Off we go.

Good afternoon, Mister Hendricks. Thank you for coming in. I'm Investigator Porter. This is Investigator Vega. Sorry about the wait. Something came up. Would you like another cup of coffee? (Because nervous and talkative can save us some time here.)

Badges, business cards. Casual toss of the pocket digital recorder on the table since the room still was not wired. All on the up and up. Joel stepped to his mark and took a lean on the wall to one side of the suspect, palms behind him in the casual parade rest of a man waiting for the welfare office to open, his face as flat and bland as the wall, except for his eyes, which traced Hendricks' profile in a seemingly endless loop. Porter used a moment to let Hendricks simmer while he admired this bio-mechanical marvel. Joel could be a computerized quality-control laser scanner probing a product for flaws, or a forensic x-ray machine peeling back layers of faked pigment on a purported masterpiece. Porter squeezed into a chair on the far side of the battleship-gray prison industry table across from the suspect. There was still a clear path to the door, but, with Porter and Joel on either side of the room, the subtle gauntlet of this arrangement could not have been lost on Mr. Hendricks, at least subconsciously. Porter went first.

No? OK. As I said, we're from the Department of Insurance. We need to get some more information from you about the disappearance of your car.

Mr. Hendricks seemed anxious to give voice to his nerves.

I don't understand. I already reported it to the police.

(Intent knit of the eyebrows. Must like B-grade movies, but sitting up straight now. That did not take long.)

Yes, Mister Hendricks. Actually it was the county sheriff. I have the report. When was that?

Mr. Hendricks' eyes did the back and forth flit between their faces.

Right after I came out of my house to go to work and it wasn't there. Um, last Monday. Didn't they write that down?

Yes, they did, Mr. Hendricks. But there's a few things that don't make sense. You want their report to make sense don't you, so your claim gets processed right away?

Well, I, uh. Sure. But doesn't that—shouldn't that mean I should be talking to them?

You want to talk to a sheriff deputy? This is about your insurance claim. I thought we explained that.

Oh. No. Yes—What?

Great. So, you went to bed the night before. About what time?

Uh, around eleven forty-five. Twelve. Right after the late news.

(Eyes up to the right. Wants us to see he's thinking hard. Mister Cooperative.)

And, you woke up around?

Six. I got to get out the door by six thirty to be at the lumber yard by seven.

How'd you sleep?

How? OK, I guess. Why?

Just trying to get the full picture. Sometimes we overlook the simplest stuff, and then have to go back and check. Saves time. So you were home, in bed, from, let's say midnight to six the next morning, the morning of the thirty-first?

Uh, I don't...yeah. I got paid the day after, the first. Hey, listen, I got to get back. I'm supposed to be back from lunch already. Can I call my boss?

I don't think this will take much longer. We'd be happy to have someone call and give them a message, though. What's the number?

They watched Hendricks ponder the implications, watched him choke.

Uh, never mind. But can we hurry up?

Hey.

Joel came off his wall. Porter showed an upright index finger to Hendricks, but it was really for Joel. He ignored Joel's look, and went ahead.

Mister Hendricks, you want to help us process your claim, don't you? You want your money, don't you?

Yeah, I suppose.

You suppose? Help us out here. Surely there's more than what's in this report that brought us together here today.

The remark could be innocuous or not, either challenge or offer, which was exactly the intent. Hendricks' eyes floundered from face to face, Porter not needing to look to know that Joel's face would be too jagged for Hendricks to try a finger hold, and Porter's deadpan too slick to grip.

You guys said you had some questions. About my claim. So I came down. That's all I know.

Porter decided it was time, for a host of reasons.

Actually, I think you know a little more than that. Mister Vega?

Joel did his best insolent lean over Hendricks' shoulder and flipped open the file that Porter had placed on the table, giving it a spin so it faced Hendricks. Joel kept his lean on the table and spoke to the subject's right ear.

Do you recognize anyone in this photo?

It was grainy, and night, but the area around the pump island was truck-stop bright, and the person filling the gas can was unmistakably their suspect. Hendricks did the death-spiral stall, pretending to study the photo, rifling through his options past any reasonable time for a response, and finally squeaked when even he had to see that any further delay was costing him.

That looks like me.

Joel snorted.

How about it *is* you? How about we look at those numbers down in the corner that show you filling that can at three in the morning next to your shiny new Mustang the night you say it was stolen, when your twin was home asleep two miles away at your house?

Now Hendricks did the whole giant octopus freak out, squirting the verbal equivalent of his colon contents in all directions in the hope that it would look like ink.

That date can't be right. That was, like, a week before. I stopped to help a guy who ran out of gas. I wouldn't have reported it if I thought I was gonna get jerked around by you guys. Why would I set my own car on fire? I gotta go. You can keep the payout, but leave me alone. You can't treat me like this.

Joel stepped back and spread his arms, his expression melting into a smug beatific, and reprised a soliloquy Porter was already tired of.

Thank you, Mister Hendricks. Once again, my faith in the perfectibility of mankind has been renewed. You want the door? There it is.

Hendricks puffed up. Either for another blow or preparatory to a, *Yeah-don't-mess-with-me* bluff as he made a try for the door. Porter had already come around the table dragging his chair with him, and sat down with his back to the door facing Hendricks. He down-boyed Hendricks with a gentle downward push of his palm, moved his chair closer until their knees were almost touching, and then did his softest co-conspirator.

You're free to do anything you like, Mister Hendricks, but there are a couple things you might want to consider before you go.

Hendricks stayed put, so it was closing time.

There's still the issue of the loan. The bank told Steadford Insurance to put a flag on your policy as soon as they got the stolen vehicle report from DMV. That's because the bank owns your car, not you, until you pay off the loan. Since you are three months behind on your payments the bank is on the lookout for this sort of thing even if the insurance company drops the ball. They even have a name for it: Flamer Claim. So, yes, you are free to walk if you want, Mister Hendricks. But your first stop should be to find a good lawyer. Not just for civil court, but criminal, too. Because, unfortunately, that's what this is, Mister Hendricks. A crime.

I'm not a criminal. Who the hell—

Joel shoved in.

You most certainly are, and not a very bright one at that.

Porter twisted in his chair to ape cocked-head astonishment at Joel, as though Joel had spontaneously combusted. Joel ignored him.

So let's stop the charade, shall we? The only way you might avoid serious jail time is to start cooperating.

Now it was Hendricks who looked about to combust.

Where's your boss? I want to file a complaint.

This was getting old. The dance. The dishrag odor clinging to the walls. The stench of terror oozing from Hendricks. The ruthless hall monitor dragnet that condemned every minor truant to extended detention as incorrigible, with Vice-Principal

Vega pinching their ears, a bully in a business suit with the weary collaboration of Principal Porter. Joel was now really on fire.

Sure, why not? Let's get the governor in here, too, while we're at it. Call the newspapers. Let's show them what a fine example of upright citizenry you are. After all, there's no money in it for you. Even if the insurance company believes you and writes a check, that check is going to the bank. But you'll still owe the bank because the car dropped a couple grand the minute you drove it off the lot. You'd have been better off to just tell the bank to come get it. Now does that make sense to you? Listen up. People steal cars to go for a joy ride, rob a bank, part them out or ship them to Africa. The only people who torch the cars they steal are trying to cover up some crime. The only people who pretend to steal their own cars and torch them are owners who can't afford the payments. But of course that never occurred to you, did it Mister Hendricks? It's a wonder you can find your way home at night. You're not smart enough to beat this thing, but that doesn't mean it's not too late to wise up.

If Joel was expecting Hendricks to do the sigh with shoulder slump that signaled the flashing white belly roll of a spent trout as it is brought alongside the boat, it looked more like Hendricks was about to leap into the boat in pike fashion, all fang and attitude. The flexing jaw muscles were certainly primed, but Hendricks managed a few words through his teeth.

So what do you want me to do?

Joel ignored the jaw and backhanded the eyes.

Do? Mister Porter and I don't want you to do anything except quit wasting our time. But if you want to write out a full account of what really happened to your car that night, we'll see that it gets attached to our report with a note that you were cooperative.

Joel stood implacably, while Hendricks' eyes thudded ineffectively off the heavy bag of his obvious indifference, looking for all the world as though he could not care less if Hendricks took an actual swing at him by way of cooperative.

Porter eased between them in a glacially slow screen of neutral pacification. He laid a legal pad and a pen on the table next to Hendricks and told him they would be back in a few minutes to see how he was doing. It was better to sit and watch to keep the pressure on in case the suspect wanted to change his mind, but he did not need to hold up a sign. Joel followed him out and down the hall to the break room, Porter ignoring Joel's *I miss something?* to make sure they were out of Hendricks' hearing. At the coffee pot, Porter got his and spoke up while Joel was in mid pour.

What's up with the barracuda-cop bit? You're lucky he didn't just flip us off and lawyer up.

Joel tried a double take, but had to watch his pouring. Had to talk to his occupied hands.

It didn't look that way to me. Did you see his face when I flashed the gas station print? I thought he was going to seize up and we were going to have to toss to see who had to do CPR.

OK, still, you didn't have to rub his nose in it. The way you got down on his whole act. That was pretty cold.

Joel set the pot back. He was still pumped with himself. Still tried to sell incredulous.

I'm sorry. I must have missed the hand-holding session at the academy. Did I violate someone's constitutional right to full self-esteem?

Porter just looked at him and sipped his coffee, while Joel turned his smile to the wall clock over the sink as if hoping for a better reception there, leaving Porter to wonder why they had bothered. Angela always turned off the pot around ten, so the coffee was barely lukewarm, with congealing bitterness visibly ringing the sides in high water marks that told of prior staff visits. They both knew Joel was out of line, now twice over. Partner rule one, or maybe two after loyalty. You had to be as familiar to each other and as dependable as a brace of mules in matched collars. The bit with Mr. Hendricks was a change-up that Joel had not tipped Porter to. Not particularly inspired, and not appreciated. He was losing control of his trainee, who was losing control of himself.

Point is, your bedside manner is getting off course, Joel, and it can cost you. Maybe you were a tough guy back on the block, but that isn't enough here. If Hendricks went after you it would be hard for me to say you did not have it coming.

So I'm a thug now?

Back to incredulous. Joel's face weighed something else, said *hell with it*.

As long as we're talking history, Mike, here's something you should know. It's no secret DOJ bounced you over here. I don't know why, but, whatever you're here for, I didn't sign on to get snowed.

So there it was. Two rounds dead center right through Porter's 10-X ring. Whatever bitter delusion he was hanging onto in thinking that the new guy might not do some asking around, would see Porter's transfer from the Department of Justice the way nobody else had either, apparently, as some flavor of voluntary, went in the sink with the spit-warm remains in his cup.

Joel now stood looking at the floor, the break room having shrunk considerably for both of them, apparently. How had this veered to finger pointing about their pasts? Joel did not look like he wanted to go there any more than Porter did.

Look, Joel, these are simple cases. The idea is to learn some finesse. Hendricks might not have overreacted if I had said, maybe, *violation* instead of *crime*. Nobody would want to hear that, so that's on me. But it didn't help coming off like you find him disgusting. That just lets him pretend it's personal, too.

What if it is? I don't care if he wants to act upset. He's holding back. And don't forget, he's the reason you and I both pay too much for car insurance.

Trying a diversion twice. Joel should have known better. OK, Porter could play.

What he did was shut down and try to bail on us just when he was on the bubble. I don't always like what it takes to get there, but we got hired to close cases. I'm also not too happy about paying for a mortgage and an apartment at the same time, but Anita doesn't want me around. I still have to come to work every day. If I can do this, so can you.

Joel's averted eye made it clear this was not exactly a revelation to him either, or something very much like it was at least suspected. It still had the desired effect of tipping him off balance, but more by brute calculation than tact, scattering personal chaff as expedient brow beating, stooping to cheap tactics. Who was the bully now? And he was caught out, divulging more than he would have preferred. Now he had to absorb Joel's hang-dog aw shucks, and whatever was coming next.

You might have said something.

Porter thought the same.

Joel sighed.

All right. I may have gone a little overboard. Maybe we should go grab a beer after work.

Porter hoped his wince did not show on his face.

The temptation to do some confessing was something Porter fully understood, but no self-respecting counterfeiter would ever dish it all, especially to a cop and, in this case, a subordinate. It was not just Porter's situation Joel was daylighting, but their shaky alliance as well. Things between the two of them had been cooling since late summer, becoming less partner, more collegial, if that. Good enough for most jobs, marginal for this, and Porter had no idea why, until now. It seemed like they were meshing at first even with the age difference. He had Joel over to the house a few times, and Joel seemed to enjoy himself. But then Joel seemed to be pulling back, finding excuses, claiming he did not want them to go to any trouble. All that made a lot more sense now that Joel had also said a good deal more than he probably intended. Porter had thought Joel seemed like a hotshot in a hurry. Now he wondered if Joel's short-fuse routine with suspects was as much of a tell as his own pedantry. Whatever notions Joel had arrived at this job with, what he thought his ideal partner would be like, they could not have included dragging around with the walking dead. So, no, Joel's offer was not for real, and he need not pretend he would consider it. And do what, blubber in his beer about Anita?

No, but thanks anyway. I only mentioned it to try to make a point. It'll work itself out.

Joel suppressed a belch. How about a distraction, then? I have an extra ticket to the game next week. Or are you still taking your kids to soccer and stuff?

Soccer and stuff.

This was a lie; Roger's youth soccer league had wrapped up for the season, but he was not about to open the door to another of Joel's invitations. He would sooner go on pretending that long walks to escape his apartment, haunting art museums, and reading the Sunday *Bee* from headlines to comics was diverting enough. Time to change the subject.

And you? How's this working out? Yeah, yeah, besides this morning. You'll be off probation soon. Are you moving on?

Joel's hands went into his pockets, seemed relieved to change subjects, too, but his rueful pucker also had a bit of the deflective.

Well, the longer I'm away from it, the harder it is to gear up to take the Bar. I wanted to get some enforcement experience so I'd be a better prosecutor or defense attorney. Now I'm not so sure it matters. I like putting cases together.

This was effluvium, of course, as Joel had just made abundantly clear: he had a reject for a partner. Joel could not take that back any more than he could pretend these were not low-yield cases even for a new guy. Well, at least he and Joel were back on familiar ground, saying whatever would get them through the day.

Some case. So what about our friend down the hall? Are we good?

Joel ground the heel of his palm into one eye like a man trying to wake up, then remembers what it was that woke him. Now he was all business.

Do you really think he did this all by himself?

They had removed half the fluorescent bulbs in the break room to meet the state's energy reduction mandate, but the dimly lit room was suddenly too bright for Porter. Of course. The scheme was so common he had not bothered to cross off the boxes on his pre-flight checklist. Now he was skimming the tree tops on autopilot with an uncalibrated altimeter. Hendricks did not have time to dump the car and hoof it or hitch it back home in time to make the call to the sheriff. Too poor for cab fare even if he could get one to come to some alley in the dry-gulch fantasia of North Highlands at that hour. No bus service, at least not at four a.m. There had to be an accomplice. Which minor detail Hendricks had surely considered and was at that very moment studiously omitting from the scrawl of his incomplete and self-serving "confession."

As for Porter, he found no wiggle room at all in filling out his own scorecard:

Efficiency	0
By-the-book procedurals	0
Credibility with partner	-1
Self-indulgence	-1
Self-delusion	-2
RATING FOR THE DAY	A trifle short of complacent

The *HAPPY THANKSGIVING* banner festooned above the microwave drooped in reproach. And it was barely noon.

CHAPTER II

THE OVERLOOK

So Porter's first thought when he found himself talking to his former supervisor, Maddie, late that night was that somehow Joel had gotten her number and made a pitch. How else to explain Maddie digging him up to drag him back to DOJ limbo? Or was the caller an impersonator dangling a cruel trick for a joke? He knew people who were capable of it. The timing was certainly perfect. Vertigo always came with the calls that woke him. It was probably there when he was starting out, but back then he could bounce up and make the right noises into the phone while marveling at the receding landscapes glimpsed through doorways that were closing in the hallways of his mind even as he became aware of them. Nowadays his dreamscape vestiges were lost in the basket of trash he was rummaging through next to his desk. He needed the back of an old letter or envelope to write down the basics so he could distinguish reality from dim recall later when all he had to rely on were his own hieroglyphics. Unless he wanted his former deputy chief to know he could be rattled that easily in having to ask her to repeat herself. If in fact it was her. It sounded like her, but it had been awhile. Added to that was waking up in his apartment, which was still as disorienting as waking to a door slam in a strange hotel after six years in the same house.

It was her. Only Maddie would call a former employee in the middle of the night and spew directions as if he should have been expecting the call. She wanted him to get over to Breakwater and see about a car-over-the-side investigation. Not because of the car, but because of the occupant, apparently deceased. A woman someone in the administration wanted to make sure had no loose ends for the papers to sniff out.

And Michael?

She had been rattling on so fast it took a few moments for him to realize there was only the little hurricane sound of his own breathing coming back at him through the earpiece. She was waiting for a response.

Yeah?

You're from Insurance on this one. Not Justice. You with me? We're not in a position to leave any fingerprints until we find out more. This came straight from the Deputy A.G. I already pulled Warren in so they won't miss you at the office tomorrow. OK, so, questions?

His Department of Insurance boss, Warren, was a fat piece of deadwood in a bottom-drawer agency, but he was nobody's fool. Porter wondered what kind of lie Maddie had told him that would let her use Porter on a Department of Justice case, with Insurance holding the bag if he screwed up.

One.

Her sigh on the other end meant she did not want any.

Yes?

DOJ hasn't wanted anything from me in over a year. Why now? Or am I the only one who answered the phone at—three a.m.?

A bigger sigh.

Did it ever occur to you that you just might be in the right place at the right time? You know auto fraud. If nothing else it's good cover. As for the rest, we've been all over that, and I'm certainly not going to take it up with you again at this hour.

So we're talking fraud?

We're not talking anything until you go find out what it is.

Right. Then—

She had already hung up. Now here was his cell's tinkle. A voicemail from Warren OK'ing his loan, and telling him to take Joel along with him.

If the call was short the subsequent drive seemed endless, and was every bit as unsettling. In fact, getting anywhere by car in Whitley County seemed to involve driving in circles. Either the local road builders just followed ancient deer trails over the mountains, or they had no familiarity with the concept of a straight line. Porter's computer map, on the other hand, relied on satellites and lasers, resulting in a travel time estimate that was off by half. The roadside mileage markers said he was still a good thirty miles to the coast when his nausea hit a tipping point of curve after curve, brake and accelerate, his weight shifting side to side along with his stomach contents which consisted only of coffee and bile. No wonder the whole county only had forty-seven thousand residents. Even if the population noted on the sign at the county line was out of date, it was clear only hicks and people rich enough to own helicopters would put up with these roads. So they had Redwoods. Impressive towering columns so tall all his headlights picked out were huge, branchless trunks, the limbs out of sight somewhere overhead in the black. Hard to appreciate when his attention was directed the other way. He was leaning on a wall of bark by the side of the road trying to decide if he might be better off if he painted this one with his insides, or if he even had a choice. Turned out he did not, but he did his best to keep it away from his shoes which were already half buried in mud and leaf litter. An odor of mold and decay crept up on him as the sweat cooled on his forehead. Freeway signs were not just getting harder to read at night. A drive in the country that should have been a vacation by comparison to his freeway commute should not be rocking in his stomach. Joel offered to drive but Porter was having none of that, not unless Joel wanted to see some of this on the floorboards. What was he doing here? Was this even legal?

This was going to take some explaining all right, beginning with the CHP patrolman who was still parked at the overlook when they arrived. He was typing intently on his onboard computer, heedless of the career back pain he was feeding by twisting his torso to type on his center console, and oblivious to the scrap of yellow caution tape snaking around in the wind against his tires. If the clerks in Records whining about the ergonomics of their work stations could see this. It was not quite dawn, so the patrolman had to have noticed their headlights even if he could not hear their car with his windows closed up tight against the chill. Some officer safety. Or was he just so cool he already had them made? Not likely from the available information; Porter had to tap on the window to get him to look up from his console. And what was a rookie Chippy doing way up here anyway? Only guys with a couple decades of seniority used to make it to places like this, where there was so little action you could get lulled by the ocean breeze into letting someone walk up on you.

Help you? was all the patrolman said as the window came down, but Porter could see his hazel eyes waking up, doing the tardy size-up. Two guys, predawn. Windbreakers, polos and khakis that might as well have been their usual business suits. Haircuts. He craned around a little more to take in their dark blue sedan, and then deflated a little.

Look, I'm typing as fast as I can. The commander and everyone but the Pope has already been by. You guys will just have to take a number.

Porter handed in a business card. I'm Michael and this is Joel. We'd appreciate it if we could get a copy of the report, too.

The patrolman sat flicking the card with his middle finger, assaying its cheap stock. What the hell does Insurance have to do with this? Whatever company has the coverage can get a copy with a letterhead request. And you guys could have saved a drive with a phone call.

Well, here we are. And we have a thermos of hot black stuff. How about a cup?

That finally brought a handshake. His name was Eric. In keeping with the institutional ideal of command-presence manhood the California Highway Patrol valued above all else, Eric stood well in excess of six feet. He had the coast from the south county line to Breakwater, at least on paper. That did not include his partner transferring out, which left Eric with the coast run from county line south to county line north until they found a replacement. It seemed that senior officers were retiring faster than they could find even rookies willing to transfer to the boondocks where there were no big box stores, and no jobs for spouses to help afford the houses that had no right to be so expensive in the middle of nowhere. Eric had been assigned there straight out of the CHP academy. He was single, so the spouse problem was not an issue, except in the potential thereof. There was so little to pursue in that regard that he was just biding his time until he could transfer himself. Porter imagined that getting stuck here would be even worse for a man recently separated from his wife, never mind the prospects for a fortyish slab of pudge, which would be inversely proportional to his profile, and thus infinitely slimmer than a sculptured patrolman's. Anita, on the other hand, would have much better luck. She took care of herself, even if her calves might be considered a bit too defined for modeling from all her running. The average guy would still drool. She might already be out shopping. Might even interest Eric here, if he were just a few years older. Eric would certainly be amazed if he knew what Porter was thinking as he showed them where the Honda had gone over.

Over and then some. The debris trail got off to an explosive start about a hundred feet almost straight down, with paper scraps, plastic and tin scattered for about another hundred feet below that. They would have needed people who knew their ropes and knots just to get down there for a look around. Tricky winching, and not very many wreckers would have a cable long enough or would want to use it like this, but there was a cable groove in what was left of the low dirt berm at the edge of the overlook, and a recovery trench scraped all the way up from a lone rock escarpment. Probably trying to make points and keep the local cops happy for future calls even if it frayed a cable here and there.

Eric pointed out the scenic highlights. The driver was ejected near the initial impact, probably out the front windshield which popped out entirely and was not recovered, a sheet of glass sliding better than skin. They probably would not have found her either, but a ways farther down was a shred of bush that, despite looking too fragile for the job, was where the body hung up. Below this was the rock escarpment where they found what was left of the car wrapped around it, minus the front half. Below that was a straight drop to the surf.

Whoo, was Joel's summation of the scene as he kicked over a stone and watched it bounce down the cliff. Then he popped a more workmanlike question.

Did all that crap come out of one car?

Porter saw that what Eric's flashlight had picked out was mostly the rusted remains of prior events. Eric explained that the location was mapped as Cape Hallelujah, but had come to acquire a certain distinction. Locally, it was Cape Hal or, more prosaically, Hell's Corner. Porter swung around to look back along the path of travel, which had the momentary reward of putting his back to the vicious wind coming up the cliff. When they pushed their doors open against it on their arrival it was a shot of pure oxygen, blowing the sweat and nausea out of the car in an instant. Now it was just damned cold and his toes were going numb. He asked Eric if there was any sign of braking or swerving.

Nope—was Eric's pronouncement, the matter of fact way one would recite the weather forecast—Straight as an arrow coming out of the corner approach. Even weight on all four. No sign of deceleration or deviation from course of travel.

Eric's take on it was suicide most likely, with one departure from the norm that left a slim chance for accidental.

She was probably only going around ten or fifteen when she launched, but being a chick maybe she wasn't all-in until it was too late.

Joel beat Porter to this one.

How'd you figure that? You said there was no sign of braking. So what are you using to run a coefficient of friction with? And this is mud, not pavement.

Skids? Don't need 'em. Just look where the car hit first. The ones that are serious catch nothing but sky on the way to the water. I've also seen gravel scattered at the pavement edge because they are really getting it on by the time they leave the roadway. That didn't happen here, and without signs of panic braking or four wheel drift you can't say she just lost it on the curve. Which makes me think she mighta been pulling off for a smoke or to see if her cell phone had a signal and misjudged the edge in the dark, or was too toasted to notice, or whatever. We'll have to wait for the tox report and see if she left a note at home. I didn't find one in the half of car we recovered. Coroner's deputies came up empty too, at least here.

Body condition?

It was a dumb question, but Porter was not ready to ask one Eric might not like.

About what you would expect. Like someone tossed a rag doll. Blunt force everywhere. Major lacerations, knees and shoulders abraded, and one side of her face all mud and hamburger. She looks a lot hotter in her DL photo. Kind of a shame.

He knew Eric's remarks would sound crass to most civilians, but Porter read the code: this was an unfitting end to anyone, made the more poignant considering her youth and beauty. And unfair, he had to agree, seeing what Eric no doubt had also taken from the driver license photo clipped to the spring catch on the lid of the Posse Box he pushed across the Bronco's hood. Twenty-nine, five-eight, one twenty, brown over blue. You did not need a photo to guess she might be a knockout. But there were those eyes, bursting with conspiratorial glee despite the ritualized face-off beneath fluorescent lights with an anonymous functionary trying in vain to hide his boredom behind the camera array. It was a long way from those eyes to despair. And if it was clear from the picture, it was even more so given that Porter had seen those eyes for himself, watched them dance across his face, racing ahead of him while he teetered between blue or green, or if they were just picking up the color of her turquoise sweater to confuse him along with the distraction of a delicate perfume drifting over to him, as close as breath after a kiss. This had to be an accident, or something else.

Joel wanted to know where he was going.

Back to the car to get my flashlight. See if I can put myself in the driver's seat. Minus the aerobatics, of course. Coming?

Joel roused his shoulders, falling back from his cliff-edge roost.

Anything to keep warm.

Porter got a light and walked back through the Jackson Pollock mess of fire truck and tow truck duellie tracks and footprints, swinging wide as he neared the pavement to avoid the remnants of two narrow-gauge imprints running more or less undisturbed from the road edge. Like Eric had said, there was nothing out of order with the way the tracks left the pavement. Like someone pulled off and just kept going.

Take the passenger side, would you, Joel? He squatted and shot a beam a few inches above the ground and parallel to the tracks on the driver's side. Shining a light like this was a trick that made even pebbles jump up out of the surrounding surface and cast mountainous shadows. Alternating tiny ridges appeared, marching along next to the tire impressions.

I got footprints.

Joel was examining something on his side.

Me, too, but I think these are Eric's. There's little roll-a-tape furrows next to 'em.

With that, they both impelled forward, examining each impression from the side, then swinging their beams wide around and behind themselves in an elaborate and repetitive ritual to make sure they were not about to disturb anything not yet seen or had overlooked in passing. Of course, either set of footprints could have been anyone's. A lot had happened here in the last few hours. But, by the time the tracks disappeared in the jumble of recovery activities, the pattern was unmistakable. Would he have looked if he had not known the woman whose face was on the recovered driver license, Holly Morris, however briefly? Porter wanted to think so, but there was no way to tell unless he had lived a different life, and then he would not be in any position to wonder at all; he would have only his procedurals to rely on. He asked Joel to go pull Eric away from his paperwork. And then he returned to the highway to do what he had started to do in the first place. He walked north down around the corner following the center double yellows, letting his eyes get used to the dark again.

Now, if he were intent on doing himself, Porter pictured himself flooring it straight up the grade, then just holding the wheel straight when he got to the corner for maximum acceleration across the wide overlook before take-off. But, walking the road back up the hill to the pullout, he could see that the car had pretty much rounded the corner before turning off. That would not make any sense unless turning off was a snap decision. Or unless you wanted to be out of sight from any traffic approaching on the long straightaway from the north. But then you could not see if any traffic was coming yourself.

Back at the overlook, he confirmed that the car's last run could be arranged to be out of sight from traffic approaching in either direction. Headlights from the south would be visible rounding curves for at least a half mile. He then walked over to the far north corner of the overlook, which provided an unobstructed view down the north approach. Just off the pavement was a compass rose of footprints. Of course, they could belong to a tow truck driver killing time waiting for clearance to do his thing. There was a single cigarette butt, perfectly cylindrical, paper unstained, still a pristine white as though it had just been dropped. It could also have tumbled clear across the pullout in the wind.

Joel was pointing Eric to the prints and roll-a-tape tracks, which Eric confirmed were his, being left-handed. And no, he did not recall walking along the driver side, but a lot of people had been through here before he got around to taking measurements.

Porter allowed as how at least one did not appear to be sightseeing. He showed Eric where the footprints on the driver's side of the tire impressions were close together near the road, and the toes were dug in, pushing up little ridges of mud. Then the prints flattened out and spread farther apart. Finally, inexplicably, the prints came closer together again and angled inward toward the tire tracks.

Eric sighed the sigh of a man whose paperwork was just getting started.

I suppose this wasn't someone running alongside, trying to talk her out of it?

Porter smiled.

I don't think there was any talk at all, unless it was between this guy and his lookout over there just before he reached in and yanked it into gear. You got any more caution tape?

CHAPTER III

CRASH REPORT

The CHP investigators who were called took their photographs, impressions and measurements, avoiding eye contact with Joel and Porter. There was not much to do for the two of them after pointing out what they had found, but it was only polite to wait around to make sure there were no more questions even though they knew better. So Porter and Joel stood to one side to watch first light dissolve the assembled headlight flares. It was boring, and cold, but it beat Porter's usual routine.

Most other days he would be on his way to his afterthought of an office, that glorified public storage unit for sundry aspirations buried in a light industrial backwater of West Sacramento. Where he ended most days was even less inspiring. Some days he even considered turning around and going back to work rather than admit he had no place better to go than a different set of boxes, a sprawling tumble of hollow plywood blocks that was his new home, peopled with the diligently uncommitted on their way to a semblance of a life, his collusion being apartment number 2511. He did not belong there. He had a wife and had succeeded in performing his biological function by producing two children, a family. They lived in that very same town. Just not with him. One of life's mysteries: why it took freezing on an ocean bluff to see he was commuting from a town he really did not need to commute from anymore.

Even clinging to Roseville for the sake of the kids was getting to be a stretch. They were running hot and cold these days, but often cold thanks to Anita and whatever poisoned gruel she was feeding them. Tina especially seemed to be imitating her mother; the I-miss-you-Daddy's fading to looks of recrimination and betrayal, and sometimes no looks at all when he stopped by to visit. Porter preferred the days when Tina was feeling small, and lonely, and sympathetic. Roger seemed to be still making up his mind whether to side with his dad or shoulder the cross of man-of-the-house and actually work a lawn mower without wheedling.

So what did he have to show for the years of weather stripping, drip irrigation hoses, brick barbeque building and whatnot, other than a regret that was worse than when they sold their first place in Mountain View just when he got it all fixed up? He could not stay there either, but at least that move had been his choice.

She probably thought Sunday morning with the kids asleep upstairs was a good time for announcements. For him, a Sunday morning was when he was most exposed, the one morning when much of the previous week might be forgotten with his wandering dreams, and a cup of coffee with the sun coming in the kitchen might begin to rebalance the other five days of coffee snatched in the dark before it was even done perking. Sundays were also his way back from Saturdays. Saturdays were usually a write-off now that he had what passed for a regular job. Just the yard, house and car repairs, and watching his kids play soccer from a folding chair with his coffee mug of bourbon.

But she picked a Sunday, so he had a bit of a head. Nothing a couple of aspirin and coffee would not disguise, and then he became aware that she was talking at him. She had her back against the sink with her arms folded, and it was not about how he had left a wet towel on the floor or tracked mud in the entry. She was just back from her morning six-mile run, and she had been doing some thinking. He had not been around the block since selling his patrol uniforms to a cadet fresh out of the academy six or seven years before. Anyway, she was talking, saying it was time to level with him, with her eyebrows set in the horizontal plane of a cement foundation she had poured over-night while he slept, and she was bolting on the sill plates, laying rim joists, tilting up the walls faster and faster, cladding them in iron. It seemed her new house had no room for him.

It should not have taken him so long to catch on. By the time he did, he was already in his car driving down the street, wondering how he got from, *What the hell?* to, *You're damned right I'm out of here*, to wondering what had just happened. Arguments with Anita had a peculiar quality about them, an interminable aspect, an excruciating and confused eternity, but, as he came to suspect with their opposite intimacy, co-joining under the sheets, were probably a lot shorter than his recollections would have claimed. This one was no different, except for the out-come. About the only thing he remembered was stuffing a bag and wondering how much the kids had heard.

In hindsight, launching without a return trajectory probably was not the wisest move considering that this left Roger and Tina alone with Anita to hear whatever version she cared to invent. And if he expected her to fold after he called her bluff it quickly became apparent that her indifference only solidified the longer they were apart. He would have preferred her everyday annoyance. But she was a distance runner, and had been putting more and more distance between them for months. Then as now, he assumed it was one of those things he had to put up with for a while until she got tired of her avoidance game. He should have known better. He knew all about evasion. People that really do not want to deal with you will not look you in the eye even when you walk right past each other in the hall even, as he discovered, when you are married. In retrospect, a closer look at the facts from the day she went sour on him might have been a better approach than filing a skeletal report and waiting for something else to develop:

<table>
<tr><td colspan="4">STATE OF CALIF.
CRASH REPORT   DEPT. OF INSURANCE</td></tr>
<tr><td>X FIRST
  FINAL
  SUPPLEMENT</td><td>DATE

10/08/09</td><td>TIME

08:30</td><td>PAGE

1 OF 3</td></tr>
<tr><td colspan="2">EVENT NUMBER</td><td colspan="2">20098712</td></tr>
<tr><td colspan="4">LOCATION: Kitchen, 1221 Sierra View Dr., Roseville, CA 95689</td></tr>
</table>

PARTIES

PARTY 1: Porter, Michael, WMA, Age 41

P-1 was identified by an increase in alcoholic beverage consumption, increased immersion in electronic media, insomnia, occasional impotence, lethargy and vision obscurement.

PARTY 2: Porter, Anita, WFA, Age 38

P-2 was identified by an increase in extra-familial activities, like her damn jogging, transference of affection to offspring, and reduced interaction with spouse, (P-1, M. Porter).

WITNESSES

WITNESS 1: Porter, Tina, WFJ, Age 13

W-1 was identified by needy-surly mood swings, infantile regressions and bedtime meltdowns.

WITNESS 2: Porter, Roger, WMJ, Age 15

W-2 was identified by argumentativeness, an increase in time spent with peers, and increased protectiveness and indulgence in mother's, (P-2, A. Porter) whims.

SCENE

The marriage was located upside down approx. sixteen years from point of departure and approx. two years off the roadway.

(Cont., Page 2)

PHYSICAL EVIDENCE

The following evidence was recovered at the scene:

1. Five (5) sixteen-ounce Budweiser cans, empty.
2. One (1) receipt for fifty (50) dollars from Roseville Family Counseling Center issued to P-2, A. Porter.
3. Three (3) condoms in frayed wrappers.
4. One (1) Fem-Glo brand personal massager, battery operated.
5. One (1) mens Irish knit sweater, gift wrapped, for "accidental" washing until a perfect fit for P-2, A. Porter.
6. One (1) emergency roadside repair kit, unopened.

STATEMENTS

PARTY 1: M. Porter was interviewed at the scene. P-1 had a noticeable odor of alcoholic beverage about his person, but he passed Field Sobriety Tests administered at the scene (Attachment 1, FST). The following is his statement, in summary: P-1 denied that he was the driver. P-1 said he was reading the Sunday paper at the time of the crash. P-1 claimed to have no recollection of the crash.
END OF P-1 STATEMENT.

PARTY 2: A. Porter was interviewed at the scene. The following is her statement, in summary:
P-2 said M. Porter, (P-1) was the driver at the time of the crash. She said she thought the crash was "unavoidable."
END OF P-2 STATEMENT.

WITNESS 1: T. Porter was interviewed at the scene. The following is her statement, in summary:
W-1 said her mother, (P-2) was always saying what a crappy driver her dad (P-1) was.
END OF W-1 STATEMENT.   (Cont., Page 3)

WITNESS 2: R. Porter was interviewed at the scene. The following is his statement, in summary:

W-2 said he noticed tension while giving his mother a neck rub the night before the crash. He remembers there was swerving and weaving, but he was playing a video game when the crash occurred.

END OF W-2 STATEMENT.

CONCLUSIONS

Based on Physical Evidence obtained at the scene, marriage condition at time of officer arrival, and Statements obtained from parties and witnesses on scene:

POINT OF IMPACT

POI was determined to be within shouting distance of the intersect of Conflicting Careers Blvd. and Unmet Expectations Expressway, approx. 100 yards south of Parent Alley.

CAUSE

P-1, M. Porter, was the primary factor contributing to this crash due to his banishment to an also-ran posting, with attendant impairment culminating in his failure to observe and respond appropriately to the off-course direction of his marriage in time to avoid a crash.

Lesser but contributing factors: Driver distracted by the vindictive theatrics of his frustrated would-be-model wife who is pushing forty, and changing family dynamics of moody teenagers in back seat.

END OF REPORT

OFFICER SIGNATURE	DATE

DOI 270a (Rev 4/2007

Like any report in his files, there was more than what was on paper. Missing was how this carload of mismatched occupants came to be on that deserted stretch of road at that hour. For clues he had to go back to the bumper-caressing days, that first dent, the days of running his covetous fingers over voluptuous upholstery. Was it really an accident? It had always felt like he was meant to run into her. She was meant to be his—*Take me for a spin*. There was such an uncanny sense of unavoidable about their first fender bender that they had laughed it off, assuming it was just their luck. The way they kept tripping over each other after their first date only made a road trip together seem inevitable. Back then she taught school across town from his beat. He worked nights. Their streets kept intersecting anyway.

He was on the sidewalk outside a strip mall coffee shop back when he was still in uniform, his Friday night having extended into Saturday morning after a pretext car stop near the end of his shift yielded a half dozen bindles of dingy white powder meth, and a late arrest, booking and paper. He was talking to his partner, Sam, enjoying the dawn, the mix of fatigue and rejuvenation that came with daylight and the rise in traffic noise. Sam, too, seemed reluctant to head back to the station. Then Sam's narrow, tanned face drew inward, went from his usual sleepy-dismal to intent, fixed on something over Porter's shoulder and he gave the slightest nod.

Partner, I think you've got a—

There came a quick skipping step, and suddenly two palms raced up his spine making wrong-right chills Porter felt right through his vest, and a woman's voice breathing up into his ear.

Oh, officer, can you—?

The flirtatious lilt was probably all that saved her because he had already begun his spin and caught one of her hands in a reverse wrist twist, which gave her an involuntary lean toward one shoulder on her way down hard. He saw her mouth convulse in surprise and shock of sudden pain, and he had just time to catch her around the waist and snatch her to his chest before she fell, her mouth now agape, her brown eyes huge with terror and thrill.

Sam produced three slow, droll claps with his evaluation.

Response time: A plus. Threat assessment: D minus. Or maybe not.

Sam gave her the slow twice over, making her blush, with an unnecessary follow-up.

I take it this is your X?

Porter made the introductions, explaining to Anita that X-ray was radio code generic for an officer's wife or, in this case, girlfriend, not his ex-wife. He could see she really was not paying attention even as she explained how she had come across town to buy art supplies for her students, her eyes going fast forward to later, to her apartment where she said what he could tell she was thinking even then, when she came to him with her hair down wearing nothing but his unbuttoned uniform shirt, and sat on his bare stomach.

Officer, I've been bad. I think you need to take me downtown.

This was only a few days after he was on his feet yelling encouragement to the Giants pitcher, Burchardt, and a woman about five rows in front turned to look up at the sound of his voice. Thinking back, he could not remember who he had gone to the game with, but he never forgot her look of surprise, recognition and delight, which she then did a bad job of suppressing as she half-turned back to the game and the gesturing fellow who had his other arm casually draped across the back of her seat. But the bend of her head, even in profile, was that of a woman distracted. Porter was distracted by the sunlight making a warm translucence of her earlobe, the stray curls behind her ear laid bare by the ponytail pulled through the back of her ball cap, his game forgotten.

Later still, she did not seem surprised at all if he got done early on court days and decided there was no sense going home for more sleep before his shift. More often than not she was subbing at some school near enough for him to show up at lunch recess. He brought sandwiches to eat while her girl charges whispered in glee from the monkey bars at the two of them sitting thigh-to-thigh on a low bench at the edge of the playground. She kept smoothing her modestly long skirt over her knees, as though the children could suddenly see that they were as gorgeous as he knew them to be. She had a dancer's legs, and was still trying to break into modeling then. She also had wide-set eyes, a narrow chin, and just a bit of an overbite that he found irresistible but the ad world did not. It seemed you had to have a face and a figure that looked good from any angle to make it into the big shoots. Otherwise, you made the best of what you had and got the work you could get. If you looked good in bras, you might get in on catalogs. Some models had fat calves but gorgeous hands, so the hands got the shoots in circulars, adorned with rings, bracelets, watches. Anita had legs.

He saw her once in a dress ad for one of the local discount houses. It was a black, sleeveless cocktail sheath, and she knew how it should be worn, with one leg turned out to accentuate her hips and give a bit of fabric shift at her waist. But Porter could also see what the photographer either did not see, or could not prevent. What was needed was a look of well-bred composure, of surety that her languid anticipation would be rewarded as she paused in her entrance and surveyed the room for victims. Instead, her eyes had wandered off. She seemed unconscious, a bit bored, distracted; it was all too much bother. Worse, it infected her posture. Hers was a body congealing, not one heating up to the dance beat, about to let go. There was no self-awareness, no imagination of grace or unveiling in her awkward stance. How could a person convey a sensibility of beauty without that? If she wanted to sell dresses, if she wanted more work, she had to show a little more ardor, light herself up with a bit of the rapt lasciviousness that Porter knew she had in her for the resolute hero bold enough to earn her devotion. That was the real Anita, so why was she keeping that to herself? Women would lust for a little black dress if they thought they could become Diana, not a school teacher standing in the hall waiting for some tardy little scruffian to skid through the door to her classroom on the fading bell. He could see how that would cost her work, and it did, to the point that teacher became her most employable face, a gradually bittering face that sensed that something was missing. It never occurred to him until later that perhaps the photographer had teased out the real Anita, and the person Porter thought he knew was the Anita she imagined he wanted. At the time, he saw only that he alone could see her. It then followed that he would always be the one to find her, would find her when she needed him most, there being no such thing as coincidence in their case.

Even, or especially on the night she delivered Roger, Porter found her when everything conspired against it. He was outside the ER having made his own delivery: a stolen-car suspect getting stitched up and cleared for booking after a foot chase that earned their guy a dog bite from the K-9 unit assisting. Porter had lost his belt radio going over backyard fences, but Sam caught the traffic. Told him to get upstairs because dispatch said his X was en route to Maternity.

Upstairs, they pointed him toward Labor and Delivery, where the nurse bounced a wad of scrubs off the front of his uniform, which was his welcome as one of their own.

Get dressed, Dad, or you'll miss the show. She's ten cents and pushing.

In between she was panting and blowing, looking over at him with her face mottled red, a crescent of black hair plastered to her temple as he burst into the overheated delivery room. She took one look at him and took it in stride, all things considered.

They run out of donuts? Where the hell were you?

Then she looked at the ceiling with a groan, which told him

she was peeved but she needed him and knew he would make it in time somehow, underscored with the squeeze she clamped on his rubber-gloved hand.

It went on this way for years, even after they were married. Different shifts, different days off, it did not matter. They were the exception. And then they were not.

Sixteen years later theirs was a rented camper full of seething reluctance careening up Highway 50 to a packed ghetto of a campground on the south shore of Lake Tahoe. His idea, naturally, the better to hold him accountable for every mosquito bite and chill wind that blew off the lake, when they could have relaxed with clean sheets at her father's cabin on the north shore instead. His attempts at appeasement went nowhere.

But we can just walk down to the lake from our campsite. I get so tired of having to round everyone up, pack up the car on some sort of schedule, and drive just to take a swim or go boating. Then someone always forgets the sunscreen, or is bored.

What he had not given enough thought to was jamming two teens into a tin box on wheels with Anita's and his expectations. Hers were still focused on water skiing, using her dad's boat, of course, while his had gone flat. In pursuit of that, he was looking forward to having his back against the warm sand, napping under a book just fat enough not to blow off his face, which was what beaches were for. But somebody had to do the cooking and washing up and run to the store twice a day for the spatula or ketchup unaccustomed campers had forgotten to bring. Piled on that was Tina's prickly ambivalence about her blossoming body and her desire to troll for boys unfettered by parents, colliding with Roger's surly refusal to contribute anything beyond expressing his grief about electronic devices he was being unnecessarily deprived of. In other words, a typical family at camp except for an undercurrent of irritation from Anita that went beyond sunburn.

Jesus, Michael, can't you get the fire going so it doesn't

smoke us all out?...Did you drink the last beer?...I told you to make the reservation sooner—the restrooms are a quarter mile hike from our campsite and I can't just piss behind the camper in the middle of the night like you.

On the third night she let it all hang out.

I need a real vacation, Michael. Waking up smelling like barbequed ribs is not my idea of a good time.

The next day he called it quits and drove them all home, where the three of them scattered like quail to their rooms, the bath and to friends' houses.

The slide probably started years before, with nights. Every cop in the department had to go through the rotation, but Porter asked for them. He liked working with Sam. Sam liked nights and was pretty much stuck with them as long as he was the least senior sergeant. He told Anita he needed to stay partnered up with someone he trusted, so it was not a simple matter of what shift he wanted after Sam promoted. He left out the part about how he wanted no part of days, even if that was how they met, even if day shifts meant sleeping at night like a human. Day shifts were mostly taking paper from cold calls left over from the night before, and too many brass to bump into.

Turned out leaving Anita with the day shift eventually had consequences for someone who was usually home to see the kids off to school but was sound asleep when they got back, or whenever they needed a ride to the dentist, or when the family needed a lift home from the train station after a visit to her grandparents. Protesting that it was not safe for him or Sam to show up at work like a zombie did no good. Nor could he blame her for getting tired of living with him in a near coma, and of all the days when he could not be counted on because he had mandatory training or had an arrest that went overtime.

Some days that were not quite nights stood out more than others, when the dust accumulating in the corners began to harbor odd, verminous creatures that neither of them recognized.

She was kneeling beside the tub, scrubbing, when he leaned in the doorway with his coffee, yawning his ironic *Morning* greeting, which she acknowledged by dismissing it.

Would you hand me a towel?

Sure. How was your day?

Finger paints and principals flipping out over test scores. And the dishwasher is leaking again.

What do you want me to hit first, the principal or the dishwasher?

She ignored him. He adjusted his priority list.

What say we do something grownup this weekend and get a sitter? Go to a museum. Have lunch. I've got some comp time coming.

She arched her back to relieve it from the tub bending, which protruded her front and rear in what looked to him like wave-length agreement on possibilities too long deferred, but she was way ahead of him.

All right, but don't expect any dry humping in the dead dude wing.

She was, of course, referring to a singular night at the Legion of Honor when they were dating and could barely maintain a pretense of interest in a travelling collection of Titians as they drifted in search of empty galleries, the better to grope each other under the jealous contemplation of *Portrait of a Man*, and despite Mary Magdalene's gaze averted heavenward in erotic disavowal of her own glowing flesh, and the hotter flesh before her on the gallery floor. Somehow they made it back to her car while fused at the hip; the night, the tinted windows and hurried gusts of fog through the pines providing enough excuse to do it right there parked on the edge of the concourse, her ankles flexing greedily next to his ears in the rearview mirror.

Some of the Titians had returned, and he thought Anita might enjoy seeing them from their shared vantage of remembrance, but the sitter was late, the traffic ridiculous for a

Saturday, making it seem like just another day on the job to fight their way into the city and hope to be diverted enough to see each other out of context, in their town clothes instead of sweatpants. As before, they drifted again, but this time apart, and several times he lost her entirely and had to go looking for her. She was on a mission, as if the idea were to tramp through it all as quickly as possible. He, on the other hand, was distracted by a surge of longing, of pride and regret that poured forth from their eyes all around him, the haunted eyes of desire once breathing, now expired. He was pulled back even as he went in search of her. She was out front hugging herself against the cold, looking sidelong at the program scrunched in one hand at her shoulder, a woman just killing time, not really expecting to find anything of interest in the brochure that might just as well have been a carwash flyer shoved under her windshield. He joined her feeling torn, or incomplete. Had she seen what he had and fled? Or had she even bothered to look? His questions came out more stricken than he intended.

What are you doing out here? Do you have your ticket stub? I don't know if we can get back in.

She folded the program into her coat pocket.

I'm sorry, Michael, I guess it wasn't a good idea. I don't see the point if we are just going to wander around aimlessly. It's not like we have a clue about any of this stuff.

What's to understand? OK, I never was much for painting either, even in college. Now—I don't know. Some of them are amazing. I mean, up close it's just cracked paint. And then you step back and it's a person. Someone who was alive just like us hundreds of years ago. I—

Porter could see she was looking not at him or the museum but out at the street, just waiting for him to finish, wanting to go. Her eyes shot back to him when she realized she had been caught, but she was not apologizing.

They all look too dark and I can't tell one from the next. My class would go ape and rebel if I ever brought them here. I'm with them. I want to see things that are alive. What say we try the aquarium?

So they traded pathos approaching the sublime for bathos submerged in a verisimilitude of ocean depths; the see-through bones of the miniature sea horses, which he found about as compelling as over-mannered toy poodles, instead of the ethereal translucence he had seen on the neck of Judith, which he imagined in the flesh of the anemones in the exhibit down the hall, secreted in the giant clams. But Anita seemed to come around, and even took his arm as she pointed out the cutest of the frolicking penguins while his thoughts were elsewhere, remembering a whiff of strange perfume or the glance of a woman on the street.

On his next court day he went back, but the Italian Masters show had moved on. He had to make do with the permanent collection, unable to see beyond the derivative, beyond a simulation of seduction in the Countess of Mornington whose infused cheeks were as contrived as the red on her lips, mocking his conceit of finding a work that would entice Anita. And although it seemed strange to walk into a museum alone, he found himself looking up other art shows within driving distance, and he wondered less and less what Anita would make of it as time went by.

If Anita did not appear to notice, she was keeping track of something it turned out, in a book of her own, deducting daily from her balance of affection. So it must have taken years, not months. Now she had closed his account as a write-off. She sounded tired the day she kicked him out, and tired the last time he dropped in while she was doing the ordinary dinner cooking thing and he thought it might be a good time to ask if she missed him. She berated her pot of spaghetti sauce with the lid in one hand, the steam in her face.

How would I know the difference? At least when you were

a cop I could tell the kids you were out fighting crime. But ever since you've been with D-of-I you've been coming home late, pouring a drink and passing out in front of the news. God forbid you ever asked for time off to give a crap about us. And just because the grammar school is across the street from the middle school doesn't mean it's always convenient for me to walk right out at the last bell to get Tina to her ballet lesson or get Roger to practice.

Of course she did not see that a lot of his days were no downhill coast either, especially with an hour commute each way, even on good days. Some days went pretty long, too, especially cases that took him out of town. But she did have him out in the open where it had been years since he had regular night shifts and working weekends as a given. She was starting to cry, and she put down her sauce spoon when he unloaded his anemic: *My job is downtown. Yours ends at three and is five blocks from home. What exactly would you have me do?*

Michael, dinner is almost ready. And I've got to make three dozen cookies for the class tomorrow in case the moms don't come through for our Halloween party. Go tell the kids goodbye. I'm too busy taking care of other people's children all day and my own nights and weekends for any more babysitting.

Which was sounding just like the day she wanted him out. He knew the script:

We're hardly babies. Tina is thirteen and Roger is fifteen, and I can wipe my own nose, thanks. But if this setup is cramping your daily 10-K runs, then why don't we swap? You take my apartment. I'll live here and pretend a jar of spaghetti sauce is cooking.

The wooden spoon caught him on the shoulder as he turned to leave.

This was weeks ago, and it was getting harder to drop by even to say hi to the kids. He still drove by the house most mornings, just about this time, just as the horizon lit. It was a pathetic way to start his day but so far it was preferable to the alternative. In those gray pre-dawns his beige former life was indistinguishable from the others in the subdivision. Except for one fugitive birch. It leaned toward the street in a vain effort to escape the obligatory cluster of exactly three saplings set too close together by the developer.

If the light was on in the kitchen it was a good sign. The family was on time, and he was on time. If only the bathroom light was on Anita was running late, or had already eaten and was doing her makeup, meaning he was the one running late. On rainy days he would pull over and walk the paper up to the porch. It would not do to ring the doorbell. Anita had already said the drive-bys made him seem like a stalker, but so far she had not complained about the paper. So the best days were also the worst, when Anita was standing at the front window with a cup of coffee and contemplating something that disappeared faster than the flash of white at her neck as she clutched her bathrobe and turned away the moment she became aware of him. One time she waved him in but it was only a clogged drain.

It seemed a death in the family had better roadmaps than a break up. Everyone was expected to die, but no one expected their wife to call it quits after sixteen years. There was no relief in simple conventions. Casket versus cremation. Viewing or no viewing. Granite or limestone. The permutations of lawyer-up and restraining order versus visiting rights and the occasional lunch were unknowable. Weeks into it and they were still trying on their roles, stepping on each other's lines, missing cues.

Yesterday the kitchen light was on but the living room window stage was empty, with no solace in the string of mute garage doors and driveways empty by CCR mandate and the halftone hour. The logical thing would be to swing by after work when he was more likely to see his son toeing a soccer ball around the yard or Anita unloading groceries, but that would also mean dodging cars and kids on bikes in the street, and the curious stares of his neighbors. It would interfere with his full contemplation of his former life, the sense of peace and order that only dawn could arrange.

All too soon the garage doors on both sides of his street would glide up and disgorge a horde of oversized station wagons and minivans. One of those had been his. How would the checklist look for someone watching him leave for work in those days? How would anyone describe the person they were years ago, much less the person they are now? Multiple guess would be the best you could do. His face would have been, what?

A. Harried?
B. Irritable?
C. Distracted?
D. All of the above?
E. None of the above?

D, obviously. No, that would have meant he was paying attention. It was E, or he would not be where he was since, still looking for redemption in his willing complicity, his submergence, in that placid obscurity. He would have looked like everyone else: self-absorbed, suffused in routine, confusing sleepwalking with wakefulness. Conflating arrangement with stability.

Driving through his neighborhood at sunup was just a vain attempt to pretend he was still that person. Porter could see the absurdity of that now as he stood shivering with Joel watching the sky lighten and separate itself from the darker ocean. Behind them the CHP guys were finishing their photos and measurements of the Morris accident scene. The sun had just peered over the ridge, lighting up the cliff face below the overlook, the weak and merciless dawn picking out the shiny remnants of someone else's shattered attempt at conveying a tidy composition. Now Porter could see the whole of it: what an unholy mess it was, a life interrupted, the work incomplete. But there was no denying a life was done here, over with. So, in that regard, this piece was as finished as it would ever be. The spew of paper scraps, twinkled glass and twisted chrome spread down the cliff face was a portrait of final ironic tranquility in its settled obliteration: violence in repose. There was no center, no point of entry, only departure, with unrelated fragments accenting the blank ground beneath, a space abandoned. Something important was absent. Some focal shape or form belonged here, positioned to gather these disparate bits and unify the whole. Which was exactly the point, as though this was the intended effect: a horror of disorder, of loss. Did this make it performance art or found art? Whichever. The exploded still life below him was a stark counterpoint to his romantic musings. It refuted his attempts to maintain his suburban fiction of a neighborhood unchanged: was a glimpse of the void in fact. And perhaps closer to the truth.

Porter saw that the CHP investigators were packing up. He nudged Joel out of his own thoughts. It was time to walk over and say good-bye. Time to get on with his own duties, his own life. He was beginning to wonder if it might take a different person to pick up either piece of work, his own or the abstraction on the cliff face below him. Both had a lot left undone.

CHAPTER IV

TOO EARLY FOR SIRENS

After Porter and Joel cleared the overlook, they had a half-hour drive upcoast if they wanted anything to eat. It was mid-morning before they made it to the Breakwater Café on Eric's suggestion for a late breakfast. They would have ended up there anyway. It was the only thing that showed any sign of life other than the flip of red to green on the one traffic light on the town's main street tumbling downhill from the highway. At the bottom of the hill was a heartbreak of steel blue washing the dismembered remains of a pier, and a rock jetty beyond. They found the café snugged up against a paint-blistered Victorian hotel that offered nothing but threadbare pretense. The café was false-front-plain, seemed to know it, and borrowed from the hotel filigree next door with wrought iron tables on the wooden sidewalk, a setup that might lure a few tourists on a day with less wind, more sun, and fewer greasy-plumed vagrants lounging on the chairs as though they owned them. The street people had the paying customer parody down, clutching dirty paper coffee cups they might have picked up out of the gutter for props. Evidently the management was either exceedingly infused with holiday tolerance, or could not be bothered to shoo them away to make room for what few solvent patrons there seemed to be, customers who were unlikely to want breakfast outdoors today. Porter gave a direct eyeball to the nearest lounger, who's anticipated: *Spare change?* wilted to a grudging and choked-off: *Morning.*

This confirmed what Eric, the CHP patrolman, had meant about limited prospects for finding a mate on the north coast.

But if Eric's prospects were remote, the blinking dawn for Porter was even worse, and his stomach lurched to consider that he might have to start seriously thinking in these terms; how little he had to negotiate with, since it was looking like his chances of reconnecting with the wife he already had were bleaker still. It was the loneliness of this place, good only for the astringent qualities of salt air separating paint from the warped siding on the storefronts into little curls right before his eyes, for whale bones on the beach bleaching in the sun. He might as well be on the moon. He might as well wish for a court order. The affidavit would go nowhere:

WHITLEY COUNTY

SUPERIOR COURT

SEARCH AND SEIZURE WARRANT

In the Matter of **Porter <u>vs.</u> Irrelevance**	*(Briefly describe the property to be searched)* **Town of Breakwater** Case No. ________________

To: Any authorized law enforcement officer:

An application by a state law enforcement officer or an attorney for the government requests the search of the following person or property located in the State of California.
(Describe the property to be searched and give its location):

Backwater town of Breakwater and nearby, equally decrepit environs located in the County of Whitley.

The property to be searched, described above, is believed to conceal: *(Identify the person or describe the property to be seized)*:

Female bearing attributes identical to those of Anita Ann Porter, with additional quality of agreeing to accept Michael Glen Porter as is.

I find that the affidavit(s), or any recorded testimony, establish probable cause to search and seize the person or property, under conditions attached.

X I find that the affidavit(s), or any recorded testimony, **DO NOT** establish probable cause to search and seize the person or property, based on the court's determination that:

Requesting officer has not provided sufficient and credible evidence to support a reasonable suspicion that he is not already in possession of the fantasy female sought. If not, submit signed copy of final divorce decree to this court.

As is?! Porter, you must be dreaming.

Date ____________ *Judge Signature*____________________________

51

A man would have to be dreaming if he thought any woman with certain advantages would be caught dead here. This was especially true of the dead woman. Then what would have drawn Holly Morris to a place like Breakwater? She was a television reporter at one of the larger regional stations. A town so small, not to mention one in the advanced stages of decomposition, was unlikely to generate enough intrigue to pull her hours north of San Francisco on assignment, so what was the attraction if it was not business? Pebble Beach or a private Lake Tahoe resort would have been more her style, not this derelict burg about ready to pitch into the ocean. It might be worth a bet with Joel about her reasons for coming here, on the chance that it would give some impetus to the otherwise bleary morning but, after yesterday, the drive to the coast with Joel had been too silent to be attributed simply to lack of sleep, so Joel was still sulking. Besides, he would first have to explain how he knew her, why he had kept this from him and Eric, and how he came to have an opinion on her tastes. It would mean trying to explain why he followed her reporting without coming off like a voyeuristic fan obsessed by a favorite tennis player, professing his admiration for the superlative talent in her arms while secretly enjoying her legs flashing to the foul line.

Morris had gone from covering the south bay police beat to sniffing out no-bid public contract kickback schemes, tax-salaried non-functionaries, and nepotised third cousins hiding their substance abuse monkeys in well-appointed back offices at City Hall. When a San Francisco station picked her up, she moved up to covering state employee pension fund directors accepting free golf flings in Scotland from Wall Street investment houses; environmental reviews rubber stamped so a new power plant or landfill would get sited next to a poor neighborhood; and all-aboard projects like a proposed high speed passenger rail alignment that just happened to run right through the played-out family farm of a former legislator in the Central Valley. She was not above dolling up in evening dress to ambush politicians at thirty-thousand-dollar-a-plate fundraisers and, like a precursor to the perp walk, the guilty stumble she instilled in her prey the moment they laid eyes on her waiting in a hall as they approached made her famous. She was so successful she had gone full circle; from having smooth-talking mouthpieces pushed forward to deal with her outside committee rooms—until the pundits and cartoonists took notice—to having her interview requests answered with sit downs in nice offices. There seemed to be no question she would not ask, but done with such polite deference that she usually got responses that made her subjects sometimes spend weeks afterward trying to reverse the spin. All done with those bright eyes, that sassy walk and those flawless nails holding the microphone up to an endless succession of nervous lips.

Morris' style was a far cry from the woman with her back to the room at the counter coffee service. She let them know she was the help by the, *Sit anywhere*, she tossed over her shoulder at the door bell tinkle. Good thing; they were not into uniforms around here, evidently, unless this was it: faded maroon T over long-sleeved T of no particular shade, set off by an afterthought of red cedar that swirled in a loose twist to her waist. Jeans well on their way to lint, which he did not see much anymore, but some women looked good in anything, and this one either knew it, or did not care.

Porter eased into his chair so as not to get his gun hung up on the wrought iron arms. Concealed carry meant not sending your piece clattering to the floor in public. He and Joel kept their windbreakers on. The table had a view of the huge rollers underscoring black cliffs across the bay. Now framed in quadrants by the divided lights of the front windows, the bay was mesmerizing, especially so early in the morning on so little sleep, with the sun catching the spray ripping and swirling from the wave tops in the face of the offshore wind. Joel was caught up in it too, enough to emulate normal collegial discourse.

Looks like the leisure specialists outside might be onto something. Tell me why we're working, again?

A hand came into view to fill his cup before he hardly had it upturned. This hand was, no other word for it, exquisite. Slim angular fingers, unvarnished nails just long enough to be noticed, and a long, elliptical thumb pad that looked adept at anything from wiping a tear off a child's cheek to jabbing a mouth in an emergent clay vase spinning on a potter's wheel. He took a ride up the wrist along a slim arm with downy dark hairs that accentuated the pale skin beneath, and was well on the way to a place that seemed familiar when she beat him there.

Hello, Porter.

There was only one woman who had ever called him Porter. She was smiling at his cup as she filled it, not needing to see his face to savor getting the jump on him. He saw first the familiar eyelids turned down slightly at the corners, more so now, giving her a dreamy, appraising empathy despite the things he recalled that were likely to come out of her mouth, which itself was showing some laugh creases at the corners. Then she turned the gray-blue eyes of a killer angel his way. In this light the gray was winning out, almost silver, as she assumed a patently blasé scrutiny to match her sneak attack.

Is it still straight up black or do you or your friend want it stepped on?

He was not ready for this. She had caught him unarmed, in an alley, without his vest.

Hello, Celeste. Uh, what? Black is fine. How are you?

She waved the pot at Joel.

Your friend?

Oh, excuse me. This is my partner, Joel Vega. Joel, Celeste Brousset. We went to San Francisco State together.

We dated, she corrected him, without clarifying whether her name was changed with the band on her finger.

Cream and sugar, Joel?

Joel allowed as how black was fine, and smiled as though she had told him breakfast was on the house. Evidently, he was enjoying watching Porter scramble. So it showed.

Uh, you look great, he offered lamely.

You look like hell.

Joel laughed, bearing down on his squint with unwholesome delight, seeing Porter transported to what was, apparently, instantly recognizable as fumbling adolescence. Here he was, married, two kids, packing hardware, and feeling no different than a stuttering high school sophomore in tights trying out for the romantic lead. She had the advantage of knowing the house, had a long run at the same venue, knew her marks, her exits. She also had a head start on him, had time to sort out her entrance, rehearse her lines. He was dropping his, and she was not feeding him any hints, enjoying watching him squirm as though that were the whole point of the scene, which she had stolen, which Joel was eating up. This was all too familiar.

So.

So.

Joel cleared his throat and made a conspicuous check of his cell. Hey, they've got service here. I need to make a call. Can I get eggs over medium with hash browns and whole wheat? I'll be outside.

Joel got up and strode to the door. Porter was left staring up at her.

What about you, Porter, are you eating or just looking?

Truth was, he would have preferred spectating to playing, especially on maybe three hours sleep, but here he was on the court, unseeded, facing an antagonist he had not studied in years, feeling his composure drain out the bottoms of his feet into the grass, remembering the embarrassment she handed him the last time. She was firing them over the net and he was just sitting there, with his mouth open, getting wind burn from the serves whizzing past his ear. Enough of this.

I'm just trying to decide if it's too early for salmonella. The last time I ate in one of these places I thought someone had ripped out my insides. But I'll have what he's having, then switch plates when he isn't looking. Maybe I'll survive.

She did not have a return for that one, just a droll grimace, made a note on her pad and walked off court without a word, leaving him at the net in a gathering anguish that he had over-played. They were not the same people, however much they might try to pretend. He was out of practice, spouting inten-tional malapropisms that might have seemed charming at twen-ty, but probably now sounded just spiteful, despite the weak smile he had tried to sell it with. He watched her make the rounds of the few visiting grandparents and fewer late-rising lovebirds scattered about the other tables while he pretended not to watch, saw her shove her order pad in a back pocket, which only made her jeans tighter. Then she made straight for him and sat down in Joel's chair.

You can't be on vacation. It's the wrong time of year, so don't try to tell me he's your boyfriend.

He shook his head, hustling again now to pick up this new thread before she got too far along with the unraveling. She was still tugging.

I see you're married. How long?

He looked at his gold band, which had not been off his finger in sixteen years, and told her. Two kids, boy and girl. His responses were too short. Barest facts. He probably sounded like an interview subject under pressure. Something to hide? Nothing but an upended life. Nothing like running into some-one from when you both had more future than past.

And?

And?

Oh, come on, Porter. Where are you living? What's your wife like? How old are your kids? Do they look like you or your wife? What's her name? Did you meet her on Broadway? How's life?

If Celeste were a dentist she could not have done a better job of drilling right to the infected root. And that wry smile with those impertinent eyes. She had him punctured that way, too. What would be the diplomatic way to put it?

Are you like this with strangers, too, or do you just save the third degree for old friends?

So, still friends?

It's been a while. How long did it take you to recognize me?

As soon as I turned around and saw you. You have this way of looking around a room as you sit down. Like you are trying to memorize it all but don't want to get caught trying. So, let's say your life is a room, and you are going to describe it for me. Paint me a picture.

That was you, not me. Um, well, life is OK, but it's been... Things are OK. They say home remodeling will make or break a marriage, but I think it's the teenage years. My wife, Anita, is a little put out at me at the moment. The kids take after her, thank God.

She must be skinny, then. I see you're putting it on around the middle.

Well, you're sure not—putting it on, I mean. My partner was giving you the up-and-down, too. How do you do it?

She colored just a bit more than a hot-kitchen flush would justify. So, she was still better at dishing it out. He had some equilibrium now, thankfully.

What about you? Have you been here long?

Pretty much ever since college. I don't miss the city much.

He could see her then, a few pounds thinner, which had made her look more tiny, more fragile, and braver as a result as she walked through the campus with her dreams on her shoulder in an oversized portfolio, its outsized dimensions in direct proportion to her desire, which made her look more than a little pretentious. His would have been, what, a cape? It would have amounted to the same thing, but would have taken more panache than he had those days in his own overloaded ambitions. Perhaps she had done better.

What about your painting? That giant portfolio you used to carry around? What became of that?

She looked insulted, as though he had asked if she still bathed regularly.

Still got 'em. I didn't run away to join the circus after you dumped me, if that's what you are thinking.

(So much for memory lane.)

I wasn't suggesting... Wait a minute. You think I dumped you?

Her insulted look was gone, replaced with tired exasperation.

Well, usually when a guy quits calling, you sorta tend to draw conclusions. I was only trying to explain how I ended up so far from the city, since that's what most people want to know. I didn't mean to cart us back to any of that. That was too long ago anyway. I'm not even sure I remember.

Porter considered changing his order:

<table>
<tr><td colspan="2"> STATE OF CALIF. – DEPARTMENT OF INSURANCE

ARCHIVAL RECORD FOR RETRIEVAL

DOI 411 (REV 8/1999) </td><td colspan="3"> ARCHIVES USE ONLY:

Date out _______________ Initials _____

Date returned_____________

File missing _______________ </td></tr>
<tr><td colspan="2">FILE TYPE:</td><td colspan="2">Case File</td><td>Photos</td></tr>
<tr><td colspan="2">TRACKING No. / Date:</td><td colspan="2">1990</td><td>Physical Evidence</td></tr>
<tr><td colspan="2">SUSPECT</td><td colspan="2">Brousset, Celeste</td><td>Interview Transcripts</td></tr>
<tr><td colspan="2">VICTIM</td><td>Porter, Michael</td><td>X</td><td>ALL</td></tr>
<tr><td colspan="5" align="center">ALLEGATIONS</td></tr>
<tr><td colspan="2">CODE:</td><td colspan="2">Health & Safety</td><td>Civil</td></tr>
<tr><td colspan="2">SECTION:</td><td colspan="2">Sec. 117555</td><td>Sec. 1871.4.(a)</td></tr>
<tr><td colspan="2">DESCRIPTION:</td><td colspan="2">Illegal Dumping: Boyfriend</td><td>False Claim: Tamper/Alter Official Record</td></tr>
<tr><td colspan="5" align="center">REASON FOR REQUEST</td></tr>
<tr><td colspan="3">New Investigation</td><td colspan="2"></td></tr>
<tr><td colspan="3">Appeal/Lawsuit</td><td colspan="2"></td></tr>
<tr><td colspan="3">Reopen Case / New Info</td><td colspan="2" align="center">X</td></tr>
<tr><td>Basis:</td><td colspan="4">Subject of investigation (Brousset) now alleges victim (Porter) was party responsible.</td></tr>
<tr><td>Action Plan:</td><td colspan="4">Review file for discrepancies or corroborate with new information.</td></tr>
<tr><td>Auth.</td><td colspan="4">Felony: No statute of limitations.</td></tr>
<tr><td>Requested by</td><td colspan="2">M. Porter</td><td colspan="2">Date</td></tr>
</table>

Celeste was looking about the room, which could have been a check on the customers or an internal reorganization. She started over.

Look, I just wanted to say it's nice to see you. What happened was I came up here one weekend for a music festival with my roommate, Patricia. Remember her, the granola girl? Anyway, we danced all night around a fire on the beach. I met a guy. I never went back. That's all.

Only it was not, at least not for him. He stalled by taking a sip of coffee and glanced out at the view. New guy in town. He might pull it off. The look of bemused concern on her face said he had not. A big part of his unease was that the woman he had known was just beginning to grow into her beauty. Was still trying it on for size, a little too quick to pretend she did not know what a traffic stopper she was, which had the opposite effect: made her seem the show-off, a little too preoccupied with her gift. The woman sitting across from him was more comfortable in her own skin, whatever discomforts might be roiling beneath. Her smile was simple, earnest, earned. What had he earned? He wondered how he fit with her then as now. She seemed to be busy all of a sudden. Then it seemed that she was always with Davon at the coffee shop. He did not need a billboard. Maybe he had it wrong, or could not remember right either. Best to just take it from now.

I guess I can see it. The million-dollar view out there. Is this place yours?

Her expression came near to drifting again, but she caught herself.

You mean, am I just a waitress? It's OK, yes. I mean no, I don't own the restaurant, but I guess you could say I have a stake in it. People need a place to eat so they'll stick around long enough to maybe buy one of my paintings. That's my main thing. Still plein-air, mostly.

So, you made it work. That—That's great.

Her look said his reflexive response came off sounding condescending.

Thank you, but you don't have to pretend to assume so much. I'm far from famous. I'm like most people here. We have two lives. There's the thing you do, and there's the thing you do to get by. I live off the grid up on the hill. This gets me into town and keeps me connected, so, yeah, I guess it works. And you?

I'm just here on business.

Just here on business. What business are you in?

I work for the state.

He left out Department of Insurance, which seemed suddenly less exalted than waitressing, and too much to explain at the moment, especially with the doorbell tinkle signaling Joel's return. Celeste slid her chair back.

I better go check on your order. Top secret, huh? So, are you guys with the governor? I thought he already left.

Joel asked Porter's question for him as he helped her with her chair.

The governor was here?

Well, not here, here, but at the Pemberton Inn just south of town. Stuff like that gets around, especially when they say he was here to meet his honey, a TV news reporter from San Francisco, Holly Morris.

Porter and Joel exchanged expressionless looks.

Hang on, your order's up.

After she brought their plates and set them down, she got herself a cup of coffee and a chair and joined them. They found out that the jetty used to protect a small fishing fleet, but that the bay had filled in with silt washed downstream from logging and the cut of time, and what fishing boats were still hanging on anchored up coast at Millfork, which had a bigger harbor. Even there they needed to dredge every now and then to keep the harbor channel open. The occasional crabber and abalone-diving tourists were about the extent of Breakwater's fishing fleet now. Just then a large and boisterous party of brunchers walked in, followed by a couple of highway workers on break, and she had to excuse herself to get back to work. All there was time for after that was her good-bye in the form of: *Stop by again sometime*, as she cashed them out. If there was more to the touch of her fingers as she put the coins in his hand, or the look in her eye, he could have imagined it.

The cold ocean air immediately outside the door was at once a head clear and a comedown after the moist, steamy air inside. The tendency was to stand there blinking for a moment to get his bearings again. Joel seemed to be in the same mode, standing in a sort of daze beside him, staring off over the water. The food had turned out to be, if not equal to the view, at least a respectable side dish, but it did not let Eric the patrolman off the hook for not filling them in, any more than the toothpick Porter grabbed on the way out was going to make up for no toothbrush on a combination of morning mouth and grease. Joel was adjusting his belt and shrugging against the weight of his shoulder rig.

So what now, Mike?

Why don't you call Eric and see if that report is ready, and slap him for not giving us the whole story. I'm gonna call the person whose idea this was and do the same.

He got Maddie's voicemail so there was nothing to do but look at the view and eavesdrop on Joel's call to Eric while a briny fecundity wafting up the cliffs insinuated itself among the pine and wild onion. Wouldn't it have been nice to find his way here fresh out of college? With less on his mind it would be so easy to let his eyes drift closed as his face luxuriated in the thin morning sun that was now breaking through the fog. He imagined waking up on the beach to that warmth, made warmer cozied up with Celeste. What was that she was wearing? A light musk with a tang. Incense, or Patchouli, on top of the dusty-sunshine scent he remembered at the back of her neck. It would be very easy to let himself follow the rhythm of the waves here, the wind stirring the trees, and let that be enough. But that fantasy was as remote as his honeymoon in Baja with a different woman, a postcard found in an overturned shoebox of his marriage, his job, the person he thought he was in college: snapshots scattered on the floor that no amount of shuffling seemed likely to ever put in any kind of order. Life was supposed to make more sense by now, not less. He had always thought that getting older was a becoming, a gradual embrace of the person you knew you were all along. Instead he was dissembling, as out of place as a business suit at the beach. In his present circumstances a place like this could be a blessing, or a curse.

Joel was not having any better luck. He heard him leaving a recorded message for the patrolman, Eric. Porter decided to try his daughter. She answered with a background of adolescent shouts, diesel engine rumbling. It pained him a little and relieved him a little to know that she had checked first to see who was calling.

Hi, Daddy.

Hi, Sweetheart. Are you at school?

Out front. It's just about to start—Stop it, Jonathon—What's up?

Who's Jonathon? Does he need his arm broken?

He's a seventh-grader, Daddy—

Porter saw the back of her hand on her hip, elbow jutting out as her eyes drolled skyward.

—You don't have to check up on me.

I just wanted to see how you were doing.

I'm OK. Where are you? There's a funny noise.

That's the ocean. I'm in Breakwater.

Where's that?

It's up the coast. I could have lunch in Oregon if I wanted.

Get out.

Well, maybe dinner.

Tina's voice dropped. There was doubt in it, and plea, and not wanting to be overheard.

Are you having Thanksgiving with us?

I don't know yet. That depends on your—your mother and I haven't talked about it yet.

That would be so lame. You have to help me make our snowman. You have to make my hot chocolate. Mom never puts in enough marshmallows.

Maybe. We'll see.

I know what that means.

It just means I have to talk to Anita first.

No, you have to promise.

I'm sorry, Tina. I wish I could.

Promise you'll try, then. I have to go. I love you, Daddy.

I love you, too, Sweetheart.

Porter put his phone away, weighing a father's worth relative to promises, and how a telephone could erase distances and just as easily add a thousand miles between a father and a daughter. Breakwater was now a continent away from Roseville. A few feet down the sidewalk, Joel had gotten through to the patrolman, and was playing his betrayal card.

Yeah, Eric. Hey what's up with the girl and the governor, and how come you didn't tell us he was here? Uh, huh. Uh, huh.

The look Joel gave Porter told him he thought it was crap.

Uh-huh. And I'm supposed to buy that? That would make for some shitty contingency planning to leave one of their own in the dark. Uh, huh, uh-huh.

Joel made a rolling motion with his free hand to let Porter know it was more of the same.

Really? What time? OK. How do we get there?

Now his eyebrows went up in a *How-about-that?* face.

Ok, thanks. Yeah, OK, you're forgiven.

Joel snapped his cell shut.

Get this. We're invited to a sit down with the D.A., the district CHP commander and the sheriff.

And Morris? Was she doing the gov?

Who knows? But he figured we knew or we would not have showed up at the scene along with everybody else from here to Sacramento. It could even have been a three-way.

What?

Well, Eric says he never saw the Morris woman beforehand, and didn't know that the governor was here until after, but he did see the D.A. leaving the Pemberton. He passed by there a little before midnight and saw her driving out in her white Mercedes SUV. There aren't many of those around here so he took a good look as it drove out of the gate. He's sure it was her. Apparently she's a looker. Anyway, his report's about ready. We can grab it on the way over to the county offices. It's one exit before.

He asked Joel to drive this time so he could look at the view, which let him pretend to be looking out the window. Unlike his fellow officers, for Porter the bit about Morris and the governor was more disgusting than tantalizing, any prurient fascination with that having backfired, like finding his cousin slithering along the bar top at a strip club. Everyone knew the governor was a sleaze, and the thought of Morris with a man like that ran counter to Porter's armchair mythology even as it began to make perfect sense as an investigation Maddie would relish. Maddie was a known commodity, and whoever called on her for a bit of hold-your-nose knew they had come to the right person for help. Maddie also knew better than to get her own hands dirty.

What did that say about him? Unlike the movies where the damaged hero has staggered off to spend the rest of his days licking his wounds in the woods, there to be tracked down in his self-imposed exile when the country is once again in need of his unique talents, and he grudgingly agrees to put his life in danger again, but just this one last time, you understand, for the greater good—who were they kidding? Like Porter, the poor bastard had to be going stir crazy out in the wilderness after having flown so close to the sun. The protestations were just for show because the hero would give anything for another shot at glory. The only difference here was that Porter had hardly saved the world; had barely gotten off the ground before getting singed. So if Maddie wanted Porter she had to be desperate, but not in a way that was a compliment to his skills. She might even be looking for a fall guy, plain and simple.

It made his chest hurt. Voyeur or not, he was due for a mental vacation, somewhere out there over the hypnotic swells. Let Joel drive. A passenger could let himself soar off the edge on each bend in the road, go on a glide along the cliffs and swoop down into the mist drifting out over the water past ghostly sea stacks the size of skyscrapers, with no concern that anything more than his resolve had taken flight.

CHAPTER V

A GRASP OF CERTAINTY

Porter's cell buzzed against his chest as they were driving up the coast to Millfork, which they had also learned from Eric was the county seat. Service was spotty but it was not Maddie. It was Warren, and spotty or not, Warren was put out.

I just got off...the commissioner...not the chief deputy...Ernest himself and...pissed...CHP commiss...woke him up...just what ...doing up there?

Warren, you're breaking up. Hang on a minute.

Perhaps the bad connection was a blessing he should have exploited, but his curiosity got the better of him. He asked Joel to pull over. That helped.

Did Ernest say what set the CHP commissioner off?

Just that a couple Insurance wannabes crapped up their investigation with a lot of horseshit theories they don't have time to chase down. What are you after?

What did Maddie tell you?

Only that it might go beyond Insurance issues of smashed cars, but she couldn't look at it directly. That was good enough for last night, but now I need details I can defend or I'm going to have to pull you back. Hang on, this is her on the other line.

Typical Warren, ready to singe his people for doing what he ordered. While Porter sat listening to dead air, he marveled idly at a tiny gray bird flitting up and down the woolly trunk of a conifer as it probed cracks with a pin-sized beak. Unlike the bird, Porter felt like he was getting a little too high to be working without a net.

He put his cell on speaker so Joel could hear. Warren was back.

Michael, you there?

Yup.

Madeline?

Still here. Good morning, Michael. I got your message.

(But you had to call Warren first? This cannot be good.)

Warren wants to know what I'm doing here and, frankly, so do I. It seems half of Sacramento beat feet up here last night. Did you know the governor was here yesterday? Why didn't you tell me? It doesn't seem to be much of a secret with the locals.

Inexplicably, it sounded as if she was laughing.

Try decaf, Michael. You sound over-amped. Warren, the governor's trip was off calendar. I didn't know where until now, but I did know he was seeing Morris. When I heard her car went off a cliff in the middle of the night, I took a chance and called you to let Michael check it out.

Warren came on.

What's it to you? Why not let CHP handle it?

Just a guess, but it sounds like CHP is too close to the governor since they do his security. She's also the wife of one of the members, so it sounds messy. Anyway, they aren't sharing and people want to know. I can't tell you who asked us to do the parallel, so don't ask.

More dead air, which Warren was the first to break.

What have you got, Michael?

Only that it might be a homicide. CHP must agree or they wouldn't have called their forensics back to the scene to look at some footprints we found. No, it's not a hundred percent, but it's not horseshit either.

Maybe, but DOI can't be sniffing up CHP's backside without good cause or I'll be the one twisting in the wind. If there's nothing like insurance fraud we have to back out. What's there for us?

Well, the low speed take-off suggests the car might have been dumped. That puts a cloud over any insurance claim, which makes it our business.

Warren gave one of his hemorrhoidal grunts.

Pretty weak. All right, you can keep him for now, Maddie, but this better be legit. While I have you, I want to talk about an upgrade to the stone-age wiretap gear DOJ loans us.

Can we get together later on that? I have another meeting in five.

I'm here all day. Michael?

Warren?

I'll need you to keep me in the loop.

Maddie added her: *Me too,* and said she had to go.

Joel gestured for the phone. Porter leaned away.

Wait a minute—I got it, Joel—Maddie, you haven't answered the big question. Whose water are we carrying here? I'm feeling a bit of a draft. Are we protecting the governor or helping someone who is looking to torpedo him?

Joel's head did some emphatic bobbing.

Maddie's tone took on the flavor of a person talking to a child.

Does it matter? I told you the request came from someone in the administration, so we have to assume we are acting in the governor's, the state's, best interests.

Joel scowled, and spoke up extra loud to be heard over Porter's cell.

Which is why no one will tell us who made the request? Come on.

You put up with that, Warren? Tell your partner to calm down, Michael. We're all on pins and needles up here waiting for the recount, since we don't know who or what party we will be working with in January. It's going to be real close, but the incumbent has the advantage so we expect Vaneros to win re-election. If he does, everyone expects him to take a shot at the White House, which is why the more eyes on this Morris thing, the better. Whether Gorman beats Vaneros, Gorman is still my boss until January. You guys just do your jobs, and let me worry about whether there is a thumb on the scale. I gotta go.

Porter put the window down to let in some air. His first impression was that the sea was totally flat, but as he watched, it became apparent that a slow heave of low swells angled in from the northwest. The two tiny geysers that shot up about a half mile offshore surprised him until they repeated a few seconds later a bit farther south. A pair of whales headed for Baja to bear their calves, trailing funnels of spray that tore sideways in the breeze. How nice it must be to know instinctively that you were heading in the right direction. Celeste seemed to have managed pretty well at that, and he was a bit envious. It had been a long time since his uniformed days when he felt that he was in a place that he belonged. He tried to recall the sudden wakefulness he had the night before at Cape Hallelujah when he began to sense this was no ordinary car crash, when the shinier pieces of debris scattered down the cliff face took on a significance beyond the rusted, self-inflicted detritus of events attributable to the actions of sole individuals, whether their ends were intentional or not. Holly Morris had help, and whatever mess she had gotten herself into, if her life had not gone according to plan, it did not deserve to end the way it did, and his might feel a bit less disheveled if he could show that. He owed her, himself, at least that much. Proving it would not be easy, but there was allure in that, too. It was a puzzle but it had a direction, and with it a feeling that certainty was out there somewhere and could be brought within grasp, an imbalance set right, chaos resolved to an orderly form.

But he was naïve not to suspect a host of less savory motivations for their involvement, and Maddie had only reminded him of that with her explanations that were not, with her dismissive condescension substituting for a moral compass. The sense that he might be onto something that needed doing, that could right a wrong, was slipping from his grasp faster than shreds of a pleasant dream. Maddie hadn't even done a passable job pretending that she did not want good soldiers as much as she wanted dumb ones, and Porter owed her zip.

So here they were sitting, going nowhere. Joel looked to be sorting it out, too, waiting for some sign from him. The smart thing to do would be to call Warren back and have him tell Maddie she could find some other fools to haul her freight. But here he sat, refusing to say straight out that, however debauched this deal might turn out to be, he could not turn his back on it. Besides, the alternative held little appeal: an endless heaping of sour, adulterated mush served up by estranged wives, corroded and hapless supervisors and lesser chiselers in his burned-out hash house office on a dismal side street. It seemed his choices were one or the other. Better to go down swinging then, even if he might be just punching at clouds, trying to be of some service to a dead woman he barely knew because the live wife he did know was no longer interested. But Joel deserved better, even if he, Porter, might be confusing lost causes.

Still wanna work for DOJ, Joel?

Joel sniffed, wrung the steering wheel.

I don't recall asking. Or being asked, for that matter. Are they all like this over there?

Porter was tempted to ask if he meant the people or the assignments, but decided it did not matter.

I think most people would conclude that the Justice Department is kind of a snake pit, Joel. You've got an A.G. who's an elected official, presiding over a department that is supposed to root out corruption in government, including elections. The mission conflict is built in.

I'll say. Especially if they have to borrow agents from another department to do their dirty work.

Most likely, but I also have to wonder...

Joel looked surprised.

You got another idea?

Well, on some level it really could be just a due diligence thing. Only the A.G. has to have some distance from it so the investigation doesn't look politically motivated. It will look like payback if Gorman loses the recount, and worse if he wins, because then it will look like the A.G. is being petty and churlish in an attempt to bury Vaneros even after he beat him.

So, why bother then?

Gorman may feel that he doesn't have a choice. Damned if you do, damned if you don't. What bothers me is wondering if he even knows about this. Much less ordered it. But somebody was with her there last night.

Joel shifted in his seat.

You think Vaneros is dirty?

Porter pondered.

I think they're all dirty, but of this in particular? All we know is he is involved with Morris, and he was in the area with her about the time she died.

Nice picture, Mike. I feel like the girl in the slasher flick going up to the attic at midnight in the abandoned house.

Porter checked his watch.

Speaking of horror shows, how long do you think it will take to get to Millfork?

Joel seemed not to hear. Sat looking straight ahead. Probably pondering his squeaky clean rep, and who knew what else. Porter tried again, but wondered who he was convincing.

What else we got? Just a pile of steaming flamer claims back at the office.

More staring out the window, but eventually Joel got back on the highway and left Porter to the view which, thankfully, needed no explaining.

CHAPTER VI

DENSE COASTAL FOG

As meetings go, it was going to be one of those. Everyone supposedly kissing cousins and thicker than blood until the will was read and it was no use any more denying that their self-interest, the one thing they really had in common, meant they would prefer to see each other dead. Porter played along with the charade because it was part of the drill, and the sheriff and CHP commander did the same. They knew as well as he did that it was bad form to brandish before proper introductions had been made or they would not have gotten where they were in their professions. So they shook hands, exchanged cards, asked about backgrounds and talked a little football while trying not to glance at their watches as discussion topics among doers not talkers dwindled.

CHP Commander Jerome Quill did not fit the mold at all. He was short, surfer blond and too young for a commander, with a flat gut that donuts would bounce off of. He was congenial but watchful. Probably a quick study, which might explain the rank. Sheriff Anthony Baylor had a pretty good donut gut going, but with TAC squad biceps that strained against his sport coat. He was much more at ease than Quill, with a relaxed body language and a manner that said, whatever their differences, they could probably work out something to their mutual benefit. It probably got him a lot of votes, but only made Porter ill at ease wondering at the depth of that sincerity, and if Baylor was the better dancer at gigs like this. Porter was also having trouble making small talk because he was beginning to wonder if the D.A. had not purposely kept them waiting out of some sort of self-congratulatory efficiency thing that was really just work avoidance, hoping that they would work things out among themselves in his absence. If so, the D.A. was wasting all of their time.

All eyes popped to the door when it opened, but it was a false alarm. It was only the D.A.'s investigator, Jeff Sentienne, apologizing that his boss was running late, but really functioning as the herald of the D.A.'s imminent arrival. He did the round of hands with the appropriate feigned regret. Porter took in his tall good looks balanced with prematurely thinning hair and a discount store suit flared over love handles, and took him for a go-along, get-along sort as Sentienne endured the weak greetings of his now clearly half-interested associates. Mercifully, the door eventually admitted the D.A., but it was not a he, which Porter had forgotten, conventional expectation filling in for lack of sleep.

When a limousine pulls into a stock yard, the cowhands tend to notice, and if east coast prep schools had a look, he figured it would look like this long neck brushed by the shimmery corn silk ends of a cut that could not be more than an hour old. Now there was a thoroughbred to join the elephant in the room, but the locals avoided any eye contact that might acknowledge what a show pony had arrived. A moment later and Porter understood why as the county D.A., later identified as Stephanie Flanders, shouldered the conference door shut with a distracted apology for running late as she continued an argument about unreimbursed per diem on her cell phone, leaving Porter with the further impression that this was her ordinary M.O.: always late and not really sorry. As an accessory, her attitude was the perfect match for her beige very-tailored blazer over cream blouse. It was a look Porter normally associated with assistants to CEO's, TV news anchors and flacks. The top half was all business, but the coordinated pencil skirt was a good four inches short and she knew she had the legs to get away with it. This woman was not above using those legs as tools or weapons to get what she wanted. What she wanted was somewhere beyond this slackwater county, and she made sure it was obvious. She set her phone on the table, glanced at but ignored its immediate buzz, introduced herself, and said she wanted to make sure everyone was on the same page, beginning with Insurance, getting right to the question the CHP commander and sheriff had spent twenty minutes avoiding.

Why are you guys here?

Porter gave her his best bureaucrat: The available facts indicated that the collision might not have been accidental. The state had an interest in making sure any resulting insurance claim was legitimate and had no regulatory or political repercussions, since this was arguably a high-profile case, as was evidenced by this meeting. And someone in the administration had asked that he be here.

Flanders fixed him with a pair of deep green drowning pools that she no doubt had practiced on witnesses committing perjury.

Quill rose to his rank and piped up that protecting the administration's officers, and the state's interests when it came to highway safety, was the primary function of the CHP.

Baylor broke in and said as long as coroner inquiries were his lead, everyone could get on *his* page when he was finished with his investigation. As far as CHP involvement, this was a simple traffic accident until proven otherwise. If there arose any question about cause of death, it was an official sheriff-coroner inquiry, and his responsibility.

Quill reminded Sheriff Baylor that state highway fatals were his jurisdiction, and whatever the coroner found would be an attachment to the official CHP accident report.

What Porter had in mind was suggesting they call a break and deal with what was really on their minds; in pursuit of which Baylor and Quill could save them all time if they would just unzip and flop their arguments on the table to see whose was more impressive. What came out was a snort that got away from him, which swiveled Quill's and Baylor's glares around at him, now two halves of a domestic whose combatants forgot their squabble in favor of settling for a piece of this interloper instead. He raised two palms in mock surrender.

Flanders tugged at the hem of her skirt with an irritated grimace.

Whenever you boys are through kicking dirt on each other's shoes, may I remind you that whatever criminality may come of this it's going to be a tar baby to prosecute, *my* tar baby, if you guys can't work together. Now, Insurance did you two a favor by finding what may be a key piece of evidence that you overlooked. My advice is we all agree this is not the time to campaign for office and work together to get out in front of this investigation, get it packaged and off our desks.

Quill's immobility and silence had the effect of emphasizing an unwillingness to concede anything, a diplomatic broadside that Porter found admirable. He had underestimated Quill, and overestimated Baylor, who had gone red in the face, prompting the D.A. to target him first.

Calm down, Tony. I'm not finished. Ultimately there can be only one official inquiry, and that should be the Coroner's, since the Sheriff's Department has the body.

At this Baylor puffed up in validation, but Flanders was not done.

But you have to start with Jerry's collision report, and you should include anything—she glanced at the cards on the table—Mister Porter and Mister Vega find out about the car or the insured. Tony, you and Jerry can also do your own legwork on that if it makes you happy. Yeah, there's going be overlap, but that will make sure nobody overlooks anything. Again. You all coordinate with Jeff and let's get this done.

There was scraping of chairs and Baylor and Quill went into

a heated huddle in the corner, effectively dismissing the rest of them. Flanders ignored them and addressed him and Joel.

If you two have a minute, I'd like to talk to you down the hall.

Down the hall meant her office, and the inescapable rear view of those remarkable stems clicking purposefully along in front of them. Joel signaled his appreciation to Porter by the downward thrust of his mouth corners and the slightest nod while Flanders put the stretch to that skirt. Porter ignored him, and not just because Sentienne was bringing up the rear. Porter saw only beauty defiled.

Her office had the pristine sterility of a person who had other people do their work for them, and a too-large desk made even larger by the dearth of papers—a desk she had to sit behind for their edification despite the couch and chairs she had to walk past to get to it. Joel sprawled on the salmon-pink couch without being asked. Sentienne took a matching chair. Porter remained standing until invited to sit, and eased reluctantly into the other chair. Flanders was no less direct in this exchange.

I want you two to know that you're not fooling anyone. I know why you're here, and if the A.G. wants you sniffing around there's not much I can do about it. But I want to know what you're doing, even if Tony and Jerry don't care, is that understood?

Joel sat up straight now and rested his elbows on his knees, signaling annoyance better than a catcher signing the high outside pitch he wanted so he could take the pitch up and away and pick off the base stealer at second. Porter accommodated him, with a caution.

Joel and I don't have any specific instructions, if that's what you're getting at. So if you think there's some sort of agenda—

Joel cut him off, and sent one whizzing over his head.

What my partner is trying to say is that everyone seems to know a lot more about what's going on than we do. So if you have information about why everyone is so jacked up, why don't you let us in on it? The governor is single, and he can date who he wants, short of maybe hookers and strippers. And even if someone pushed her car over the side with her in it, I don't see the governor out there getting mud on his Florsheims.

Flanders stabbed her desk pen in and out of its holder a few times before she replied, with Sentienne looking at the floor, making it plain he wanted to be anywhere else.

She's not just a reporter. You knew that, right?

Joel, as usual, was not up for twenty questions.

We might, if we hadn't spent all morning going to meetings.

Flanders gave Porter a *Get-your-partner-in-line* look and was now clearly addressing him, not Joel.

Do you want information or not?

Thanks to Joel, he now had to play suck-up to this woman.

Sorry, we've been up all night. It might be best if you assume we know nothing except what we got at the scene. We haven't even read the CHP report yet.

Flanders put both hands flat on the desk, and spoke in clipped bursts that made it clear she was not happy about being asked to serve coffee to the help.

The governor is single but Morris is not. And her husband is Assemblyman Thomas Biel. If you guys are so bush league that you don't know this, then you should turn your fog lights on because you are a hazard to yourselves and others. Politics is about appearances, and if you involve the governor without good cause you could end up working out of Yuma, because that will be the closest town to your next assignment.

This was news, but it was not his job to remind her he worked for the insurance commissioner, not the A.G., even if he was ostensibly on loan. And certainly not for the governor. Short of whittling their budget, there was not much the governor could do if he was unhappy with another elected official's investigation. Flanders also might be holding back, which was more the issue at hand. He decided it was worth a shot.

I have a report that you were seen at the Pemberton Inn last night. Is that true?

Flanders looked at him as if he had asked about vomit on her coat sleeve.

Where did you hear that?

A stall was not the answer he expected. A subject never answered a question with a question unless they were shook. The thing was not to give her any more time.

From a witness. Well?

Too late. She was back in her comfort zone.

It's my job to know what goes on in my county. It was a courtesy visit to make sure the governor felt welcome. Now, are we done here?

Sentienne rode in to the rescue.

I was just going to get some lunch. You guys want to join me? I'll show you the best Mexican in town.

Flanders was on her phone before Porter could answer, so there was nothing to do but follow Sentienne and Joel outside. Sheriff Baylor and CHP Commander Quill were still in a forehead-to-forehead that had progressed no farther from the conference room than the parking lot. Sentienne extended the lunch invitation to them. Quill begged off, claiming another commitment and unlocked his black, unmarked Crown Vic. Baylor, by contrast, acted like he had run into old friends.

Great idea. You buyin', Jeff?

Sentienne just laughed and said to meet at Hermosa's.

Porter and Joel hitched a ride with Sentienne, who seemed to lighten up the farther he got from the county courthouse. It seemed like a good time to float an observation.

Jeff, your boss doesn't seem like she really fits in Millfork. What's her story? She's not from around here, is she?

Sentienne considered for a moment.

Actually, she was born and raised right here in town. But,

you're right. Most people let their hair down after a while, even the transplants. She went the other way. I think she thought she had escaped. She got a degree from Columbia on a full scholarship, and went to work for a big criminal defense firm in L.A. At some point she got religion and swapped hats to become a lead prosecutor. Then her mom got sick. She's not thrilled to be back here, but you have to cut her some slack. She could have just put her mother away and sent checks to some home.

Joel was not so easily mollified.

Well, her manners could use some work.

Porter determined that the town could use some work, too, as he took in Millfork's offerings on the way to the restaurant. Even the main street had a scattering of boarded up storefronts. The shops were mostly faced with extruded aluminum sash work that might have been an upgrade in the fifties, but now looked stark, tawdry.

Hermosa's was a laminate countertop and red plastic tumbler affair, but the grease was minimal and the portions were huge. Porter was half way through his enchiladas by the time Sheriff Baylor came in. They watched him work the room like he had all the time in the world. By the time he joined them it was only coffee he wanted. Baylor had given some thought to his own manners, apparently, since the first meeting. He was all smiles now.

So, what did Mizz Flanders want with you two?

Porter had his mouth full and waved Joel ahead. Joel nodded his regrets to Sentienne as he fired away.

With apologies to Jeff, here, I think his boss is a cunt. She wanted to know if we had some kind of agenda. I think she mistook us for two guys who have more on their backs than just doing their job. I didn't appreciate it.

Baylor found this amusing, and leaned in so the other diners and loungers would not hear.

I keep having to remind her she's not my boss either. If

anyone has an agenda, it's that woman. She got elected promising to clean up the large-scale pot grower operations and leave anyone with a patient or caregiver card alone. Only now she's tossing back cases on technicalities where we give her five thousand plants on a property trespass tied up with a bow. Some of my task force guys are wondering if the money we spend on C.I.'s might be better spent on a contract to take her out. Just kidding, of course.

Baylor sat back with a satisfied smile.

Sentienne looked a little hurt.

Some of your deputies are better at chopping bales of dope than finding the growers responsible. And I think you have to give her credit for trying to find some balance between the law and what the county voters want. You should work up more meth cases. There's a public safety issue if there ever was one.

Baylor's self-satisfied smirk now turned sour.

Oh, please. If I hear: *Bring me the white stuff,* one more time I'm gonna puke. We've run most of the tweaker labs out of the county already. Meanwhile, the Mexican cartels have gotten the message your boss is soft on pot. My guys are bringing in bigger and bigger hauls because the grows are getting bigger and bigger. The voters are sick of it, which is why they re-elected me twice. I'm not after mom and pop, or some cancer patient's backyard pot. Hell, I don't have the time or the manpower.

Then why don't you work with Stephanie to put Prop 14 on the ballot next year? It will let anyone have a small garden for personal use, not just medical.

Because until the feds make it national it would only attract more dirt bags here. The cat's already out of the bag, Jeff, but I don't have to feed it. The voters get that too, which is why it'll get a big thumbs down.

Sentienne looked over at Porter and Joel. Baylor noticed.

Don't let Jeff and me give you two indigestion. This is just how we play checkers up here in the sticks. I gotta go. I'll give you all a call as soon as the Morris tox report comes in.

Baylor stood and shook hands around, holding onto Porter's an extra beat.

You guys have fun with Flanders, but watch she doesn't turn you into panty sniffs like Jeffy here.

He tossed a wink at Sentienne, and was out the door with a wave to the other customers.

Sentienne chased a few fugitive beans around his plate with a fold of tortilla, his retort as dyspeptic as his expression.

Tony reminds me of one of those letters to the editor. The ones where somebody writes in to object to raising the county sales tax and you find out later the guy owns a local car dealership. The cartels are definitely getting a foothold here, and they're getting violent about protecting their grows, which makes them a popular target. But mom and pop? Mom and pop went to dope school and are converting every abandoned garage and warehouse into year-round grow houses with genetically twisted seeds, space age hydroponics and weird spinning light clusters that turn out weed that will kick your ass. Some of them are getting plants that produce a pound or two of bud per plant, and getting better than a grand a pound, even with the prices collapsing with the current glut. Until recently the best stuff was going for around three grand. So mom and pop went and got second homes in Aspen and Cancun. Tony knows this, but he also knows they support the local nurseries, the hardware stores, the auto dealers, truck and equipment rentals, the agricultural supply businesses, the plumbers, carpenters, electricians, and you name it. People who vote. As long as the operations are indoors and he's not getting complaints about the stink from the neighbors, Tony is better off siccing his limited staff on the outdoor grows that generate big numbers of low-grade plant seizures on paper and don't ruffle any of the establishment growers. Call it job security. His deputies are just seasonal harvesters with guns and pensions since the outdoor growers just come back and replant year after year knowing the task force can never get to them all, much less hit them every year or catch the grower in the act. I guess what I'm saying is Tony is no different than Stephanie. He's just doing the best he can with what he's got and tiptoeing down the middle of the voters. Come on, let me show you something.

On the ride back to their car Sentienne swung around town past former company houses identical except for the upkeep. Next to ones with fresh white paint, a neat yard and a clean but faded American pickup—the signs of people long used to industry and self-reliance—were places being rapidly weather beaten into shacks. These had muddy, rusting Toyotas in the yard, against which lounged working-age men of the sort that Porter associated with no visible means of support; men whose industry consisted of observing closely any strange passing vehicle, especially ones with exempt plates. Sentienne's tour continued in a loop that took in the harbor while he explained that the town's two biggest industries, fishing and timber, had succumbed to the disappearance of the things that had sustained them. Dead was the operative word at the harbor all right. A few corroding fishing boats huddled shoulder to shoulder against brooding warehouses under a stillness that could not be explained by the off season alone. He wondered why someone would leave a large forklift out in the weather to rust, and why there were no transients scavenging around. A waterfront that was too lifeless to attract bums was something new.

Deader still was the abandoned mill at the south end of the harbor, its acres of scattered sheds giving it a deceptive scale without any human activity or device to settle the buildings into the familiar. They looked like ordinary sheds and shops, some wood, some tin, some both, until Sentienne steered toward one and let it fill the horizon. Under the blank regard of phalanxes of broken windows, Porter could see there was space inside to park a Hindenburg, which would be easy since the structure was stripped of equipment to bare walls he glimpsed past the languid swell of torn canvas doors the size of sails swelling out in the breeze. Where there should have been a cacophony of shrieking saws, calls of men and the rumble of trucks, there was now only a loose panel of corrugated tin siding beating in cut time. Sentienne put the millworks behind them and parked on a featureless cliff above the waves, got out and walked to the edge, and pointed down.

What do you see?

Porter saw only the cliff face, with the butts of a few old tree trunks jutting out of the face twenty feet down.

So?

Sentienne pointed at the tree stubs.

See how the ends are cut off? They didn't get here by themselves. Even redwoods would have rotted long before now if they were washed downstream and left behind by seafloor uplift thousands of years ago. They got there from a century of millworkers pushing cull logs over the side just to get them out of the way, and bulldozing the gullies flat to make room for more mill buildings, log staging and stacks of lumber.

Porter looked around the open plain and realized they were standing on the castoff bones and skin of entire forests converted to a graveyard of ocean frontage made only more vacant by the empty buildings. There was not a tree to be seen for a mile in any direction, and so much open terrace was grossly out of place in a land of hills, tortuous valleys, and giant conifers. Yet here was clearly once the center of life for the town, a convergence of trucks, people, ambitions and energy now drifted away on the wind with the smoke from the collapsing teepee burner not yet torn down for scrap.

Sentienne palmed his tie which was beginning to flap in the increasing wind.

This is what we're up against. Dope growing was only a hippy sideshow until so many families lost the work they had been doing for generations. Some moved away. Some stayed and took up other trades like construction, took up art, sold real estate to retirees, or opened B and B's for tourists. Some weren't into bagging groceries and started talking to the hippies who were driving new pickups and paying cash for generators to run their pumps, lights and fans. The rationale is that they just found a new natural resource to sell downstream. Dope is just a symptom of people trying to adapt to changes they can't control.

And hell with the law, shot Joel.

Sentienne looked discomfited but resolute, with arms crossed as he examined the dust at his feet.

Government has never been popular up here. They blame Uncle Sam for closing off the fishing and making too many rules to make a living harvesting the pecker poles that are all that is left after all the big trees were sold wholesale to Japan to pay off some junk bonds.

Joel had something to say about that, too.

You sound sympathetic. The government didn't cut down all the old growth and chase all the fish out of Dodge.

Sentienne shrugged.

Sympathetic and public safety are two different things. There's also the home invasions, rip-offs and shootings that catch up with a lot of them. The lifestyle sucks. My wife knows people who turn down invitations to certain parties because the only people there are growers sitting around smoking, drinking and paranoid.

Porter did his best to organize his impressions of the county from Sentienne's tour and what he had gleaned from the other agency representatives. The picture he got was a little skewed:

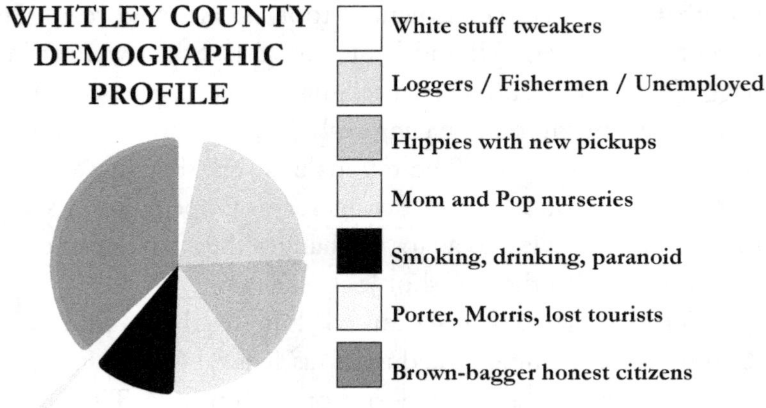

It was also pretty obvious there had to be a lot of overlap.

They thanked Sentienne for the tour and headed back down coast to the Pemberton Inn, where Morris had last been seen alive. Porter had little interest in the passing coastline that had so enthralled him earlier. Despite the view, the backdrop was not what defined this county. You could not eat pretty scenery any more than a local grocer could fail to notice an abundance of reeking greenbacks in the till every fall. It seemed there was a lot that had to be overlooked living here. Curiously, amid wondering if there was any place on earth man had not yet found a way to demean, he found this reassuring.

CHAPTER VII

BREAKWATER TIME

Celeste's bedroom looked out on an open ridge of tall, fall-seared grass poured downhill into a meadow surrounded by redwoods. She knew there were similar views anywhere from the Santa Cruz Mountains to the Canadian border, but this one was still spectacular. More so because it was hers. Because it was home. She liked feeling that she was still connected to where she grew up—the sun and fog here that walked her back to streets and sidewalks flung up over soaring hills, tight houses all squeezed skyward out of their narrow allotments, eucalyptus and coffee smells—but what remained of San Francisco was an unconscious affection for these reminders, a trait that she had simply inherited. It was always a part of her like her mother's eyes. She had a more visceral attachment to her adopted home. What she held here, and what held her, was a gathering memory of irretrievable and priceless investment in a landscape that still called her with a faded promise but yet a persisting hope. Each passing year was a reflexive inhalation of her changed and changeless surroundings, absorbed, distilled into her blood, if now more by habit than will.

Today it was both sun and fog. The fog was out there on the horizon in a thin smudgy band that might come in or not, or might drift away. She would not be here to find out, which made her want to sit on her deck and enjoy her perch. She knew there was only the distant Pacific beyond, her gaze pulled to the visible curve every morning for close to twenty years, but she wanted to sit here watching, and sip her coffee.

The march of shaggy tree crowns down grassy clearings

tipped nearly on edge straight down to the sea pulled the eyes of her guests down there, too, giving her a secret mirth to watch them struggle not to drift from her face even as they said their hellos. She understood that feeling. What she did not understand was why the view so completely unbalanced many of them after they haunted her for invitations and then drove hours to escape the city. What were they expecting? Maybe she was the one with expectations, forgetting that people who grew up in noise and lights could not just flip a switch and merge with the landscape. Most proved unequal to the scale of so much ocean and sky and became determined to find something out there to set their eyes on: a freighter, a whale, a passing barge with the tiny tow craft so far ahead it seemed disconnected. China maybe. Had she been like that? Now she preferred days like today. Endless cobalt with barely a whitecap upcoast. Straight out it bled to a titanium she was forever trying to approximate, which would become silver down the coast in the afternoon when the low sun skipped back at her, provided the massing black clouds down there held off with the fog. Her infinite canvas.

Wealthy retirees bought ridge tops for similar views, or plunked down millions to build at the water's edge. Both paid a price in wind and fog that pretty much kept them indoors. Winters especially she was glad Owen's family had the good luck to be fourth generation locals and the good sense to buy land off the south side of a ridge. That shoulder blocked the coldest storms from the north and made most days a deck napper's heaven, even if only for an hour or so around noon when rain or fog generally drifted downhill and the sky emerged. On days when the sun never showed, the house was still bathed in light from tall windows on all sides that Owen installed to celebrate the lack of any neighbors at this height, and a plethora of sky-lights that he had a special thing for, although he was always on the roof chasing leaks. Like him, she had to have her light. And some space. And she woke up every morning blinking in renewed astonishment, imagining how a prisoner would feel, unexpectedly pardoned, that she had both, even if it was just a consolation prize. So no, she had not forgotten. She just had the luxury of resetting her balance on her own terms every day when she woke up.

For her, for her work, it was mostly the light. Compared to the greenish cast of this north coast air, San Francisco might as well have been Los Angeles. It made no difference that she was brought up in the Sunset District, or maybe because of it. Light there was all one or the other by turns. So bright it hurt her eyes, or so fog-submerged the gray washed out everything, even the pastel stucco same-but-different houses in the avenues. Coming north up the coast was a lot easier on her eyes. It was months before she realized she had misplaced her dark glasses and had not noticed. But the forested valleys had too many redwoods, which suffocated her. They completely swallowed the light, dripped itchy needles all summer and rain all winter. She soon concluded that redwoods were best admired from afar, and at first she hung close to the ocean, nudged to the curve of beach sheltered by the stone breakwater at the head of the bay, taking the foggy days as penance for the sunny ones that set the deep green trees and opaque blue water buzzing against each other. How people lived in the dimness of the year-round pall in the tree-choked valleys was something she would never understand. But then Owen invited her up here.

At first she thought it was all this openness that made her fall for this place as much as for him, but when she saw her first sunrise she knew it was the light. Either way, it doubled her love for him immediately, irrationally. Any man that had a need for these things knew what was important and, while she had learned a lot about carpentry in finishing the inside of the house, in his honor she never got around to putting the wood trim around the inside of the front doorway. That way she was reminded of him whenever she left, just before she walked out into that wash of light, when the exposed shims in the gap between the stud framework and the door casement jumped out and carried her to the time when they picked the site and framed this house together. Missing baseboards and skylight trim went unnoticed after a few years, receding into the fabric of the house, a dropped stitch in an embroidered design that she lost because she was too close to it, was wearing it, but the unfinished doorway always startled her no matter how distracted she was in chasing down her car keys, or how hurried she might be to get to town after lingering too long over her coffee and the sea. Which she had done again.

Halfway down the hill there was a Doug fir across the road. Of course. Roots letting go in rain-softened ground and mudslides seemed to conspire to do so only on days she had to be at the café for the breakfast shift. But do-able she had already decided as she climbed out and reached in the bed of her truck for the chainsaw. Like many locals, she kept a saw handy the way people in Tahoe probably had snow chains in the trunk, or people in Death Valley must carry extra water. The tree was only about a foot thick where the road passed under, and even a former city girl could deal with this one. She'd just have to remember to brush the wood flakes out of her hair so someone did not order fish and chips later and get wood chips mixed in.

Ches, the owner, flipped his usual greeting over the hot shelf for waitresses who showed up late for their shift.

Good afternoon. Running on Breakwater time I see.

Which was his way of chiding her for emulating the town people, who Ches said lived a five minute walk from everything but always arrived a half hour late for anything, be it a council meeting, a haircut, or their own funeral. Inexcusable to him, but for her it was understandable given the years she lived right across the street from her high school. You had all the time in the world until you did not, and at least a couple times a week the final bell would ring while she was still brushing her teeth.

She would run out the door backhanding toothpaste off her mouth, and come flying through the door of first Algebra, then Civics, then Spanish, then Trig because first periods were the bane of her four years at Lincoln. Miss Gibbons would just fix her with that tight little smile which meant she could expect two additional problems to solve for her homework.

Her response was to exploit her favored status as Ches' most dependable employee, at least most days, by apologizing profusely for leaving him to fend off the crush of a pair of deuces rattling around in the otherwise empty café. He kept his time, she kept hers, and on foggy days she wondered if Breakwater time was not something else again, more in common with the life she imagined an abalone lived. The things clung to submerged rocks, moving imperceptibly as they grazed the algae or whatever it was they ate, turning a hardened back to the breakers overhead, to the strong currents and predators, fastened firmly, absorbed in their tiny, timeless, hermetic lives.

Katy, her favorite niece, joked that people moved to Breakwater to sit on the porch and die. She loved to visit, but soon chafed at the lack of internet at Celeste's house and fled back to the city. Well, yeah, there was that, but it was no more annoying than co-existing with so many panhandlers—if you could live wherever you wanted, why not live somewhere beautiful?—and who could blame them? A sunny day here was to die for. Idlers were just the dingy froth on a shining wave of people who came looking for the same thing and found a place where each moment held at least a shiver of possibility, where everyone and all things often connected in ways that were unexpected but not really surprising. It was not that the place was so small that anyone you talked to probably knew someone you knew too. And it was not that anyone could show up here, and eventually did, which was why she was delighted but not particularly surprised when Porter turned up. The realization made her smile all over again. She had poured coffee for movie stars, famous musicians, and countless familiar faces whose names she could not recall, but whose faces she had seen on the covers of newspapers, magazines, and flyers for fundraisers that pulled celebrities out of their local hideouts along with their musician/artist/actor friends from elsewhere. On balance, things seemed to turn out in a way that more or less made some sense here, more so than any place she had ever been. Even some of her mistakes turned out later to have at least OK outcomes, which was why she came to accept having to waitress. Call it her penance. It was what honest people did, and people belatedly honest with themselves. Others, like with Owen, she was still trying to figure out. Taking his crab boat south that day was just a cover, a timely excursion to blend in with boats from as far away as Washington converging on the waters off San Francisco for the start of crab season. A season that conveniently coincided with his need to get a hundred pounds of cannabis to market without risking the checkpoints that could appear suddenly on the only two roads out of Breakwater. But twenty-foot swells announcing the arrival of a cold front from Japan could appear just as suddenly. He had not figured on that, but went anyway. She went along with his side job as a disagreeable trait you tolerate in the person you love, like poor table manners or bad teeth. And up in their sanctuary, surrounded by woodsy freedom, she convinced herself his activities were fairly benign, unwilling to admit the size of the bet not just he, but she had wagered. Where could she go now that would not sever her attachment to a man that was so caught up in this place? And Porter, how did he figure into that, and why was she even wondering? His face held the serene desolation of a man who had been that way so long that he was no longer particularly bothered by it, or aware that it showed. Why should she find that intriguing? She had enough on her plate.

Be here now. Beverly surely intended the electric eye beep at her gallery door to alert her to an entering customer, but for Celeste, it always gave her a mental startle reflex, compelling her to take stock of herself and her surroundings. Here she was, with no recollection of the two blocks between the café and the gallery but the chill. It was cold in the gallery, too; Beverly saving money. How to tell her it might also be putting a chill on sales? People buy when they are happy. People are happy when they are comfortable. Beverly's short gray bob popped up from her desk behind the front display case and she stood up and came around, rubbing her hands together. She took both of Celeste's hands in hers, which encased Celeste's in two calla lily leaves, dry and cool as her greeting.

Crap it's cold.

And your nose is red, Bev. Why don't you turn on the heat?

It is on, but I turn it off at night now and it takes forever to heat the place up again. But your hands are so nice and warm.

Maybe we should trade jobs. Between the walking around tables and the kitchen, I'm always too warm.

Beverly threw and snatched back a quick glance over Celeste's shoulder, returned dubious.

We could, but I think you might do better where you're at.

Celeste followed her look and saw that her three latest works were still on the wall, answering the question she came in with.

Still slow, huh?

Doors are open, which is about all I can say.

Celeste remembered. She pulled away and produced a shortening-spotted napkin from inside her hand-woven Guatemalan shoulder bag, unfolded the paper, and there were two glistening bear claws.

The café was slow this morning, too, which is how I came upon these.

Beverly gave a little schoolgirl squeal.

Oh, you bad, bad girl. I'll put on some coffee.

While Bev was in back, Celeste cleared a corner off the desk, which seemed covered mostly in bills, not orders and invoices. When Bev came back with two mugs celebrating Breakwater

Days from two different years, Celeste asked her why she did not just close up for the holidays.

Well, I'd love to, but it's a funny time of year. One day nobody comes in at all and the next day pays a month's rent. Like Christmas Eve year before last when a guy who said he was Carl Strand's drummer came in and bought one of yours. That made a nice Christmas. Alan says the hotel is about half booked, so that might help bring in a few. You working on anything?

Celeste wondered if this was what it felt like to tell someone you were pregnant. What was in her mind was a distant staircase of steepled firs and redwoods tumbling down a dramatically steep mountainside to a bed of impenetrable blue going in and out of focus, an image shimmering in heat waves from hot grassy hillsides in between, there but existing half in the imagining. How to put it into words?

You'll probably laugh, but I don't know why I never thought of it before. It seemed like cheating at first. You know how gas keeps going up, so one day I got looking at Owen's telescope and pointed it down the hill. It's a whole new perspective on places I used to have to drive to. At first it didn't seem to bring enough into focus, but then I thought, what the hell, go with what you have. The colors are different and sometimes I have to guess what's around the corner or behind a fog bank. What I'm turning out is not so representational. Then it got me looking at pieces I did on site, and I'm borrowing from them but experimenting in different hues. I haven't got one I'm ready to show yet, but I might have something in a week or two.

Beverly grinned over her cup.

And look at you all excited. I knew something was up with you. I can't wait to see what you're doing. I just hope I'm still open.

It's your coffee, Bev. But, really, are things that bad? You know it's always dead in the winter.

Yeah, but not like this, and not two years in a row. If this keeps up I might be trimming buds by next fall.

Bev was not a gardener. She could only mean the other kind.

You? No way.

Bev's small, narrow face was a mix of astonishment and feigned affront, her tiny bird-set eyes unequal to the larger task of owlish challenge, which she seemed to know, so she let them flutter with ironic insult that Celeste should find her incapable of participation in that enterprise. After a moment she gave it up.

OK, so it wouldn't exactly be ornamental horticulture. But remember when I let Erin go because there wasn't enough framing to keep her on? Well, she showed up in a new used car last week and said she was doing just fine, getting thirty dollars an hour working for one of the growers. Maybe they could use an off-the-books bookkeeper.

Celeste snorted some coffee, and had to wait out the coughing fit.

I can just see the headline. Former assistant to Fortune Five Hundred CEO popped for laundering drug profits through her art gallery.

Beverly brightened.

There's an idea. You think I could find some rich dealer to underwrite me? For all I know, they're doing it indirectly already, all those all-cash people. You never know if they are rock stars or what, but you sure wonder, especially the ones that come around in late fall after the harvest is in. People in their twenties driving fancy cars. I love to see them walk in, but sometimes I wonder.

Celeste swigged from her cup and stood up.

Anyone with that kind of cash has to be way outside the medical marijuana limits, and who knows what else. You just hang on. Things always pick up by spring. If not, you can always come stay with me.

Beverly put out both arms and wrapped her in a hug.

You're so sweet. But you're not really looking for a room-mate and you know I could never live way out there like you.

And I don't think I could live in town. I have to scoot. I need to go by the art co-op and I promised Owen's folks I would pick them up a few things at Wendell's. I'll see you Tuesday.

The door sensor beeped her good-bye in unison with Beverly's. Outside, the rain fired a couple of warning splats and then unloaded a slanting fusillade that she felt right through her chore coat, the kind of Pacific storm that peeled paint. Still, she managed enough squint through the sting to admire the headlands across the bay, black and enormous one moment, then obscured behind drifting shreds of the explosive down-pour, not much different than looking through a telescope that was a little out of focus. For years she had worked to portray exactly the concrete thing that was in front of her, to render a landscape precisely as it stood and fix it in time. Later she enjoyed nuancing familiar subjects with the infinities of season, time of day, weather and, most enjoyably, her own emotions translated into shadings and texture and volume itself, whether she was feeling tentative and off kilter, or overflowing. There was a lifetime in exploring those connections and so she was at first apprehensive moving from there into experiments with how sight itself could be altered, not just the thing seen. And now here she was getting soaked, wondering if there might be more behind a moment than what was even visible. Time itself could be a vantage point, even if it had no fixed position. Memory could be blurry. Funny, how Porter's recall of their divergent lives was so at odds with her own. What if she turned the seeing around? If she were the rock and not the painter, what would she see? Was her life any less precarious than Beverly's? Than Owen's? A mere thistle to be taken away by the next gust? A terrifying thought. An exhilarating idea. As she rode the buffets in a wavering path along the boardwalk, it occurred to her that some things were worth getting wet for.

CHAPTER VIII

A SQUAT IN THE BUNKER

They missed the Pemberton twice, and when they found it, it was easy to see why. The turnoff was marked only by a small brass plaque that had been allowed to weather on a cypress trunk deep in the shade beside a rare stretch of straight road. Evidently this place wanted to be located but not easily found, and two city boys used to freeway signs ten feet wide were forced to stop at a water tank converted into a roadside art gallery where they learned that they had passed it. After they missed it the second time, Porter deduced that freeways were in their blood in other ways; the drag strip stretch of asphalt among the curves enticing Joel to drive too fast for either of them to see the turnoff or intuit why not. They found it only when they quit looking for signs, and slowed to examine any opening big enough for a road apron. *Up Yours*, was what came to mind as he pieced together the scripted lettering; whatever satisfaction there was in finding the place smothered by such a bald display of vacuous arrogance. Who would go to such lengths to proclaim their exclusivity at the expense of ordinary function?

Joel swung the car off the road, and the low winter sun glare rose up and was gone as the tree shade swept up the windshield. Now Porter got a better look. There was a stone gateway farther in. The gate alone had to cost thousands, which seemed even more extravagant since it was swung open, elevating its purpose further from utility to a custom artwork of immense driftwood logs bound in hammered copper bands just sheltered enough from the salt air to go red-brown instead of green. From there the road took a turn and widened, and the cypress trunks on the ocean side were trimmed up to make an advancing series of framed water views, any of which would have made a fine subject for a Japanese woodcut. The road curved back again as it swept down a long hill, bringing glimpses of a modest, slate-roofed gable into the foreground, then curved again, opening into an expansive gravel turnaround at the front steps of a structure that Porter could now see he had been subtly deceived about. The cottage he thought he had seen was actually an overwrought aggregate of sandstone block and timber that sought a promise of massive and timeless solidity within sight of a homecoming that was familiar, fleeting, nostalgic for a perfect time that may or may not have ever existed. Where were the human proportions hidden? Somewhere in the architectural details had to be clues. His best guess was bastardized gargantuan prairie farm house in the wide roof overhangs and tall windows set low in the walls. Deep-set sills, splashes of shingle siding and inlaid rough timber trim broke up the mass, tricked the eye into seeing the whole in half scale. The thing wanted to look hundreds of years old while leaving no doubt that it might have been built yesterday. And out of it all was the unmistakable intent: this was not your three-and-two in the suburbs, right down to the pea gravel under their tires that they were audibly sullying by their arrival. Evidently the Mexican gardener raking the gravel next to his wheelbarrow had a full-time job, the management not wishing to disturb the ambience with anything so crass as a leaf blower. It would take half a day to rake this, and would still leave a few fugitive leaves behind to demonstrate a veneration for Nature, albeit tamed within an inch of her life.

So I guess this would be how the other half scrapes by, hey, Joel?

Joel had his face squinched over the wheel, getting wowed no doubt the same as Porter by the chimney count, the strings of copper cups serving as downspouts, or perhaps the brass urns at the foot of the steps, probably costing both of their monthly salaries. The sharp angle to his neck gave Joel's voice a bit of a squeak.

More like one percent. Where the hell are we supposed to park?

It was obvious Joel shared Porter's sense of being out of his element, which made him irritable. Whoever had designed this place, however attractive and inviting it might appear at first look, had also made sure that people like Joel and him would be suitably impressed as well, and hence relegated to delivery boys. The only thing to do was ignore it and advise his partner to do the same because, despite all the subtle architectural sleight of hand, the only way into such a massively contrived edifice as the Pemberton Inn was to know damned well who you are: a personage clothed in the requisite style and poise needed to convey an assurance that you both possessed and deserved a surfeit of hidden assets; someone who wore the fashion so effortlessly, carelessly, as to impart a mass of character the equal of this building's true scale. He anointed Joel.

My guess is people that have to ask don't belong here. Just leave it right in front of the steps, and let's pretend we own the place. Otherwise, that gardener over there might think we're here after him or his job.

When Porter looked up from closing his door there was what would be called a handsome woman of a certain age on the porch, looking as if she had just stepped out to take the air in a heather, thigh-length Eileen Fisher cardigan over a white silk jersey and black Capri's. The outfit was a good complement to her white hair, swept back from her face and wrapped loosely at the back, relaxed but business-like, not the Dutchboy popular with older women under the mistaken hope that it looked sporty when it just made most of them look butch. He wondered if paying guests would have been greeted at car side or at least at the foot of the stairs. The porch-top venue evidently was her compromise between establishing her status for these arriving functionaries, and providing a reasonable approximation of a personal welcome if her profiling turned out to be wrong. The warmth of her smile was genuine enough, a happily surprised grandmother greeting an unannounced but favorite niece. She moved to greet them when they reached the top of the stairs, her fingertip handshake the only indication that she would not have preferred to give them hugs instead. The handshake clinched it. He had felt the urge to let himself be taken in, but he was nobody's niece. He examined her alley-cat gray eyes looking directly at him, knowing she was doing the same. He could see that the corners of her eyes and her washboard neck wrinkles had some training, either coming up the hard way or working show horses for hour upon hour in the sun, he could not tell. Either way, she could probably well afford a facelift now if she wanted one. This woman had more pride than that.

Welcome to the Pemberton, gentlemen. I'm Katherine Monteith. Won't you come in?

So she was not going to talk business on the porch in front of the gardener. And she knew they had not driven all the way down the hill just to ask directions. That was fine.

Inside was a broad alcove leading to a lounge that would have comfortably held a gathering for fifty, but the details again reduced it to parlor feel. A Middle-Eastern area rug bordered with glistening plank flooring and tall baseboards shrunk the floor space, fat wood beams and crown moldings dropped the high ceiling, and dark leather furniture absorbed the middle. Monteith gestured them to a couch and she immersed herself in an armchair, at which point a much younger and attractive blonde in a navy pantsuit appeared with a tray of coffee. She set the tray down and disappeared without making eye contact, as though the idea were to make the stuff appear as if out of nowhere. Monteith poured. It was savory and medium bodied with a robust finish. Kick-butt stuff, brewed seconds before.

She must have ordered it up as soon as she saw them, or when they triggered a sensor or camera at the gate, more likely. After glancing at their business cards she set them aside, asked where they were from, how they liked the drive out, had they ever been up this way before and had they any trouble finding the Pemberton. It was just small talk, part of a routine to put guests at ease, but it had the effect of doing anything but. Finally, she directed her attention to him, assuming correctly that the one with the girth and the receding hair was the lead, even if she missed their titles on the cards.

How may I help you today?

We're hoping you can give us some information. There was a highway fatality last night just south of here. We're assisting CHP in the investigation. They're looking at the mechanics of the actual collision, and we're gathering information on the driver and the vehicle's background. We understand that the woman that was killed may be acquainted with one of your guests, Governor Vaneros.

He sat watching the response, which was slow in coming. Other than that, she took it like a pro.

It seems you're fairly well informed. What is it you would like to know?

I have to ask your cooperation in keeping this confidential until her next of kin have been notified, but, under the circumstances, you'll understand we have a need to gather all the facts as quickly as possible. Her name is Holly Morris.

Holly Morris? Is Dead? Dear God.

Their hostess turned this over while she sipped her coffee for a moment.

Pardon me. I really liked her. She was a reporter on Channel 7, you know.

So she was here?

Would you excuse me a mom—

Monteith set her cup down and made as if to get up, then

must have thought better of it. She retrieved her cup and settled back into the chair.

We had no one registered by that name here last night. That isn't to say that she wasn't here. Or was. Our guests are certainly free to have visitors, in any event.

Monteith was being a good soldier, but she was the one who was out of her element now.

Miss Monteith—

Mrs.

I'm sorry. Mrs. Monteith, do you have security cameras on the grounds?

Of course.

He watched her ruminate on that piece of gristle. Then she attempted a little face saving.

I'm sure the governor's security detail has his visitors well documented. You really should talk to them, but, yes, she was here.

She had a point, but now that he had her talking, he was not going to concede it.

We're working closely with them, but it's best to confirm all the facts from a variety of sources in these matters, to make sure nothing is overlooked. Do you know what time she arrived, and what time she left?

She got here well after dark, around eight-thirty, I think, but I have no idea what time she left.

Are there any other staff that might?

The only staff who were on after eight, besides myself, were the cook and a porter. Their instructions are to stay in the kitchen and an adjacent lounge unless I call them. I let them go at midnight, and I left shortly thereafter.

Did the governor have any other visitors?

Monteith seemed to visibly relax now.

Just one that I know of. His aide asked to have the Cézanne meeting room stocked from seven on. Stephanie Flanders, the county district attorney, joined him there. Around ten-thirty, I think.

Joel wanted a piece of this.

Kind of late for a meeting, wasn't it?

Monteith was smiling now.

It's been my experience that people in the governor's position can keep whatever schedule they choose.

This made sense, or at least a good cover, but from Porter's perspective, a scheduled meeting between the D.A. and the governor was still a problem, at whatever time. Flanders had mentioned only dropping by as a courtesy. Joel seemed to have missed it, and was pressing on.

Other guests? Other visitors?

Just one of his staff.

Her response was as brief and emphatic as it was spontaneous. She would have to be a very accomplished liar to fake that. This was not getting them much. He let Joel carry on with the routine, watching closely.

Did you notice what time Miss Flanders left?

Sorry. I let the CHP security guys handle the comings and goings after everyone got settled. I was in my office most of the time looking over accounts.

Now this was more like it. When Porter heard someone say they were down in the bunker and knew squat, it was more likely they knew plenty. And doing the books with the governor on the grounds? All the training and discretion in the world could not have kept her from snooping a bit. Joel may have caught this one, too.

Did you notice anything out of the ordinary at all last night?

Other than the people I mentioned being here? No.

Where are your security monitors located, Mrs. Monteith?

In the porter's lounge, and another set in my office.

Anything catch your eye?

I'm sorry, no. There's no sound, so most of the time it's just, let's see, an empty hallway, the parking lot, and the front gate. I was working on ordering, so I would have had to look up at just the right moment to even see anyone on the screen.

Too much explanation. She knew something. Porter had a question, one he had been saving.

Do you serve alcohol here, Mrs. Monteith?

We're licensed, if that's what you mean. The guests serve themselves unless there's a catered event. Last night was informal.

Did you happen to notice if Miss Morris was drinking?

It wouldn't be for me to say if I did. But actually, no, I didn't. Her or anyone else, for that matter. I can check our inventory, but that won't tell you who drank what.

And the meeting with Flanders. Would you have any idea what the meeting was about?

I most certainly would not. And forgive me, but I wouldn't tell you if I did. You would need to ask the governor. By the way, I never said he had a meeting, or a meeting with D.A. Flanders. I just said he asked for the room and she joined him there. And no, I don't mean to infer anything by that.

I understand now. Thank you for clarifying. I heard *meeting* or *meeting room* in there somewhere, and I thought, if there had been something scheduled, knowing what it was might give us a sense of whether it might have included Miss Morris. I didn't mean to infer anything else, either. Forgive me. I didn't mean to put you on the spot.

He made the eyeball handoff to Joel, who picked it right up.

Mrs. Monteith, you've been very helpful. There's just a couple more things. Are the employees who were here last night available for a few questions?

The cook is home on call but the porter is downstairs somewhere. I'll get him up.

That would be great. We won't keep him long. And if you could give us a download of the past twenty-four hours on the camera feeds, I would really appreciate it.

He handed her a thumb drive as the three of them stood up. She took it from him with two tweezer fingers, as thought he had asked her to hold a controlled substance.

I'll get Tim and be right back.

Tim was dressed in the same vein of casual but presentable, just more so on the casual, appropriate to someone's idea of his station, in beige khakis and sage polo shirt. He was probably close to Porter's age, but athletic and tanned. Porter figured he was the coastal equivalent of ski bum, and probably did this only to support his surfing or diving or fishing. He was nervous, but eager to help. His recall of the night before jived pretty closely with Monteith's except he had seen Morris leave, around 11:30. She had been in a hurry, and seemed upset. He appeared relieved to hear Porter's: *Thank you, Here's my card, Please call if you think of anything else.*

Monteith came back and she exchanged looks with Tim on his way out. Tim's look was sheepish and interrogative. Hers was noncommittal. She handed Joel his thumb drive and a couple of discs, with an explanation.

Captain Rappel with the governor's security office said it would be better to put the video on a disc. Here's a copy for you and one for him. He asked if you would drop his off and have a word when you get back to Sacramento.

So Monteith had made a Mother-may-I? call to clear their request with her contact at CHP. He watched Joel accept them graciously, wondering if Joel had his same reaction: CHP could do their own fetching.

It had started to rain serious rain, overtopping even the Pemberton's deep gutters. Joel politely declined her offer of an umbrella. Porter did the same, adding his effusive thanks for her cooperation, and he and Joel did some more damage to the pristine gravel expanse in front. There was no checking the ocean views on their way back up the hill since there was an ocean of rain in the way. Joel was clearly nonplussed; kept looking back over his shoulder. Porter imagined most people probably would be, not wanting to leave the beauty and opulence behind without a last look around to file the experience in with movie star sightings and other rarefied occurrences. Joel could have it. To live here would be to proclaim that you were trapped in your own façade, a concrete example of how people of means were so often distracted into amassing trappings of ever larger and more questionable taste: The more you had, the more you might have to hide, and the more you then had to justify, increasingly to yourself. This was confusing technical acting with method acting and confusing both with life. The self-imposed tension would be as unbearable as it was inescapable.

They emerged from the trees and the highway came into view. Unlike Joel, what Porter felt was closer to relief.

CHAPTER IX

PRETENDING THE INNOCENTS

It being too late to face the drive back to Sacramento, they made their way to Breakwater to check out the hotel. There was no one outside, and the torrent had washed the street clean of cars as well, except for a few abandoned sedans snugged up to the boardwalk as though longing to be tethered to the remnant hitching rails in case the flood rose higher and floated them away. Joel cleared the lake at the curb with a tremendous leap. Porter's leap was more of a sodden lunge that sent him surfing with flailing arms along the wet boardwalk to Joel's splattered applause. They burst through the door as though pursued, then stood shaking like dogs on the rug inside while they brushed sleeves and took stock of the damage. Nothing some heat and food would not remedy. There was a huge fireplace earning its keep, and Porter felt himself immediately drawn to the low upholstered chairs scattered about.

First there was a bit of tedium to take care of, but the beggars were on top tonight. The desk clerk's face in the cold glow of his computer monitor was a study in what he failed to convey: a hint of desperation, resignation, disgust, justifiable anger or condescension in his trim, neat profile as he performed the altogether superfluous inquiry into the status of, at most, a dozen rooms he probably knew by heart before acknowledging, with no expression whatsoever, that he could offer them accommodations at the state's third-class hotel rate reserved for government minions, leaving unspoken that it was the off season in an off year. In that event, they could haul their own baggage, but all they had were their laptop cases, which they flung on the cutesy ironwork beds upstairs, and made their way back to the parlor and the adjacent bar whose attractions were much more to their liking. Joel went explorative and got a bottle of local micro brew. Porter's needs were simpler. Straight up bourbon, and a double since they were done driving. The per diem would cover it if the hotel did not exact revenge on the price of a steak. Soon he had a small fire of his own stoked in his gut, and his wet shoes were down there somewhere, but not making themselves a nuisance because they were baking inside and out. Dinner was a vague notion. This seemed a good time to see if he could get Joel talking. They had some smoothing over to do, under the guise of which there might be no reason to move at all for a while. Part of him did not care much either way, but part of him thought there ought to be more going on with drinking buddies, albeit circumstantial ones, than just drinking, even if he preferred his drinking alone. It was out of his mouth anyway.

So, Joel, you said something yesterday about sticking around DOI. Nothing lasts forever. Where do you think you're headed?

Hmm?

Joel was somewhere else. He should have just let him be, but he had already knocked.

I mean, from here. There are three kinds of people in DOI: Incompetents, people like me some other agency didn't know what to do with, and people on their way to someplace better. So where are you headed? I don't see you staying put in a finger-in-the-dike agency like Insurance.

You sound like Warren—What's your five-year plan, young man?

Their combined sardonic coughs wedged a well-needed crack in the stuffy parlor, even if Joel's came in a little late, as though unsure if he might have overstepped the bounds of deference expected of a probationary employee toward the vengeful deity of the boss, even in absentia. Porter could do disciple, dumbed down for the unwashed.

Well, Warren has a point. You stay here too long and you'll get typecast. You should look around.

Joel sighed and burrowed deeper into his chair.

Actually, I'm having a pretty good time right where I am. What about you?

Looking around? Or having a good time?

The first. I know the other.

Doesn't matter. I'd like to move on but, as you can see, I've been blacklisted. Quit dodging the question.

Joel shrugged.

Caught me. This is going to take another beer. Ready yet?

Porter realized he was holding an empty glass. He handed it to Joel.

While Joel fetched, Porter did the side-by-side. Joel could be a younger version of himself, more enamored with the wallet badge than his function merited. Joel's energy, his singularity of intent leapt off the laminate of his agency I.D. card, reminding Porter of his freshman photo in his high school yearbook: naïve straining to project earnest with hair in his eyes. It was embarrassing to be reminded of those times. These days it was a struggle even to imagine coming to work with a shining certainty other than the conviction that his day would be spent in an accumulation of pursuits amounting to no more than so much pitchforking sand uphill in a wind storm, surrounded by people doing the same as they dug furiously in the wrong places for salvation, producing only their own shallow, anonymous graves.

His former job as a policeman was nothing like that. There you had the sense at least that you were actually shoveling, as one, in more or less the same direction, and the back-slapping satisfaction that you were on the front lines together. But adrenalin was a high like any other drug, and ultimately as corrosive as the worst of them, burning his nerves and his nerve both raw and in no shape whatsoever for accepting a boy dead at his hands, no matter the reason.

So he hung up his blues and limped into the Justice Department, hoping for some sort of halfway house, which it was, but in the wrong direction. Every day there was a competition: for a bigger case, for an office assignment with more status, for a plusher cold-plate car, all pursued as ruthlessly as the bad guys. By the time he realized that fitting in required an aptitude for alliances of convenience, deals and payback, it was too late. He was still on probation when Maddie called him in for the execution. He could go back to being a cop somewhere or apply for a job at a second-tier agency that was hard up for investigators. She had a friend at Insurance that might be willing to try him out...no promises...an opportunity to build an inter-agency connection while gaining experience so he could come back some day. He had been too upended to absorb the rest: He was a great analyst but he was analyzing to death...He needed to be more aggressive...He needed to close more cases...He had to know he was swirling the drain.

Yes, but it was hard to tell which direction to swim when he was spinning in circles and being pulled down. It got so he was convinced people could smell it on him when he walked into the complex at midtown; people edging by him in the halls not making eye contact. He was a marked man, stinking of death. When Maddie handed him his last probation report he did not bother to read it since she had already pronounced sentence. The official reasons would not jive with the real reasons anyway, which he could have written himself:

STATE OF CALIFORNIA – PERSONNEL ADMINISTRATION

REPORT OF PERFORMANCE FOR
PROBATIONARY EMPLOYEE

STD 666 (REV 9/2002)

NAME PORTER, MICHAEL	**SSN** XXX-XX-9847	First
CIVIL SERVICE TITLE Special Agent	**POSITION NO.** 3588465766	Second
DEPARTMENT Justice	**DIVISION** Consumer Fraud	Third
		Final **X**

CIVIL SERVICE RATING (Last or Final Report)

ACCEPT		REJECT	**X**	Date 04/07/08

PERMANENT CIVIL SERVICE STATUS DEPENDS ON SATISFACTORY WORK PERFORMANCE

	RATINGS ARE INDICATED BY "X" MARKS

QUALIFYING FACTORS	Unaccept.	Improve Needed	Meets Std.
Cutting warrant corners	X		
Guilty-Until-Proven-Innocent M.O.		X	
Badgering Victim / Suspect	X		
Cherry picking facts	X		
Fluffing witnesses for prosecution		X	
Seeing zero-sum forest for the trees	X		

Supervisor Comments: Investigator Porter can't seem to get up to speed in terms of butt kicking and name taking, but has a bright and secure future as a nice bank teller in a small town.

Supervisor Signature	*Madeline Menhaden*
Employee Signature	

Well, he had to wring from his circumstances what he could. Joel would have to do the same. For now, this fire and his drink were really hitting the spot.

Joel came back and set down their drinks, then pulled his chair aside and began to drag up another between.

Look what followed me home. Can I keep her?

Porter looked over his shoulder. It was Celeste, with one hand going to her wet hair and a glass of wine in her other, looking embarrassed.

Hi, again. I hope I'm not interrupting, but your friend insisted.

She set her glass down.

I'll be right back. I'm going to get a towel for my hair.

He grilled Joel while she was gone.

You insisted?

Why not? You have plans?

She was back in a flash, tousling her hair with a bar towel that left her looking waifish and wild, and altogether fetching.

I thought I'd drop in to bug my friend, Spence, the bartender, and have a glass of wine. And there was your friend—

Joel.

—Joel at the bar. I thought you two were just passing through.

Whatever else Celeste had done with herself, she had developed a superb sense of timing. This morning Porter had been half awake. Now he was half lit. He struggled out of his chair and motioned her to the one Joel had added.

I guess we are passing through only in the figurative sense. What brought you out on a night like this?

I'm still trying to get home, sort of. Waiting to see if the rain let up seemed like a good excuse to put it off. Did you guys get what you wanted done?

Hardly.

Joel did a better job of saying little without seeming to.

I think we're only getting started, but we ran out of daylight before we ran out of work. We're putting off the drive home, too. Can't see, anyway. They need to invent faster windshield wipers for the rain here.

Joel helped her off with her coat, and Porter saw it was the same outfit from that morning, which confirmed it had been a long day for her, too. She settled herself in the chair between them while Joel did a bad job of trying to avoid eye contact with Porter. Joel could pretend the innocent gentleman bit all he wanted, but he had no doubt jumped at the chance to watch his partner squirm some more, and to learn more about Porter's past than he was likely to get in another year of shared road trips. Porter saw right through it but could not exactly hold it against him, which Joel also knew, which rendered any attempt at remonstrance off limits. What he could do was try to even the score a little.

Joel was just about to tell me what he was going to do when he gets off probation at the Department of Insurance.

Joel did some ineffectual huffing and puffing about how that could hardly interest Celeste. She assured him otherwise.

But first you have to tell me what you did to wind up on probation in the first place. Did you do something naughty?

For Joel she had a face that was only innocent curiosity, but Porter caught a mischievous glance from her. This was more like it. The two of them tag-teaming on Joel with Porter doing the set up and her sealing the exits. He watched Joel take a pull like it might be his last. He brought the bottle down too quickly, which set a cascade of froth down the sides. This gave him a momentary reprieve while he mopped up with all their cocktail napkins, but he still seemed too bothered for such a minor mishap as he wiped and dabbed extravagantly before he let go.

Uh, let's see. Mike can't understand why anyone would want to stay doing what we're doing any longer than it takes to find something else. I guess my answer to that is, then why is he still with the department? And working insurance fraud cases isn't just flipping burgers for some of us, especially if you consider I'm not supposed to be here in the first place, and not just because a funny thing happened on the way to the lawyer I started out to be. Anyone from my old neighborhood was a long shot for any job that takes a college degree. My parents worked six days a week at their dry cleaner's in East Palo Alto so I could be the first Vega to get past high school. I don't know about your families, but that was some load to dump on a kid. I studied all the time because every minute I hung out with my friends I felt like I was stealing from my folks. I mean, everything had to tie into school. The best I could do was Science Club this, Chess Club that. And no, Mike, I was not the neighborhood bully. I was a lot skinnier then. Got my trombone stomped on behind the seven-eleven, the whole bit. When I got accepted to Cal they pretty much just shrugged. They acted like it was expected, the same as brushing your teeth at bedtime. Then we found out I got a full scholarship. You should have seen my mom's face. My dad threw a block party.

Porter had not heard the part about the trombone before. Celeste looked enthralled. Joel looked anything but, but started up again when he won or lost some internal debate.

You could say I don't owe them anything, but that wouldn't be true. I feel I owe a lot to the state, too, which is part of the reason I'm happy doing what I'm doing, I guess. Keeping people honest. But what I think Mike really wants to know is what's up with my law degree? Simple. I got my degree and I'm still trying to pass the Bar. Sometimes he sounds like my dad.

That left out a lot. Celeste must have wondered, too.

Couldn't you work for an attorney doing something or other in the mean time?

Joel looked a little pained. Porter threw him a rope.

Or play trombone?

Joel waived him off, with a scowl that said Porter was

handing him an anchor.

I did a couple clerkships with the San Mateo County prosecutor, but those things are short term. It's designed to be a conveyor belt. As long as you're moving along, you get moved along. If you hit a snag you get shunted off to the side. Now here's the funny part. It's a lot more fun catching bad guys than trying to make a case out of somebody else's weak police work. I thought this would make me a better lawyer, but it seems to be working out the other way around.

Porter had to agree.

He's come a long way fast. But, Joel, it's the same thing here. You can't stay in one place too long or they'll figure this is all you're good for. You're a guy that's meant to go places, even if you don't realize it yet.

Joel turned to Celeste.

He was giving me this line just before you came in. We've only been working together about six months. I must have B.O. or something.

Celeste leaned over to sniff Joel's shoulder, which should have nudged a laugh, but Porter was wondering how Holly Morris could be so blithely reciting the day's news on the TV in the corner. Then the frame reduced to a corner shot, Holly Morris doing the teleprompter bit in archival footage, and the real newscaster filled the larger portion.

Hey, Joel, there she is.

Joel and Celeste looked where he was looking. Joel remarked that either the family had all been notified or the story was out anyway so it did not matter, explaining to Celeste's *What story?* that she was killed in a car crash the night before.

Celeste looked stricken.

I met her once. That's just—

Porter was more interested in what the TV had to say about the how and why of it. There was just:...*tragic accident...solo occupant...esteemed colleague...wife of Assemblyman Thomas Biel...services at...investigation continues...* Nothing about Vaneros or what she was doing up the coast. That would not last, at least not on the more salacious channels. Even Celeste had already connected the dots.

If she is married to this Biel guy, what was she doing up here with the governor?

Porter raised his glass to her.

That's what a lot of people are trying to find out, including us. At least insofar as it might help explain how her car went off a cliff.

So you guys are detectives? Forgive me, Porter, but you're the last person I would ever have guessed would be doing that. You were a theater major.

Joel pounced.

Acting? You?

She could not have cost him more partner points if she had said he tended toward the rote in bed. His fencing instructor pretty much said as much one day in the spring of his junior year, just after his thing ended with Celeste, which helped not at all. Fencing lessons seemed logical for an aspiring actor, but there was a lot more to that, too, than he imagined. He had been hung up on a simple drill of cross parry-disengage-drop the point in line-riposte, reduced from the intended exercise that had included footwork and timing. If he was not rushing the disengage, he was hurrying the thrust and landing off target. Knowing that Creswich was just trying to break it down into fundamentals was no help. The simpler he made the exercise the more Porter locked up until all he could see were those hyper-whitened teeth grinning behind the wire mesh face shield. Creswich tore off his mask and stalked right across the blade distance separating them and put his face in front of Porter's, demanding to know what the hell his major was. When he told him, Creswich's laugh echoed around the gym, underscored with an emphatic—*You haven't a prayer!*—and he whipped Porter across the upper arm with his foil, producing a reflexive flinch. If he could not learn to loosen up, if all he could do was memorize words, he was wasting his time. Fencing was a *conversation.*

With a—*Very funny*—to Joel, Porter explained that he eventually had come to the same conclusion, that acting was a road to starvation. Switched his major to A.J. and went that way. Real drama instead of pretend, with a public benefit. Police work was a bit of a morality play anyway, wasn't it?

What he did not say was, yes, but not the way he intended; how he went full circle, from surprise and delight that he stumbled into a job that compelled routine acts of bravery he had not thought himself capable of, to one where he ended up in an act full time. These days he troweled on the thick stage makeup of diligent civil servant, tough-guy investigator, the loyal partner, the shrewd interrogator, the law-abiding citizen, the role model dad and the attentive husband (no Tony award there), constantly looking over his shoulder for his blissfully self-assured understudy.

Finding himself in this gray flannel role was not in the game plan. Ditching his police uniform for plain clothes was liberating invisibility at first, but it meant walking the streets as this nebulous entity. The gun and badge underneath only made it an act within an act. *Hi, I'm just a business schmuck on the outside, but underneath I'm an armed bureaucrat, so no sudden moves.* He missed the clarity of the uniform—This is me, this is what I do—because for a while it was simple. You geared up, went to briefing, and went out to shake things up for the better. Sure, ninety percent of it was scooping up the same drunks, bums and perverts over and over. People loved you or hated you, depending, but when they really needed you it did not matter how you came dressed. The department still forwarded Christmas cards from a woman he pulled out of her burning car while she sat too stupefied from the exploded airbag that saved her life to undo her seatbelt and open the door. He missed the knowing that everything could be at stake on any night. When life beyond the street, even your own, took a backseat to the imperative of *now*, and you were invincible as long as you believed that you were. For that there was no substitute, but it came at a price. So did going without. So he could keep his fingernails clean now. So what? Maybe Joel was all-in, but there had to be a more legitimate engagement out there than this cross between social custodian and professional busybody. More than a bit part as a muck miner in a shallow trench that ran all over town. The problem was, what? Even the Morris investigation had a tabloid taint, and was a diversion that would not last forever. What then? Porter suspected he would not recognize a better script if someone slapped him in the face with it.

But at least he was still looking, even if he often suspected he was no better than the rest, all digging in the wrong places. Why else hang around art galleries on his off time if he had not studied art history since college? In that respect he was a man who dug up rocks he could turn over and over in a futile attempt to discern their molecular structure. It was deluded but so diverting. What did his kids think about all day? Damned if he knew. If they needed advice for much of anything besides their homework they went to their mother. Where did Anita go on her daily jogs except slowly nuts, apparently, with shin splints? How long had it been since he had taken her out for a real night out, and treated her like a date and not a school teacher? Not that he got much encouragement for that, but still. He was turning into a walk-on ghost in a triple mask: husband, bureaucrat, man, phoning in his performance most days, losing a bit more of himself each day he pretended that even this off-Broadway gig did not deserve his best effort, knowing that even a hack had to live the part because the day could come when he would need more than a throwaway line coughed up on reflex, more than a cheap dress shirt crammed with wishful thinking or he would end up tossed out a side door to land face down in some alley, like he was pretty much there already with Anita. What he ought to do was—?—*Line, please!*

Celeste was asking how he became an insurance investigator and not, say, a policeman.

I was a cop for nine years. But I took the cure.

Joel tipped his bottle back and stood up.

I've heard this one. And you two probably want to talk about old times. Mike, I'm going to go look at that stuff we got today. Give me a call if you want company for dinner. Otherwise, I'll just have something sent up.

Celeste watched Joel disappear up the stairs before she spoke.

That's twice he's bailed on us. Do you think he's trying to set us up?

Doubt it. He knows I'm still married.

Still?

She was right. That was a funny way to talk, but it was what came out. He tried again.

We're not living together at the moment.

Celeste looked to be thinking about that before she was going to venture a response. When she did it was as diplomatic as it was not.

At the moment sounds like someone is happy with the arrangement, and someone isn't.

It was a pretty fair summary of a situation he had not been able to put into words, or was not willing to. He still wanted it to be more complicated than that, and maybe it was. He wanted Celeste to be clear on that, too.

Anita's not talking a lot right now, so it's hard to say what she's thinking. Me, I'm still getting used to the idea, which wasn't mine, if that's what you were wondering.

Celeste looked flustered.

I'm sorry, was I prying? You looked like you might want to talk about it. Of course, that wouldn't be like you, would it?

He did his best never-mind smile to let her know it was OK.

What about you? Isn't somebody going to wonder why you aren't home yet?

Oddly, she did not seem particularly flattered. More reflective.

Oh, there's a guy. I suppose I should say was. His crab boat capsized year before last. They found his boat, found his two deck hands, but not him. Everyone but him. I don't think I can explain what that's like. I still half expect to see his truck come out of the trees and up the hill to our house someday.

She was right. He had no idea. Or maybe he did, except from the other side. Why else would he haunt his old neighborhood? To get a glimpse of Anita? His kids? Would a divorce be funeral enough? What was Anita waiting for if she would not talk to him? Anita knew where the body was; she had pulled the sheet over it. Until some smiling idiot walked up pretending to be an old friend, just long enough for him to answer to his own name so the guy could press a legal envelope into his hand, he was neither among the living nor the departed. He could think of few tortures more excruciating. If that was where Celeste was, then they were drifting in similar limbos. Celeste's would be worse knowing that the nightmare that had been visited upon her was entirely capricious and undeserved. He would forever be haunted with the likelihood that his was anything but. Still, his situation might not be irreversible, while Celeste was stuck in a cruel fantasy. Maybe she was not alone in that, either. But it was selfish of him to let her sit there while he wallowed in his own troubles.

I'm sorry, Celeste. How long were you together?

Ever since I came up here. Owen was the man I met at the beach bonfire I told you about this morning. It wasn't what I was expecting, but there he was and there was just something about him, and I knew. He was the guy.

Porter had not been that guy, probably knew it from the start, but he gave it a go. Or rather, Celeste gave him a go, who could tell? She had her easel set up on the light rail platform right in the middle of 19th Avenue, making the other students squeeze around her to wait for the next car, generating frosty looks that she seemed impervious to. He found himself standing next to her, unwilling to pretend that the space was somehow contaminated, abandoned by the others having crowded away from her as if she were one of the deranged shopping cart monologuers from downtown. What he was pretending was that where he stood did not matter. He would not have wanted to be standing anywhere else. She was painting a tree across the street, of all things—like her, surrounded by pavement. It was more than a little vain. Would she look for telephone poles in parks? Paint meadowlarks in gutters? But looking at her was harder. She was unbearably pretty, her hair aflame in the late afternoon sun. She was using her jeans for a paint rag, which made her grubbily angelic, as incongruous as her subject and her mere presence on her island in a sea of asphalt clouded over with phone and streetcar wires. So he made a pretense of examining her tree.

Do you like it?

Evidently she was not entirely immune to her surroundings. He was anything but immune to the stares of the others, especially now that speech was required, and said the last thing he wanted to say.

Wouldn't it make more sense to go to a park to paint a tree?

She did not even look up.

It would if you wanted to get lost in them. But look at this guy. He didn't choose to be here, but here he is, saying, *Look at me.*

He thought she must be a freshman, talking like that, even if her tree looked pretty good. He was older than that.

You and the tree seem to have an affinity for each other.

Now she looked up at him, backhanding her hair out of her eyes, baring fingertips of black forest green. And he was completely unnerved, frozen in place by those eyes, pale, crystalline blue shading to gray, coming at him from a far-off place they had not quite left. He hurried to smooth it over.

It's a good likeness.

She was not fooled.

You like art, do you?

I'm supposed to, as a minor. I'm actually studying drama.

She turned back to her work. He could breathe again. But she was not finished with him.

So, what, you think art and drama are mutually exclusive? There's more drama in that tree than any of those people over there—she conjured with her brush as if that would make the cluster of students vanish—with all the attitude. Yours, too.

So she was not to be put off by convention, just put out. His was showing. He owed her an apology, but he had his pride, too. He sighed.

I'm sorry. Maybe you're right. Maybe I just can't hear the voices. If a tree is painted at a bus stop, does it make any sound?

She kept painting, but he saw a wisp of smile in her profile.

The bus stop?

Now she was being intentionally obtuse.

The tree.

She made a big show of examining her brushwork before she responded.

Forest, trees. If a guy wants to ask a girl out, why doesn't he just say so?

And like that he, they, were off, Porter wondering if she came to feel the way he did about their time together, as though he rounded a corner and saw a cable car going his way, decided on the spur and ran gasping to catch it, only to have his arm nearly torn from its socket as he grabbed the rail. As a conveyance her painted-wagon tour was picturesque, but the trip was pretty fraught. It was not just the strange neighborhoods. The ride itself was unlike any swaying MUNI bus or chattering trolley he could have imagined. His was standing room only, hanging by a strap. He did his best to affect the nonchalance of the regulars he had seen swaying effortlessly with their coffee cups and newspapers on passing Powell Street cable cars, oblivious to the bench-shaking rattle, the subterranean hum of the cables, the haphazard lurching and heaving, the clangs, the sun transitioning to shade on her arms, the constant wind off the bay swirling fetid Chinese cuisine, asphalt and steam with the warm, sweet and sour scent burrowed under the hair at the back of her neck. It all left him dizzy, but he did his best to shift his weight from front to back to avoid being flung out into traffic as they invaded wet intersections, jerked to a halt, crawled through skyscrapers up precipitous slopes while he gaped at the sprawling view at the top before plunging down the backside, hoping the cable brakes held. When they did stop, it was no street he recognized.

Along the way she took him to gallery openings, art museums, hoping to convince him that the spoken word was at times inarticulate. He took her to comedy clubs and plays, hoping to divert her from the fact that she had already seen his best performance on the day they met, and so she would not see that her dance partner had only the one step, invented on the spot. For common ground they pretended they could afford even the desserts at expensive restaurants, tried to impress each other with their disdain for anyone majoring in business, politics, or anything resembling a trade. She could discuss painting all day long and for him it was good cover, since as long as she was talking he had no need to demonstrate his weakness at even a walk-on, or any exercise that was more than superficial improvisation, much less a more traditional role: boyfriend at ease. He held his own for a while, but she was always a beat ahead of him. He was not surprised and, on reflection, a little relieved to see her cozied up with this Davon guy on a bench one day the next spring. So that was that. He played the speared former lover lurching off stage, but after a while even that became a self-imposed farce not much different than the person he now had to admit he had been even after they were together a while: half of a stand-up, acting as the straight man he thought he was supposed to be. He could not tell her he felt miscast. Had only himself to tell after.

Then she disappeared entirely, no doubt having met a rock star or something. She was the sophisticated city girl and he was from Tracy, a valley farm town that existed only because it landed at the crossing of two highways to somewhere else. He was out of his league, or worse, trying to learn a new sport without a rule book. It made running into her again all the more disconcerting, just when he was feeling the same way about where he was now, which was nowhere. Only now he had the benefit of more practice. Of course, so did she. She wanted to know what he was thinking.

I was just wondering if we wind up where we are supposed to. What do you think?

It took her a long time to answer.

In coming here, meeting Owen, I'd say yes, but I'm not willing to accept that losing him was spelled out somewhere.

So where we are comes down to only those things that happened that we wanted to happen? What about the rest?

No, it's just being thankful for anything that feels like it was meant to be. There's nothing that felt right about him not coming home one night.

It was time to change the subject, for both their sakes.

And how does this feel?

What?

Running into me, or me into you.

Everybody turns up here sooner or later. But I'd say it feels—I'm not sure. All I've done is bore you with ghost stories and cry on your shoulder. I hope that's not how you remember me. I always had the feeling I was doing the talking for both of us. And then you would say the strangest things, like just now.

She had always made him feel like he was talking twice as much as a person should need to. Was doing it again.

As I recall, you were anything but boring, Celeste. Don't get me wrong, I don't think either of us is looking. That doesn't mean I can't say it's good to see you again. If there's no hurry to get home, why don't you stay for dinner? I'd like to hear more about how you managed to stick with your art all this time.

She looked at her watch.

I really should go. I have groceries in the car for Owen's folks, and at some point they will begin to wonder what happened to me. If you get a chance tomorrow, go by the Shore Pine gallery. They've got some of my work, mostly seascapes. It's just down the street.

They stood for good-byes. The wine was having an effect on her, one way or the other. She went to kiss his cheek, lingered briefly with a tenderness beyond the expected tentative or perfunctory, surprising him with an electrical charge along a circuit he thought was decommissioned.

Uh, look, I might be back up this way in a day or two. Can I call you?

He could. She gave him her cell number, but told him it only worked when she was in town.

Joel was too engrossed in his laptop monitor to turn around when Porter came back to their room, but not too distracted not to want an update.

That didn't take long. Either you did the two-penny upright in the back hall or you struck out. Which?

If you wanted the blow-by-blow you should have hung around. What have you got?

Nothing. Or plenty. I'm not sure. Most of it is watching the paint dry, but check this out. This is the front lot looking from the porch.

Joel turned the laptop so Porter could see the screen. Porter sat on the edge of one of the beds for the sake of his back. As usual, the security video quality is unequal to the promise, and the night swallows up most of the gravel turnaround anyway. Then headlights come down the hill, turn into the gravel area, flare the screen white as the glare hits the camera straight on, and then a black and white backs up across the bottom of the drive, lights up the hedge on the far side of the turnaround and cuts the lights. Moments later, a CHP officer in full regalia including platter hat ambles over to the car and stops on the driver side. The hat gives the officer a sinister aspect, his face in the shadow of the brim. Now the officer is looking up in the direction of the camera, and the head and shoulder of a woman are seen from behind moving into view in the foreground, now descending and moving out of view around the fender of a pale car. Now the woman is walking over to the other car and the officer beside the patrol car steps back out of the way as the woman shoulders in to address the driver's side window. There is no soundtrack, but her body language says plenty. Whoever is in the patrol car is getting a piece of it. Now the woman is walking back to the other car, trailed by the other officer who splits off and walks up to and under the camera. The woman is gone, too, but a few moments later the pale car backs into view and heads up the hill. It is a Honda. Now the patrol car fires up and heads up the hill also.

Porter pointed at the bottom corner of the monitor, which showed a date stamp of 00:37:42/23-11-09.

Is that accurate?

I'm guessing they forgot to put it back to standard time with the time change. That would put it consistent with Monteith's statement about when Morris left. There's something else.

Joel pointed to the front gate monitor, where the Honda is now coming into view. It turns south and is gone. A few moments later the CHP rig exits, and heads south also. Then nothing for five minutes or so of fast forward blur until another set of headlights flares into view from the left, backlights the shrubbery along the pullout next to the gate and stops just shy of the camera view. A minute or so later the car leaps into view and yaws suddenly toward the highway in a soundless eruption of dust and gravel, rights itself southbound on the asphalt with an attendant wake of white smoke, and is gone.

Joel backed up to a frame with the car ass-ended toward the camera, mid peel, displaying the four-ring-circus emblem of an Audi, and something better, which made Porter exclaim even as he realized its superfluity.

That's a member plate. Is that an A or an S in front?

No telling. It's crappy video but I got the two numbers: 81. Senate numbers top out at 40. There's an Audi registered to Morris and Biel with a plate ending in those numbers. But they also own a Mercedes in both their names, as well as the Honda, so there's no guarantee that was him in the Audi.

Or if he was alone. The chippies might know. We'll do some horse trading with this video. Hungry?

Dinner at the hotel restaurant was pretty much a repeat of the breakfast crowd next door, or lack thereof. It was so quiet Porter could hear the surf over the tinkling piano recording. It would be a perfect hideaway for newlyweds, or an affair.

This is really relaxing compared to Sacramento.

I don't know, Mike. It's kind of slow, don't you think? How would you ever get a date in this town? Well, maybe you. But this chop is top drawer. I'd be eating microwave glop at home.

You should have taken me up on a few of those dinner invitations you turned down when I still had a wife who would cook for us. Did you get food poisoning when you came over on the 4th?

No, Anita's cooking is killer. I just felt I should give you guys a break, especially since I can't reciprocate. I'm not much for cooking.

You shouldn't have let that stop you. Anita was always asking about you. She said you were cute.

Anita had looked pretty good that day too. He recalled her sunburned shoulders set off by a soft white sleeveless top and her cheeks flaming like shame as she fussed with the place settings in their back yard. All he wanted to do was walk over and take her in his arms, but she was unapproachable after they had one of those surrogate arguments before Joel arrived. It was all about the marinade, and nothing about it whatsoever. He had hoped Joel would not notice, but Joel's talk was forced, and he seemed unable to look at either of them, especially Anita. And no wonder. The more Anita fussed and fidgeted, the more she kept getting up and down to refill Joel's glass or fetch him another chicken leg, the harder it must have been for Joel to feel at ease.

Joel stopped chewing and looked up from his plate.

Do you realize you are talking about Anita in the past tense? If you were a murder suspect I would think you had offed her. Are you guys really kaput?

This was getting caught talking in his sleep, with the benefit of hearing it coming out of his own mouth. Sometimes there was more to what people said, not what they did, and not the other way around as conventional wisdom had it. Joel had an ear for it, too. He hoped Joel's ear was off this time.

The only one who can answer that is Anita, but she's not calling and she's not returning my calls. I have to stop by when she's there or I can't get the time of day, and then I'm lucky to get that.

What do your kids think about all this? Are they taking sides?

It's hard to say. They seem angry when I'm there and angry because I'm not. Come to think of it, that pretty much describes Anita, too.

He wondered how much that applied to himself as well. Sometimes it seemed they were all torn between figuring out how they really felt and putting on a front of how they thought they were supposed to be: the hurt wife, the collateral-damaged kids, the husband spurned. It was a good distraction for avoiding sorting out their emotions and what they thought they should do about them. He was taking the easy way even now, with his *Woe is me, wife's a bitch.*

How's your love life, Joel?

Joel was equally noncommittal. Either he was trying to spare Porter's feelings by not gushing on about some new girlfriend, or he was in a mess of his own and was too caught up in it to have a posture figured out. Well, it had taken a while to admit his own situation to Joel. Let Joel figure out his own problems. He was fresh out of advice anyhow.

The next morning he left Joel to settle the bill while he walked down to the Shore Pine gallery. The gallery was still closed, but he could make out a few paintings through the window. The seascapes hanging on the back wall were too far away for him to form much of an opinion about. His eye was drawn anyway to a figure drawing at the side of the window display. It was two figures, actually. One was a last blush of sunset pastel, so dark it was almost a falling shadow, the other incendiary, hot as a ghostly, yellow-green comet, either just searing into or shooting from the frame. Together the pair vibrated off each other in a wistful soft-focus dreamscape dance that veered off in an imbalance of disquieting mechanical movement or blind grasping, sabotaging any expectation of harmonic human connection suggested by the opposing hues, the dance undone by their disjointed juxtaposition, subverted by the bent perspective. There was emotion, yes, but the contorted, embryonic emotions of subhumans, or androids. There was no telling if the figures were supposed to be aware of each other or if they were trapped in unconscious parallel dances that were doomed never to connect. Or if he was seeing a figure chasing a severed soul.

It was tragic and beautiful. It was signed *C. Brousset.*

He wondered how much his response to the drawing was due to the gray morning and the deserted street, and if he would have had the same reaction on a bright summer day when the empty boardwalk was more likely to be relieved with strolling vacationers sticking their heads into the shop, determined to carry away something to remind them that they were here and carefree, if only for a day or two. Would they see the dancers as joyful models of themselves, exploring life with abandon? He found only mocking irony in the warm and cool pastels. How could anyone miss that? Here was Joel.

Hey, Joel, do you like this picture?

Joel folded his arms and stood there.

I don't get it. Are they supposed to be dancing? I'm not much into guesswork. Or chalk drawing. If it's supposed to be people they should go back and look at a few. They're almost sticks. And they don't even have faces. Isn't that kind of a cop out? Look nice in a motel lobby, I suppose. I take it you like it.

Why do you say that?

Joel just smiled.

Porter had not given any thought to the fact that the figures were expressionless, much less faceless. The expression came entirely from their incoherent juxtaposition. They could be evoking the essence of longing, or an antecedent striving, older than regret, the emergent forms standing in for raw, primitive need. He found nothing shallow or humorous about it. How to resolve this? Here they were looking at the same thing and seeing both ineptitude and the profound. Was Joel that obtuse or was he just unwilling to put himself out there, refusing to admit to anything that might show his true colors, a vice cop disparaging the haul from a pretense buy as *garbage* before palming a handful and going home to roll himself a joint? No, it would not do to seem too open or unorthodox, would it? It was part of the problem with working with Joel; he was so badge happy that he fronted the whole cop persona to a fault, leaving Porter feeling he had no choice but to spend all day surfing veneers with him.

Or were they both tourists—the late, stunted novice too quick to embrace, and the other, jaded beyond his years, too quick to reject—making Porter a Friday nighter who had the misfortune to be partnered with a Saturday nighter? The house was usually one or the other, as he found out when he did his college drama internships. Friday night audiences were mostly students, irrepressible, ready to conspire in their own enjoyment with little or no experience for guide. He could feel the theater suffuse with complicity as the seats filled. Punch lines got laughs before they were fully out of the actors' mouths. Halting deliveries and clumsy entries might generate a rustle of nudges, but they usually stayed. They wanted to be part of the show. Saturday was sclerotic couples lugging in their latest quarrel, daring the cast to entertain them. They sat there stiff, expectant, having said and heard it all years before. Curtain up on some of those nights was a visit to a casket showroom, all sound smothered in heavy drapes, thick carpet, and a surfeit of yawning, overstuffed appliances waiting for a dropped line to complete their destiny. Then it was empty seats, stodgy backsides crawling their excruciating crawls up the aisles, the cast deflating into the expanded space. Porter was glad he was not one of the leads on those nights. He could hardly endure them even from the wings while he waited for his cue to squeak the walk-on line the director bestowed on him purely in deference to his major, the best that could be done for a mannequin who thought he wanted to be an actor.

But Friday's were a gift for the cast. The pace was usually a little faster and the actors took more chances. It was one indelible Friday that one of the down-program cast members threw out a line with just the merest change in inflection and tipped the stage into an entirely transformed theme. It was momentarily a show stopper for the actors, their mutual, unspoken epiphany shocking them into an unscripted tableau, and the respondent was, in fact, off half a beat getting out the next line. Off stage the crew exchanged looks: *Did you hear that?* But it was the only version the audience was going to hear so the cast flung themselves ahead into the netless unknown, wishing those out in the seats could appreciate the high-wire act they had the unsuspected privilege to attend.

He would always miss that, the surprise center of it; no two performances could be the same. The audience was never the same. The actors had good and bad nights. The thing that happened was in the middle. He had never supposed a painting was anything so fluid or alive, more than a single performance fixed in place however much skill and passion was there. You could argue all day about what it meant, how each person saw it, but a painting was not going to change in front of your eyes. Now Joel's complacent dismissal had brought something else to Celeste's pastel, had given him a better insight. So was Joel the only Saturday night husband dragged to a play his wife had heard about from a friend? Porter's insulted superiority was no match for Joel's derisive taunt, even if he got it wrong. Which suggested that Porter, much as he wanted to imagine himself the carefree Friday nighter, had been exposed as a Saturday nighter with Friday night memories, a rigidly opinionated knee jerk, the same as Joel, whose ignorant smirk was from the same coin; one that was two-faced, on edge.

Yes, you had to be a little oblivious to your own denial to be a sniffing good poseur, the Saturday nighters distancing themselves in their disdainful dissections. He had taken steps to avoid being labeled as one, sneaking off on his lunch breaks to wander through museums and galleries while Joel spent his lunches jogging or at the gym. Which meant, if anything, Porter's police persona was the bigger wig, an affectation pursued to the absurd point of avoiding any serious effort at art education beyond dim memories of the college survey courses he had abandoned with his art history minor. He subsisted on morsels gleaned from exhibition notes snatched off tables in lobbies, unwilling to admit that he had an enduring interest in anything beyond killing a lunch hour.

What he did was random patrols of the halls, trusting to serendipitous turns at gallery intersections, or tagging along with tours for a few minutes to make discoveries and comparisons he could claim as accidental. He once endured an entire guided tour and learned more in an hour than he probably had acquired in all his excursions up to then, but the experience also left him feeling a bit tainted, doubting whether he would afterward see the featured artists through his own eyes, or instead through the eyes of historians nodding in concert to the beat of the central committee's party-line dance rhythm. One could see the influence of this artist on the technique of that artist, and so on; Cézanne was dismissed by the avant-garde until the retrospective exhibition opened their eyes to his genius, etc. Porter was especially mystified by the thrall that seemed to infect art experts who tended to assume that biographical details of an artist's life somehow imbued them with a deeper understanding of the artist's body of work, as if Mark Rothko's muse could be inferred from the brand of shirts that he wore.

He preferred to search for relational order on his own terms using whatever tools were at hand. He particularly liked finding echoes in one piece and then backtracking to the source of the recognition to compare the two, developing an internal map of art movements, at least in the twentieth century, more or less on his own. One day he happened to be standing at the junction of two galleries, in his business suit since it was a work day lunch excursion, when a gray-haired couple from St. Louis mistook him for staff and asked him if he knew where the Paul Klee was. He did indeed, since there was only one at the Hopkins Museum, and he pointed the way, suggesting also that they might enjoy contrasting that with a Robert Delaunay in the adjoining exhibit, experiencing a mix of pride and a touch of being caught in the open, unthinkingly admitting he knew a little about pursuits above his office.

What a smug little delusion, as Joel had so casually exploded. Pretending otherwise would not erase the pretension of his studied disregard, a disavowal of interest every bit as tainted as Joel's. There were good reasons people put some effort into art study, and he was probably dodging some vantage points that could enlarge his appreciation. But he was not about to accept that he had so much invested in his artistic peregrinations, even if it made him no better than painters in Paris who at first refused to admit they had absorbed some influence, even a bit, after being confronted with Matisse's *Woman With a Hat* in Gertrude Stein's salon. He had clung to a stubborn faith that his sporadic forays through the galleries would lead to a refuge of discovered beauty he could call his own, ignoring the likelihood that he might end up following a woman he chanced upon in the street merely because she wore a dress the shade of red favored by his lost love, the one she had worn long ago on a Friday night.

None of this changed the fact that Joel was still a philistine who could not be bothered, with no expectations beyond a cheap entertainment, at least when it came to art and goading his partner. What kind of aesthetic was that? Or was he just irritated because Joel seemed to have his number without doing any heavy lifting, his shot from the hip seemingly on target, tossed off as a glib ad lib that he could hardly have worked up at the racquetball court on his lunch breaks? Was he that easy to read? Well, if that was the best he could expect from his partner, then it was a mistake to dip his poseur mask for Joel because the rest was wasted on him. Even now Joel was looking at him strangely. Porter was not meeting expectations. Or was. He turned away.

Joel, you wouldn't know quality if it came with cheese on it. Let's go.

As they folded themselves into the car, Porter kept his face neutral, but he was still irked. They could have made a good team with less time wasted at opposite ends of perception: clashing attitudes, size-ups and responses. He had to intervene when Joel was about to explode the Hendricks interview, but Porter had overlooked a crucial detail in that investigation. Yesterday, Joel had seen that Porter and Celeste could use some time alone at the café, and later at the hotel, and had the mature sense to disappear. Today he rudely claimed to be unmoved by Celeste's pastel. Porter had been looking for a moment to mention he had met Morris before. Now that was impossible, especially given the time lapse. Joel had just confirmed that he would see this as proof that Porter was blindly infatuated with Celeste and Morris both. He did not need Joel looking at him the way he had looked at him outside the art gallery: Joel's smirk painting him as an abandoned husband ready to lap up an amateur art work, or let a dirty case foul his judgment, because he was mooning after every skirt, living or dead. But Joel had a good nose for character. It left him wondering if a dilettante detective was dangerous to himself and his partner if he was just dabbling, the former cop on holiday to be distracted by the first window display, or by the death of a woman he barely knew.

On the road back to Sacramento he examined the landscape they had groped their way through two nights before, as much as he could see through the fog insinuating into the canopies of impending redwoods and spruce extending overhead far back into the coastal hills, next turning vineyards into ghostly ranks in the hidden pocket valleys, then, as they emerged into the broad Central Valley, reducing the sink of black, flooded rice fields to a silenced foreground edged in solitary egrets and the occasional migrant hawk biding its time on a fence post. Anything beyond was obscured.

CHAPTER X

A TOSS IN THE HAYLOFT

By the time they got back to Sacramento they were both digging out their dark glasses against the glare bouncing off remnant patches of tule fog only to carom back at them from the china crest of the Sierras to the east. Then they passed the airport where they joined a race track of cars jostling to be the first to get back to, what, another case of late again? He and Joel had no place special to be other than to make sure they got to town before the governor's CHP security heads were all at lunch. He moved to the slow lane so he could enjoy one of the best views in town. Not the vertical black extrusion designed by an adolescent sensibility and known on the street as the Darth Vader building. He wanted the stair-stepped pale blue number with the curved wall of windows that reflected the city's moods as the sky, the clouds, the sun swung around it, captured within the lesser arc of freeway. In late afternoon it would go from lamé to tinsel fire, an intentional testament to lofty purpose and a glimmer of success without the arrogance and pretensions of some of its urgent, looming neighbors, or the expedience in that sea of chunky beige flat tops lapping up against its flanks. The Capitol Protection Section headquarters was one of these: a nondescript stucco storefront a few blocks from the capitol dome that yet achieved a spectacular failure of anonymity, like a plain brown wrapper Crown Vic with diamond E plates. If anyone bothered to look there was a war wagon bristling with antenna, black bullet-proof glass and gun ports hulking in the side lot. He made sure to squat the Taurus in one of the *CHP Only* reserved spots in front since they were not privy to the security gate code for the concertina-fringed parking lot, and were not likely to be.

The uniformed gal behind the counter looked to be about twenty-eight going on fifty, all sandy rayon, smoker pallor and hair the color of dirty straw, cut as if it were. It was a tiny room and she was the only person at the only desk back of the counter, but she did not even look up from her console when they came in, as though the crescendo of traffic that washed through the glass door with them could be ignored along with her ostensive utility. It made him want to check the counter's baseboard to see if she had lifted her leg to piss on that, too.

Captain Rappel in?

She answered without looking up or seeming to notice the flop of his wallet badge on the counter.

Who's asking?

Porter, D of I. We have something he wants.

I doubt it.

She rose and went through a door, still without looking at either of them. He noticed two things. Stenographer's spread would have its revenge on her, and her console was topped with insets of shots of the street by the front door and a view of the gate to the side lot. And this room. There was a shiny black half ball sticking out of the ceiling above the desk. He was careful not to say what he thought to Joel, but put as much of it as he was able in the look he directed up at the ceiling. A tedious minute later she returned, preceded by a sinewy Army Ranger type who had to duck to get through the door, showing off a cranium that was shaved so close there was not even a shadow, just gloss. His gray eyes were set so close together they were only good for hunting, and they came up immediately on target. The handshake was just as accurate, dispensed with while the eyes never left his, trusting to a finely tuned sense of every molecule his corporeal self displaced while Porter fumbled in delayed reaction to the flash-bang introduction. This was the top, or at least the end branch of a very specialized order.

I'm Rappel. What have you got?

Now he knew where the clerk got her manners. Evidently they selected for lots of talents, but civility was not one of them. This was a strategic deficiency, since common courtesy had its uses. And a tactical error in this specific instance. He had something they wanted. Rappel was going to have to back up.

Good morning. I'm Michael Porter and this is Joel Vega. I understand you want a copy of the Pemberton security video array from night before last. Perhaps you could reciprocate with a log of Holly Morris' cell phone calls from that day. I assume you've tagged that base? We could save each other some leg work.

Rappel just looked at him, like he would like to squeeze his head and watch it explode.

What I want I can have delivered by a local patrolman to any vacant field where my helo can land and have it back within an hour.

Porter wanted to do some squeezing of his own.

Perhaps, but that's an hour out of a twenty-four-hour news cycle, which is probably this close to daylighting speculation about a love triangle between Morris, Assemblyman Biel, and your boss's boss.

More stare down, while the clerk typed away as if they were discussing a fender-bender counter report. Rappel shifted position.

You're the guys who came up with the extra footprints by the tire impressions, aren't you?

I wouldn't call them extra. I would call them pertinent.

Another head squeeze look.

You're an asshole, you know that?

Porter picked up his wallet badge. There were only so many hours in his day, too. Inexplicably, Rappel stepped to the end of the counter and swung open the half door. It was not exactly capitulation, but what he had taken for mere posturing was prelude to Rappel's brand of professional courtesy.

Come on back. Let's have a look. Karen, print me a copy of the Morris cell phone activity for her last twenty-four.

Back included a room that any state, and perhaps a few nation states, would covet for an emergency ops center. Rows of wired console tables fronted a wall covered in large monitors. A conference table with a smaller bank of a mere half dozen monitors on the wall at the far end of the room could be glass-doored off from the main room. Rappel made his way to a tower of electronics, and busied himself there for a few moments, then stepped back with a remote as the room overheads dimmed. Three of the monitors came to life, with a Pemberton Inn vantage point in each.

So what am I looking at that I don't already—?

Joel stepped forward.

The gate shot. Move it up to just after Morris leaves. It looks like one of your guys followed her out. Any idea why he left?

Standard procedure.

You follow all the governor's, uh, visitors?

I don't get paid to assume anything. No one was supposed to be in or out after twenty-three hundred until morning except on my say. She wasn't happy about it. I had my guys escort her to the county line. At a respectful distance.

No disrespect, but, you sure about that?

Rappel's head turned and his face was a shadow in the backlight of the monitor, but they had already seen that look.

What's your name, again?

Joel Vega.

Well, Joel Vega, all my men are hand-picked. Who the hell are you?

Joel volleyed.

I'll take that as a no. Which leaves us with an unknown. Cape Hallelujah is still in Whitley County, maybe three miles north of the line. Shouldn't your guy have seen her go over or lost sight of her and wondered what happened to her?

False dawn became first light, then Joel's and Rappel's faces resumed a ghastly fluorescent opacity. Rappel leaned over and slapped the black starfish in the center of the conference table.

Rachel, get Herl in here.

He's just pulling out. I'll turn him around. Say two.

Rappel now relaxed into the composed determination of a man who expected all situations to go to shit, and that he would triumph, regardless, because he always did. He punched the lights down again.

That all you got?

Joel still had him by the cuff.

What's the deal with D.A. Flanders? She left around midnight. Was she hand-picked, too?

Cute. No, not by me anyway. She was on the appointments schedule. And it's not like she's an unknown quantity.

Joel should have had a follow-up, but he seemed eager to move on, speaking before Porter could, which would do for now. He was enjoying watching Joel take bites out of Rappel because it was good medicine for a chain-of-command guy like him. Porter did not even need to raise a sweat to scuff Rappel's spit shine. He had people for that.

OK. Move it up about another five after Morris left. Be about twenty 'til. Was this guy part of the escort?

Rappel had nothing to say about this one. Porter imagined him trying and failing to get any traction on the Audi flat-track action. Joel continued.

We think it's Assemblyman Biel's car. Did your team have any contact with the driver? Do you know what his car was doing in the area?

Rappel was probably thankful the lights were low, but he seemed more distracted by something else on the screen; his response was merely dismissive.

I got no reports.

Well that just leaves us with why we came. We could use his cell activity, too, if you can get it.

Rappel was jabbing the remote with a machine gun finger.

Where's the rest of it?

If it was a stall, it was a good one. Joel answered, regurgitating Porter's nauseous premonition.

The rest of what?

The other camera feed. The one in the meeting room.

She didn't—we didn't get that there was one.

Porter now recalled the camera inside the meeting room visible through the transom just above the lobby door. It covered the whole room, including a door at the far end leading to a deck overlooking the ocean. He had assumed it was for recording meetings or video conferencing. He should have asked if there was a camera outside the back door, or if the one inside the meeting room was on at any time that day. Monteith had weaseled them.

Rappel punched up the lights and popped the disc with the offhand toss of a man removing a burnt slice of bread from a toaster oven.

Who imaged the hard drive?

Now Porter was thankful that Joel stepped up so he did not have to.

We didn't. We just asked the manager to make us a copy. In the interest of time.

If Joel thought that might give him cover, it was only an admission that he knew better. Rappel gave him, them, the reception it deserved.

In the interest of time. Vaguely fucking interesting.

On that last bit, the doorway was occluded by a black man who was all shoulders and thighs, the knife-edge ridge of his starched sergeant chevrons stretched almost flat against enormous biceps. Whatever big and tall uniform shop he challenged must have had to take in and cut off a good four-inch taper of shirt on either side from his ribs to his waist. He paused in the door frame despite the tactical misstep, doing a room scan to reassess whether entry might be premature or altogether imprudent. Rappel cleared the way.

This is Sergeant Herl. Wayne, these guys are from, what is it, the Department of Insurance. Couple things, Wayne. Call Air Ops and see what's available, have Rachel pull twenty-four hour cells for Assemblyman—

He looked at Joel.

Biel. Thomas Biel.

—Biel, while she's pulling the Morris traffic. And find out who was outer prim mobile Wednesday night.

Herl backed into the hall with a smooth retreat that was a beat too eager to be gone and an appraising glance toward Porter and Joel, putting two and two together.

That would be Walt Henry. Back in a minute.

That left just the three of them again, looking at each other. Rappel was the first to crack, and pawed his digital device out of his pocket and began furiously thumbing God knew what to God knew whom. Porter and Joel could do nothing on their cheap two-ways but bark, so they could not pretend to be busy without looking like second-rate bureaucrats. Thankfully, Herl demonstrated an efficiency that returned him in no time.

AdamStar Nora Two's on station and unassigned. Rachel is on the other.

Have it hot in ten. You come, too. Gentlemen?

Joel and Porter looked at each other, staggering between confusion and trying not to look confused. Rappel clarified.

Would you like to pay another visit to Mrs. Monteith?

That got them to their feet, Joel stammering something about their car out front, triggering Rappel's deadpan:

I already had it towed. You can ride with us.

They made it to West Sac in under ten, with Herl drifting

the Crown Vic through corners like it was a code three run, only without lights and siren, as if this were his normal mode. The helicopter's blades were already a blur when they arrived at the field behind the academy, and the exhaust shimmered the poles and fields beyond. The pilot held the door and gestured down, but Porter did not need to be told to approach like a supplicant. He would have crawled if Rappel and Herl had not demonstrated such nonchalance in ducking under the slashing rotor whir. The closer he got the more his brain rattled with the clashing whine against a continuous release of massively compressed air. Then everything was hot wind and pointing fingers until he made a seat facing backwards against the far window, Joel beside him, with Rappel and Herl opposite, facing forward. He had just about congratulated himself on finding and fastening the ends of his seatbelt when the flashing rotors increased in speed and pitch to a frenetic buzz and his seat tipped backward, slamming Porter in a recliner gone insane. He grabbed the seatbelt because that was all there was to grab as the tail came around and twisted over and he was now looking straight down out the side window at the receding H painted on the asphalt below. Then the horizon tipped back up more or less in place. Rappel and Herl leaned forward on their knees with the languid aspect of two spectators at an unimportant ball game waiting out a conference on the mound.

The sense of ascent and progression diminished as the spread of earth dropped below the window edge until there was mostly sky, and he was suspended almost motionless between the Coast Range and the Sierras. An inbound Southwest commuter lumbered into view as a dot followed by a smudge out the left side, quickly overtook them, and descended to Sacramento International trailing a black plume. So much disparity in size and speed made Porter consider what flimsy tin was all that elevated his perspective. What an arrogant idea that such an insubstantial and overly complex device could be trusted with his life when a loose bolt or tiny design flaw could breezily convert climb and thrust to the resolute pull of the earth disdained. Speech was unequal to his thoughts and the noise, and so he busied himself as a man in thrall with the view, which in fact he preferred to the inner landscape of his unease.

Presently, on some unseen signal, Rappel and Herl removed two headsets from the rear wall and hung them across their craniums. Talk ensued with some kind of interrogatory from Rappel directed at Herl. Herl nodded and plugged his cell into the headset, and punched the faceplate. After a few moments Herl had a one-sided conversation with the side window, distraction merging with consternation growing in his forehead crease. He turned to Rappel and mouthed a few words. Rappel began stabbing an index finger into his opposite palm to emphasize some point, underscored with the only lip read Porter could pull out of it: *Got it?* At that, Herl snuck a glance at Porter, as though he had been caught out and was hoping Porter had not noticed. Porter gave him a blank look of incomprehension and apathy, but that was only half true.

Now the horizon devolved into mounded loaves of brown ridges not yet gone green with winter rain, dotted with tiny ragged umbrellas of oaks throwing long winter shadows. The higher slopes developed little green spires, and soon these masked the sharpening landscape beneath their merging canopies, transitioning the tan ridges to the black-green of redwood, spruce and fir. This went on seemingly forever, the entire earth serrated into a maze of snaking dark crests and clefts, until the western slopes thinned to brown again, pie-sliced with forested promontories that dove into the sea. The helicopter tipped and followed the falling lead of the terrain, gradually drew closer to a speck of flint at the edge of a cliff that became the roof of the Pemberton Inn, flew past, and settled in a nearby field or pasture that had been invisible behind a grove on Porter's visit the day before. A CHP four by four waited at the fence line.

Monteith was at the foot of the front steps this time, a look of dismay she probably intended for concern on her face.

Captain, I had imagined we were settled up. Did we overlook something?

Rappel gave her a handshake that rattled her shoulders as he all but marched right by her, then caught himself.

I need to see your security DVR.

I don't understand. I already made copies for—

She turned to Porter, with a look of beseeching incomprehension. Porter looked back at her, giving nothing. She turned back to Rappel.

I think you know the way.

Porter and Joel followed Rappel and Herl, and she followed them up the stone steps, through the lobby, past the front desk which was a real desk, through what would be Monteith's office, and into a large closet that had shelves of office supplies, a copier and fax, and a DVR that had a monitor with four views, not three. Herl did the honors while the other three men crowded around and Monteith hovered in the doorway. Herl tossed a perfunctory: *Password again?,* as he addressed the keys. Her reply was submerged in resignation.

Pembviolet101.

It was not like in the movies, even with motion-sense recording. Herl had to hunt around a bit while Porter became aware of the pressure on his heels, a cramp in his lower back and the soft computer hum which took a while to insinuate itself through the ringing in his ears that had not yet subsided from his helicopter ride. The longer Herl took, the more the anticipatory air pressure increased in the room, with Monteith either refusing or afraid to offer any assistance. Herl typed and clicked as if he were unconscious of the others, or was unwilling to imbue his trespass with any awareness of consequence.

Here we go.

Porter was as startled as he was relieved that they now had

something to do.

On the upper right monitor is an empty conference table, a side table is being set with coffee by Monteith herself, with the hall entry door out of sight below the camera. It is night, with only black outside the far wall of glass. Monteith exits. Herl advanced the clock, and a ghost that appears to be mostly legs blurs into the room, settling into the personhood of D.A. Flanders as Herl cut the fast forward. She paces around a bit, and consults her watch twice. Finally, she comes to rest inches from the rear window with her back to the camera, but her face is reflected in the black glass while whatever thoughts she has possess her. She certainly is not admiring the view. Rappel turned to Monteith.

You're excused.

Excuse me?

We'll call you if we need anything else.

With that he closed the door in her face. Having done so, he offered his dismissive edification.

Nothing she hasn't seen. Any gaps, Wayne?

None obvious. I don't think she has it to fake it, but I'll have Eddy double check back at the office.

More fast forward. Now two gray ghosts fly onto the monitor, then slow and become substantially and unmistakably the governor and another man. They shake hands with Flanders. Everyone seemed content to watch, except Joel.

Who's the governor with? Not the D.A. We've met. The guy.

Herl explained that it was one of the governor's aides, Adam Suhr.

Porter had little time to make any sort of assessment, other than a mid-thirties white male in a dark turtle neck under a medium color, patterned sport coat who looked like he got it about right except for his hair, which looked like he forgot to comb it. He is there only long enough for introductions, then he is gone. Flanders and Vaneros take adjacent seats across the far corner of the conference table. She is wearing white over white over legs. The governor is in slacks, oxfords and a light shirt, no tie.

Flanders is feigning a relaxed comportment, but she gives it away with high shoulders as she fidgets with a pencil. Vaneros has one elbow on the table with his ear resting in one hand, doing a much better job of tired-and-show-me despite his microscopically perfect Kennedy cut with gray temple upgrade. There's some back and forth, which Porter guessed might be about the weather, the recount or something that might better explain this meeting at this hour. It would have been nice to know.

You sure there's no audio?

Herl confirmed that this camera was audio featured, but it was turned off. Porter could only watch and wonder like the others. Presently it becomes apparent that the pleasantries have gone by as gradually Flanders and Vaneros forget themselves. The conversation pulls them both forward onto their forearms, and soon they are nearly forehead to forehead across the table. Flanders has her hands clasped as she is making some point. Now she opens her hands palms up on the table and leans over them. Vaneros' head does a ponderous little side-to-side tipping *Maybe*, then he pushes himself straight back in his chair, and considers his fingernails. Now he stands and wanders over to the coffee pot, followed by Flanders. He pours her a cup, sets the pot down and then moves in close to her with most of his back to the camera, almost in front of Flanders. At first she seems not to notice and is talking into her cup as she stirs it, but she is holding the cup up a little too high in front of her chest. Now she sets her cup down awkwardly on the credenza behind her back and looks up at him with a tight little smile as she puts her other hand up to the governor's chest. With Vaneros in half profile she could be straightening his tie, but the look on her face says she is putting a flat palm on his chest gently but firmly as she leans slightly backward against the credenza. Now both their heads snap to something below the camera, suspending them both in a frozen imbalance that says nothing if not way too much. Vaneros does the slow pull back of a mollusk retreating into its shell. Flanders turns and busies herself with her coffee cup. Vaneros steps toward the camera with one hand coming up in a welcome, then drops it to his side and stands there. Flanders looks back to the door and then sets her cup down. They turn and face each other. Vaneros' shoulders quake up and down a few times and he smiles at Flanders from under his eyebrows. She smiles back, but with her lips still a little pinched. She walks over to the table, retrieves her purse and steps to Vaneros with her right hand extended, elbow locked. She says a few words while they shake, and then she is gone. Now it's the governor's turn to walk to the far windows and look at his reflection. Then he removes an object from his pocket and holds it up to one ear.

The room stayed quiet while Herl poked around some more. Where to start? Joel said it.

Looks like they were interrupted just when it was getting interesting. Who came in?

Rappel opened the door. Monteith looked up from her computer at her desk outside.

Mrs. Monteith, did you enter the conference room at any time while the governor was in there?

No. His aide said he wasn't to be disturbed.

Did anyone else?

Not to my knowledge. It wouldn't have been any of my staff. Of course, feel free to ask them yourself. Mister Suhr came around a little before midnight to say we could clean up any time we wanted.

Do this for me. Get signed written statements from all your staff, and you, about everything you all did and the time it was done from the time everyone got here on Wednesday through the time each of you left. And have it to me by tomorrow morning. Where else is the DVR networked?

Monteith looked nonplussed.

Just to my desktop. The kitchen monitors are just monitors.

Scoop 'em, Wayne, and check the kitchen, too.

Herl was already pulling cables from the DVR. It was amazing how fast he worked. He did it like he drove, and was at Monteith's box with a pro forma, *Pardon me*, before she could work up half a sputter.

This has all our books. Our reservations. Everything.

Rappel pointed to a small box next to the big box.

Don't forget the external hard drive, Wayne.

Monteith dug in.

Now, look, Captain. That's my backup for all my files. I can't work. We'll be out of business. You—You need a warrant to do this.

Rappel stepped in front of her.

Do you really want me to accommodate that? I can do it with a phone call, but every second of my time you waste is a couple more items I'm going to add to the affidavit. You may also wish to review your contract, which gives us access to all grounds, structures, systems, facilities, personnel records, deliveries, utilities and equipment for ten days before and after the governor's visit. As for your business, your professional good will has already taken a hit here. If you want to try wading into obstruction of a homicide investigation, that's up to you.

There followed only the sound of Herl grunting under the desk. He backed out and stood up, handing the boxes to Joel, then addressed Monteith.

We'll get these imaged and back to you as soon as we can, Mrs. Monteith. Promise.

The four of them then edged past Monteith with their haul, failing to sell the exaggerated deference of men who had stepped on the toes of a reluctant dance partner.

Outside, the patrolman was on his car microphone standing next to his rig. He did the come-here hand wave to hurry them up. He was telling the handset he would ask.

There's a home invasion with a medical up in the hills. County wants to know if you can respond with the helo. The S.O. helo is in Redding for training.

Rappel did not hesitate.

Tell them yes, and have Steve start crankin'.

A few minutes later they were airborne again, the helicopter laboring to pull itself up a forested canyon, dodging shreds of drifting clouds through which Porter glimpsed a twist of muddy current overhung by shaggy extensions of massive crowns. Then a spur ridge opened to the south, revealing a handful of structures huddled up to the forest edge, except one, hanging just off the ridge top. The pilot made a fast orbit of the hilltop. A house at the toe of the slope was partially in the trees and had no sign of activity. A dusty curl lingered around the chimney of the upper house, but nobody was showing, which was strange given the racket they were making. Rappel pointed it out and said a few words into his headset. They made a rapid descent on the hilltop behind the upper house, turning the tall grass into a frantic crop circle. As the skids rocked and settled, Rappel and Herl were undoing the latches of two AR-15's attached to the ceiling. The things were bristling with laser sights and twin thirty-round clips. The two busied themselves with their hardware in a methodical, business-as-usual manner, checking chambers, switching safeties, extending collapsible stocks, while Porter blew the dust off what he knew of building search basics and perimeter containment, burdened by the sense that he was having an out of body experience. Too much was happening too quickly for someone whose patrol experience was getting dated and was on different turf: alleys, public housing projects, business districts. His gut was not keeping up, either, thanks to the aerobatics. He looked over to see how Joel was doing. Joel was following suit as far as he could, doing a press check on the chamber of his pistol, which did not take long. Porter did the same. Of course he had done it already when he dressed that morning, but there was nothing like the prospect of impending mayhem to compel a sort of neurotic compulsion to double check. All it did for Porter was to reinforce the disparity in armaments, the more so as he stepped into the grass and could now better appreciate the distance to the nearest house, the tree line and his exposed position. He and Joel might as well have carried pocket knives or slingshots. Rappel pushed a black jump bag with a reflective blue medic cross on its side at Joel, and pointed him to the tree line.

You go with Wayne and clear the left tree line and hold there for my signal. I'll take your partner and clear the upper house, then we'll flank right along the other side of the meadow and meet up with you at the lower house. They're probably long gone, but we'll do it by the book. They could still be in the area.

Herl stepped off toward the trees with his rifle in high ready; hunched over the stock, elbows in tight, sweeping side to side. Joel set off in his shadow, then seemed to remember himself, and moved off to one side.

Porter swung the other direction with Rappel, feeling like a fool trying to sneak up on the upper house in plain view from the knees up, with the snapping rotor blades contributing only the useless effect of covering the rustle of their footsteps. The house was set just above mid slope, of a plywood-siding style that he had always thought of as contractor, or owner-built, meaning it was designed by the same person who built it, a person who thought that an ability to pound nails was qualification enough. They got one thing right though; you could see all the way to the ocean. Porter wished he had time to appreciate it.

When the slope intersected the rear of the house they moved in for pop and peeks of the rear windows, seeing nothing. Rappel tried the back door. It was unlocked. They took turns doing diagonal looks to pie slice the interior, which was only a laundry room, so they did it in two bites. Then Rappel motioned him down and in, probably because he had the shorter, more maneuverable gun. Or was more expendable. Passageways were death traps, especially ones with doors to side rooms midway leading to a fatal division of attention, especially for cops in a hurry. And here he had talked himself out of the need to wear his vest when he put on a suit. He gave his: *Police come out and show your hands*, with no response. He stayed low so Rappel could shoot over him, peeked left into a kitchen, then right, which was an empty bathroom. They continued down the hall with Rappel's hand on his shoulder, which meant there was a rifle muzzle somewhere over his head. The main room was empty, as was the bedroom, and a room that was being used as some sort of artist studio. One down.

They were on their way out the front door when a photo on a shelf drew his eye to a woman with her arm around the waist of a sunburned man on a dock next to a fishing boat. He was in rubber boots and yellow, bibbed rain pants with suspenders, and he was red curly-hair handsome. The woman was Celeste. The smile on her face said she had clearly landed a trophy. He looked around the room again with eyes that were no longer blinkered by building-search tunnel vision. Those were her landscapes in the other room. There was her coffee cup. This was her view. His intestines did the twisting cringe he used to get on the way to rapes and battered-child calls. Please let her be in town at work.

Coming or sightseeing?

It was Rappel, and he was already on his way down the front steps into the open hillside below the deck.

Hey guys.

It was the helicopter loudspeaker. They looked up the hill and saw the pilot pointing down behind them. There was a fore-shortened figure in the clearing in front of the lower house, wig-wagging its arms over its head at them.

Rappel did an overhead point downhill to indicate he

understood, and to signal Herl.

See you there, came over Rappel's radio.

Porter followed Rappel's sprint across the slope to the opposite tree line, holstering after the second time his street shoes sent him skiing across dry weeds onto his butt. There was a jeep road in the trees that made the going easier, except for the dirt sifting into his shoes to nourish the grass seeds that were already poking his ankles. The road flattened and spread into a clearing that was the de facto front yard of the lower house. Celeste was on the wrap-around porch yelling at Joel and Herl to hurry up, all but shoving them through the front door of the prairie one-story.

Porter and Rappel crossed the clearing and clattered up the front steps, and found the others in the already overcrowded living room that smelled of old people, dust and kerosene. And urine. And if he had a category for ransacked it would be like coming upon a dog with rabies; you might never have seen it, but there was no mistaking it when you did. It took a particularly unhinged sort of animal to leave a house ankle deep in such ruthless and brutal disregard for whatever this family had fashioned from their dreams and memories. But he had to give them credit. Whether through practice or a frenzy born of paranoid expedience, the most surgical and methodical warrant search would be no match for a completely heedless room toss like this. Treasure hunt by court order might eventually turn up someone's stash of cash, but there was nothing that would make hidden greenbacks explode from pages faster than the entire bookcase slammed to the floor and the remnants kicked about in what looked like a white-powder-enthused spasm of break dancing. Cops would go through drawers. These guys did the fast forward to the jerk and smash, with greedy eyes alert for hidden keys doing the spin and flash of tossed coins. Cops took photos, made inventory lists, diagrams. These guys took family portraits and sailed them against the nearest wall. Envelopes that might have been hidden in the frames would flair and flutter like hapless doves caught in a spray of glass shards.

Yet, somehow, the creeps must have come up empty, at least until their presumably tweaked brains exhausted themselves on their demolition side trip and stumbled from accumulation to elimination; looked about and noticed there were one or two things they had not pounded on yet, as evidenced by the dried bloody clump of mustache, the congealed drip on the chin of the stupefied man sagged into the burst easy chair in the corner. He had ruptured plums for cheeks, and various crimson fissures insinuated in his sparse white hair. A strip of duct tape lingered on one pant cuff, as inconsequential as a piece of fugitive party crepe.

Despite the man's condition, all the action was on the couch, where Herl had two fingers on the wrist of the man's matronly counterpart. Her face was blotchy but otherwise unmarked. Herl put a B.P. cuff on the woman's doughy upper arm and slipped the business end of his stethoscope under the edge of the cuff at the crook of her elbow, and pumped the black rubber bulb with the other. Celeste was spewing it out the whole time, as if apologizing to the woman.

I should have been here yesterday. I found them tied up in the kitchen when I came down this morning. Al said there were two of them. She was in and out of consciousness. I know she's got heart problems.

Herl asked for quiet and for a few moments there was only the sound of him squishing the rubber bulb, then the diminutive hissing of released air. Herl sat back and made his pronouncement.

Pulse is barely there and thready when it is. B.P. is sixty over forty. We need to get her out of here.

Herl fitted her with an oxygen mask while Rappel radioed up the hill, asking the pilot to pass along the gone-on-arrival and get a trauma flight helicopter. Then came the skidding arrival of the local deputies and Rappel walked out the front door to greet them. Porter touched Celeste's arm.

Are you OK, Celeste?

She opened her mouth without taking her eyes off the woman on the couch, but nothing came out. She might have been deciding, but then she turned and looked at him strangely.

How do you—

It's me, Michael.

The day's events had clearly heaped upon her too fast. He watched her scrutinize his jacket, his hair in the dim parlor.

Why? How?

He walked her through his just-along-for-the-ride, and his diversion with the CHP to her 9-1-1 call, assuming it was hers. He pointed at Joel by the door. Joel gave her a shy little smile and a simple—*Hello, again*—which did more to bring her in from the cold than all of Porter's explaining. She unfolded her arms and shoved her fingers in the back pockets of her jeans, a person waking up but still not knowing what to do with her hands.

I could kick myself. I had groceries for them last night but I didn't get back until after nine, and their porch light was off and the house was dark, which means they have gone to bed. I went on up to my place and didn't come down until late this morning. If I had come home earlier I would have known something was wrong.

You might also have walked in on something you didn't want. Did you see any strange cars, or anything out of the ordinary?

She shook her head, and turned back to the woman on the couch. The deputies walked in and Rappel did the hand off. Attention now focused on the man in the chair since Celeste was only the finder and the woman was in no shape to talk. His voice was thin and raspy. There were two of them. No, he did not know them. Two white guys with long hair. Kept asking her where the money was while they beat him, but she just screamed at them to stop. When they went for her instead and said they would cut off her fingers he told them. He kept it in a plastic bag in a hollowed out loaf of frozen venison sausage. The deputy had to ask him twice how much they got. About nineteen thousand dollars.

Porter looked at Celeste, who looked at the floor.

One of the deputies looked at Rappel.

Have all the buildings been checked? For suspects? If not, would you give Charlie a hand?

Celeste excused herself, waded through the remains of a coffee table into the kitchen and ran water over a towel at the sink. Porter went with Joel, Rappel and the deputy to have a look around. There was a shed out back that had the well pump and odds and ends. A lean-to attached to the barn yielded a soft: *Yeah baby*, from Deputy Charlie.

Ten KW generator. You could run a small carnie ride with that. Let's check the barn.

It took a moment for their eyes to adjust, but there was nothing to see except rotting floor timbers, empty stalls down one side and the smell of mouse droppings and decay. They followed the deputy up the newer-looking steps to the loft. Also empty, except for a track of scuffed dust bisecting the floor between them and a door at the end of the loft, and a skunky odor. The deputy had a different take.

Here we go.

Whatever it was, it looked to Porter like a mad scientist surgical theater when they went through the door and the deputy found the switch, starting with the walls which were lined with foil and plastic from floor to ceiling. The ceiling suspended an array of wires and lights with box-shaped light reflectors set over low greenhouse tables trailing tubes from a grid of plastic pipes. Large fans on floor stands marked the corners. Whatever happened in here put out some light, and heat. The deputy did not seem very impressed.

Just your average hayloft, eh, gentlemen? We must have

caught them between grows, which means they're new at this or not very ambitious. You can grow year round with this setup.

Joel toed a few stray curls and asked what came next. The deputy was somewhere between resigned and dismissive.

With them? Nothing. Even if they were still in operation they probably have medical marijuana cards, which means they could be cranking out up to fifty plants at a time, all the time. Of course that means they could smoke themselves blind and never make a dent, but getting a cultivation-for-sale isn't going to happen here. Least not today, or anytime soon.

Why not?

The deputy ushered them out and palmed the lights off.

Sorry to say, but this is small time. It's not worth our resources. They may think twice after last night anyway.

Porter pondered the relativity of victimhood as they made their way back downstairs and outside. Another set of rotors was approaching from all directions at once, then was right overhead as a blue and white boxy helicopter popped over the ridge from the east. Around the front of the house, Celeste was getting into a pickup. He jogged over with as tactful a question as he could come up with.

Where to?

She seemed impatient, about a lot of things.

They asked me to drive up top and fetch the medics.

I'll come with you.

She looked everywhere but at him.

There won't be room on the way back down.

When he did not answer she added: I'll be right back.

Look at me, Celeste.

When she did, her eyes were hiding and seeking.

It's going to be OK, Celeste. Really.

She put the truck in gear with a: *So you say.* And turned the wheel.

CHAPTER XI

THE LIFE DRAWING MODELS
RELUCTANTLY DISROBE

There was a certain rhythm to incident response that he came to divide into three phases. The first was the blur of radio, sometimes phones, followed by jotted essentials, tunnel-vision driving and chaotic decisions usually based on incomplete, often erroneous information. Everything happened too fast, unless things really went to hell, and then moments stretched to infinity. After the drama got sorted out nothing happened soon enough, whether he was waiting for an ambulance or just a tow truck, because the steps were so repetitious as to be almost interchangeable incident to incident. The same questions. Same blood. Same forms. The same assurances and victim handouts. He called the middle part the forever phase. Then suddenly everyone would be packing up and rolling away, time advancing again, sped up to normal, the getaway. The middle never quite showed up this time. Events were still moving a little too fast to suit him, which was odd considering the banality of the incident, which was not even his to begin with. But too soon he saw Rappel conferring with the deputies and it was obvious that their services were no longer needed. They exchanged contact information and then Rappel told him and Joel they were out of there.

They had packaged the woman and sent her up the hill in a litter in the back of Celeste's truck to get flown out to a hospital with her husband for a go-over. Celeste wanted to fly out, too, but they told her two plus crew was all they could handle. She would have to drive to Redding, a four hour drive. Someone needed to stay and secure the property anyway, which Porter thought took some nerve under the circumstances of there not being much left to lock up that was not already gone or trashed. In any event, the medic helicopter soon left, and there was no reason or excuse to hang around looking over the deputies' shoulders as they filled in their forms and took their photos. The lead deputy, named Ed Tierney, thought he knew at least one of the idiots, based on Al's description of a slug tattoo on the guy's neck: one Bernie Haddock. Not Porter's problem, but what, then?

Rappel declined Celeste's offer to drive them all back up the hill. She had done enough, and probably had her own affairs to attend to. He thanked her for her help and began the return trudge up the jeep road, followed by Herl. Porter held Joel back.

I'm not done here. You go. Check the Morris and Biel phone records and her tox report and I'll tie in with you tomorrow. I want to talk to Flanders again, too. Tell Rappel thanks.

Joel looked past him at Celeste, who was looking about the yard like a person getting her bearings.

She know about this?

Porter followed his look.

She'd just say, no, if I asked. I'll hitch with the deputies to get a rental car if I can't talk her into a ride.

Joel smirked.

I'll bet you can.

Porter dropped his chin and stepped inside Joel's reach in the manner of a submission fighter, blading his left shoulder up close to Joel's chest, his back to Celeste.

It's not like that. It just doesn't seem right to walk away and leave her with all this. I'll get with you tomorrow. Fill Warren in for me.

Up to you. I'm going to miss my ride.

Joel hustled up the road and left him and Celeste looking at each other across the yard. She called over as he moved her way, with her chin a little too high for the confidence effective sarcasm required.

Are you going to arrest me?

Is that a question, or a request?

She ignored his grin.

You know what I mean.

This approach needed some de-escalation. Porter waited until he had closed the distance so he could lower his voice.

I thought you could use a hand straightening up. And I could drive you to the hospital. You probably shouldn't be driving.

She did some appraising.

I don't need rescuing, if that's what you think.

The helicopter up the hill was doing its ascending warm-up whine.

Well, I'm here, and I have some odds and ends of my own to take care of, not just this.

They both turned as the deputies reappeared from inside the house and clomped down the steps, snapping their Posse boxes shut, juggling cameras and a handful of small paper bags. Tierney called out.

You need a lift, detective? It looks like your friends are leaving you.

The CHP helicopter reached its crescendo of buzz and then passed overhead and was gone in a dopplered descent of the canyon. Porter looked at Celeste. She took and released a deep breath.

You want to do housecleaning. Dressed like that. Porter, you are so full of shit.

Porter held up four fingers for the deputies, who gained apprehending looks, and then got in their car shaking their heads.

Moments later it was so quiet he could still hear the crunch of gravel from the deputies' tires even though they were long out of sight. A bit of wind bowed the tops of the conifers in soft counterpoint to the push and ease of blood in his ears. A pair of ravens slid overhead, trading groks transposed by a fifth, an effect soothing, nearly soporific, accompanied by a rhythmic pulse of air that rose and fell, which he realized was the beat of their wings rendered audible in the stillness. It would be so easy to be lulled into a daydreamy routine here, sleepwalking through the day. Celeste must have felt herself slapped awake when she walked in on that scene, here where speech itself seemed an intrusion. She wanted to know where one started. He did his best. It was just a lesser form of triage; look for the thing that seems to need immediate attention.

Let's say we clear a path through the living room to the kitchen, if that's where they keep soap and mops, and go from there.

He trusted that any progress toward setting things in a normal direction would further contribute to a therapeutic result, and he was right. He concentrated on gathering armfuls of splintered furniture and piling it in her truck for disposal, in effect removing the worst of the battered homestead, while Celeste made progress behind him with a broom, picking out photos and salvageable bric-a-brac as she went. There was one big item that had not yet been carried out. She was sweeping around it. Porter gave it a nudge.

You, uh, knew about the barn?

She answered but kept sweeping.

Yes, but that was their thing not mine. Hard to avoid it on hot days when the smell comes up the hill.

He thought that was all he was going to get, but she was just chasing her thoughts into a pile.

Al always fished. He never had an income other than what he caught, and then he couldn't any more, and Owen was the same way. When we lost both Owen and the boat there was nothing. No insurance, him or the boat. Ruth worked the order desk at the mill years ago before it shut down, but her social security check is tiny, and her medical bills got to be more than they could handle. People up here are used to doing for themselves.

What she left out was how two people as old as Al and Ruth managed a growth industry they seemed a little beyond. Maybe their son taught them, or they did their best to take over the business after he disappeared. Sentienne had said the fishing industry had dried up. It could be that mom and pop were not the only ones short of cash. Porter also wondered about the rental arrangement that kept Celeste in the house of their dead son when they were supposed to be so short of money. Simple logic would point to her involvement, but if the locals did not much care, why should he? He let her know that the sheriffs did not seem to be too interested in going after Owen's parents, much less her.

Celeste now seemed as equally uninterested in that topic, or discussing any theories about who might have robbed them. The damage was done. It might have been one of the workers snooping around when they had their road graded in the spring. It could have been some poachers or mushroom pickers wandering through the property. It could have been someone who followed their buyer. He was supposed to sell it to a patient co-op in Oakland, but she was not even sure about that anymore.

After some mopping it became apparent that they had done all they could short of hiring someone to repair the holes in the walls and a splintered door jam. The sun was going behind the trees anyway, and a chill was settling down the hill. Porter's stomach was growling back from its helicopter queasiness.

How far is it to get something to eat?

You mean a restaurant? A good hour, and I haven't eaten since breakfast. I'm not going there and back this late in the day, especially with a truck full of junk. And I want to call the hospital while we're down here with their phone. You OK with leftover spaghetti and a couch?

He hesitated over the permutations, which she misinterpreted.

I'm sorry about how I was earlier.

He could set that right.

People aren't always at their best at these things. No, I didn't want to impose, or give you the wrong impression.

Finally, after all day, he got a genuine smile from her, and something that sounded more like conversation that was not defensive, was not second guessing itself.

As if. At this point I think I could use the company. I could sure use a glass of wine.

In that case, spaghetti sounds fine. Wine too.

There was no news yet from the hospital. There was nothing left to do but call it a day and head up the hill to her place. The advantages of her house extended beyond the view as the truck came out of the trees and brought them back into the sunshine, reddening but still giving off a little warmth, especially on her deck with their backs in sun-warmed chairs. But the silence was almost eerie after the way his morning had gone. He wondered what she thought of that.

It can get pretty quiet around here, can't it?

Everyone says that. Nobody ever comments on the absence of noise. Do you still live in the city?

San Francisco? No, I left after college. I moved to Sacramento for my job about seven years ago. Before that was San Jose. They both have enough noise, though.

And when you're not at work, what do you do?

Well, I've been pretty busy getting resettled since I moved out. I'm on call a lot. When I'm not, I like to relax and regroup. Do some reading. Visit museums. I got more interested in art over the years.

She smiled at some private joke, then decided to let him in.

And you think my life is quiet. Did you make it by the gallery?

It was closed. But I liked the pastel in the window. Do you have any others?

None worth seeing. I came to kind of a dead end with figure drawings. They weren't selling anyway. Like the one you saw. The gallery owner says people say they like it but can't imagine what room they would hang it in. Bev thinks they find it a little disturbing. She says it still brings people into the shop so she leaves it up, but I think she is just humoring me.

What about the landscape paintings?

The seascapes sell. From what Bev can tell it looks to her as though tourists fall on them with a kind of relief after seeing the figures, and then out comes the plastic. But I can't say I get the same satisfaction from them. I've been kind of in a rut, or maybe I did so many I'm boring myself. Lately I've been trying to imagine more that isn't there and suggest some of that. Would you like to see one? Come on, while there is still some light.

He did not know what he was expecting, but he did know what a burglar might feel returning to the crime scene, walking through rooms he had already been through without his hostess. There was an orderly chaos to her studio, which was the only impression he retained from earlier. Mismatched canvases loitered in the corners. A traumatized kitchen table occupied the middle, covered in paint tubes, brushes and soiled rags, with an easel next to a north window under skylights that ran the length of the room. She stood next to the oil and was immediately lost in some problem or contemplation of her own, leaving him to take a good look for himself without feeling compelled to lean one way or the other. It was a fairly pedestrian seascape that looked like it had been pretty far along, but the left foreground had been scraped clean and whitewashed, which blasted a hole through whatever had been there before, creating a porthole view of a tremendous mass or cloud forcing its way into the scene. The effect was destabilizing, the form at once smashing into and obliterating the background above and to the side of a trembling remnant of sea stack refusing to give way, the orphaned and heroically doomed promontory remaining to challenge the impending march of anticlinal sea crests while the bigger threat appeared to be the white mass at its back. There was no judging scale of any sort, since there was no foreground, and most of the painting did not exist anymore, but this only increased his impression of irresistible and immovable immensities clashing blindly while pressing heedlessly into the absolute void of ocean. He had no words for it.

There's something about the scale that throws me a little off balance—of course, I know it isn't done yet—but, for a coastal scene, all the formal elements seem to be at war with each other, not just land mass against crashing surf. You sure the tourists are up to it?

She folded her arms, acknowledging his observation with a defensive reflex before she even spoke.

I wonder about that, too. This one might have to be just for me.

Or some other gallery?

She now busied herself with rolling a brush in a rag.

I couldn't do that to Beverly. She's carried my stuff from the beginning. Things aren't that cutthroat here.

Porter considered what he had seen so far of Whitley County.

Could have fooled me.

She continued cleaning her brush, but looked directly at him, looking for the joke, looking disappointed.

I think people get what they expect. I'm not looking for that.

Porter supposed that this applied to him, too, and was momentarily chagrined, but hers was also a triumph of wishful thinking. Even if he were to accept that she did not have a direct hand in their enterprise, did she really believe that all of the pot from Ruth and Al's barn went to ease the exits of cancer patients? Well, if she wanted to cruise through life smelling the flowers and ignoring the weeds, who was he to judge? Her outlook might even be healthier if she did not drive off a cliff while admiring the view. He knew what that was like. He was going to keep his eyes on the road, watch for potholes. And hope he had not missed a sign and was on some bumpy detour he could have avoided. In that case, her roadside-attractions approach might make some sense. But anything could be overdone. Surely she could see that?

I suppose, Celeste, but it's harder for some people not to see what's right in front of them. Me anyway. If that makes me a skeptic, I guess I'm stuck with it.

She stopped her brush wiping and gave him a look that was without the benefit of doubt this time, merely hurt outright. His shrug came too late, and was not mitigation enough. She had abandoned him and was speaking to the window.

Skeptical is just thinking all you have to select from are bad options. I don't think people are selective enough, not in the right way. You have to want something good to find something better. If you look, it's usually there.

She had him on that. There were couple of possibles in his immediate vicinity, but he was doing a poor job of cultivation. He was only willing to risk discussing the less obvious one, the one he had formed an opinion about.

Well, I'm sure this oil of yours will work out, but I don't think your seascapes compare to the dancing figures I saw in town. Do you think you will ever get back into those?

Now she pulled her brush through the rag with renewed vigor.

You would bring that up again. You want to know the truth? I just locked up on portraits and figures. Can't do 'em anymore, which you'll probably think is funny, because I still teach figure drawing at the art co-op. If there is something in front of me I can correct technique, make suggestions. But when it comes to my own, expressing people on a blank sheet? It's like I'm starting all over, with nothing to say and no way to say it. Did you ever see a Japanese calligrapher go at a big sheet of expensive, hand-made paper with just a brush and a pot of black ink? It's like a dance, and they only get one chance. I feel like that, except

I've forgotten how to draw any of the characters. I suppose it would bother me more if I hadn't found a substitute, but this seems to be working out.

She was being too hard on herself—art was art. At least she was engaged.

Well, as long as you are painting you are still in the game. I wish I had half your dedication.

She seemed surprised.

For painting?

It seemed lately he wanted nothing but to embrace women he had no rights to. Bring her back to the here and now. Make her see concentration could veer into obsession. She was making her life so complicated because for her it was so simple. Or did she mean him, Porter, with a brush in his hand? For him it was a color wheel reduced to the clash and drab. It made him sigh.

For lots of things. OK, except banjo and tap dancing.

What about your job? You seem pretty successful at that. Isn't there some creative aspect to what you are doing?

Whoa. He had to think about that. The bare palette, the stark stage set of his shrunken interview room. Opposed actors, with one on a fool's errand of reconciliation. He found his hands going into his pockets as his cheeks expanded. Pictured himself completing some investigation, signing off on a criminal complaint form with a calligrapher's flourish, or channeling a bullfighter's élan as he slapped the bracelets on a pair of reluctant wrists. *Olé*.

I think that would be stretching things a bit. If there is, then I have a bitch for a muse. I think you could make a far better case for calling your life an artistic pursuit than mine.

She thumbed the wooden point of her brush handle at her canvas.

Now who's being charitable? Right now things are about as messed up as this painting. And going backwards. A work in progress is about the kindest way you could describe it.

She was not getting away with that.

You've just had a bad day. It's a matter of perspective. I find you, what you are doing, very inspiring. Take it from a cop art critic. Those who can, make art, those who can't, make life miserable for the ones who can't pull off a boring, respectable life. But there's no warrant out for you. You're—

He was forgetting a few things, and not just Ruth and Al's dope operation. Anyway, she was not buying, even with the little extra push she gave to his chest to clear her way to the door.

What I am is getting hungry.

The tour was over. She led him out of the room and hit the refrigerator, leaving him to his thoughts and the view. Time to take stock:

Field Interview Card				**Date**			
Subject: **Last, First**	**Ht**	**Wt**	**Hr**	**Eye**	**DOB**	**Age**	**Race**
Brousset, Celeste,	5-7	130	Br	Bl	1971	39	W
Aliases: (None)	**Reason for Contact:** May lead to more contacts. Explore confidential informant arrangement of mutual benefit, terms to be negotiated.						
Comment: Subject knows more than says; associates with undesirable elements; displays maddening mix of artifice, openness, practicality and equivocation. Potential as high-value C.I. with fringe benefits. (Cautionary note: Such an arrangement would violate current policy.)							
Follow-up Needed: Seek to maintain contact. Don't get made as just the stand-in.							

DOI 426 Rev 3/11/09

For leftover spaghetti hers was beyond adequate, helped along by the wine and the scenery inside as well as without, where the last scuds of low clouds on the horizon were losing their maroon to black. He thought they both were having the sense of being two places at once: the people they were turning out to be, and the people they thought they were when they had known each other before. It was behind the news of whatever happened to friends and teachers that they once had in common. Porter decided he could risk another compliment without having it misinterpreted again. After all, it had the benefit of truth.

You know, I wasn't kidding before. From the moment I met you I always admired how you could paint, make this thing out of nothing and have people look at your art, knowing they were making judgments about you at the same time.

Her eyebrows went up in wry disparagement as she gave her wine glass a superfluous swirl.

You had a funny way of showing it. You were teasing me that first time.

I was just envious, and a bit in awe. Of you, and your painting.

Now she dropped her head a bit and her look up at him from under her eyebrows was dubious, even if her reply sounded willing to let him off the hook.

My, you have learned a thing or two. You would never have admitted that before.

Porter shrugged, not knowing how to respond to that. She was getting some other thought together anyway, her eyes up and away now, picturing, so he waited her out.

Besides, Porter, you should talk. Painting is easy compared to getting up on stage in front of an audience. I could never do that.

Porter's *hmph*, escaped him, and he could almost see his dismissal filling the room. It was clear that she wanted to change the subject, but it was false flattery considering it had been twenty years since. He had never put it into words, but Celeste, of all people, might recognize the attempt.

Turned out I couldn't do it either, as you can see. I mean, it felt like I could as long as I was reciting somebody else's work. Then it wasn't me they were looking at, just how well I could pretend to be this fictional person. But then it became obvious that the only way to be good at that was to leave some blood on the stage, invent or dig out pieces of me that I wasn't sure I had, and somehow connect them to the other cast members who were right there trying to do the same, and have it amount to something that made sense. I couldn't make any sense of it at all. So I gave it up to earn a living. Cops and robbers seemed more straightforward. I haven't been to the theater in years. For jollies I go to museums and galleries and admire what other people produce.

It was so quiet Porter could hear the wind outside rolling around the house and across the ridge above. Celeste looked at the dark windows, listening as well, or looking for relief. This was not what he had intended.

But at least one of us kept at it. I'm happy for you, Celeste.

Porter saw that he had not opened a door for her escape as much as admitted an awkward guest as he watched Celeste fidget in her chair.

I don't know, Porter, the longer I do this the more I wonder how much is just substitute for more of a real life. Look at you. You're out and about doing work that sounds real and exciting. That seems to matter. Isn't that life as good or better?

Porter thought what he could not say. He would not be the first person to find that wearing a bulletproof vest to work was false protection, so now he did not bother. The problem was all the other stuff that went with cops who could not leave their work at work. That trying to impose some order on a disorderly world only reduced his own life to unending chaos. He could not explain this to Celeste, except in outline form.

There's real, and then there's conventional. I'm not sure I know the one, and I don't recommend the other. What else you got?

Celeste sighed.

Probably the same as you. I wake up in the morning and just try to do the best I can. Why don't we call it a day?

Porter had long since decided this was not the time or the place for either of them, but he could not end the day like this. He gave it another try as she was handing him an armload of blankets for the couch.

Don't get me wrong, but you're selling yourself short, and I think any guy at least would agree with me, art or no art. I bet Davon is still broken hearted about you leaving him and moving up here.

Thank you, but it wasn't like that. He tossed me over for this girl that worked for the campus paper, Karyn. He was into writing, so I guess he saw her as a step up. That was part of why I came up here that weekend, to get away. He had a motorcycle and liked mountain climbing. Looking back, I think he just had all the right props. It was just stupid.

Girls always fall for the guys who seem dangerous.

He saw her looking at the photograph of Owen by her side at the wharf. She laughed a small, half-smothered laugh.

Maybe. Actually, I think it was more of a thing where he seemed like he knew what he wanted, at least as long as it was me he wanted, whereas you were, if not exactly aimless, pretty unfocused.

She gave him a glance from the side, and picked at the blanket. He was caught speechless, and as the silence shrunk and expanded the space between them in mockery of his arrested breath, his paralysis bounced between protest and grudging capitulation. She handed him a fig leaf with the blankets.

You were dangerous in a different way, making me see right

through what I was painting. I wasn't ready for that. And I guess I was avoiding you, especially afterward. But you left me alone. It made me like you and resent you at the same time. You were always so decent about things, even when I wasn't.

Unfocused Porter could handle, maybe even *aimless*, but this pretty much boxed it. He made a paltry attempt at face saving.

You know, of all the things you can call a man, there are two that are sure to make him cringe: cute or decent.

He could see she wanted to laugh again but did not.

Worse than unfocused or aimless? Well, you're still both. Deal with it. Good-night, Porter.

And there he was, sitting on her couch in the dark with a lap full of blankets, wondering which *both* she meant.

CHAPTER XII

OFFERINGS AT THE TEMPLE OF HEAVEN

He awoke to the sound of footsteps on stairs, his mouth gummy, and an awkward teeter.

On the one hand was a wobbly sense of waking in the house of a one-nighter amid the question of whether the previous night had been a fluke—in this case the fluke being that absolutely nothing had transpired. So, far from floating in a steamy vessel overflowing with afterglow, there was no remembrance at all of whether expectations had been met. There had been no sweating intimacy to provide any of the usual clues, much less a sense of even what those expectations might have been. Yet here he was, on her couch. For strange, it was about up there with, say, regaining consciousness only to find he had passed out on her porch, having never progressed past considerations of good-night kiss or not.

On the other hand, and about as much use, was a hazy recollection of a succession of nights with what might have been this same woman, an untrustworthy memory well past the statute of limitations to have any comparative value, especially without a more recent tumble to place beside it. She could be a nun now for all he knew, chattering away as she came through the front door as though unaware of the Japanese bathing ritual they had forgone the previous night, giving every indication that it had been so long since she had enjoyed a good soak herself that she had forgotten what it was like, or was past wondering.

Or had she woken with a start of dismay, jumped into her clothes and fled the house so she would not have to risk being misapprehended by him if she emerged with negligee and tousled hair to inquire how he had slept? About that last part he was probably still half asleep. Thankfully, she was too busy talking to notice his befuddlement, or was talking over it to spare them both until he woke up. All he could make of it was, if Celeste had a cheery, *Good morning*, as she burst into the room, as though refreshed in every aspect of her being, he could take none of the credit, much less have any inkling why. He would have to listen for hints.

She had gotten up early to go down the hill to phone the hospital again. Both Ruth and Al were going to be OK and could maybe be released on Monday. Al had a fractured mandible and a probable concussion, but his Irish heritage was up to some bumps. Ruth, although she needed some new meds, was apparently no better or worse for wear. They were just going to hang onto her over the weekend to make sure her blood work stabilized. Still, Celeste wanted to get to the hospital to see them, declining his mumbled offer to go with her. Of course, taking him as far as Millfork for a rental car was the least she could do to thank him for his help, this smirked from behind a superfluous: *I have to go to the dump, anyway.*

The road out took them into the trees down canyon from the two houses, then shot out into a disturbed landscape that was in the process of becoming overwhelmed with shrubs in a race to outgrow sprouting redwood stumps dotting the hillside. It looked like a desecration, but Porter tried to be charitable.

I guess this is where you get your firewood?

Hardly. This sale paid for Owen's boat. It'll be forty, maybe sixty years before they can do that again.

Hence the barn?

Hence the barn.

Couldn't they sell some of the land?

They could. They could also sell my place, although they've said they never would. But Al's going to have to do something about Ruth being so far out for doctors and hospitals.

In that event, what would you do?

What anyone would—something else.

Porter reflected that he needed to get on with his life, too.

Can I ask you a question? How is it you knew Holly Morris was in town?

She took her eyes off the road to give him a look.

You've been awful quiet this morning. I thought you were going to ask me if I was still carrying a torch for Owen. That's easy. Shin Maeda, her co-anchor at KXSF, told me. I've known Shin since high school. I met her once at one of his parties. She went to Sacred Heart, so we had a dead end there. She liked my hair. I asked her about makeup for TV, which I have no clue about, but I told her I do paintings and we ended up comparing combinations of pastels for face tones with shades of concealer and eye shadow. I think we were both a little curious and envious of each other, without really wanting to be each other. Her life seemed pretty exciting but also a little hectic and unreal, like she was living in an abstract painting or a movie.

What do you suppose she thought about you?

Oh, probably that it would be nice to make something creative that you could hold in your hands, but it wouldn't be worth working in an unheated garret and giving up designer jeans.

Was she with her husband, Thomas Biel?

She wasn't with anyone that I could tell. And if the governor was there, I would have remembered that. There were a couple county supervisors and the mayor was supposed to show but didn't. This was at least a year ago. Shin was trying to put me back in circulation. I got really drunk and had to get a cab to my mom's.

Do you think you could put me in touch with Shin?

About Holly? Sure. I'll give you his number when we get to town. Just don't mention I said he told me anything.

Town was a concept more than a destination for over an hour of a full body workout up, down and side to side on the bench seat of her truck as potholed dirt switchbacks merged with a decayed promise of blacktop that betrayed his hope with teeth-cracking sinkholes that were even worse than the unpaved parts. A freeway commute was boring as hell, but the body toll was normally limited to cheek cramp and an overworked leg from hitting the brake.

How often do you make this trip?

Twice a week, Tuesdays and Thursdays to work. Every other Saturday to teach.

Once a year would be too many.

That mean you're on your way out? I was going to offer to put you up for the weekend. What happened to all the real men?

He had to put a hand between his head and the roof as she slammed the truck into a particularly deep and precipitous hole on his side.

I think I'm getting mixed messages here.

No more than I'm getting. You're just too easy to mess with. Seriously, if you need a place to stay, you could use my place. I'll probably spend the night in Redding.

With what Anita would call typical male gestalt, he noted that proximity made a compelling argument as his attention was diverted to the joyful pneumatic flight of Celeste's breasts against the marginally adequate confines of her sweater with every bounce and shake. Should he take her up on her offer? Did she expect him to do what she was flirting around and want him to try and talk her into staying? The problem was he could not even admire another woman's attributes without Anita's thumbprints all over his mental imagery. On top of that, while there was no denying that Celeste's mood had lifted the farther they got from her place, she was tossing him too, her teasing pointless, too little, too late, so any discussion of an extended stay at her place was out, for a lot of reasons.

I'll have to think about that. I've got to make a few calls.

It was another hour up coast from Breakwater to Millfork,

where Celeste dropped him at the one car rental in town. They did their good-byes, he having decided that the drive back to Sacramento and the dubious appeal of his apartment beat driving back to her place, alone, as had become abundantly clear in the interim, teasing or no. Like it had been the night at the hotel, and even when she was skinnier, her hug was surprisingly strong. It had to be the waitressing, because he sure could not see a paintbrush doing that. She would be noticing his appreciated bulk.

Thank you for hanging out with me, Porter. It made last night a lot more bearable. Please come see me again, just not by helicopter.

He assured her that particular possibility was unlikely, although preferable to the drive, even with the airsickness, and thanked her for Maeda's number.

Is there some secret password that will let him know I'm legit? He won't know me from Adam.

It's his private number. If you have that he'll know you had to get it from me or someone else close to him.

He let his mind go blank on the road home, letting the rental car radio substitute for thought. The Millfork station was stuck in the hippy sixties. A novelty but, my God, at some point you had to realize there was more to music than the Grateful Dead. Unfortunately, the Sacramento stations that returned with the small cluster of high rises on the horizon were familiar but no better. They were a good match for a place that had grown up without figuring out what it wanted to be when it did, bypassing any attempt at regional pride and going straight from hick to corporate-focus-group format: synthesized embarrassments from the middle of the pop charts as accompaniment for the tiny blue huddle of earnest glass silos thumbing their noses at the surrounding flats. Just because he had to return to the disappointment of his bare-walled apartment did not mean that a bit of Zoot Sims or Esperanza Spalding would not improve his mood. He popped in one of each when he got back, while he scraped the crust off dinner dishes from two days before, cleaned himself up and changed clothes. Then he picked up the phone but changed his mind. He wanted to see his kids anyway, not just hope to talk to them.

He pulled into his driveway with the self-absorbed frontal focus of someone who did not need to see what notice his neighbors might be taking, or care, almost knocked, then walked right in. Roger had commandeered the couch so he could enjoy his zombie attack game on the big TV screen. Porter got the formal greeting of seeing him put the game on pause, which would not have happened when he lived there.

Hey, Dad.

Hi, Roger. How are you? How's school going?

OK, I guess.

What's this one called?

The South Shall Rise Again. It's about a jail built on top of a civil war cemetery, and all the dead soldiers come back to life as zombies for revenge. You get to choose if you want to be a guard or a prisoner. You, uh, want to play?

Roger was being polite, as though he were a guest.

Sure, why, not?

He never did this, since he had made it clear that this was intellectual masturbation. The unexpected deviation from his former parent role was not lost on Roger as he handed Porter a controller and pointed out what buttons to push with a bit of impatience; a grumpy uncle explaining how to drive a car to a bothersome three year old who had no need of the information.

You'll want to start out as a guard. Prisoners can rack up points faster, but they have to get out of their cells first and steal a gun from a guard or they're toast.

In no time Porter found his avatar being dismembered and eaten by a slobbering cluster of ravenous specters well on the way to ragged maceration, but somehow capable of mastication. His grisly death was still preferable to the bloody—*You Lose, Turnkey*—splattered on the wall that made in-your-face insult of the obvious. Roger expelled a contemptuous snort and then was lost in his own point amassing. This left Porter sidelined for the duration, which gave him ample time to recall the hoots, laughs and shoulder-lean intentional fouls Joel had traded with his son that summer afternoon while he stood by uselessly, taking counterproductive consolation in rapid pulls of beer. Joel was not that much younger, but they might as well have been from different generations. Porter could not help that, and there was no use trying to fake it. It was almost a relief when Anita walked in, her face alight with happy expectation. Then the inquisitive arch of her welcoming eyebrows for one of Roger's friends went flat and crowded her eyelids.

What are you doing here?

Can't I see my family?

You should call first.

A fat lot of good that would do.

Tina's not here anyway. She's at Cynthia's.

I'll settle for two out of three. I'm not here to pick a fight. How have you been?

Too busy to humor uninvited guests. And Roger looks about as interested.

Roger did not even look up:

Don't drag me into this.

Porter looked at Anita, who looked back at him over the insistent minor dirge, the random explosions and muted screams. Like most women, she would have no idea how beautiful she looked with her hair half up in a haphazard pin, a misshapen sweatshirt and a favorite pair of jeans that were getting just a little too clingy.

He's right, Anita. Let's not. Come on. Come have a cup of coffee with me. How about lunch at the Purple Pagoda?

That would be tea. Are you asking me on a date?

Sure. Unless that would make you want me to go away.

She looked from him to Roger and back.

That's not fair.

OK, let's just call it lunch.

He really was not all that into Chinese, but she knew that too, so the olive branch would be obvious. She sucked her cheeks for a few moments in the kitchen doorway, then disappeared and came back with her coat, but would not look at him while he took in the sweater upgrade from the sweatshirt, and her hair, now up all the way, the way she wore it to her job at the grammar school, the way she looked the day he met her.

He was working Traffic with San Jose P.D., a rare day shift assignment for a guy fresh out of the academy who was used to graveyards. A beater compact rolled around a corner on a red light right in front of him and he lit it up on reflex. No big deal. A dime-a-dozen citation for a dime-a-dozen California stop. What he got when she rolled down the window was this feisty little brunette, all up thrust chin and sharp cheekbones, blaming him for making her late to her substitute teacher job, spitting how she was not the least impressed by a man who must have a tiny dick so he went around trying to compensate by wearing a big gun, and congratulating him for making asshole of the day even though it was only seven-thirty. Teacher, teacher. Most of it went on by, not because he had heard it before, but because she was so completely in his face that she was oblivious to the rain running down her own, and down her neck, and between two very nice ice cream scoops peeking out of her blouse, quivering with indignation.

Back in his car he wrote her, but took his time because she deserved it, and because he was thinking of something else. He had to go over it a couple times to make sure he had checked all the boxes. When he walked back to her car she was giving him more of the same even as the window came back down, as though she had never let up the whole time he was gone. He gave her the: *Press hard, three copies*, and an encore that was totally outside of policy, explaining that letting her off was not an option, but if she wanted to write down her phone number he would like to take her out and show her it was nothing personal.

She did the big blink, but it shut her up. Then she gave him the up and down like she was seeing him for the first time, and he knew he was screwed because she was going to want his badge number. When she spoke, there was still the defiance, but her demeanor was teetering on the edge of collapse.

Will it make you go away?

Her voice was so small he could barely hear her over the tires tearing by behind him on the wet asphalt, but he was gut shot.

So he was surprised when he called the number the next day, the grocery receipt she had written the, he assumed, phony number on already crumpled in his hand, and it was the actual Anita who answered. More surprising was how apologetic she was, explaining how it was not like her, but she had this thing about authority, and he had been the frosting on a burnt cake of a morning. Much later she told him she had been too stunned by his nerve to make up a number to write down. He had never asked her if that was really the truth. It was too late to ask her now. She was too deep into domestic mundane:

I'll be back in a while, Roger. If Tina calls, tell her I'll still pick her up at three.

Her only comment on the way was how clean his car looked. He told her it was easy to keep clean without grubby teenage fingers all over it all the time, and immediately regretted it. That left the expansive silence to soak in. The radio would be too much. What would fit the mood: The traffic report? The forced hilarity of Bill and Ted? The oldies station? He left it off. They were stuck in a pot overflowing with the unsaid as traffic noise pressed in from all sides.

The Purple Pagoda was more of a dinner place. Daylight revealed the chipped table edges and the joints of wallpaper beginning to curl. He wished he could have arranged the softer light of the Chinese lanterns at night when none of this would show. There would also be more customers than the thin scatter of lunch lingerers, which made him feel more exposed because there was not enough background noise to speak above a whisper. She ordered the Dim Sum special which she knew he could not stand, leaving him with either the fore-ordained burnout of a monotonous bowl of pork fried rice or a large plate of Mandarin beef and snow peas, like inflexible co-workers on separate checks, instead of sharing plates the way they had done when they were first together. He could at least pour her tea, for which he got an actual thank you. She asked him how he was getting along.

You mean my apartment? It's one or the other. It's too quiet and then there's too much other people's noise coming through the walls. You?

It's nice to have the whole bed to stretch out.

He wondered if she said this without thinking or meant it on purpose.

How about the kids?

Tina asks about you, believe it or not. Roger's been extra helpful. Believe it or not.

What's happening on Thanksgiving?

She looked up at him, looking startled.

You mean, can you come? I think that would be too weird. I mean, it's going to be weird anyway with just the three of us at my folks, but it would be even stranger if you were there. I think it would confuse the kids.

Not you, though?

She put her cup down carefully, solidly, with both hands, and gave him the cemented look of a loan officer being asked for a large sum on no collateral.

What are you asking?

I'm asking where are you at with this?

I think I've made that pretty clear. We aren't anywhere because we weren't going anywhere, and I've already been there.

You make it sound like we never were. I'm willing to see if we can work through this. We're just not in a good place right now.

Right now? Five or six years ago you wanted to quit San Jose P.D. and take a job up here. I didn't like it, but we did it. I had to quit my job, too, and settle for a worse one three hours farther from my parents and my sister. Did it make any difference? Not that I can see. You wanted off the streets. You miss the streets. You wanted out of a uniform. You hate suits and ties. You think you know what you want. You don't know what you want. I need more than that or I'll just be settling for more of the same. I thought when we moved up here you'd snap out of it. But it's been like you're dead. You used to be fun. I'm sorry, but I'm tired of waiting. I need more than—more of this. You think I just woke up one morning and said, *that's it?*

This was a frontal assault that was uncalled for, especially in the face of his white flag. Porter found himself flushing the *Oh, Honeys*, even though he knew it was his only hope. But he gave it one shot. A squib load that lodged halfway down the barrel.

Oh, no. You made it clear you've been pissed off at me for a good long time. I'm supposed to be a police chief somewhere by now so you don't have to work and can stay home. Well, there's no more chance of that than you getting a call anymore for some photo shoot. So you're not the only one who's tired. I'm tired of looking for a magic wand that is going to make you happy. Tired of tip-toeing around you while you sulk and grind your axe. Tired of feeling guilty if I can't just scrape off my day on the front doormat and bounce into the house like some game show host. You miss your mom. You miss your friends. So you're unhappy. What do you expect when you won't let it go? What I want to know is, what now? Is this the way you want to carry on, or do you intend to make it permanent? I'm stuck in limbo over here.

For a dud, his aim was pretty good. Now she was just—the old Anita.

Limbo. What would you know about limbo? Limbo is living with a ghost. With somebody who won't admit they have a problem. You're the one who bailed on the counseling.

Porter had his own version of that, too, but Anita could not see it for what it was back then, either, so why bother? As if that bronze-haired career academic could have told them anything. He could not decide if she was a lesbian, thrice-divorced or a never-was, but her idea of roll play was as cheerily inconsequential as it was an insulting farce of engagement. Which was what they did every day. Meanwhile, Anita was hitting her stride.

The problem is it's always had to be about you, and now you're in a hurry, as usual. So don't go pretending—

Her face turned scrutinizing, parsing, arctic.

You've met someone.

It was a statement, not a question. In some ways she had really missed her calling, but she was off base. At least he thought she was. She was looking out the window now, a woman surveying a new landfall. He hurried to steer her back to their neighborhood.

Now where did you get that? All I'm trying to say is, OK, I'm not perfect, but neither of us is, so why keep pretending? I want to know if you think we might still have a future. Look at me.

She did, but blankly.

I still love you, Anita. You know that.

The food would arrive just then, allowing her to draw herself up and away into a singularly disengaged composition of wife and wife-not, who would now pretend to be his circumstantial lunch companion. No more, no less. He prepared a restaurant review while she smothered her Dim Sum rolls in plum sauce balanced with a bland mixture of Roger and Tina's grades, her relatives' most recent illnesses, and pointless teacher-lounge gossip poured over the rest of the "date."

PLEASE TELL US ABOUT YOUR DINING EXPERIENCE	
Category	**Comments**
Ambience	Walk-in freezer
Attentive Staff	Not now, you fool
Dining Companion	Exploding blow-up doll
Food	?

What he ate he immediately forgot.

CHAPTER XIII

WHY SWITZERLAND
IS NOT ON THE EURO

He talked Joel into meeting for coffee on the outskirts of Sacramento with the excuse that it would be more efficient than meeting at the office just to compare notes, but he really just wanted to avoid a Monday morning that started there. He got to Buster's first and looked around at the other diners, imagining what their lives were like. Two crusty journeymen in overalls hunched in a window booth boring one young apprentice in jeans and a work shirt who was trying to look eager and impressed while fighting to stay awake. Twin geezers at the counter in pathetic matching Kings hats, silent over coffees, having no new lies to tell. A young woman in a knit dress and heels standing with an order binder in the back, waiting with obvious impatience for the manager to appear, and in no mood for the admiring glances of the men present for her impressive frontage which would translate into a backache by sundown. Here was Joel. What did they look like, a couple of real estate salesmen? He guessed that was the point of a suit and tie. You could be anybody, but at least you were employed, or trying to be. Joel's was accessorized with a conspiratorial grin as he came swerving around the tables, like a sharp-faced dancer.

So how was your weekend? Was there a happy ending?

Porter considered that he was 0 for 2, but it was none of Joel's business.

For someone so clammed up about their love life, you sure want to know a lot about mine. How was yours?

As if you would care, but great. I got the phone records. You owe Rappel a blow job. Morris had three calls from her husband about a quarter to twelve. All under a minute. Plus one she never picked up. But here's the kicker. His calls hit the same towers in Whitley County as hers. So he was there.

Or will have a helluva time explaining that he wasn't. Anything else?

Rappel wouldn't admit it, but I think he owes us one, too. Herl told me he talked to the officer who was supposed to be escorting Morris to the county line. He followed her only part way and then turned back, on the assumption that she was out of their hair. I think he'll be escorting wide loads for the foreseeable future. There was another car going the same direction as her that he passed after he turned around and was headed back. It could have been Biel, but it could have been anybody.

Why do you think Herl told you this? It leaves them looking pretty careless.

Not necessarily. It depends how much gets out. Their interest in her should have ended the moment she hit the highway. Anything more than that could also be construed as overkill, harassment, or worse. It's to their benefit to be able to say only that they ensured that she had exited their governor-security jurisdiction, and leave it at that. I think Herl is hoping we'll see it that way, too.

Porter mulled this. If the focus was so much on butt covering, there might be more to cover up than they were letting on. Joel had the benefit of longer contact.

Any reason why we shouldn't?

Joel looked up over the rim of his cup, as though he were checking to see if Porter was kidding. He took a long sip and swallow before he answered.

That would assume that the governor had a problem with her and that his crew was into that kind of problem solving. I think it's much more likely that there is a bigger screwup they don't want to daylight, or else hubby deserves more of our attention. Or a random encounter that isn't on our radar. Did you see the news this morning?

He had seen it, but calling it news was a stretch. The pretty faces on the daybreak ersatz news shows were wetting themselves while repeating love-tryst conjectures in such a way that you had to listen carefully for the unnamed sources appendages that otherwise would have made the pronouncements indistinguishable from headlines reported as fact. Roundtables of the jowly red-tie set immediately set about speculating whether the recount would have been necessary had the governor been faced with this "crisis" before the election. Inside of twenty minutes, any discussion of truth versus gossip was trampled in a dash to put this "November Surprise" in context with the tightening recount results. All this could be affecting their assignment.

I haven't talked to Maddie or Warren since Friday. Any change in the terrain?

No, except Warren wasn't too happy with you racking up rental car fees when you had a free helo ride home. Was it worth it?

I never got ahold of Flanders, it being a weekend, but I did get a lead on one of Morris' co-workers, a Shin Maeda. Her relatives might know something, too. Maybe you could track them down. Or have the CHP or coroner's people already talked to them?

Joel scoffed.

The boys at CHP keep making a lot of noise about getting to the bottom of things, but I think they just want this to go away. The coroner, I have no idea, except I got a text that her BAC came back point zero four. Negative for anything else. So she had maybe one drink in her.

OK, so if you would talk to her people, I'll talk to her co-worker and Flanders. And I think I'll swing by Biel's office. Unless you want to. You put him at the Pemberton, you should get first crack at him.

No, thanks. I'm not in a hurry to visit the capitol. I hear bad things happen there.

If Joel could have seen how many skirts seemed to be skipping about the state capitol grounds he might have changed his mind. Ladies that seemed to be all legs were everywhere, and all were on a mission to be somewhere other than the general vicinity of riffraff like Porter, who should have followed them instead of climbing the broad marble steps. As if sensing the intimidation that the massive columns pressed down upon him, the grossly proportioned oaken slabs of door failed to yield for either push or pull. He beckoned at a CHP officer inside who pointed him down and around the corner. Only then did he see the small notice directing him to a side entrance for security clearance. This meant retreating back down the steps and backtracking around a broad concrete meander of walkway for a forced return stroll past long, broad beds of annuals that had no business being there in November, then across the driveway leading to the underground garage where members presumably avoided the glorified proctology exam he was headed for. With the immediate reversal of vantage he could see now that the capitol was on a slight rise of ground that imposed an imperceptible boost, revealing a desire for height and grandeur while concealing the mechanism, the conceit of a short politician in elevator shoes obscured by extended pant cuffs of huge conifers draped to the ground, and a few leafless giants whose tiny labels distinguished them as originating from distant lands. There were coastal redwoods intermingled with sycamores, palm trees, valley oak, and giant sequoias that under ordinary conditions existed only in the Sierra mountains. Others wore green droopy clusters that were unidentified, but existed nowhere on the continent as far as he could tell. Under it all were acres of lawn that was indistinguishable from any Midwestern park or cemetery, inviting a promenade past the floating dome of actual gold leaf and the tiny flags snapping at the peak; a theme park mashup of main street idealism tossed off with disparate and hoary remnants of Aegean pomposity. Any endeavor that went to such lengths to trumpet its power in such a calculated juxtaposition with pastoral benevolence was surely confused about a lot of other things.

When he showed his badge, the guards inside the basement entrance waived him around the detector and into a vestibule where he left his gun in a bank of tiny lockboxes common to courthouses, which he was quite familiar with. The mundane aspects of the routine must have lulled him, because he then became immediately lost, despite the simple-sounding directions the guards had provided. His mistake was walking past the jammed elevators fronted by a throng of tourists and school children, and feeling quite smart about finding a tiny back stairwell. Four flights deposited him in a hallway with doors numbered in the three thousands. That did not make much sense. He went back to the stairwell to check the floor number and saw his error; he had miscounted somehow and had exited on the fourth floor when he wanted the fifth, never mind why offices on the fourth floor were numbered in the three thousands. But when he went up another flight he was confronted by a door that was also marked *4*. This made no sense at all. He was standing there looking at the sign stupidly as another set of shoes tapped and scuffed with increasing volume from below.

Back stairs lend a timeout for the mind which gives itself over to its own thoughts as reward for the bare walls and repetitious activity. This man was no exception. Porter had ample time to size him up as he waited to come into the man's vision, which was directed in the general vicinity of the fellow's own ascending feet. A good head of black hair with a good haircut to match. Natural shoulders and thin lapels of a dark blue suit, off the rack, but from a high end store. It needed a splash of tie to relieve the dark expanse, but the shirt, though richly thick and crisp white, was open at the collar. The tasseled loafers were not the surprise—the sockless feet stole the show. He looked up suddenly as if struck by some aspect of Porter's plain oxfords that was equally at odds with expectations.

If you want to have a smoke, I wouldn't. The smoke alarms in these stairwells are fiendishly sensitive.

Well, if he knew that, he probably was not a tourist. Not that he looked like one. This guy was on duty, socks or no, and the friendly gaze was a bit too direct; the brown eyes busy sorting through an internal file of faces. Porter's would not be among them.

Maybe you can help me. I seem to have gotten turned around. Either that or there are two fourth floors.

Actually, there are. The floors in the old capitol are taller than the ones in the new wing, so they don't line up. What are you looking for?

Room 5012. Rev and Tax Committee.

The man extended a hand.

You can come with me. Howard Zephur, chief consultant. Have we met?

Porter told him his name and did the handshake while reaching for his wallet badge in his inner breast pocket with his free hand, which was a handy arrangement for just such occasions, but mostly it left his gun hand free. He thought better of the badge and came out with a business card instead. Zephur angled it toward the dim stairwell light.

Insurance. Did Toby Sim retire? I used to work with him on proposals. Oh, you're an investigator.

Yes, I was hoping to get in touch with Assemblyman Biel, the Committee Chair. It's about the death of his wife. I assume he's away on bereavement, but I figured his staff would know how to get in touch with him, at least if I came in person and not by phone.

You would be right. And yes, you won't find him here, but

maybe there's something I can help you with. Perhaps we should talk in my office.

Porter followed him up another flight and into a hall that had the vacated chaos of campus dorms during summer break. Here and there were office desks, side chairs and bookcases abandoned against the walls, piles of files and documents, and boxes, lots of boxes. Zephur explained that, although the session did not officially end until the end of the month, legislative business was over. Members that were termed out or forced out by the election were already abandoning ship. Elections always resulted in office shuffles anyway, even for the members staying on, because power shifts could get you a bigger or smaller office, depending. They were not all the same. Some were barely closets.

The Revenue and Taxation Committee office was far from a closet. It had a spacious foyer with one of those leggy staffers in front to greet them, and a suite of offices and meeting rooms beyond. Zephur led him into one with a window looking out over the lawns, closed the door, and settled himself behind a desk. Porter took a tucked and beaded chair of dark burgundy leather, cool and slick against his thighs, making him think of brandy and cigars. A similar relaxation of enterprise seemed to have occurred with Zephur, whose frank expression had drifted to wearily bemused. He would be easy to trust in a negotiation over a piece of proposed legislation. He had to have as many questions as Porter did, but something out the window seemed to have gathered his attention, leaving him talking to Porter in a desultory show of interest. He was curious to know how a person came to be an investigator, which seemed like the sort of idle question Porter might expect from a man who had all the time in the world and was in no hurry to get anywhere in particular. It might also be an indicator of someone avoiding a topic, or who had not figured out what they wanted to say. Or it could be just a man tired to the bone and ambling through the moment. He knew enough about the legislative process to know it could be a grinder. Porter's sojourn at SF State brought Zephur around, so it had all been pro forma; a sleep-walked routine of ease putting and seeking a common connection as precursor lubricant to slip into or out of whatever crass proposal was sure to follow.

A Gator? Me too. What year?

Ninety-two. From the looks of things, I should have skipped AJ and majored in whatever you majored in.

Poly Sci, but getting into Hastings was the difference. You never can tell. My counterpart in Water, Parks and Wildlife majored in Environmental Science. I told her she was wasting her time. It was all survey courses: Bird Watching one-oh-one; Posey Sniffing one-oh-one. I told her to pick something and specialize or she would starve. She had the last laugh. She ended up riding a wave of EIR's to bigger and bigger planning firms, and suddenly she was the one who hired the 'ologists to feed her the data, then cut them loose. She became an expert in CEQA and the Coastal Act, became a staffer on the Coastal Commission, and ended up down the hall, with a bigger office I might add. As for the suit, it's just a uniform. A prop to impress the rubes. How may I impress you today?

Whether he was being softened up or not, Porter liked this guy. Maybe he could play along and return the favor, both.

I apologize for intruding at a time like this. I imagine the press has been after Assemblyman Biel. Maybe you, too.

Actually, that's what I thought you were at first.

(Some compliment.)

Did you know her well? Miss Morris?

About as well as anyone knows the boss's wife. What she's like at home, who knows? But she was a real firecracker when she was out campaigning with him. She lit up a room better than he could, which you would never guess if you saw him on his own. Women seemed to admire her, even when it was obvious she also had every guy in the place salivating. A lot of women can do one or the other. A few can do both, but not at the same time. She just made everyone feel like they were her friend. It's been pretty rough on the whole staff.

Well, I have no desire to add to anyone's burdens. That's why I think it would be to his benefit if I could talk to him right away.

Zephur leaned back and clasped his hands behind his head.

I don't know how you would do that. Even if he wasn't in seclusion, Thomas and Harold are friends, and not just because they both have a D after their names. They go way back to walking precincts together in the eighties. Would he like to strangle the governor for spending too much time with his wife? No doubt. Is he looking to commit political murder-suicide by trashing Harold over this? He won't see it this way with her funeral coming up on Saturday, but I guarantee you by next week he'll be moving on, and taking the high road. Living with failure is what politics is all about. A pitcher can't be thinking about his last pitch, only the next one. He won't give you anything.

Zephur was smooth, but it was still a stall. This was taking an exit to a town with no filling station.

Perhaps you misunderstand me, Mister Zephur.

Oh, Christ, call me Howard.

Look, Howard, the facts are going to come out one way or the other, but in the meantime the rumors are running wild. My experience with these things is that the truth is always preferable. All I'm trying to do is get the facts straight, file a report, and this will probably die down before the January swearing-in. But to do that I need to talk to Mister Biel.

Zephur looked out the window some more on this first.

OK, answer me this. You say you're from the Department of Insurance. Forgive me, but I don't see what that has to do with this. Nobody else from law enforcement has been around asking questions.

I believe you make my point for me.

How's that?

I think there are enough questions floating around that a reasonable person might begin to wonder if there might be a bigger question if they aren't answered. At best, my role is to provide a parallel check on the process. At worst, I'm here to ensure that there is a measure of independence surrounding this inquiry. I've got no personal stake in this and, as far as I know, neither does my boss.

Aren't you under the Attorney General?

No, Insurance Commissioner Havens. Why?

It's just that, if you were, I would have to call you on that one. Gorman's bound to be sniffing around this. Say Gorman loses the recount, which is going back and forth every day now, but say he does. Our spanking new lieutenant governor, Surlitz, would have preferred to work with a governor who also has an R behind his name, which is why he and Gorman campaigned arm in arm. If Gorman loses he could help a fellow Reep if he can use the Attorney General's resources to dig up some impeachable dirt on Vaneros. The LG assumes the governorship if that were to happen. Then Surlitz could return the favor. As close as this election is, Gorman would be a shoe-in to step up the next time around if he had the backing of Surlitz as sitting governor. Of course, he'd have to convince Surlitz not to run himself if Surlitz got comfortable, or wait him out, depending on what the party prefers, but—Is everything OK?

Porter was not OK. He was a rented clown at a birthday party who had just been asked why he always wanted to be photographed with little boys, but not little girls. He was a long haul trucker who had himself convinced he liked the open road until the day he woke from a dream about falling under a crush of hysterics stampeding out of a burning nightclub, and now had to wonder if really he just did not like people. He was a night watchman who had just found out he was guarding an empty warehouse.

I'm fine. Probably the stairs. I guess I'm a little out of shape.

Hot in here, isn't it? You should try sitting in a committee hearing all day in a suit coat and tie, in July. Hang on a sec.

Zephur disappeared and Porter looked around the room for a distraction from his nausea. There were pictures of Zephur with the Speaker next to a golf cart, Zephur on a small sail boat, and a large framed Assembly proclamation with a gold seal recognizing him for his work on something or other. No family photos. Here was a man with obvious accomplishments. But at what cost?

When he came back he had a large glass pitcher of water and two glasses. Porter resisted the urge to dump his down the back of his neck and drank it instead. It was a simple gesture of hospitality, which he now had to tamper with.

Thank you. Can we focus on your boss for a minute? As things stand, there are some gaps in our investigation that only he can fill. We would like to find out what he knows about his wife's appointments and movements the night she died. If you don't think that will convince him to get in touch with me, tell him this: to complete my report I also need to ask him about his own whereabouts that night. It would be in his best interest to do this sooner rather than later. I'll meet him anywhere he wants. It will only take a few minutes. And please be sure and give him my condolences.

Zephur stood up and walked him to the door.

I'll do what I can. Was there something else?

Porter realized he was taking too long fiddling with his tie.

You're probably not the one to ask, but I'm going to take a shot. Would you have any idea why the governor would want a private meeting in the boonies with the Whitley County District Attorney? That county's a hangnail compared to L.A, or Orange, or San Francisco, even if the DA is good looking, which she is.

Zephur stuck out his lower lip and folded his arms while one shoulder drifted toward the door frame, as though in accord with his redirected thoughts.

The skirt alone might be enough to reel in Vaneros, with Holly Morris being exhibit A. If it were a larger county I'd say it could be about fundraising, block grants, a key vote, or who knows?

She's a Republican.

Really? Now that is interesting. You know, there's been some discussion of an initiative to totally legalize marijuana. Some of the north counties are quietly suggesting that it might be preferable to continuing to drain their enforcement budgets, clog their courts, and keep county government at odds with free enterprise.

Would Whitley County be one of those?

Let's just say our committee has been approached with questions about the revenue implications of such an outcome.

What might those be?

I think it could make Big Tobacco look like bubble gum, and all that goes with that. It's the wild west, and it's starting to remind me of the scramble for Indian casino dollars; every office holder and would-be office holder preaching against it while reaching for handouts behind their backs. The marijuana industry is becoming like that, a country unto itself, with lots of marbles to share with friends or punish its enemies.

And the governor? Where's he at on this?

Zephur had roused himself and reached for the door, but hesitated with his hand on the knob and turned back toward Porter.

Are you asking if I give a damn if Vaneros sinks or swims?

Should I?

Don't.

Porter missed the alcove to the back stairs and found

himself in a backwater of the uppermost floor whose dimness was unrelieved by a succession of picture-window sized governors' portraits stretching back a century and a half. They were almost unfailingly setups of the heavily proportioned and the heavily dressed, potentates rimmed in darkness as they stood or sat at their ease with the relaxed satisfaction of visionary resolve rewarded in leading their people forward into the light of their leaders' esteemed proximity. The exception was the oil portrait of Jerry Brown's first term, a close-up bust of near abstraction lurching forward, crowding into the frame, with the unsettling challenge of a subject gazing straight into the camera's eye. Moreover, in contrast to the stuffy bits of revisionary hypocrisy apparent in the window dress of most of his predecessor deities, Brown's eyes conveyed a forthright mixture of steadfastness in triumph over distrust, even fear, caught in a snapshot glance of pragmatic self-doubt as revealed in the blotchy cheeks, shadowed upper lip, shiny forehead, the world-weary eyelids. Here was a man who had made some pact with the devil and was not afraid to admit it, the jury still out on which one had gotten the better part of the deal, even to the point of allowing the commissioned artist to render his eyes the deep black of pools so clear and clean that you could see all the way to their black bottoms. Porter knew for a fact that those were some of the deepest blue eyes he had ever encountered, which were only apparent at the closest proximity, in his case blundering into an elevator with the governor after a commission meeting at Insurance headquarters. The guy had to be the gutsiest of all those bastards.

He made his way back downstairs and walked past the dioramas lining the main floor hallways, each window display a county fair cornucopia overflowing with one of fifty-eight claims to fame: oranges, golden sunsets, palm trees, mountains, forty-niners with picks and shovels, railroad trains, proud Native Americans, surfers, rockets, movie stars, wine bottles, mission bells. Whitley County's was fishing boats, a Paul Bunyan knock-off and vineyards. Noticeably absent was the county's largest cash crop: a marijuana leaf. He nodded to the guard doing the heel-toe rock outside the double doors to the governor's suite, noting the short trip it would be from there to Biel's office for someone wanting to use the one to excuse a visit to the other. Too soon he had his gun back and found himself outside blinking in the glare off the white granite, so bright it made his eyes tear. He started walking anyway although he was essentially blind, and almost fell when he reached the top step, wondering how it must feel to the lobbyists and legislators to emerge from the interior dimness after a big win on an important bill, or a crushing reversal. Some would have a bounce to their step as they struck out into the shining promise of a brand new day. Others, like him, had to satisfy themselves with just putting one foot in front of the other as they sought to put themselves at a distance from this place. There was no way in hell he was going to tell Joel about any of this. Joel was sure to take a walk, a walk with real purpose. Besides, the least he could do was give Joel the benefit of plausible deniability. Zephur could also be wrong, just guessing, or stringing him along with some game of his own. The possible permutations were endless. If they wanted to give visitors a taste of the real California, they should have lined both sides of the capitol hallways with mirrors.

CHAPTER XIV

STUPID IN LOVE

As glib as Zephur was, Porter still had the feeling he was holding back, perhaps unconsciously; a person lying to himself. It seemed he wanted to help, but kept hauling up short on some principle or allegiance so deeply ingrained as to be as automatic, involuntary as blinking. It was clear Zephur had a lot of respect for Biel, and none whatsoever for Vaneros. His first instinct would be to protect Biel, and his wife who it was clear Zephur had a soft spot for as well. He needed to talk to someone who might know Biel, but who would not necessarily owe him much. Zephur had mentioned having worked with Toby Sim on Department of Insurance legislative proposals. Porter knew Toby as a former DOJ district chief investigator who had some kind of falling out with higher ups and migrated to the Department of Insurance. Once at DOI, he had made the improbable leap from the Enforcement Division to departmental legislative advocate on the strength of his regulatory knowledge juiced with his DOJ background and a masters in Poli Sci. He picked up on the first bounce as though he were expecting an important call, or was extremely busy and was in a hurry to dispense with the interruption. When Porter told him the reason for the call, Toby the former cop was suddenly available.

You had lunch?

Porter checked his watch.

It's after two. You haven't eaten yet?

Too busy 'til now. Besides, the Senator Club doesn't open until two. You in?

That would be great. I'm hoping you can do me a favor…

The Senator Club was old school, like Toby Sim, who the department called a legislative liaison instead of what he was—a lobbyist. What the Senator club was was a dive. It was dark inside, with furnishings as thin and shiny as Sim's pants seat; slick past its pull date, more than a little disreputable. Sim was all that, even though his reputation was also muddled up with integrity to a fault. The Senator Club was just the place to have the kind of discussion Porter wanted to have with him. In the bad light Sims looked like a bloodhound on a bar stool: bags under bags under weary eyes that said he was still game for the trail, or a good drunk, as long as it took. He ordered bourbon with a side of water for lunch, which explained plenty, and looked at Porter. Porter declined, and ordered soda and a sandwich.

I'm on duty.

Suit yourself, it's on me anyway. What's this favor?

I heard you've worked with one of Biel's staffers, Howard Zephur. I was wondering what you might have heard about Biel and his wife, Holly Morris.

Sim smacked his lips over his empty glass, which the bartender refilled automatically in passing, as appeared to be their routine. Sim only gulped half of this one, having found his stride.

The fact that you're here asking makes we wonder what you don't already know. What is it you really want to know?

I want to know what kind of relationship they had. What was her relationship with the governor? Did Howard ever say much about that? What kind of fellow is Biel? What's Morris like? Anything that might better explain how she wound up driving the coast highway at midnight the other night. The department is interested, for reasons I'd rather not go into.

Toby made a disparaging blow through pursed lips.

I can imagine. Biel's a chump. Who knows, maybe I would be, too, with a dish like that. But he was stupid in love with her. Let her run wild, even let her give his staff orders. And meanwhile it's all over L Street that she's bouncing from one populist crusade to the next no matter who gets walked on, and diddling the gov. That about cover it?

What if the blinders came off? Is Biel capable of violence?

Toby made a skeptical frown.

You're giving him too much credit. This is just what I heard from people. I worked mostly with Howard, not Tom. And I don't think Tom would confide in me even if we were close. I do know this: he comes from the Central Valley, where a person's word, their reputation is everything. My impression of him is that he is what used to be called a stand-up guy even if he's not so bright when it comes to her. The way Howard describes him, he wants to see the best in everyone, and generally gets what he expects. Sounds about right. I'm guessing people admire him so they generally live up to their better inclinations. I can't imagine what would happen if he ever figured out he'd really been burned. Those houses can come down hard. But murder? His gorgeous wife who can do no wrong? I doubt it. He's too straight-laced and he's too hung up on her.

To Porter, this sounded like just the opposite, setting up an unbearable tension between the immovable object and the irresistible force. There had to be some compromise or there would have been hell to pay. Or had Biel and Morris done too much compromising, with disastrous consequences? What fantasies had to be entertained to make the thing go, and how many were too many? A look at his own situation had to make him wonder also: what was the dirt on him and Anita? A start would be asking if he was on his own crusade and taking his marriage down with him, or whether his marriage was already a lost cause and this was the excuse. How a person could wake up one day and find himself digging dirt on people he had never met, or just barely, while his own wife was going A-B-C in front of a class of third graders as though her husband would still be home that night. Neither had died, but it was a far cry from the summer they moved in together and he could wake up from graveyard shifts and have breakfast waiting, and sometimes more. Sim seemed to be thinking along similar lines:

You talk to his family?

I'd like to, but they aren't returning calls.

That probably says all you need to know. Don't spend a lot of time there. They'll be circling the wagons without some axe to grind. Concentrate on her family. They will either have something to say or something to hide. Either way, pay attention. These things almost always come down to a spouse, a relative or a known associate. And don't forget to talk to Biel's enemies.

You know any?

You might try Ira Coombs. Biel took his seat from him in the last election.

Porter could not get Coombs, but he did get a call from one of his staffers, who said his name was Ellis Craig. Craig was understandably standoffish:

I don't know what I can tell you that isn't a matter of public record. Biel outspent Ira two to one and the results speak for themselves.

So, it wasn't just his straight-arrow image that got him elected?

Craig could not resist this one.

Oh, the image helped, but so did hefty contributions from tobacco and drug companies. He was playing both sides of the fence. Both are looking for favorable regulations and tax treatment if the marijuana laws loosen up. Ira wasn't going to touch that.

Who else knew about Biel's backers?

Who didn't?

Including his wife?

She was a reporter. How could she not?

CHAPTER XV

THE RIGHT THING FOR THE WRONG REASONS?
OR
THE WRONG THING FOR THE RIGHT REASONS?

A visitor had only to ponder the roofline at the Department of Justice to know this was no library or hospital, what with its pitchfork and bayonet array of antennas beneath the totemic pole of microwave tom-toms looming in mute testimony to the soundless secrets being signaled and gathered in all directions. Porter had never given it much thought when he worked there, even though he saw it lots of mornings like this one, spent days under that phalanx. Now it looked like what it was: a citadel of state-sanctioned paranoia, and the implied threat of the place applied to him as well as anyone. He would have the benefit of all the minor insults that came with the downgrade. His gate code had long since been de-activated so he had to park in the front lot, go through the doors, cross the lobby and pass inspection like a supplicant or salesman by whoever floated in the green dimness behind the bullet-proof glass of the kiosk. It was Arlene, still. He showed his badge like a good soldier. She gave him an insulted moue, and hit the buzzer along with the intercom.

Skipper, there's never been a nastier suit than yours in the whole shop. Go on.

She had always called him Skipper since they had been introduced and later fumbled for the recall; Hopper? Warner? Skipper was what stuck. He pantomimed writing on his palm.

What about the destination card?

I'll forge one for you. Where to?

Maddie's office.

Here you go.

She slid a plasticized card with a lapel clip attached through the document chute under the glass. The card was imprinted *VISITOR LEVEL 3*. He put it in his hip pocket and went through the doors in the two-story glass wall beyond the kiosk, through which he could see other staff in shirt sleeves and skirts going about their important rounds, a sheaf of papers in hand here, a cell phone there, trotting up the open stairs ascending the sky-lit atrium or scurrying along one of the walkways on either side. He took the stairs, enjoying the light and the weightless spaciousness that were not apparent from the outside. Another flight and he took a left at the hallway signed Tennessee Street, stuck his head in the unmarked door of Communications and Surveillance to razz Sanchez about the Niners. Sanchez was hunched over a task light on a bench top covered with miniscule screws, scraps of wires, circuit boards and odd bits of black plastic. Porter told him not to sit with his nose in the solder smoke. Sanchez did not even look up, just pointed at a fly-specked placard on the shelf above that said: *DO NOT DISTURB GENIUS AT WORK.*

Genius, huh? Is that what you call that Niner offense?

Sanchez turned his head and tilted it down so he could scrutinize Porter over his magnifying lenses.

Says the safety who got benched.

Whoa, touchy today. How much did you lose?

Twenty.

I see. And I suppose that would mean lunch is on me. Is that your recovery plan?

Can't. Deadlines.

The civil servant as zombie. Have at it. But did you happen to get a requisition from Maddie for some gear for Warren Tell over at DOI?

Nope, and no, I don't need to look.

Sanchez turned back to his circuit board. Porter then continued down to Chestnut and popped in on Maddie. She was on the phone, and gave him her own deadlines look. No one would ever accuse Maddie of sleeping her way up the ladder. Supposedly she had a husband somewhere, but the idea made Porter resist a shudder. Her hair was the brown of a rotten board, stiff, and splintered at the ends. She had on some sort of faux leopard-spot blouse under a black coat that strained at the shoulders, topped with a string of pearls that set off the creased wattle of skin at her neck. He plopped down as though she had given him a big smile and a welcome wave, while she went on and on about some subpoena screw up. Eventually she hung up, which was all the greeting he got.

So. What?

I'm just fine. How are you, Maddie? Oh, I don't know. I thought we might talk some more about how I was blessed with an assignment by your agency using my agency for cover. Lately, I'm having to explain that I'm doing a check and balance kind of due diligence number but, from what I'm hearing, it's sounding more and more like I'm just somebody's water boy.

Where are you hearing that?

I'm hearing it from people who should know. Even if they are speculating, the fact that they are has to make a person wonder. So what's going on?

You know what your problem is, Michael? You're too busy tripping over your goody two shoes all the time to just shut up and do your job. You're an investigator. So investigate. Let somebody else worry about the politics.

And if the politics are picking the investigations? You have a thousand things you could be working on. What's driving this one? Who wants to know? I need to know.

Maddie got up and came around the desk. Thankfully, she was in pants, so he was not forced to contemplate those lumpy thighs. She made a show of leaning back against the front of her desk while she consulted her toes for the right words to mollify her clueless child.

Let's talk about the investigation for a minute. What have you got?

I've got a dead woman that nobody wants to own, which leans more and more away from suicide or accidental. I've got CHP doing a duck-and-cover. Whitley County doesn't seem to care as long as it wraps. We're still doing background on Morris, and the county D.A. is at least a peripheral witness. I'm going to talk to her but first I could use a come to Jesus. This whole thing smells, Maddie.

OK, OK. Tell me, Michael, what do you get paid to do?

Investigate, but—

That's right. You're not the governor. You're not the legislature. You're not the commissioner. You're not the courts. You're an agent of all of them and, by extension, the electorate. You're paid to make observations and report facts, period. Nobody is telling you to do otherwise.

Oh, please. Don't patronize me. Like I shouldn't mind what?—torching poppy fields in Afghanistan trying to flush out Osama Bin Laden when he could just as well be in Tahiti? Or dodging bullets in Iraq for democracy when it's just a cover for some oil company takeover?—that's just bull.

Maddie exhaled audibly through her nose.

So, you want to make this a career decision over your save-the-world notions? Again?

This was too much and, as if to underscore his disgust, his chest was in a bear hug.

You want to make threats? I'm just a hired gun? Is that the best you can do?

If that's the way you want to look at it. OK, then Bingo. Class dismissed.

Porter seethed, shorting out in an attempt to run down his go, no-go options, which there was no form for. Nor was there a table or spreadsheet he could imagine sufficient to organize, much less equate, the scramble of knowns all jumbled up with his suppositions and speculations, his oath to serve justice and the public trust, his glacial wife, his smell test, his blameless kids, the lack of a smoking gun, his chest pain, his future job prospects, his self-respect and what was owed a loose-cannon reporter and her family if nobody else cared how she died in any sense that was more than self-serving. What he thought, what he did or didn't do, wasn't bringing Morris back any more than he was likely to convince Anita to take him back, so who was he kidding? It was a little late to be getting religion. It made as much sense as a man deciding to take up jogging again just after the doctor tells him he has inoperable lung cancer. What did that make him? No saint, and maybe no better than the rest of them; exploiting a woman's death just to further his own denial. Then why not let it go? What was he sticking his neck out for? In this, his was a terminal case in the final stages, and he was now reduced to bargaining, with Maddie of all people.

There's something wrong about the way she died. Is it too much to ask why it should matter so much to your precious agency, or to whom?

Maddie showed him her dingy teeth, the result of her up-bringing in some white-washed ranch style on the Colorado Front Range drinking well water with high concentrations of natural fluorine. Cowgirl up.

Maybe because it matters to you. Just follow your nose. No-body expects more than that.

Out the window a commuter jet made its tiny progress be-hind her head. It had a place to be. All it had to do was follow its nose, as long as it did not suck a fat goose into an engine, have a midair with an octogenarian private pilot day-dreaming in his Mooney, or get taken over by terrorists and get diverted into a skyscraper. He was not on autopilot, at least not when it came to this case. If he went along on her terms he was going to lose more than sleep over it, maybe a lot more. He could not imagine how she slept at all. He searched his closet for even the thinnest blanket.

I'm not going to work off the books on this. What I could use is a signed request from the Deputy A.G. to Warren asking for my services. What you put on it for justification is up to you.

Maddie turned this over and then took a deep breath.

Fine. I'll update Warren.

He wanted out of there, was already at the door.

When you do, find out what that gear was he wanted. They never got a requisition ticket downstairs.

He knew Maddie would drag her heels on his request, too, find excuses why she would have trouble tracking down the Deputy A.G. for an investigation order, would know Porter was not going to let this case get cold while he waited for a piece of paper they both knew he was never going to get. He had let them both off the hook. If he had pushed it, she might have had to show her hand. But if she called his bluff—*Ok, then you're off the case*—What would he have said? She really did have the right man for the job.

Halfway across the parking lot his cell phone buzzed with a voicemail. Somehow the building had smothered the signal on his unsanctioned phone until he was released. It was Flanders getting back to him. He punched the numbers and waited with his hip against his fender. It would have been quieter inside the car, but he wanted the air.

Mister Porter? Good Morning.

Good morning, Ms. Flanders. Listen, I need to talk to you again. It's about your interaction with the governor at the Pemberton.

With who? Since when is what I do with anyone your concern? You're supposed to be focusing on the vehicle.

If Porter were a prosecutor himself, and if they were in court, this would have been the point where he petitioned the judge to treat the witness as hostile.

Sorry, I'm past that. And I've never been in the habit of

taking direction from witnesses.

A long pause. Then:

You've got about two seconds to explain why I shouldn't hang up on you.

How about a video of your meet with the governor that is at odds with your portrayal?

Another pause.

And you want to discuss this on the phone? That's not going to happen.

What are you doing this afternoon?

I'm not in Millfork. I'm at a conference in Redding. Tomorrow I'm gone until after the holidays.

Give me a time this afternoon and I'll be there.

I can meet you around three thirty, but it will have to be short. You know where the convention center is?

He was doing about eighty on I-5 north when he realized it would be barely noon when he got there. What was the hurry and what was he going to do in the meantime? He did not know a soul in Redding. Maybe he did. Sure enough, Celeste answered, and she was indeed killing time at the Redding hospital. Ruth was still waiting for clearance to be released, after which Celeste would be driving them home.

I should be there around noon. Can you get away for lunch?

I guess—I thought I had run you off. Sure, that would be fun. It's supposed to hit seventy degrees here today, if you can believe it. Maybe we could brown bag it at the new park by the river. I'll get sandwiches and meet you at the museum.

Porter knew the place, but only in artist renditions of its most eye-catching feature designed to put Redding on the map, the result of a bit of political back scratching that had blessed Redding with park bond funds far out of proportion to what the town's population would seem to justify. Besides the museum, there was a new water park, an Olympic pool, a paved bikeway along the river complete with fish viewing windows in a tunnel dug into the bank and—the flagship enhancement that had Porter gawking like a rube in Manhattan—a sailboat-white suspension bridge over the river supported by a soaring sailor's needle of mast at one end with a fanned rigging of cables draping to the deck itself. As a statement it was overwrought for the woodsy setting a hundred miles from the ocean; the thing overloaded with mixed imagery, appearing as both a vessel of racing-sloop aspiration and a mythically-proportioned Aeolian harp floating above the river for some god to strum the rigging while singing heroic songs of the region's conquests. The deck itself was paved with giant glass blocks, ostensibly to provide natural light for the fish. It had to cost millions, and it was built just for bikes and walkers. It was far bigger than it looked even in pictures. He almost overlooked Celeste, who was watching him near the sculptured bike racks. She evidently had been enjoying observing him unawares.

You look like a kid at the new spaceship ride.

That thing is gigantic. And it's just to walk on? You could drive a truck across and still have room for people on both sides.

It's got a secret, too, but let's eat first, and I'll show you after.

Once again, he was self-conscious to be the only suit and tie in sight, especially with a woman who made jeans and a red pullover look so good. She did not even have jewelry, just those long, expressive fingers as she unwrapped his sandwich on a nearby bench, almost knee to knee with him. Now that he was with her he did not know what to say, but he should say something. He had called this meeting.

Roast beef and Swiss. How'd you remember that?

Sorry, just luck. Most guys are into red meat.

And you found a great spot. How did you hear about it?

The hospital staff suggested it. I've been coming here for lunch every day. Don't you love all the light? It's brighter. It's like the air is lighter, too, easier to breathe.

She meant compared to the greener, damper coast, but

Redding was a far different country than Sacramento, too, even though they were cities in the same valley, just opposite ends. Despite being separated by a hundred and fifty miles there was still the same river sliding by in front of him, with the same mossy smell, but the air was distilled, astringent. She had her head back now, tracing a brooding oak, marveled aloud at the twisted branches, brought her sandwich up to her mouth, stopped, then examined it.

It's so dry after the coast. My sandwich bread is already drying out. Look, the edges are curling.

So they were. So was his. Even his skin tingled with desiccation, even so close to so much water. He had the air conditioning on in his car most of the time even in the winter, what with the suit, and after so long living in the valley it was only the contrast of his recent exit from his car that corroborated her observations. It could not be good for the skin but it seemed to have no effect on hers. Just the opposite. Maybe all those years soaking up the damp coast was part of her secret.

That's funny because your hair looks straighter, but it looks good on you. You look more relaxed, too.

I've been able to get in and see Ruth and Al, talk to them, forget about myself for a while. I think the change of scene helps, too. Breakwater's always been my little piece of heaven, but getting away helps me see it's not perfect, either. I think I was getting a little too wrapped up in what's been and not what is.

She looked out at the river for a minute, absently chewing, while he watched, admiring. She noticed and came back.

How about you? How's the bachelor life?

My wife thinks I'm having an affair.

This put the skids on her banter. She looked uncomfortable, then brave.

Are we?

Not unless they've changed the definition.

It was a reflex thing to say for a stall, but it was better than saying he did not want to give her the satisfaction, his wife. Unfortunately, this left Celeste looking less than satisfied. He also had not foreseen wondering, sitting here confronted, how anyone married managed an actual affair. Attempting that would be like trying to drive two cars at once he could see now, separated or not. She, they, he deserved better than that, which was a sour spice added to the torment of just being with her. What did he expect, calling her up like that? Did he really think they were just going to do lunch? Wouldn't he have been disappointed if that were all she wanted? What a jerk.

Don't get me wrong, I'm very much enjoying the feeling of who I'm with right now. I just wish the circumstances were different. It might be easier to be friends again if we try to forget that we were more than friends for a while.

Friends.

He could not tell if she was talking to him or herself, but she was clearly crying and trying not to show it. He sat there stupidly, watching her fold her wrapper into a careful square. After a bit she looked out over the river, speaking to it, not him.

You used to be a lot more fun to tease. When did you get so serious?

She was trying to save face. He had better let her, but he could think of nothing to say. Teasing was out. That just left the shushing river, the chattering starlings, the shouts of a couple of boys passing on bikes growing louder than words. She came out of it first.

Come on, I have something to show you.

She led him onto the bridge where he found it a little unnerving at first to walk on the large translucent green paving blocks, especially in street shoes which threatened a slip. Celeste left him to his ginger stepping and ran ahead to the cables that plunged right through the deck to hidden attachment points beneath, and she did an unexpected thing. She laid her head against one of cables and slapped the three-inch-thick braid with her palm, which produced a smile.

What are you doing?

Try it. Put your ear right up against it.

He did so and then heard a sound out of a space war movie; a ba-choom-choom-choom-choom that went on and on, finally falling beneath his hearing. A trick of physics made the tiny vibration of her slap shoot up and down the cable with an effect greatly magnified, as though a gnat had somehow managed to pluck a giant guitar string and make it pulsate in slow motion.

Cool, huh? Bet you weren't expecting that.

No, he was not. He also felt faintly ridiculous standing there with his ear pressed to the cable as other strollers passed with expressions both quizzical and amused. But he also could not help reaching for his keys to try a tap of metal on metal, which produced the same effect, but higher in pitch, more of a ka-ch-jew-chjew-chjew-chjew. The tension on the cables must have been astronomical to exaggerate such a miniscule influence. He nearly allowed himself a smile, not at the phenomenon as much as the realization that such a tiny surprise infused him with a taste of her resurgent good humor, if not actual delight. The cables were not the only things that were wound a little tight. His head was still full of that sound when he joined her at the rail where she was staring intently at the dark green flood passing beneath, a quarter mile wide and humming full.

What are you looking for?

There. Two salmon almost side by side. See them?

He looked and saw nothing but flashing water, hints of green.

Don't look for the fish, look on the bottom for their shadows, then look above and to the left more toward the sun.

And there they were, just as she said. Two shadows surfing the bottom, not quite parallel, not quite in tandem, emerging and submerging beneath the flicker and shine of the surface. The fish themselves were even harder to find, just mottled ghosts swaying above their own shadows that he almost had to imagine in order to see, requiring an act of faith to believe in specters or fairies before they would show themselves. He wanted very much to imagine a different life at that moment, a life going in the right direction, the same direction with someone relying on the same instinct, adjusting effortlessly to the smallest vibrations sensed directly through the skin as water flowing by transmitted minute changes in temperature and pressure at the merest finnings of the fish beside. It still took work, of course, to stay in place, the one in front taking more of the force of the current for the other, and trust that the other was as constant, and would be there to trade places when the first tired. He was acutely aware of the faint warmth of her shoulder against his, of a bit of reluctance and relief that this lunch date had a time limit. It was nearly three o'clock.

I should get going. Let me work out some stuff. I'll come see you.

She looked at him directly now, a stray wisp of hair on the downstream breeze across her wonderfully sleepy eyes, which she pulled aside.

It's not that far, is it?

Breakwater? No, I don't think so.

His day was piling up with less than savory outcomes, and this one was even more confusing. He had only a few minutes before a very different appointment, but he had to make a start on a Field Exercise Report while the experience was still fresh.

FIELD EXERCISE REPORT

EXECUTIVE SUMMARY

This exercise was initiated by host agency to identify and evaluate agency preparedness, roles, responsibilities and coordination of resources in response to a hypothetical new boyfriend (BF)–new girlfriend (GF) interaction.

EXERCISE OVERVIEW

A training incident of limited duration was conceived and initiated at a neutral location to test responses of participants.

EXERCISE NAME Cheap Date.

LOCATION

Picturesque riverside park as far as possible from bedroom of either participant.

SCENARIO

Host agency issues transparently noncommittal happen-to-be-in-the-neighborhood invitation to minimize exposure for either participant. Upon acceptance by respondent, participants marshal resources (cover stories, sandwiches, breath mints, transportation, etc.) and interact at training complex.

TYPE OF EXERCISE Picnic Table-Top Exercise.

PARTICIPATING ORGANIZATIONS

Host Agency:	Porter	Role: (BF)
Respondent Agency:	Celeste	Role: (GF)

FOCUS

Clear Mission.
Prioritized Objective(s).
Adequacy and Coordination of Resources.
Clear Communication.
Identified Deficiencies.

EXERCISE REVIEW

Host demonstrates good initiative in beginning phase of exercise, then cedes incident command/control to Respondent when Host is unable to efficiently deploy sufficient resources to process a direct BF/GF? interrogative from Respondent. Communication of both participants then becomes tentative, veiled and ineffective in facilitating coordinated incident management, resulting in regional disaster.

EXERCISE EVALUATION

Undesirable outcome has implications for Host preparedness and lack of practice…

He'd get back to it later. For now, it was hardly worth getting back in the car for the short hop over to the convention center, which gave him little time to recalibrate, hell, re-arm for his meet with the D.A. As a bookend to his day, this was right up there with his Maddie visit, and he would rather have skipped it, but he needed answers only Flanders had. She was standing stiffly by the entrance doors in a flawless black pantsuit with the look of someone who was disappointed in their hope that the other party would not show.

Hello, Ms. Flanders. Thank you for making time to see me.

So it is you. You didn't seem like the type to make telephone threats.

I'm not the type that enjoys making them, but I needed to get your attention. Is there somewhere we can talk?

She led him into a large presentation hall where the heavy humid air of people too long confined lingered over rows of long white-clothed tables where sundry suits and ties languished amid castoff handouts, plastic water bottles and paper cups. A lot of them looked like cops; bodies at least one-time athletic, cheap haircuts, cheap suits, and that relaxed but wary look. She kept walking to one side and into an empty room of more modest dimensions that looked to be superfluous to the action in the larger room. There was no place to sit unless they wanted to wrestle some plastic chairs stacked along one wall with folded tables on edge. She simply closed the door and faced him. She wanted him to get to the point, as usual. On that they were in agreement.

There's two things you can clear up for me. You led us to believe that your visit with the governor was spontaneous, and was a simple courtesy call. Unfortunately, we have witness statements and closed circuit video indicating your visit was anticipated, and more formal in nature than you suggested. The room where you met the governor had been prepared especially for your meeting with him, and you were his only scheduled appointment for that room.

And this matters to a car crash how?

You were interrupted by someone who may have been Holly Morris. I need to know who that person was, and what he or she may have said or overheard. Can you describe the person that came into the room?

She didn't actually come into the room, just opened the door and stuck her head in. It very well might have been Holly Morris, but I only saw her for a second, and the overhead lights in the hall were brighter behind her, so it was hard to see her face since she was more backlit.

Did she say anything?

Just: *Excuse me*, then she closed the door again.

The governor seemed to know her. What was it he said?

He said something like: *There you are. I'd like to introduce you*—I guess, to me, but she had already closed the door.

Did that strike you as odd?

If you saw the video, you know I was struck by a lot of things.

Weren't you curious about who she was and why she blew off the governor if he knew her and was inviting her in?

Not really. If I thought about it at all it was a piece of what I was getting, and I was getting out of there.

So the governor was making a move on you?

Is there some point to this?

I was hoping you could tell me. The other question. What might she have overheard to make her react the way she did? What were you talking about when she opened the door?

Nothing business related, I can assure you that.

Maybe she heard more than you know. Couldn't she have had the door open and been listening for a while before you noticed her?

Maybe. But I think we had concluded our business before then.

On the chance that you are mistaken about that, what was it you were there to discuss?

Flanders' answer was delayed.

Nothing she would have cared about. I wanted to brief the governor on some of the enforcement issues we are dealing with in the county and see if I could get his support for reforming some of the drug laws that are having unintended consequences for us.

Reform. One of my favorite words. One person's reform is another person's wrench in the works. What kind of reforms were you after?

I'm not going to go into that. Vaneros wasn't ready to commit to anything anyway.

Then why do you think he agreed to meet you in the first place? Who's idea was it? Did you ask for the meeting or did he?

I did.

Then same question. Why would he go all the way up coast to a meeting with a small county D.A.? No offense.

It wasn't like that. He was already coming, I just asked for a few minutes of his time. I think he was less interested in what I had to say than some other things.

Do you think Morris might have noticed that?

His intentions were obvious to me. I really don't know what she saw, heard or thought.

Holly Morris is a reporter.

Yeah, I know. So?

OK, think carefully. Could she have overheard anything that a reporter might find interesting?

Political or social?

Either. In this case they might be connected.

Flanders stood with arms folded, and pored over it for a very long time.

I think that would involve too much speculation on my part. And if I follow your thinking, I'd be a fool to answer anyway because you're putting me in the position of a suspect. And the governor, if I follow you.

About Vaneros. Did he say anything to you after she left?

Nothing of substance. Something like: *What are you going to do?* He was referring to what had just happened, her going. I left right after.

I saw that. Did you ask the governor to contact anyone, or did the governor mention any calls he intended to make after you left?

No.

Have your people turned up any suspects or anything new?

No, again, but talk to Jeff. She was essentially sober and she went off the cliff. That's all I've heard.

OK, thanks. You've been very helpful. By the way, what's the conference about?

She made a thin smile.

It's for the six northern counties with DEA and BNE. Drug interdiction strategies.

CHAPTER XVI

THE SEARCH IS CALLED OFF

It was not a lie exactly. She just was not up to wondering what to do with Porter for another night at her place. So she led him to believe she was on her way to Redding, when she had a class to teach first and could not afford to skip it, much as she wanted to. Even a community art class was a small kind of performance, and she was not ready to pretend that everything was back to normal, not after seeing Ruth and Al as bashed and scattered as everything in their house. She would still see Ruth's pallor superimposed on the smiles of her students, mostly women of similar age, except for Amelia, who had talent, just not the means to attend a real art academy. Her teacher was an imposter trying to give advice to a girl so naturally gifted. Amelia had an innate sense of relational balance, of how to expose mood with the lift of a brush. She was sure to pick up on her teacher's distraction and share her disappointment, be embarrassed for the two of them. Better to be the only one who was ashamed in her hope that Amelia would not be there, her star pupil.

Porter had been the only man in her house other than Al since Owen had disappeared, and the only one to spend the night, even if it was on the couch. Walking in her door with him made the place seem small, just two rooms besides the living room-kitchen combination if you did not count the bath and laundry, and Porter seemed to overflow the space just standing there. Owen's photos were everywhere, his coats and rubber overalls too much in evidence on hooks in the hall, his smell, which was part of the house when she first walked in after being away, gone as quick as she closed the door, immersed in it again.

These had been thin substitutes for his laugh, the ascending boom of his arrivals on the front steps, but they were all she had room for. She hoped she had pulled it off, but the sense of intrusion was nearly as intense as walking in on Ruth and Al that morning, only in this case she was the recipient. Yet, a glass of wine and suddenly she was showing him her current painting, something she never did with anyone until it was finished, including Owen, including Beverly. Her studio was off limits to the point of superstition. Not that Owen could not look in any time he wanted, but the understanding was enough even if it was a transparent curtain. She was convinced he never cared that much anyway. It was her thing, and he was inevitably admiring of the results, but never in a hurry to see them. To him a fish was not a fish until it was in the boat. To her, having someone turn up in her studio was like having a stranger in her bedroom asking questions first thing in the morning when she woke up, before she could even recall who she was. Worse than entertaining a cop, wondering what trade secrets she might have forgotten to hide away; her paints and brushes more sacred and precious than any commercial plastic bag sealer or postal scale. And there she had gone offering to show Porter her unfinished work even without being asked. How did that come about? Figure drawing. There was another how come. He had flushed out her secret shame just by praising her last pastel, as though he could see what he was too kind to say. Showing him her other work was, at the time, a diversion perhaps, but she suspected it was also validation she was looking for, which was infuriating. She had not realized how much she had come to depend on Owen's offhand approval, as constant and unremarkable as her wedding band. She knew her new seascapes were good, yet Porter had seemed appreciative while he was clearly though politely underwhelmed, gently insistent in his suggestion that she had done and could do more with her figures, which she took as tactfully implicit that she had more work to do. She had never felt so exposed with a man and he seemed not to notice, or was too decent to let on that he had. He had not handed her a robe with averted eye but one better, dissolving her bit of panic at being in a crowded bus station having forgotten both her clothes and where she was headed in the first place, only to wake up in exactly those circumstances, but with Porter the attending physician who had seen far worse standing there going: *Yeah, so?*

Still, it was too much, too soon, especially on top of the upended life she had walked in on down the hill. Living alone so long meant it took longer to process things than she wanted to admit. Pretending otherwise took a lot of work and she went home exhausted from her days in town. What she was aware of, disconcertingly at first but now almost cherished, was that she liked her people in small doses, which she had every reason in the world for not being too concerned about.

It turned out there were a lot of no shows at her class, everyone out shopping or getting ready for company on Thursday, including Amelia unless she was just home sick. And now she would have to hide her disappointment because she could see it was going to be worse with Amelia gone than with her there, without her joy and enthusiasm that might have made showing up take her out of herself for a while. Amelia gave her an excuse that she was making a difference in someone else's life. There was a gathering apprehension that she was a fake, teaching something she was not doing. Even her most inept students were braver, risking so much in revealing their clumsy blotches and over-weighted strokes, the perspectives as jumbled as the proportions, standing back with their deluded sense of accomplishment. Who was she to judge? At least they were alive while she busied herself with her own make-believe landscapes, attempting the impossible, trying to imbue a glance of ocean with enough emotion to warrant even the paint, certainly not the effort, which was counterfeit.

After she closed up and wished her students a happy Thanksgiving she could not face the drive back home, especially now with neither Ruth nor Al there for company. She was not ready for the imposition of overnight guests blowing wayward gusts through her routine, but she was not ready for her empty house now, either. The ordinary disorder of her things scattered about had been revealed as nothing more than a futile attempt to make rooms in an unfinished house look full, a mindless and haphazard pass at a carefully raked design in the gravel of a Buddhist garden that was really no better than the tangle of blackberry vines behind her house. The foundation of her hilltop vantage point had shifted. Vandals had tipped over the grounded rock centerpiece in that meditative space, smashed the painted shoji blinds she had framed her sanctuary with, knocked out the walls, leaving her stranded on a precipice, her haven obliterated, as gone as a cloud that had drifted away or dissipated into nothing before her eyes.

She took a walk out the empty pier in the thin last rays of the day, out past the *DANGER—STRUCTURE UNSAFE* sign to where the deck began its inexorable sag and tilt into the water, and stood exposed to blasts of spray off the whitecaps that flung up even above the boards where she stood. It was bitterly cold, and she hugged herself, wishing Owen were there to hold her. He was her best friend. He was always supposed to be there, and in a way he always would be. But this life was two-dimensional, with a vanishing point somewhere off the canvas in a place she could not see. If he were here now, what would he tell her? No doubt something clear and uncomfortable only a true friend could say—This was only a sort-of life. She could use a friend like that again, even if she had to make room, even if she was not looking for a lover. She turned her back to the ocean, wrenched off her wedding band and flung it over her shoulder, a reluctant bride tossing a bouquet to the crowding waves, not bearing to see who caught it.

CHAPTER XVII

SOME HOUSEGUEST

Shin Maeda had him repeat how he got his number.

Celeste Brousset. She didn't think you would mind.

Celeste. How is she?

Having some ups and downs. Her husband's parents got home invaded and she was the one who found them tied up the next day.

But they live right next to her, way out in the woods. That doesn't make sense. I'd better give her a call. How is it you know her?

We were friends at SF State. She mentioned that you worked with Holly Morris and might be able to give me some background on her. I'm part of an official inquiry into how she died.

You're saying it might not have been an accident?

No, I'm saying we want to make sure it wasn't anything more. You're in the business. Surely you've heard some of the rumors.

And I'm in no hurry to perpetuate any. I see you're on a restricted number. What's your office number or a number where I can verify who you are? No, forget that. I'd rather meet you in person.

Well, the earliest I can be in the city wouldn't be until say, eight o'clock this evening. Otherwise—

That will work. It's dinner time for me by the time I clear the studio and get in a workout. If you like sushi, we could meet at Taka Rio on Sutter. It's a couple blocks above Van Ness.

I'll find it. See you there.

Sushi was not Porter's idea of a good time. That was the raw fish stuff. Lumps of gluey rice topped with pieces of what looked like severed tongue, the better to lodge in your throat the same as if you had swallowed your own. Just the thought of it triggered his gag reflex. But he wanted Maeda relaxed, so his own comfort could wait. He could hit a burger place on the way, say he already ate and just have tea or whatever. The tough part was going to be the drive from Redding when he had already spent three hours getting there from Sacramento. The dirty little secret of all those tall, handsome fighter pilots was that they all had hemorrhoids from pulling all those G's all day. The dirty little secret of bureau investigators was the same, from all the driving, bad coffee and long hours. If there was a positive, it would give him some more time to think. He was tired of being a step behind every step of the way on this one. Hopefully, Maeda had some missing pieces. To do her in the manner they found her would have taken planning, or people who did enough of that sort of thing to follow her around until they saw an opportunity, and could patch a workable plan together on the fly. Nothing detected in her system so she was not drugged and dumped. That meant someone had to get close enough to her to hit her with something and send her over to mix that up with the other trauma. Not a robbery. CHP disinclined to pursue any theory that did not lead to case closed. Either they were really asleep at the wheel or covering. His guess was a little of both, but only as a result of their misfortune in having her on their hands that night, not some ultra-conspiracy. As for hubby, if he had half the brains his office would suggest, if he wanted her dead, he would not have been anywhere near her, consistent with the axiom that smart people, methodical people, are not the ones that get caught. Unless it was a spur of the moment thing; rage would have been required for Biel to do it himself, in which case he should have left more evidence behind. There were the lookout's footprints, if that's what they were. Bringing an accomplice would be more in line with cold planning, but stupid for other reasons. Either way had built-in contradictions. Maybe it was something else entirely. Reporters had to have lots of enemies. He needed to get a better handle on Morris if he was going to make any headway. And on Biel. Seeming contradictions could begin to make sense if you had all the facts, especially in relationships. Look at his own. His feeble attempts at reconciling with Anita were increasingly at odds with the amount of time he was spending with a woman he had not seen in close to twenty years, even if most of their recent encounters were arguably accidental. Hell, Anita seemed to be able to smell her on him, and was drawing conclusions to questions he had barely drafted. What was her reasonable suspicion, much less her probable cause to go off on him like that? If the world worked like that he could just as well accuse her of the same. After all, wasn't she the one who called it quits? She had a good nose though for someone with absolutely no evidence and no experience in philandering. It was a good thing she was not a private eye on his case. Evidence or not, it would be Porter as person of interest, especially after his trip to Redding. Celeste had certainly called his bluff and he had choked, so that was over before it, whatever *it* was, began, but Anita would never see it that way. If she knew about his *I'll-come-see-you* nonsense, she would fling it in his face as a smoking gun of in flagrante conspiracy with no wiggle room for the bit of face saving he had intended.

Somewhere south of where the eroding Lassen lava flows swaled into Cottonwood and Corning and oozed into the flooded rice fields of Sacramento River bottomlands, his cell chirped as he was envying a solitary white egret dozing with one leg up on the highway margin.

Hi, Joel, what's up?

Well, I had an uncomfortable visit with Morris' folks, and I managed to get ahold of her sister in Pasadena. They were all supposed to meet at the family home in Belvedere for the holidays. Parents have no clue. She was bright, ambitious, blah, blah.

Sis says Morris thought Biel was exciting when she met him during his campaign, but lately it sounded like she had buyer's remorse. He's really a nuts-and-bolts guy with his head down on revenue and taxation legislation. Sis says Morris felt like she was married to an accountant or a preacher, and he was married to his job even more than she was. But Morris wouldn't call it quits even when it was obvious she was losing all respect for him. He wanted her to stay home and start a family and she didn't. Morris got pregnant last year—sis says it was an accident—twins, boy and girl. But she miscarried late in the pregnancy and she lost them both. There was a lot of blame as a result. Add to that, Morris had started complaining that Biel was letting too many corporate backers call the shots, and he didn't see he was being used, or didn't want to. Morris told her sister she wanted out, but it wasn't a good time, politically, with him up for re-election next year. In the meantime, sis thinks Morris was doing a pretty good job of acting out, like she was trying to get back at him. Almost like she was trying to provoke him. And every time she wanted more rope he let her have some. Sis was surprised to learn he had followed her up north. She thought that was out of character. Maybe he finally had enough. But sis also wants us to look into one of her projects. Something to do with campaign finance and initiative fundraising. All sis knows is that Morris told her there were buckets of money everywhere she looked and it was making her—sis, not Morris—a little nervous. She said Morris laughed at the notion. I don't doubt it. Sis came across as a little angry and paranoid. It could be just her way of coping. How you doing? Did you get a date with Flanders?

If you call a five minute face to face in a hallway a date, sure. She was pretty coy about it, but she made it clear the governor was more interested in her than talking about what she wanted to talk about: drug law reform she called it. The person that came into the room was probably Morris, but no reason why, or why she took off, unless she saw or heard something she didn't like. Flanders wouldn't speculate. I also ran into Biel's chief of staff. I'm trying to set up a meeting. Biel is between a rock and a hard place because he has always supported the governor, so I don't know how this will play out, but I did my best to convince them he needs to come forward. Right now I'm on my way to see one of Morris' co-workers.

He did not tell Joel about Zephur's disturbing speculations, his lunch with Celeste, or his going to see Maddie. Sneaking around on your partner was inexcusable, but he did not see any practical benefit in involving Joel in any of that. Maddie would keep her mouth shut at least. Of course, if Joel found out later, they were done as partners, but he was willing to risk it to keep Joel on the case. He needed Joel for corroboration for whatever this turned out to be. He was already way off the reservation as it was. Maybe Warren could give him some cover. He owed him a call anyway.

Michael. I was beginning to wonder if you had gone off a cliff yourself. Where are you?

Physically? I'm halfway between Redding and San Francisco. Case-wise, up to my ass.

There's no fraud, is there?

Warren had said it as less question than pronouncement on his case. And why not? Not too many people kill their wives to collect on auto insurance, and Biel was not likely to need her life insurance that bad. Still, they would need to check. Maybe she was covered for a gazillion and he was over his head in campaign debts, and she was expendable and...

To be honest with you, Warren, I haven't really looked at that angle. Not when there are so many more likely motives like jealous husband, or somebody doing her to keep her quiet.

Did you forget what I told you?

That if there was no fraud, I was out of there.

So why are you still out running around?

What Porter was tempted to say was curiosity, leaving unsaid that it might also be a possible way out of DOI, or maybe just distraction from his own problems, at least at first. It would be saying too much about what he suspected was consistent with both of their situations. Warren would never believe the real reason either. Even if Porter could put it into words it would sound like he had lost his objectivity, had merged his inability to let go of a woman he knew with one he hardly knew at all. But Warren would understand that once you dug into a slice of pie you could not put half of it back uneaten:

Because I think it would look worse to back out now than to explain how we got involved in the first place. If it blows up you can always say Justice was short-handed and came to you for help. Which is pretty much true. But if you pull me off now it could look like you didn't like where this is going and pulled the plug. This was always Maddie's gig. Let her own it.

He changed lanes and passed two semis in the time it took Warren to answer.

You think you're pretty cute, don't you?

No, Warren, I just want you to see what I'm seeing. Joel and I seem to be the only ones looking at anything that doesn't point to accident or suicide. Her husband was in her vicinity around the time she died, and she may have had information some other people didn't want daylighted. Am I supposed to just walk away from that?

More dead air, a lot this time, interrupted only by the creak of Warren's chair.

Warren, are you there?

Shut up a minute. I'm trying to figure out what to tell the commissioner.

Porter found it disgusting to be emulating Maddie, but it fit the bill.

Tell him we still have to do our jobs. Even when it stinks.

Yes, I had forgotten how simple life can be for you tenured civil servants. Unfortunately, I'm an appointee.

Well, at-will works both ways, doesn't it? Don't you have civil service return rights to a job somewhere?

Warren hmmphed.

It's too late to reverse the lobotomy. Just get going. You're caseload isn't getting any smaller while you're out chasing dead pussy. You've got—forty-two pending, and you've only closed—four, five—six in the last quarter.

Going down the Eastbay shoreline was more direct, but that would have meant dragging through some really depressing scenery in Vallejo and Richmond to the inevitable slowdown in Berkeley even if the evening commute was mostly headed the other way. It would also have meant missing the best view of the Golden Gate. So he took the Novato cutoff across the north bay flats and then south, following the curves up the last set of coastal hills, enjoying the anticipation of gathering momentum down the other side, resisting the urge to pick up speed with the other cars around a steep descending right where he got just a glimpse of the north tower lights above the black silhouette of the Marin headlands. In the thickening dusk the towers were arterial, as though still glowing from the setted sun, appearing huge and other-worldly against the foreground hills in an effect similar to manmade harvest moonrise. Then he shot through the tunnel and burst out to see both towers marching into the twinkling city, whose jeweled hills were just disappearing behind a rush of fog spilling through the cables. It was a wonder they did not have more collisions between the people trying to actually get somewhere and people like him, trying to look everywhere at once.

There are not many fat people in SF. Even with his police placard, he still had trouble finding even a yellow curb open to leave his car, and had blocks of hills to huff his way up, propelled by the downtown smells of steam, exhaust and urine. It was the same, even if skinheads were more in evidence than he remembered. Their heads must freeze for style. But the tiny ubiquitous Chinese women with plastic bags dangling from each hand looked the same, as did a few secretaries striding home late in their tennis shoes, having left their heels at work, and men in cheap dark suits lingering in doorways: drivers waiting for clients, waiters on break, or questionable hangers-on killing time. He had a pretty good sweat going when he found the place, more glass and aluminum storefront than restaurant. He must have had the look, because an Asian in a black sweater and blazer at the end of the bar waved him over as though they were old friends having the usual. It was Maeda, looking the same but different, more boyish and animated than his more serious broadcast mask. That and the wave went better with the Japanese-American face, which was more open, less reserved than a native Japanese would be meeting a stranger. On the assumption that Maeda and Morris might have been close, he extended his condolences along with his wallet badge. Maeda made a noncommittal shrug, waving off Porter's tin.

Yeah, yeah, you've got cop written all over you. Get you a beer while we order?

Evidently Maeda had already had one or two, a no-effort bonus from the looks of him. The *No, thank—* was almost out of his mouth. What the hell.

Sure, but I grabbed something to eat on the way. Can I just get some nachos or whatever with that?

Like everything Japanese, even the snack crackers came in tiny bits, but they were good and salty. There had not been time to eat on the way after all, so this would have to do since he was not doing raw fish. He nibbled while Maeda inhaled a small bowl of seaweed and cucumber slices, then stirred up a saucer of soy sauce and green paste with his chopsticks preparatory to attacking a succession of unidentifiable fish chunks. Without taking his attention from the main task, he mumbled his *So what can I tell you?*

Pretty much anything that would give me a sense of what she was like, what she was working on recently, what her state of mind was. Did you know her long?

A couple years, since we picked her up from KTSC in Santa Clara. If you watch our station you would have seen us side by side on the five-thirty segment. What was she like? She was a motor mouth. You didn't see her coming, you heard her talking before she hit the set. So and so said this, and what were they going to do about that, and had you heard…? You always knew what kind of day she was having. I felt like I knew her a lot longer than it was.

She talk about her family much?

All the time. Loved her mom and dad. Got along well with her sister, even though it sounded like sis was a drag. Holly had it figured out that she was the luckiest kid in the world. Her family had money. She went to good schools, and she wasn't going to waste it. I called her the whirling dervish because she was into every feel-good cause out there. Even here at the station. When management tried to cut back on research staff, she organized a revolt. I thought it was hopeless, but she had me swearing I would walk, too. And you know what? They found the money somewhere. We were her family, too.

Safe to say, then, she had strong opinions about social issues and an interest in people?

That's a pretty dry way of putting it, but sure. I would add irrepressible. Talk about a wicked laugh. Station management was always after her to tone it down, do more the network news deadpan. I think if they had just let her go our ratings would have been better. It was all we could do sometimes to keep a straight face after the commercial breaks.

What is the deal with her sister?

Emily? Emily married a director at Simmons Memorial Hospital in Pasadena. It was pretty clear from Holly that she wasn't happy making babies and playing tennis and second fiddle. She's really angry right now. I think it's a cover for feeling vindicated. Holly would never see it that way. She would just say it's Emily's maternal instincts, still trying to protect her kid sister.

Holly and the governor. Anything you know about that? What she was working on? Her sister thinks she may have been researching a story that might have put her in danger. Was she acting different lately, or expressing any worries?

Maeda did a little one-handed snare drum with his chopstick on the edge of his plate while he thought.

Actually, there was this other thing, but it didn't occur to me until just now. There got to be a point about a year ago where I wondered how things were between her and her husband. You know, when people first get together that's all they talk about— each other. It's just what's on their minds. Later, if I hadn't heard her mention Tom in a while I would ask how he was doing, and she would say, oh, he's doing this and that. I didn't think any- thing about it until it seemed like she never mentioned him at all anymore, and if I asked about him she was noncommittal, saying, he's fine, and then she would go on to something else.

Add to that she was a hell of a flirt, which probably didn't help. I think she met the governor at some charity function. I don't know who was playing whom. He started sending her press invitations to lots of events. I think she saw she was meant to be flattered, but she was also not going to turn down an open door to a source like Vaneros. Most of what she brought back was just political gossip, nothing we could use even if it was entertaining. I could tell she got a kick out of it though. At first it was, the governor this, and the governor that. Then it was, Harry this, and Harry that. Then, after a while she quit saying much of anything about him, and generally changed the subject. You're the cop. Does that look like a pattern? I don't know if that meant they were getting heavy, the thing had already run its course, or never went anywhere in the first place. Maybe she fig- ured out he was just stringing her along with back fence stories to stay on the good side of a major news outlet. Whatever, she was getting pretty quiet about the governor, too.

Did she seem particularly preoccupied with any project, or scared?

Preoccupied, maybe, but with what I couldn't say. Scared, no. She was just a little too normal the past few weeks. Not as whacky as usual. More businesslike, a little boring even.

Anything about campaign finance or the initiative process, like undue influence by special interests? Her sister thinks she was getting into something with those.

Sure, but that stuff's a perennial. It's just business as usual, boilerplate reporting on the board of supervisors' meetings or election polls. Or the DOW. It goes up and down, the names change from time to time, but on it goes. If she was interested in anything lately it was the state costs for illegal drug enforcement compared to the value of those drug sales for the state's underground economy. She used her husband's staff to get analysts at the California Research Bureau working on some numbers. But she wouldn't be the first person to try and compare the societal costs and benefits of the drug trade.

Is there going to be any follow-up on her story?

Not by me. I'm the local guy. She did the statewide stuff. I'm sure they're looking at a replacement, but nothing is going to happen until after the funeral, for the sake of appearances if nothing else.

Did you know she was meeting Vaneros last week?

Not directly, but when she dropped everything to meet a friend in Breakwater, I guessed. Did they find anything wrong with her car?

Porter was not able or willing to talk about how a car would just roll off a cliff at slow speed.

Nothing on that yet. Anything else I should know? Anyone else you think I should talk to?

No, that about covers it. I think I was her closest friend at the station.

I'm sorry. Was it always just friends?

Maeda took a swig of beer, and drew the foam down the corners of his mouth with thumb and forefinger.

I guess you had to ask. Nope, but secret admirer, I'll have to say yes. Can I ask you a question?

Sure.

I thought cops weren't supposed to drink on duty.

We're not.

In that case, would you like another beer?

I shouldn't. I'm driving. Why not?

Which turned out to be another first, which began with the first beer, then seconds, and thirds. He could later say that he was already twelve hours into his day and was arguably on his own time, which would never wash. He could say he was just trying to put a witness at ease, but there was no policy for that either. No, it was just that his back hurt and it had been a long, dispiriting day. He would just have to make sure he did not get in a shootout, with small chance of that for a bureaucrat with a gun, or get in a car crash and have to give a blood sample. He wished he could trade places with Maeda, who could do whatever and grab a taxi home as long as he did not slur his words on camera the next day.

More beer made him rethink that. Maeda expressed his dismay at being a reporter pursued by other reporters for a story—How long had Morris been screwing the governor? Did she talk about him? Did Biel know? What was he doing about it? Had there been any fireworks? Were she and Biel separated at the time she died? Did she have a drinking problem? A drug problem? Did he think she committed suicide? Had she ever talked about it?—Questions that only served cheap ratings, and it left Maeda feeling embarrassed for his profession. He also remembered being asked if it was true that Morris had stolen the boyfriend of her best friend, a Carolyn Stevens. Morris had mentioned her to Maeda, but he could not recall where she lived. San Leandro, San Lorenzo, one of them.

The more Porter thought about it the more he wondered if any of that should matter to him any more than the ravenous small minds at large. It was just vulgar and immaterial. The one piece of information that might have a follow-up—if he could track down someone with a name as common as this Stevens woman—what was he likely to find out? She was bound to be an ex-friend who could have no way of knowing if so-and-so was out to get Morris, and had proof. Maybe he was just tired, but if you talked to everyone a person ever knew, you still would not know them. Even a best friend could be surprised. Look at Stevens. What might be tucked away in Celeste's closet? Or his own? What the hell was he doing pounding down beers with a gun under his coat? This was not television. If anything happened after he left the restaurant he would be in the wrong right from the start. This person holding his beer glass was a shadowy specter of himself, slamming around his old haunts on some piece of business undone, with no hope and no means of putting it right. And then Maeda had to go and ask if he was related to a cop that used to work for San Jose P.D.

Maeda had long since excused himself and left Porter to finish his beer alone. It was time he was going, too. He tossed off the rest of his glass, the foam smothering a momentary regurgitary reflex, and thrust himself in a slow-motion hurl back outside, the street slope now a vertiginous descent into the dark as he wobbled his way through self-absorbed stragglers, none to be bothered looking up at some inebriate who was failing at pretending to walk like a person who had not had two or three too many on an empty stomach.

And now he was not sure exactly where he had left his car. He could add that to a day remarkable primarily for a still-accumulating list of precipitate decisions. What he needed was a search party, but not for his car, for his stranded hiker lost on a fool's errand of continuance. How many of these people he was walking by were doing the same sort of spectral routine, plodding along, groping blindly for pretexts for reasons to persist? Were any of them other than bit players in someone else's deluded excuse of a one-off TV drama? What was he supposed to do, take up bowling, stamp collecting, skydiving? Have a drink, get lost, get laid, get bent, it did not much matter. He was still going to wake up the next morning and have to decide what clothes he belonged in. He knew one thing; he was sick of these.

Even downhill turned out to be too much. He grabbed a passing parking meter to catch his breath, his attempt to rest his elbow on the meter top in a nonchalant pose abandoned for a snatching hug as the pole spun by. Cigarette butts and flat road kills of gum along the curb beckoned him to spit out what he had grown tired of. Lugging too many pounds was one. A good start might be getting back in shape, whatever that was.

But it is really his head that is too heavy, his brain lolling around his skull chased by the approaching sirens that crowd out his vision until all he can see is Sam looking at him looking at Sam, as Sam waits outside the black gridwork security door on the porch of the east San Jose man-with-a-knife call. It is night. It is hot. Sam has his gun out along his thigh same as Porter, his flashlight by his ear, listening, as the triple bash of his flashlight on the door grate fades. No answer. Is this a setup? Where is the mother who called in that her son has flipped out? She should be waiting outside to give them the story if she is so concerned. It sounds like a party in back with the tinny hip hop bouncing down the side walkway to where Porter waits at the house corner. He jerks his head toward the back to signal Sam, who turns and starts back down the porch steps. Porter starts down the walkway. It is all of four feet wide from the side of the bungalow to the fence, just a straight shot of sidewalk with nothing to relieve the corridor except a gas meter sticking out of the house at knee height. That and a motion detector light that bursts the walkway into high pressure sodium glare before he is halfway to the back. He can smell his own sour sweat, feel the sticky cling of his vest against his chest. The dog must have smelled him too, or jumped to the light. He comes around the corner at a forty-five degree slant, claws ripping to get a grip on the concrete, and has Porter by the thigh before he can decide gun or flashlight club. It is a medium-sized Lab or Rottweiler mix, but it has a big head. Teeth that slice to bone like serrated knives. Its filthy slobber mixing with Porter's blood in a guttur-al roar. He watches the white stripe on the dog's forehead flip back and forth as he pounds it with his flashlight to no effect. Then he sticks his muzzle against fur and pulls. The dog expels a throaty whine and quits shaking its head but holds on, is hanging from his leg still.

You shot my dog.

The boy, maybe fifteen, is coming at him. Damn big for a teen, but still a pretty low-grade threat, except the small cross flashing at his neck is the wrong companion accessory for the shiny pointed object pumping up and down with his fists as he charges at Porter in sightless fury. He is already twice as close as you are ever supposed to let a man with a knife get, even a young man, and he is filling his view.

Later, Porter had no recollection of Sam yelling behind him. What he could recall was mostly just standing there, frozen, his ears ringing in the confined space from the shot he put into the dog. He never heard the two that went into the boy. He saw him go down though, and struggle up almost to his knees, his face a confusion of astonishment and fading hope, then drop. The boy squirmed over to the fence, snuggled up to it, fingers of one hand scrabbling at the rough wood like he had seen his own son do in his sleep in a feeble attempt to pull the edge of his blanket over his shoulder. Then his whole body sank with his relaxing breath, as though he were melting into the deep, soft mattress of concrete. The dog fell at Porter's feet. The three bloods co-mingled. He had a metallic taste in his mouth.

When he resurfaced, the night sounds were exploding in his ears in a surround of stadium roar with Sam yelling, siren blares growing louder, a woman, two women screaming bloody murder. Mom, they learned later, and a cousin from around the corner where she had phoned since her own service had been cut off for nonpayment. The boy was distraught. She was worried he might harm himself. Did he have a weapon? Well, yes, he was cutting up scraps for the dog. Porter limped around doing his best to help Sam handcuff the women to keep them off him and his partner.

Every amateur agitator that could hobble or crawl converged like zombies locomoted by unholy curse to the scent of the gunpowder, all claiming they'd been *right there* on the deserted street when it happened, screaming a collective: *Cold blood, bitch, cold blood.* It did not help that they could not find the knife, and word quickly spread that the boy was unarmed, was merely trying to save his dog from a brutal and senseless execution, a dog that would never hurt *anyone.* By the time someone thought to look under the dog's body there was no way to get out in front of the wildfire of outrage that consumed the neighborhood. White cop. Young man of color. Again.

There was a small riot, but it was not his concern any more. Someone was asking for his gun, and he was getting into an ambulance, wishing they would hurry and close the doors to block out the noise, give him up to the mindless rush of cool air within. A woman was shouting: *Officer, officer.* He would not have looked over but she sounded matter-of-fact insistent, like another officer trying to let him know he had left his lights on, or dropped his keys. She was an attractive woman, the wrong color and dressed too well to be from the neighborhood. She looked familiar. As soon as he made eye contact she let him have it:

What happened to your leg? Were you shot?

Then he noticed the tiny red light lasered at him from the videocam on the shoulder of the burly man standing next to her. Sam was sitting in the back of a patrol car farther down the street, just like any criminal. Porter was tempted to say: *Make something up. Everybody else is.* This was not the time or place. In the end he just looked back at her, and climbed in.

He'd had many imagined conversations with the boy since, Alejandro Emilio Hernandez Osario, but there was no comprehending, much less absolution. They had only the self-serving hysterics of his relatives: the good boy, the bad night of drinking and pot smoking, the breakup with a girlfriend. None of that sounded like it should have amounted to so much. If only he could have talked to Alejandro for a few minutes. Was he even aware that he had a knife in his hand? His mother said he had been cutting up scrap meat for the dog. That should not have taken long. Had they interrupted him as he contemplated suicide over breaking up with his girlfriend? Did he want Porter to shoot him? Was he thinking of anything at all when he came at Porter other than protecting his dog? There just had not been time, and now there was too much.

They took his picture, his leather, his clothes, his blood, and swabbed his hands. Sam was off in some other room to prevent any opportunity for collusion. The union trotted in an attorney for him. Stick to basic details, do not embellish. Fifty-one-fifty man-with-a-knife call for service. No RP at scene, no additional information. Exigent circumstances; there could have been a hostage or injured person on the premises. Dog attacked you. Armed juvenile attacked you. No opportunity for retreat or lesser force. You fired your weapon to stop them from killing or completing great bodily harm on you and your partner. Period. Do not add anything. Do not speculate. Do not second guess or suggest alternative outcomes even if pressed. You had no choice. You would do it exactly the same if it happened again.

Policy-wise, it should have been an open-and-shut, but policy was two-edged. It could save or hang you. The chief was diplomatically supportive and went so far as to suggest a preliminary indication of justifiable, which did not go over with the mayor, who had a progressive constituency to mollify. Why hadn't he used his Taser? Why hadn't he waited for backup? Why was his gun out in the first place? Had he properly identified himself? Could the police helicopter have surveyed the backyard beforehand? Why didn't he try talking to the boy first? The district attorney would be looking into these and other issues to determine whether there had been any criminal act on the part of the officer involved, and if there had been a possible violation of the victim's civil rights under state or federal law.

All this meant that an investigation that should have been completed in a few hours went on for days, then weeks, while he sat at home steeping in the broadcast conjectures of people with no training and no experience, but plenty of agendas. He and Sam kept their distance on the advice of their attorneys and by mutual agreement. Sam was a sergeant, which left him open to charges of dereliction since the senior officer got to own responsibility for whatever happened on a call. The time off must have been the same for him as it was for Porter, just like a life on the run. He was afraid to use the phone, leave the house, even use his email in case it had been hacked.

At first, Anita made all the sounds any cop had a right to expect from their wife, telling him she knew it would turn out all right. But, as the investigation dragged on and the papers spread rumors, she would come home in the afternoon and flow around his rock in her stream of routine, which did not include him sitting with the shades drawn when she walked in with the groceries, especially after, as she described it, her day spent fronting the brave and dutiful wife for a street full of whispering neighbors with their nosy interest. If he did not want to look like a murderer, the least he could do was go out and thank them for their concern even if he could not talk about it yet. What was *she* supposed to think?

What he thought was this was not just some houseguest they both suddenly realized had overstayed. It was a heap of stained linen that had been piling up for years, now hard to ignore when magnified under the hand lens of circumstance they took turns training on each other. Was his arguable notoriety the reason or the excuse? Whichever, she, they, focused on this eye-catching ornament to their mis-mannered style of cohabitation as precursor to admitting that the required accommodations were no longer no bother; apparent now in a sour-mouthed accretion of graveyard shifts, the coin toss whether he was home to see her and the kids going off to school, groggy when they came home or snappish if poked while still asleep from a double shift or the daily, unremarkable overtime; a sleepwalker on court days. She wanted to know why he kept at it if he had nothing to tell when he got home on any day, not just this one, never getting close enough to see or imagine that the actual taste and smell of ordinary headlines: children shot by children for no reason, toddlers beaten and burned on purpose, and all the mundane and grotesque mutations, child or adult, of mayhem, rape, suicide, overdose, and the infinite ways people invented to betray one another, often in blood, were disastrous recipes unfit for dinner table consumption. She was not going to see any of that, even if he had to add a daily layer of deferrals between them, thin deposits of grit that nonetheless accumulated over time, because she would never understand until she had to put her own uniform in a paper evidence bag, then stare at the shower wall for far too long before she could face the street again.

So, on these terms, theirs was a success story, as was clear from the looks of pity and terror she would snatch away if he looked up at the feel of them burning into his back. When she began to say she would just have to trust the process because she did not understand these things, it was clear she really did have no understanding of their situation, not at all, not after eight years together while he was a cop. Which allowed for the possibility of doubt. He knew what she meant but he knew what he heard. By the time he was cleared it really did not matter. He walked away from the wreck with a permanent limp, and whatever he had left with Anita—that was on life support.

The city had no clue, or much apparent interest except in seeing an end to the headlines. They just gave him back his gun and leather with a welcome back, reminded him of his right to counseling, which he declined again, and told him in that case to get back to work. Simple in concept, but from then on everyone was second guessing everything from his patrol patterns to his reports, including himself. It was not harmless roll play, it was impersonation—of a person so committed to an ideal that any act in that service, even homicide, was excusable as long as he meant well. His on-views dwindled to nothing unless Sam initiated them. Days when he patrolled alone he was just a full-shift station snake, tracing and retracing the blocks nearest the yard, responding only to calls for service. That lasted all of two weeks before Sam was after him to get over himself—he'd have shot the Osario boy himself if Porter had not been in the way—and the lieutenant was coming down on him. He started looking when he thought no one was looking and saw the DOJ opening. Somehow he had thought it would be simpler. He could come home with clean hands.

Word got around pretty quickly that DOJ was backgrounding him. Sam withdrew to some corner of betrayal along with a lot of the others. His shifts now were just marking time, keeping his nose clean, taking care of unfinished business. An opportunity for some of that came one day when he saw her, Morris, doing a sidewalk interview with the owner in front of a liquor store that had been burgled the night before. He pulled over and stood off to the side while she finished her take. She was good.

She recognized him and came over, removing her blazer now that the camera was off.

Officer Porter. It's good to see you back. How's your leg?

I'm not here for an interview.

She saw, too, that her cameraman had followed her over. Seeing Porter, he must have thought that this might be some associated footage they could use.

We're done here, Steve. I'll see you at the van in a minute.

As she spoke, Porter watched the turn of her neck, saw the short ponytail, the tan, athletic shoulders against her turquoise sleeveless sweater. She had pixy ears and a pointed chin that would have been a handicap of weightless, if charming, irrelevance, but she had a large, ravenous mouth and big white perfect teeth that Europeans would instantly hate and envy as the trademark American birthright. She was too short for serious volleyball. He guessed the shoulders were from water skiing, or tennis. She would look great on the water, or racing after a ball across a grass court. Those shoulders would look fantastic above a strapless evening gown as she skipped up the steps at the War Memorial Opera House. Then she gave him the full benefit of those avid eyes, curious and bemused with barely a hint of wary, which he thought was quite a feat considering how many cops must have asked her out.

All right, officer, I'm all yours.

About the last time you saw me.

The day of the shooting?

Yes, that day. I just wanted you to know that you might get more cooperation from us if you didn't jerk us around at times like that.

Now her exuberance was dissipating.

By asking about your leg? As I recall, everyone else outside the crime-scene tape seemed to want a piece of you. I thought I was pushing my professional objectivity pretty far with that.

Was that what that was?

She looked to be making up her mind whether this was a conversation she wanted to continue. When she did, it was down a notch.

OK, so I still had a job to do. They weren't about to let me near the boy, and we couldn't have run the footage even if they had. But I still need to get the facts and put a human face on a tragedy if I can, and there you were. If I was trying to do a little of both, you can sue me. No one else seemed to give a hoot about you just then.

Porter was between stools now, between ingrate and incensed, but had to wonder if she was not just—still, working him. She did not look like Mother Theresa, and his experience with news people was they thrived on conflict, not resolution. Certainly not reconciliation. If they could not scare up some controversy from the police scanner and the whisperings at city hall, they would whip up a batch from whatever squalid root of rumor or day-old innuendo was at hand. He needed more information.

How did you end up covering the blood and guts beat, anyway?

She did not have to think about this one.

You make it sound like siren chasing. Because I'm good at it? Because I think people need to see that these things can happen to anyone? Because there is always more to the story than just another one bites the dust? Why are you a cop?

The answer, if there was one anymore, was not to be found in the gutter. He brought his head up. Now here was his car across the street with a traffic ticket under the wiper, directly over his official-duty placard on the dash. Nice. Some meter maid having her fun. The things people did to make it through the day. Did she think she was contributing to the betterment of mankind? She, if it was a she, was kidding herself. But she was accomplishing a damned sight more than he was at the moment. Maybe he should see if SFPD had any openings in their parking control division. Hardly. He had things to do. Easy or not. Agreeable or not. Things Holly Morris, at least, might appreciate. But the picture of himself tootling around in his three-wheeler was sufficient inspiration, ludicrous as it was, to help get him on his feet. The spinning in his head had slowed and begun to subside. He felt steady enough to chance, if not the drive home, at least the short distance to the garage over on Sutter Street. He only needed a few hours.

He managed to mash the ticket button, squeeze through the toll gate, and back into a stall in a dark corner without clipping the wall or the concrete pillar. Then he crumpled himself into the back seat and pulled his coat over his shoulders up to his chin, and drifted away to distant door thumps, tire squeaks, and the ticking steel of his nest.

CHAPTER XVIII

SOMEONE ELSE'S FAMILY REUNION

Mostly he came back after wandering the upper halls of some high rise searching for stairs in a vertical labyrinth that never seemed to have an elevator. Times when he managed to find his way up from the depths of some basement or subway took longer, especially when approaching fire trucks were over-flowing the tiled stairwell with shrieking sirens and brain-rattling horns. It was his cell phone, its diminutive tinkling resolving itself from the transmogrification of his dreams.

Porter? Michael Porter?

Hmmmbf.

My God, it's eight thirty. Is this your day off or do you hogs at the state trough get to show up any damn time you please?

Who—What?

Tony Baylor. We're—you were supposed to be keeping in touch. You've got our tox report. What have you got going with Flanders?

Hang on a second.

Let him think he needed time to grab a robe. He was already dressed—still dressed. Mostly he wanted to wake up. Baylor could have had any deputy give him a call, so if he wanted direct contact it could only be to get or give information of particular interest, personal interest, interest he could later deny ever hav-ing with no intermediary to say different.

Let's see if we can get Quill on conference so I don't have to repeat myself. I don't want CHP thinking I'm playing favorites.

Well, you've got a funny way of showing it, sneaking out of town for a roll in the hay with the D.A. Did you do her?

Baylor certainly had his spies. Probably one of the conference attendees who recognized him. Or Flanders mentioned it to Sentienne who passed it on to Baylor who was just humping his leg to put him off balance.

I'm afraid you've been misinformed, at least about the humping. She's not really my type and I'm sure I'm not hers, especially after I had to ask her some questions she didn't like.

Namely?

Let's get Quill on, too. I'm already repeating myself.

Jerry could care. He'll have his guys file their DUI's with whatever pretty face is in that office. Me, I've got to know my people and I are well away from her ship if it's going down.

I think you're hearing things I'm not. I just went to see her after it came out that she might have been one of the last people to see Morris alive, and I wanted to see what she recalled. Flanders had a sit down with the governor at the Pemberton and Morris walked in on it. That's about all I got.

What was the meeting about?

Look, Tony, why don't you ask her yourself? All I got was enforcement issues and what she called drug law reform.

So it's true. That bitch.

Sounds like you know more than I do.

Only that she's trying to get re-elected by running me over. She wants his support for an initiative to legalize marijuana. In the meantime, she's dragging her feet on prosecutions I hand her so she can save staff costs and court overhead on the way to looking like a white knight for the county budget while she makes the dope economy happy on the side. That leaves me trying to get re-elected with her painting me as the one losing the drug war, calling my cases weak. Tell me you've got something else.

Sorry, there are no more details than what she told me, and she's not dating the governor, if that's what you were hoping. It wouldn't be a crime if she were.

No, but it would be damn embarrassing if I can put her in bed with a democratic governor on a drive for free dope. It's still against federal law, and this is still a red county, barely, but we're poor. If it starts to look like she's trying to split the voters into choosing law and order or fiscal solvency she'll have to spend her campaign explaining how she isn't throwing the election to the pothead Liberals and Libertarians.

Well, you know what I know. What you do with it is your business. Did any of your people talk to the tow truck driver? Is he a smoker?

His name's Andy Horman. Breakwater Tow. We use him all the time, same as CHP. No, he's a health nut, so the butt wasn't his. The fire department used his cable for both the body recovery and the vehicle recovery since the fire department winch wouldn't reach that far. So he wasn't standing around much, and when he was it was at the cliff edge with everybody else, not over by the highway where the footprints and butt were.

Did the coroner investigator come up with anything, then?

Nada. No note, no mental health issues, no financial problems, no civil or criminal actions pending, no criminal history, no vendettas. Just a million parking tickets. What prints we were able to get off the wreck were just hers and her husband's. Hubby owns a Smith and got a concealed carry permit after some nutjob threat, but she wasn't shot so nothing there.

Has anybody talked to the governor's staff?

About what she was doing there? The official line is coincidence, just another guest who happened to be there, with the suggestion that perhaps she was there to meet someone else or ambush the governor for some story she was working on. Who knows? I'm not going to turn over any more rocks there until we clear Biel, especially now that he's hiding behind his attorney and the grief thing, but that may never happen. We managed to get a consent search for the car he was driving without having to spell out what your partner and the CHP turned up, just that we were aware of his being in the area, but his car was clean. Beyond that he's just a person of interest until we get something more.

I talked to his chief committee consultant and tried to convince him it would clear the air faster if he came in for an interview.

Well, if he bites, I want my guys there.

I'll let you know.

Yeah, and hey, if you do get Flanders alone again, you should go for it. I'll bet she bucks like a three-second rodeo bronc.

Sounds like I'm not the one you really want to see stick it to her, Tony.

Stick this.

Porter flipped his phone closed, not needing to listen to dead air to know that the call was over. It was time to drag himself to the office anyway, but first he needed to find some coffee, drive back to Roseville, swing by his apartment and change. It was late morning before he made it home and did the restart. He got the coffee maker going because his road coffee had barely made a dent in his haze, shaved and did the fast pull and pour while the last drips sizzled on the warming pad. His routine was now to sip with his back against the counter, looking for whatever there might be to look at out the tiny kitchen window above the kitchen trash. Most of the parking slots at the apartment house over the back fence were empty by this time, which allowed the garbage truck to swing in for an easy shot at the dumpster corral. The driver got out, undid the gate latch and twirled his chunky little partner in a spinning arc to face the truck, got in, speared the truck's forks into the box's side slots, and gave the can a lindy hop flip backward over the cab to empty the contents in the truck's bin, dropped the dumpster back on the ground, got out, gave the lids an insolent flip closed and spun the box back into the corral. The whole thing took maybe a minute. Porter wondered if they had trash truck rodeos where the drivers competed for time. What else did they think about all day? I'm too hot. I'm too cold. Shit, it's raining again. Should I take the supervisor interview? When's lunch? This box is about rusted through. Should I say something? Stupid politicians. That Niner's coach better get his shit together. Damn, the cute blonde with the Camaro is gone already.

Would that be enough or, like his barren apartment, was that where you just woke up one morning? Boredom the tradeoff for being able to come home and shower off the day, which looked pretty good at the moment.

He had his own cleanup to deal with when he got to work. His desk was littered with *While-you-were-out* pinkies from some of those backlog cases Warren had been huffing about. He thumbed through them idly. They were about as exciting as a stack of someone else's family reunion photos shuffled through in vain for a familiar face, or a pile of campaign mailers and credit card come-ons that held no prospect of a personal letter buried therein. He would have to show interest if he found a note that might wrap at least one of his cases: the postal inspector who had found the phony drop box, the bank examiner who had noticed an interesting deposit-withdrawal pattern, the subject who had panicked at their offer of a lie detector test and was now ready to give it up. Sometimes there was real money involved. Sometimes there was significant jail time involved. But whether or not they had it coming, the problem was not that he felt like a perverse rubbish guy making his rounds, checking bins to see if they were full enough to dump on somebody. The problem was his increasing dread that a suspect might indeed flash a recognizable family trait in their fraud, making his involvement akin to that flaw, a sort of accessory or extension, a party to the crime even if in reverse. Dump he would, but the dumping smelled more and more like unwholesome reciprocity, a casting of stones, adhering to him a more persistent odor with an indelible reek. The image was unseemly, and dejecting. He made a few calls, tried to set up a few appointments. A lot of people were out of town already for the holiday coming up. By early afternoon he still had little to show for the day except a growling stomach from skipping breakfast. Joel was not helping. He could hear him in the next cubicle rattling his spoon around, chasing the remains of one of those ridiculously tiny yogurt cups before making a dash to the gym. The pointless noise hurt his swollen head and his empty stomach at the same time.

OK, already. Why don't you just lick the thing clean or buy a bigger container next time?

Maybe someone should put a cork in it. I can smell you from over here. Are you off the phone?

So it would appear.

There's a guy up front waiting to see you.

What's he want?

Wouldn't say. Just wanted to know if you were in.

Damn, Joel, and you said I was? It's probably a process server, and I want to go eat.

I could bring you back something, but I won't be back for an hour.

I'll be in hypoglycemic shock by then.

Then just walk out. He probably doesn't know what you look like.

He'll just be back. Probably just some chump trying to earn a living anyway. Never mind.

It was no use trying to avoid the inevitable. He grabbed his coat so he could do his legal reading and fuming in the privacy of his car.

The man in the alcove was more of a kid who looked to be in college earning money between classes, and he stood up from his chair with a little too much alacrity for a process server. They were generally older, at least in town, the old guys getting to cherry pick the short drops in the metro area, leaving the youngsters to chase dead ends way out in the sticks. Usually they sidled up to you on some innocuous pretense just before they slipped the envelope between your ribs. But he was fumbling for something in his cheap tweed sport coat, so he was probably both: a college kid making easy money while trying to learn the business from dad.

Michael Porter?

Yeah, you got me.

Insult to injury, getting served by this five o'clock shadow for a haircut. Pants too tight. A fucking earring.

I'm Dylan Frank, from the *Sacramento Sun.* Is there somewhere we could talk?

Porter gave him a: *What's this about?* while he perused the laminated press credential.

I heard you were leading the investigation on the Holly Morris death, and I was hoping for a minute of your time.

If there was one profession Porter would rate below process server it was anybody connected with the *Sun*, a schizoid bi-weekly that was as famous for the dirt it managed to scoop the majors on as it was infamous for sloppy editing, quotes out of context and a glaringly anti-government slant.

I'm afraid you've been given a bad lead. The only thing I'm leading is a charge to lunch.

So, you're not part of this investigation? I'm looking to share some information, not just get some.

Say you are. I can't really discuss an open investigation, and I'm not available to be used as an unnamed source.

Look, I'm taking a chance here, too. I don't know anything about you other than my source thinks I can trust you.

It was a cheap bit of flattery. Even if someone had told him that, they just could have been trying to get rid of him. The kid looked a little desperate. Maybe he was a stringer who had promised more than he could deliver. Question was, was there really a source, and who might it be?

Ok, I'm willing to listen at least. Come on back.

He led the way down the hall, giving Joel's raised eyebrows a responding shrug as they passed. They took opposite chairs across the table in the interview room.

This is about as private as it gets. Do you have a pocket recorder? Put it on the table, off.

No problem. I wouldn't record this anyway. It could come back to haunt both of us.

Yeah, a lot of cops find that out every day. Mind telling me who your source is? It would help a lot.

I can't tell you that.

Well, this puts us at kind of an impasse.

What if I told you I was working with Holly Morris on a story?

I'd find that hard to believe. She's broadcast news. You're free print media that clogs gutters after it rains. I don't see those as competitors in the same league, or colluding even if they were. She could get a story on the air in minutes and leave you with crumbs.

We had it worked where she would pick up the story the day it came out in the *Sun*.

Why would she agree to that? Why would you agree to that? She could scoop you and broadcast any time she wanted.

She had her reasons, and I trusted her. She has a good reputation.

You don't, so back to square one.

Frank laced his fingers together and placed his hands on the table. Porter was going to get the truth now, or as much of it as this guy was willing to risk.

Here's the background. If you've been reading the papers, you know public sentiment is starting to tilt in favor of loosening the laws that supposedly let only sick people have marijuana. It's resulting in an unseemly scramble to corner the market, not just by the larger dispensaries currently in operation as so-called patient co-ops, but by drug companies, tobacco companies and who knows who else. The lobbyists are bankrolling legislators they can tap to set them up as legal monopolies. Holly has been talking to Biel's staff and others trying to find out who's involved, but she's been keeping a low profile to keep her husband's name out of it. I'm not sure Biel even knows. That's why she was going to let the Sun have the scoop. She was supposed to give me some names this week.

Porter had a sense where this was going, and he knew more than Frank did, apparently, but he was not about to lay out a spread for this guy. He passed the plate back empty.

Well, there's already speculation that Morris was sneaking around on her husband. This is just a different flavor of that. Am I missing something?

That would depend on whether you think she was murdered or not. She was setting this up to embarrass a lot of politicians. Did somebody want her out of the way? If they did, I need to know if I need to be looking over my shoulder.

Porter was way ahead of him. Rationally, there could have been some tradeoff, payoff or political threat that might have convinced Biel to get his wife in line if it was brought to his attention that she was stirring up trouble, but it was also clear that Biel's M.O. was generally to just give her more slack. They might even have been on the same page for a while. Had she gotten out ahead of his political wiggle room or decided she was in bed with the wrong politician? Had her probable fling with the governor finally snapped the link that held Biel and her together? Biel, most likely, or someone else might have concluded that it was past time to stifle Morris, but Porter was not about to corroborate Frank's suspicions. His first instinct was to give him the party line again. Then he had another thought: if a reporter got the idea that there was definitely a homicide, the news would get around and might smoke out another suspect, or help get the goods on Biel. This guy Frank was a sleaze, but was that any different than working with a confidential informant?

Tell you what. It would not be inaccurate to assume that this investigation is looking at every scenario. More than that, I can't say. But it wouldn't be a bad idea to alter your routine a little until this is resolved. Just to be on the safe side.

This last bit was not really called for, but Porter could not help himself. He had overdone it by the look of Frank, who now shifted nervously.

Can't you give me at least a hint of who you are looking at? I'm not liking what this might mean for me. This isn't what I do.

Porter thought this was a bit disingenuous.

Maybe it is. Sorry.

They traded cards and promised to keep in touch, but as he watched Frank trudge out to his car, Porter caught his own reflection in the window, a mix of weariness and regret. Was this what *he* did?

Joel had his desk chair rolled to the doorway of his cubicle when Porter came back.

Long lost brother?

Turns out he's from the *Sun*. Says he was working with Morris on a marijuana legalization story, some unholy mix of politics and big business. Thinks somebody might have found out and wanted her gone. I let him believe we are on to something. Maybe he'll spread the word and break something loose for us.

Or get in over his head.

Yeah, well then we would all be brothers, wouldn't we? I'll see you in an hour.

Why don't you hit the gym with me? Lose a few pounds before the holidays.

I'd rather take a walk in the park where I can think, thanks. Don't you get tired of jogging on the treadmills or whatever?

Nah. I listen to music. Sometimes a book. And they have a weight room and showers. I can hit the bricks after work if that isn't enough.

There had been Porter's own overly ambitious attempt at

that, which Joel was never going to hear about: the time he pulled himself into a glorified jock strap and launched himself into a freezing splashdown at the local pool. He found he could kick, or pull, or draw great gasping breaths, but not in any semblance of the flying bodies in the adjacent lanes slamming flip turns off the walls before sailing past him again and again. If they were racing sloops, he was a broken paddle wheeler adrift, a prisoner of the current, hopelessly derelict. There was no reprieve beneath the surface, either, where the pool itself mocked his lack of form. Nothing in his floundering would measure up to the broad and bold and straight black stripe on the bottom, no matter how much the black cross on the wall at the far end suggested something achievable. He had no goggles, and the chlorine burned his eyes every time he opened them to check his progress. The cross was still up ahead, beckoning, apparently no closer as he sank lower and lower the more he flailed. When he finally made it across to hang on the edge, belching and hiccupping in the flooded gutter, he turned and considered the same black stripe on the bottom, the same black cross on the wall at the other end, and had to contemplate how the return trip would be an identical struggle to gain an objective that was always a little out of reach and of no consequence when he did, beyond agony. He climbed out.

He liked his thinking with a bit more peripatetic to it. He drove to the park, but soon gave up trying to keep up with the power-walking secretaries in tennis shoes and veered into the Artesian Museum. This was his favorite museum because it was mostly modern art by American artists. Inside, the dimness was a relief from the outside glare of a rare warm, sunny day in winter, and his shirt began to chill on his back, but there the relief ended. The works were implacable today, and conspired to rebuff his escape attempts. Where the angular black and white shapes of a tilted Manfred Mohr cityscape had captured him in the past, today the jagged angles of shadowed canyons with lurking silos exploded into crystalline fragments and arrowed shapes flying off a blue-green that was a mockery of ground. The effect struck him as broken window shards of data raining out of holes in the computer that generated them. There was a walkway through the painting in an angular path that led from the bottom out the top, but he would never get out alive.

Hill's red and gray grid did not work either. Today it was just a maze even if he let himself see the design in three dimensions, in which case the apparent dead ends among the fluid pattern of gray box shapes devolved to changes in elevation, telling his eye it had only to step among floating flagstones, or perhaps the flagstones were pools among bloody tiles, but how deep? All he got was a dizzying balancing act between slippery gradations of venal reds amid stone grays that bled from hammered steels to glistening slates.

Even the Barnet could not save him, his favorite. It was the treat he saved for last because it was so approachable compared to some of its brasher, more self-involved companions. It was warmer, more whimsical, a meander through catlike receptacles, dozing owls and precarious cartoon stucco houses. But today he saw the surreal roots had long since been teased out, absorbed in the vernacular, leaving him aloof. There was no escape in these dreamscapes unless he was lying to himself, clutching at fantasy sets where he could hide behind a painted backdrop; pretending he still had a functional marriage any more than he had a case he could solve. What he needed was a new medium for his own disarray, a less formalized compilation of his trite circumstance, a found-art collage of disparate observations that might lend his amateurish work an appreciable sense of order even if beauty was unattainable. But really, his tools and talent were unequal to the attempt. All he could envision was a sort of bastardized whiteboard exercise of incongruent elements posted in some drab squad room, with tentative and unbalanced connections lacking anything resembling harmony, focus or resolution:

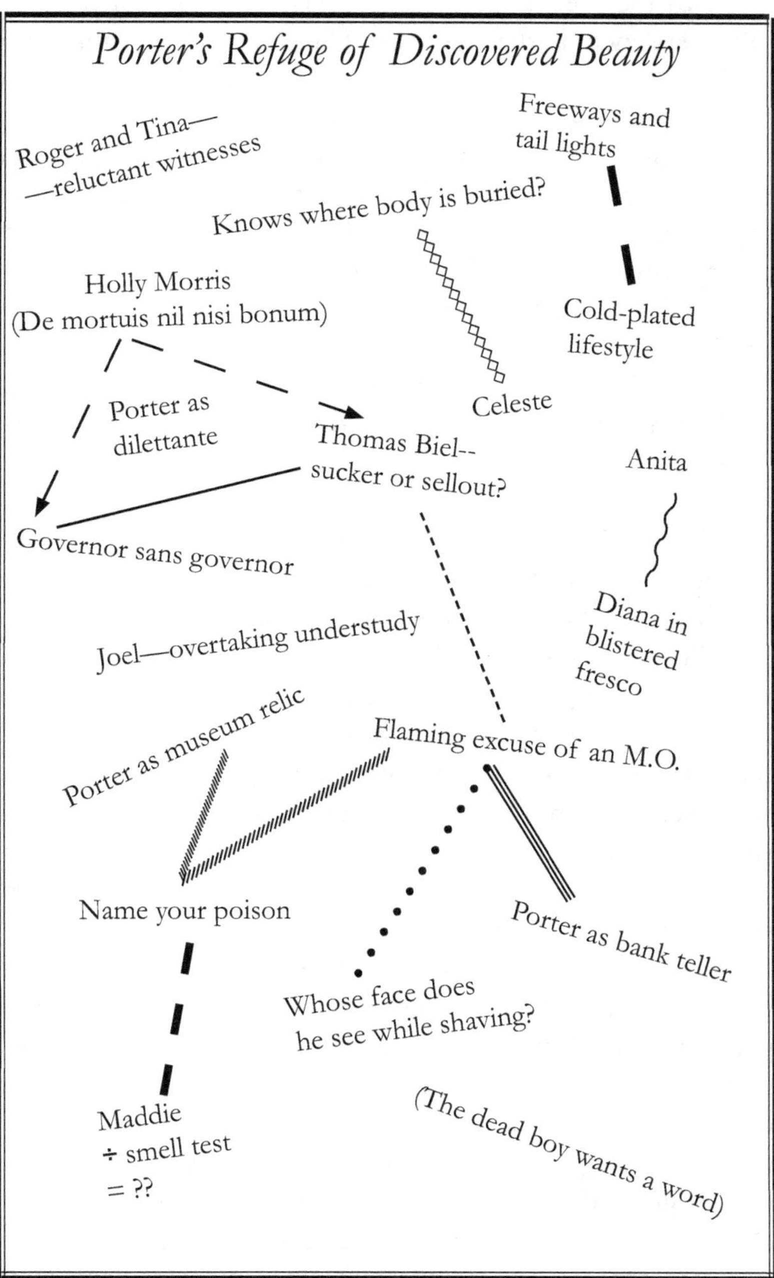

Porter's Refuge of Discovered Beauty
Roger and Tina—reluctant witnesses
Freeways and tail lights
Knows where body is buried?
Holly Morris
(De mortuis nil nisi bonum)
Cold-plated lifestyle
Porter as dilettante
Thomas Biel--sucker or sellout?
Celeste
Anita
Governor sans governor
Joel—overtaking understudy
Diana in blistered fresco
Porter as museum relic
Flaming excuse of an M.O.
Name your poison
Porter as bank teller
Whose face does he see while shaving?
Maddie
÷ smell test
= ??
(The dead boy wants a word)

With the predictable result: stillborn even in concept, the premise as inept as the execution. Thus reduced, his entire body of work stood as derivative of the Neanderthal school for the blind, a walking-dead end of a dabbler branch incapable of replicating even the simplest implements and techniques of the more advanced races; devoid of any sense of design or purpose, much less transcendence. His cell buzzed. It was Joel. Life happening while he was making a mess of it.

You know a guy named Howard Zephur?

Sure. Biel's chief of staff I told you about.

(Or had he?) Joel was in talking mode, so it did not matter.

He wants to set up a meet tomorrow. I said ten. All right?

Fine. He coming in?

No, at the capitol.

That won't work. That's his turf.

He said it was there or nowhere.

He would. I'm on my way back. We need to gear up.

When he got back to the office he sat down with Joel and they went over what they had. They had very little, actually, at least as far as a conspiracy to hush up a TV newscaster. While the influence of the dope industry seemed to stretch from the back roads of Whitley County to the halls of the capitol, it also seemed to be an open secret. Nobody was getting too concerned about it as long as there was enough cash on the street to prop up rural economies supported by "alternative agriculture," and for tucking cannabis contributions into the hands of ambitious politicians. Those in office produced votes for interdiction grants to local law enforcement that had the dual benefit of salving their consciences, while acting as a price support for a commodity that would otherwise flood the market with cheaper and cheaper dope. On the other hand, nobody wanted to be the one caught with their hand in the cookie jar. Morris was on to something that was likely to embarrass her husband, whether by virtue, if one could call it that, of her direct involvement with the governor, or as a deductive result of information she had gained from it. The available evidence did not indicate the governor was all that concerned with Morris, even when she caught him with his hand reaching for another cookie.

Biel was another story. The odds were good that Biel was at the scene, since it was probably him in the car picked up by the camera covering the Pemberton Gate. Whoever it was, something incited them to blast off down the road after Morris. That was not much, but Biel could not know that, and probably had no prior experience of being in a position to learn how to keep his mouth completely shut. But he could afford good representation. They would just have to deal with that. Biel knew something, and Porter knew something: Biel was not getting a pass, not with ample opportunity and two possible motives, even if one required a true psychotic of a political lapdog. Politicians were a strange bunch Porter did not think he could or would want to relate to, which meant dealing with a lot of unknowns and putting aside a few prejudices. The handful of questions they settled on were not very encouraging. Even Joel was not optimistic:

Not much there, is there?

No, we're going to have to wing this one. Our best card is probably his desire to protect his political image or his self-image. There seems to be a disconnect there given some of his campaign bedfellows. And there's his friendship with the governor. Poke at those and see what makes him flinch. You be sure and sit where I can see you. We're going to have to be extra nice, at least until we can get a sense of just how he's involved. So far everything points to him.

Joel showed him both rows of small, even white teeth.

Nice guy. I can do that.

CHAPTER XIX

GONE FISHING

It was going to be a superb day to be skiing in the Sierras according to the weather lady on Porter's television. A stable air mass had moved in, and snow in the mountains the day before had dropped an early base of what passed for powder in California. You could even get a sun tan judging from the weather cam shot of Boreal Ridge that showed slopes sparkled blinding white in the crystalline air. And if dodging commitments was a momentary attraction for Porter, the prospect was sure to entice snowboarding truants to the mountains, at least working-age truants in better shape than Porter. The schools had long since capitulated to half-empty classes on Thanksgiving week, giving kids the whole week off. Maybe Tina and Roger were there already if Anita followed the annual routine and shipped them off with her folks to their cabin at Lake Tahoe. She would want to be skiing all week, too, even if Porter preferred a book by the fire, but neither of them had ever spent the whole week. A week of that would only mean cabin fever for him, and for her there were always papers to grade and lesson plans to write. So, nothing new for the kids so far, just their parents, until tomorrow when Anita would drive up to join them on Thanksgiving Day and arrive without him. Thankfully, the clear weather meant the roads would also be clear. He would not have to consider her alone in the car by the side of the road, snowflakes sifting through the slot of the steamed window she had lowered an inch to finger a couple of twenties to the chain monkey. Well, whatever the weather did on Thursday, she was on her own this year. Of course, so was he.

The lights were off when he drove by the house, which he should have expected. She would be catching up on her sleep before hitting the stores or housework, or grading her students' homework, or however she had her day off planned. The newspaper was not in the driveway, either. Nothing to do but find his way back out of the subdivision, the variations on neutral stucco slipping back behind anonymous curtains of tule fog that were of the same stuff as snow, but a corruption of the sunlit purity heaped on the uplifted mountains. This was winter's curse on the Central Valley, and going nowhere without an approaching storm or unsettled front to bluster in; inspire the slumbering layer to get up and move along. The fog could be here all day today. It could last for days, a viscous oppression poured all along the river bottomlands and floodplains from Redding to Sacramento to Fresno, forcing cars to slow, instilling a somnambulance in every step ventured in the heart of the state, defusing street lights, merging downtown buildings into alien ranks that could be three stories tall, or thirty, or blown to kingdom come somewhere up above him in the mist. It could also be that some banker in the Darth Vader building had bought himself an office shot clear through to the blue and was sitting there now, warming in the sun, contemplating those snowy peaks. Would that be dispensation enough for whatever sins put him there? It might seem so on a day like today. Down here there was not a prayer of elation to be had with this morning. It was hemmed-in weather. East looked the same as west. Everyone stuck in it carried the same burden. He watched as a woman in a long dark coat plodded a side street with her head down, manifestly unequal to the day, no doubt wishing she were someplace else, constrained by her own condition on her way to some poorly analyzed assignation that had probably sounded like a good idea at the time.

Joel was another story altogether. He was pacing around the front offices in the barely contained exuberance of a kid on the last day of school before a big holiday. He was giving Angela hell about keeping a candy dish full on her desk for passersby just as an excuse to eat most of it herself. Angela was a boney redhead with skin so white it was almost the translucent blue of skim milk, so Joel knew he could get away with it. He was still in bounds, but pushing. If Angela was in at seven-thirty, it could only be because she wanted to get off early to go finish her Thanksgiving shopping. The look she gave Porter said as much, as she ignored Joel to give him the message that was on the machine: His ten o'clock was still on. A Mister Zephur would meet him with Assemblyman Biel at their office at a quarter 'til.

Thanks, Angela. Come on, Joel. I've been doing some thinking.

About interview versus interrogation? I think we at least have to Miranda Biel.

Porter thought Miranda was a stretch without more to go on. The pedigree was spotless: Born in Modesto, math degree from UCLA, master in economics from Stanford, settled in Rohnert Park, partnered accounting firm, then city council, board of supervisors and assemblyman, his campaign slogan: *Making A Difference*—(Wouldn't we all?)—member of Stanford Business Roundtable and Governor's Asian Economic Development Council. Only child, married a little late, at thirty-eight, Morris his first wife. Hobbies and interests: foundation to send underprivileged kids to summer camp, collector of rare coins. What Porter got was a portrait of plain white bread on the rise, and a very analytical, methodical mind who liked things a certain way. An organized mind. The bills in his wallet would be in denominational order, if he even carried currency. The socks in his bureau drawer would all be folded neatly inside themselves and aligned in rows by color. His car would be immaculate. His home décor would be like Porter's apartment, on the minimalist side, unless Morris dressed it up. All of which could be suggested by the scant evidence they had found at the overlook where Morris took her last plunge, as well as not. Someone as fastidious as Biel seemed to be would not have wanted to get his hands dirty, and could have arranged to have someone slug her somewhere else, drive her to the overlook and send her over. Was Biel that cold? Was he capable of that distance? Not according to Toby Sim, who saw Biel as hopelessly infatuated. A less organized mind could have invented the whole thing on the spot; attacked her in a sudden rage, and then taken the immediate and obvious step of pushing her car over the side with her in it. That should have left more evidence behind, and did not sound like Biel. But Sim had also mentioned the possibility that an orderly and very contained personality could be stretched to a sudden breaking point. This did not sound like Biel either, a man with enough self-control to make it to the state assembly. Someone else then? Sim's advice was to stick to probabilities. Probability was lining up behind Biel, but which one? Suspicion was not going to pry Biel out of his shell unless Porter found the right crack. So was it the result of icy deliberation by a rigid idealist, or a so-called crime of passion committed in the sudden collapse of an edifice? The most likely way to tell depended on whether there was an accomplice—the lookout. That would take planning. But would a hermetic control-freak invite an accomplice into his private affairs? Porter was unable to fathom that possibility.

He had looked Biel up online the night before while flat on his back on his apartment floor, his head on a pillow, the laptop propped on his stomach. All the driving had seized up his back. It made him nearly cringe to watch Biel bound up the steps of a rickety stage at some county fair rally for a pre-bout victory strut, his smile at once humble and guarded as he played the part, his arms thrust skyward with palms extended to his supporters to feel their heat, to salute their accolades, to mirror the foregone conclusion that his prize-fight foe would be carried out on a stretcher. The microphone was poorly muffled for the wind tear, but Biel's words carried over it:

Are you ready for a change in Sacramento?

(The crowd and paid shills yell their more-than-readiness, and jab their *Make-A-Difference* signs up and down in the air like pitchforks.)

Are you tired of seeing your water shipped out of state, your fish harvested by Canadian trawlers, your trees shipped whole to Japan and your jobs shipped to China?

(Cheers)

Are your schools run down, your roads full of potholes and your pocketbooks picked with nothing to show for it?

(Cheers)

Do you want a better life for your children?

(Cheers and sign waving)

Do you want a leader who will make a difference in Sacramento?

(Roars)

Then I humbly request the honor of your vote on November second. In return, I promise I will fight for you. (Fist doing controlled little bumps on the podium to convey commitment, but short of an unhinged zealot that ought to be committed.) I will fight for you. (Bump) I WILL FIGHT FOR YOU.

(Cheers, roars, applause, and canned *Rocky* theme music)

Biel looks to the side, off camera, and Holly Morris strides across the stage, pecks his cheek, and puts her arm around his waist as she turns to acknowledge the cheers of the crowd that have now increased in intensity, distorting the microphone pickup so all that is heard is a shearing, warbling buzz.

A lot of what Biel promised would have been a mouthful for any congressman, much less a down-ticket member of the statehouse, but if assemblymen had running mates, Biel could not have made a more strategically inspired liaison than teaming up with Morris. Style, smarts, commitment to public good, she had the whole package, and Biel clearly basked in her reflected glow, apparently more than content to let the bridesmaid show up the bride, wearing nothing more than a purple Kings jacket, a white silk tee and jeans. Porter imagined himself up there with his arm around Morris, having made the same promises, which were vague, the same entreaties. Who wouldn't? Even though Biel's delivery was short on specifics, it was long on emotional strings. Porter found Biel's words stirring despite himself. What was he selling? It was possibility. It was renewal. It was hope.

It was also just words, words that Porter could imagine coming out of his own mouth just as easily. Who would not want these things—a more perfect union—especially with Morris standing beside him, lending him more credibility with her white-hot smile than all his words and podium thumping. By comparison, Biel came across as more reserved than fully involved. He was saying all the right things, but Morris was the one on fire. She oozed passion and confidence just standing there. He looked out of place, like he would have preferred to be looking over his coin collection rather than a crowd of potential voters, and he could not quite keep it from showing. But it was not a failed attempt at subterfuge so much as an inability to mask a forthright character, one that was not fake so much as a little sheepish about his public appearance as the devoted attendant who stood ready to move heaven and earth to prove worthy of the electorate's trust projected, embodied in her. She was the visionary. He was the true believer, shyly professing his faith, all the while juggling unavoidable sins under his robe; his visible unease less that of a scoundrel, more that of an honorable man who aspired to his eternal perfection, even if he had to roll dice with the devil. So, Miranda for this guy? He wore them uneasily, but he had the trappings of a would-be saint. A heavy-handed interview would amount to slapping a novice who was buried in ritual even if Biel might be a disciple who had reason to question his faith, had perhaps strayed, but was looking for atonement. What was required was a persuasive return to the doctrine, not the rack. How to convey that to Joel?

I don't know, Joel. There's still an outside chance he's just a tool or a witness. Let's not force our hand just yet. I was looking at some of his campaign speeches and interviews last night. I think it will go better if we go selective. I'm getting a mixed read on this guy. He doesn't seem very comfortable in his own skin, at least the public one. Underneath I think he's an idealist who leans more toward introvert and control. How a guy like that winds up in public service is beyond me. A private guy in a very public job would make for a lot of stress, which could help explain motive with a wild card wife like Morris, but the personality doesn't seem to jive with the brutality of what the scene would indicate. About all we can do is stick to basics, guilt being the common denominator. If he had a hand in it then he needs a fig leaf to admit it. If he didn't he might be blaming himself anyway. Either way it'll be a booger of an interview. We're going to have to go easy on the pedal. What?

Joel had a good scowl going, and the folded arms of a subject shutting down.

I don't think we need kid gloves, Mike. You said it yourself—he doesn't know what we know. Let him think we matched his tire tread pattern with impressions we took at the scene. Ask him what size shoe he wears. Let's hammer him on that and the front gate video, then slam him with the cell records. If he's got anything left after that, let's pile on his public image and anything else we can leverage.

It can't come across that way, Joel. I'm going on the assumption that he's no dummy and he's going to be with counsel.

He's just another perp, only in a suit.

Maybe, but if we go in thinking that way we might as well have blinders on. He's stiff-armed the other agencies. Either he thinks we're stupid or Zephur convinced him we can give him something he wants. I want to let him think we're good for whatever he needs to open up.

He hoped he sounded more convincing to Joel than he felt, which was all the pumping up he could muster for the actual interview. They went over their scripted questions again, but it was really a fallback option. What he wanted to do was just see if they could get Biel talking and let him tell his story. There was bound to be more in that to work with than anything they had cooked up. They went through the exercise in the desultory manner of a couple of chefs checking off a list of meager ingredients—stone, onion, turnip—as pretense of a savory outcome neither of them really had much expectation of realizing, however much they tried to spice it up. But if Sim was right, Biel's still waters might not hold up if a rock were tossed in. Not just any rock, though. It would have helped if he had a clue about the dynamics between Biel and Morris, the daily cover stories they must have invented to carry on with each other, but they probably had no better understanding of their own fairy tale than he did with Anita. It was a tangle that had kept Porter awake half the night. What was Biel's soft spot? His wife was one, certainly, and she was gone, with both the lock and maybe the key.

It was a relief and a bit of hope abandoned when it was time to go. Joel had gone internal as well and there was not much talk as they set off for the capitol building. The fog still had the city under submission. Traffic was lighter than usual. A lot of bureaucrats must have taken the week off. He led Joel through the ritual of leaving their hardware in the little locking boxes in the room next to the metal detector at the capitol public entrance, and they headed up to Biel's office suite. Zephur was there, but Biel was not, and Zephur had traded his casual sartorial for jeans, a plum cashmere V-neck and a pair of ankle-high suede hiking boots for climbing summits of style, there to survey the lowlands of utility with a triumph of disdain.

My apologies, Tom's running a little late. Can I get you some coffee?

Joel said: Sure.

Porter declined. He was jacked up enough as it was, since fishing expeditions were not his thing. He much preferred to go in like a lawyer ready for trial, prepared to ask no questions he did not already know the answers to. Zephur may have picked up on that.

I think you'll find that Tom has nothing to hide and is as eager as you are to clear the air.

Porter took this to mean Biel had everything to hide and nothing to gain with transparency, but Zephur had given it a good try. He continued his easy bedside manner as they made their way downstairs and onto the Assembly floor through the large dark doors and right up the center aisle past the stanchioned sign that said *Members and Authorized Staff Only*. For a large room it was serenely, expectantly quiet, the ornately patterned green carpet and two-story-tall drapes gathered at the windows and columned entrance doing a good job of that. Porter saw his passing was an immediate attraction for the tourists on their guided tour in the gallery above, there being no other activity but his group on the floor amid the chevroned rows of double desks and the vacant dais. Enormous chandeliers above gave off a lot of light, but the space was so large there was still that dialed-down dimness of a mortuary. Joel asked if there was some significance to the huge portrait of Lincoln presiding over the Speaker's desk. Zephur explained that the Senate chambers had already glommed on to Washington. The Assembly chose a portrait of John Sutter initially—illustrious California pioneer or profiteering scoundrel, take your pick—but nobody recognized him, so they swapped him for Lincoln.

Zephur led them through a door behind the dais and into a low-ceilinged but no less ornate lounge set with steaming silver coffee urns, bottled waters, sodas, and an assortment of fruits, muffins and sweets along one softly lit wall. The room's sole occupant, a stocky middle-aged man with a thin comb over, white shirt and tie, no jacket, sat facing the room with a newspaper spread precisely flat and centered in front of him on an otherwise empty table. He had just turned a page and was lining up the corners. This was a guy who would read every page thoroughly, secure in his role of being exactly where he was supposed to be and doing what he was supposed to be doing, an attendant at an exclusive club engaged primarily to be simply available. His greeting was his resumé.

Good morning, Mister Zephur. How are you? The quarterly is out for that Telmex stock you like. Their net is up nine point six percent over last year.

Thank you, Bill. Yes, I saw that. I hope you took my advice.

I would, but I prefer safer investments, like ponies.

Well, you should have listened to this tout.

Good one, sir. Maybe next time.

Have a good day, Bill.

You, too, Mister Zephur.

And with that they moved on through the room and out a door at the other end. Bill had already gone back to his paper, giving no sign that he had even seen Porter and Joel. It was an impressive performance. Bill had let it be known that he knew eighty-one assembly members, forty senators and their key staff on sight, and something currently of interest to all of them. More important, his formal deference to Zephur, with no acknowledgement of his companions, indicated he had sized up this procession instantly as one that included participants whose passage was intended to be invisible or of no account, it being Bill's charge to neither note, differentiate, or recall. Was Zephur trying to make some point with this tour? There had to be a more direct route to wherever they were headed than through the assembly chambers and past this human Rolodex. They crossed a corridor and came into a conference room with a mini assortment of refreshments similar to the room they had just left, and a large conference table that could seat a dozen easily with high-backed chairs all around. Otherwise the room was empty.

It was awful. Porter had to consciously resist the impulse to grind his teeth. You could call it a juvenile game or a breach of protocol, but when you invited somebody to your house you did not march them around and then keep them waiting unless you were trying to make a point about who was in charge. The empty room was rubbing his nose in it; the fact that it was such a transparent bit of primal crotch grab making it no less effective. If it were not, every self-styled potentate from the pyramids to the Kremlin would not have felt compelled to erect edifices to their own exaltedness. The promenade through the tribal trappings of office here was proof of that, but this room was the capper. There were three separate entrances. The chairs were too comfortable, the table too big to allow for a subtle coercion of intimacy, the lighting too subdued to capture fleeting expressions from across the table or compel an expectation of truth, and the ones who were kept waiting to ponder the import of all this were the interrogators. All of which made Porter distracted, off balance, and his awareness of it made it more so. He did his best to concentrate on his breathing while listening to Zephur's breezy time wasting, wondering what it was going to be: door number one, door number two, or door number three.

—coming to this side of the capitol, with all this history just sort of oozing out of the architecture. The annex could be any modern office building, so I always feel like the important work is getting done over here. You can't help but feel the eyes of history are on you when you are working in these rooms. Not that there hasn't been a lot of sausage cooked up in this one, but the grinders can never say later that they didn't know better with Minerva here looking over their shoulder. You guys doing anything special tomorrow?

Porter was caught contemplating the portrait of the goddess of wisdom and war; how her presence, at least, seemed appropriate to the proceedings. He looked at Joel hoping he had a more standard response at hand, but Joel's face had a mixture of caught off guard and a scramble for prevarication that Porter hoped did not show on his own. So he went first.

No special plans. Staying close to home.

Joel took the hint.

Yeah, same here.

Doing the family thing, huh? Must be nice. You guys have kids?

Porter said he had two teenagers, if you could call that nice. Joel just shook his head. Zephur was not really listening.

Well, as soon as we wrap here I'm off to the airport to catch a flight to Denver, then Vail. I'm going to eat powder for Thanksgiving.

Porter saw him appear and disappear amid clouds of white as Zephur sliced down an impossibly steep slope, came right at him, then lifted his hips and replanted at the last second as he shot by on his way to a rendezvous with some hot snow bunny, sending his advertent rooster tail of icy crystals right in Porter's face. Porter's plans for Thanksgiving? Table for one.

It was door number two. Biel looked nothing like his website hero shot, the suit and tie and carefully haphazard Kennedy forelock. This Biel was a bit on the short side, sporting a rumpled-hair, rumpled-suit, rich wino look that had gone out in the nineties. Face with eons of acne merged into overlapping lunar impact craters. Basset eyes and matching bags. There had to be a hell of an intellect here, because Holly could not have swooned over the wrapping. Porter opted for an awkward reach across the table because he had not worn hiking boots for the trek around. His tie fell out of his coat. Biel was unburdened by same, which made Porter's accoutrement a regrettable grasp at deference, an unnecessary formality or an affected accessory cummerbund to be buttoned back out of sight as quickly as possible. Off to a great start.

The intensity of Biel's handshake matched the look in his eye. Both of them were doing the fast size-up. What Porter got was smarts and anger behind a weak mask of engagement. There was a good chance that Biel got the same from him. Probably. Anita said she could always tell when he was lying. This interview was going to be a disaster if both of them were coming from the same place, circling the room, two dogs in a pit. The idea was to *get* to the same place, whether one of them wanted to get there or not. Maybe he should have let Joel take the lead. No, that would not do. It was his case, his lead. And Zephur had said he had convinced Biel that Porter was the man to talk to. The room had at least one confidence man.

Biel's attorney had entered behind him so unobtrusively that a person could be forgiven for assuming his role was attendant at best, not crucial to the proceedings, as he busied himself with the clasp on his large leather satchel. Three-piece charcoal matched with a graying little goatee. A pince-nez would have been perfect, but he had on a pair of those ubiquitous idiot slits set off with iridescent green temples to clash with the coat. Porter disliked him immediately, but chastised himself for indulging in a non-productive observation. Zephur was doing the introductions.

Tom, this is Michael Porter and Joel Vega. Mister Porter, (all formal now) this is Assemblyman Biel and his counsel, Robert Briar-Gold. Won't you be seated?

Pleased to meet you. I'm very sorry about your wife, Mister Biel.

Call me Tom. It's a pleasure, gentlemen. Thank you, Howard. Have a safe trip, and use some sun block this time.

Zephur left them alone. Porter and Joel exchanged cards with Briar-Gold. Porter laid his pocket recorder on the table. Briar-Gold objected immediately.

That won't be necessary. My client is here voluntarily.

It was expected. Porter, over Joel's objection, went along

on the gamble that Biel would give up something they could use, whether he intended to or not. At the moment they had nothing, much less trust. He removed the battery and placed it with care, upright as a talisman on watch next to the device, and there they were looking at each other across the burnished Serengeti of table, or almost. Biel angled into his chair, coming to rest with his ear in his palm and his elbow on the table facing forty-five degrees away from the edge, and Porter. This gave him a clear view of the two of them, with his attorney also in his range of vision. Porter mirrored his posture as both an attempt at rapport, and because it allowed him the same advantage in keeping Joel in view. Biel seemed to be talking to no one in particular.

Thank you for coming over on such short notice. I'm sure you gentlemen had better things to do the day before...

Porter resisted the urge to complete the sentence for him, which would have been a social misstep but, more important, a tactical blunder. Yet the seconds dragged on, and soon it became apparent that Biel was off on some errand that had carried him away from this most trite of ease-puttings. An uncomfortable silence swelled.

So, um, Tom, I hear you collect rare coins. How did you get into that?

Biel rubbed the side of his face as though the remembrance took some effort.

I sorta backed into it. My father died and left me a couple Civil War coins that were in the family. I like to think about them jingling around in some cavalryman's pocket as he rode around the countryside raising hell.

What's your favorite, north or south?

Either one, but if you ever hear of an original CSA one-center, let me know. It's the Holy Grail hole in everyone's collection. Are you a collector?

Only as far as checking my pocket change for Lincolns with

a double-struck obverse. I guess that makes me a pretty lazy collector.

Well, that might actually be a good approach, because if you ever get lucky you could be screwed. That's the kind of thing that could hook you good. You have kids, Michael?

Uh, yeah. One of each. Boy and girl. One's in junior high. One's in high school. Why?

No reason. Just—you're a very lucky man.

Thank, you, I suppose you're right. Sometimes we forget. Listen, as to why we're here, I'm sure Howard explained that we are looking at your wife's death to make sure we know exactly what happened, which I'm sure you want to know, too. That being said, there are some holes in our understanding of what caused your wife's accident. I'm hoping you can help us with that. Probably nobody knew Holly better than you or was in a position to know her routine and, hopefully, her frame of mind on the day she died.

No response from Biel. He just looked at Porter with his chin in his palm like he was waiting for him to finish, but his body was still facing away at an angle. It was meant to look more relaxed than it could possibly be.

First off, did she mention having any mechanical problems with her car recently? What kind of condition was it in?

No, she didn't mention any. It's only two years old. We got it because she does a lot of commuting and we wanted something reliable.

Biel was checking the fingertips of his free hand, bit a hang-nail. For a control question he was not enjoying it much.

Who would your wife say are her enemies?

Nobody that I'm aware of. None that would want to hurt her anyway. She gets flame mail same as everyone at the station, from what I hear, but nothing like the rants I get from people saying I'm not doing enough to create jobs in my district. I'm on a committee looking for ways to expand trade with Asia.

Porter wondered if Biel was just following his own train of thought or was trying to get off the subject of Morris, enemies, and mayhem. And Porter had not said anything about anyone physically harming her, just inferred it.

Yes, but, about your wife, did she ever express any concerns or mention that anyone was bothering her, or following her?

No, unless you count getting hassled by panhandlers and street nuts. That's just part of working in San Francisco.

When you last saw your wife, when was that? What did she talk about? Was there anything that was bothering her?

It would have been the Sunday before, at home, but we talk every day. I usually make it home weekends. Sometimes she comes up. It was just office stories, plans for getting the family together, for tomorrow, what she was going to cook. Nothing jumps out.

To Porter, that sounded a little pat, but maybe he was projecting. What would he have to say about his last visit with Anita if someone were to ask? He'd serve them some Dim Sum and they could kiss his ass about the rest.

Porter could not see Biel's face front on now, but Joel could. Joel drew a little line straight across his page, then crossed it out, meaning Biel was not being completely straight with him. A check mark would have been an OK, a circle a big fat circumvention.

OK, so that I can be clear, you last saw your wife on Sunday, and you last spoke to her—?

Briar-Gold intervened.

I believe Tom has already answered that, and he's demonstrated an extraordinary degree of cooperation by his presence here. Perhaps if you gentlemen would reciprocate by telling us exactly what it is you want to know, we can move this along a little faster. What is it you want?

It was none of his damn business, of course, certainly as long as this was an open investigation, and Briar-Gold was all too aware of it, but they had to give him something, be it a carrot or a stick. He wished he had Sam's knack for telling people to go to hell and making them happy to ask for directions.

Mister Briar-Gold, what we have is a need for some help from Tom if we are going to learn the truth about how his wife died. I think the most productive approach would be if Tom recognized this as his opportunity to set the record straight. We all know there are a lot of stories circulating. He'd be doing us a big favor if he could point us in the right direction. For our part, we'd like nothing better than to tag this base and move on.

OK, let's cut the crap, shall we? Howard said you wanted it known that it was in Tom's best interest to clarify his movements on the night of his wife's death. What exactly did you mean by that?

Porter was not sure which was more irritating, Briar-Gold's attack dog bait and switch or his thinking he could do a reverse good-cop, bad-cop on him and Joel. He was not going to bite on either, but it was so tempting. There were other ways to put Briar-Gold in his place.

Tom, if it's all the same to you, I came here to talk to you, not your attorney. I'm not at liberty to discuss the progress of our investigation, at least not until we know everything about that night that you know. This is a regrettable although crucial step in the inquiry, as I'm sure both you and Mister Briar-Gold can appreciate (even if Bowser here would pretend otherwise). I would like nothing better than to conclude this with as little drama as—

Is my client a suspect? Yes or no?

This was Porter's own fault. He should have dropped the drama. Cards on table, sort of.

I'm sorry, I didn't mean to suggest there is anything dramatic that we expect out of this conversation. What I meant to say is that I know this is a difficult time for you, Tom. The last thing I want to do is add to your difficulties. Just the opposite.

If you are straight with us it would help us expedite the official record, which would hopefully put an end to the media scrutiny as well. But you are a key part of that, Tom. You are a witness who knows more about what happened that night than is in any report. We know that. You know that. I think you also know that your continued silence is detrimental to your standing. You need to look at this as an opportunity to end the speculations concerning you and your wife so you can get on with your life.

Biel came out of his palm.

My standing? What would you know about that?

Now this was an interesting response. It had challenge, opportunity and plea written all over it. It was also overly defensive and a distraction. Who was this guy? Or was Biel's reaction to be expected even without the excuse of his exalted office? How would he, Porter, explain the reasons behind his own car wreck with Anita and the position he now found himself in? Would all his ready-to-wear analyses look like anything more than diversions, flimsy masks for his refusal to face up to his role in their breakup? He was losing focus. Get back on track.

I was referring to our attempts to get a clear understanding of how your wife died. If there are other concerns you would like me to know about, I'm all ears.

I'll bet you are, but the point is, it's none of your business.

This was not exactly hitting it off. How to sound conciliatory without the patronizing?

For the sake of progress, I'm willing to go with that for the moment. Let's say your other concerns are none of our business. Maybe we don't have a right to know them. That doesn't mean we may not need to know them. But let's not get ahead of ourselves. We just want to understand what happened that night.

I'm sure you do. Wouldn't we all. I don't think I can help you.

He did not think. As long as Biel was thinking of himself in terms of what he might have to lose, this was just going to keep going in the little circles Joel was penning round and round on his legal pad. Biel needed a reason to see beyond something in it for him, something else he cared about. He was too wrapped up in himself. But first it was past time to get the bad news down while Biel had a mouth full of bile for condiment.

Maybe we should get this out of the way. I have to ask this. Did you kill Holly, Tom?

No, no, I—

Briar-Gold cut him off.

Tom—

Joel was giving Porter a *What-the-hell?* look. He would have to come back to this, but not yet.

Thank you. It's just part of the drill. Sorry. You love your wife, don't you, Tom?

Sure. Of course.

He said it with a little shudder shrug toward a dropped ear that could easily pass for unconscious denial, but Porter knew he had gotten through. It was the face saving of a shy kid trying to downplay his admission of something he cared deeply about. The fact that Biel did not correct him for asking it in the present tense meant he still had not accepted her death, which was odd given his response, and Briar-Gold's reaction, to the kill question.

There's a lot of people saying she killed herself.

Biel got a dyspeptic look.

She didn't do that.

Nobody knew your wife better than you. So help us out. How do you know that?

She wouldn't do that.

True or not, in the absence of proof, people will believe what they want to believe. Is that how you want her remembered, Tom?

Why should they believe that?

Joel was looking at him intently. Was he serving up an alibi? At least Biel was talking.

Isn't it at least plausible?

Porter knew the answer he would get before it was out of Biel's mouth.

No, it's not.

Stupid, asking a closed-end question. He was going to have to shake the cage now, just a little.

You don't think she might have killed herself when things didn't work out between her and the governor?

Let's leave Harry out of this.

OK, do you think she might have killed herself over you?

Why would she do that? I've never done anything to hurt her.

Wouldn't that be reason enough? Shame can make people do a lot of things. You have to have thought about this. What do you think happened?

Biel disengaged, leaned back and looked at the ceiling. Joel was giving him the small frozen wince of a man watching helplessly as his partner slid below the fractured ice.

I just know she didn't kill herself.

OK, what else could have happened to her? Her death wasn't just an accident.

This drew a physical and a verbal response: Biel sat up, and he looked over intently at Porter for the first time since they sat down. His voice rose a bit, insistent with conviction or over-selling.

Yes it was. It was dark. She lost control of her car. She went off a cliff in the middle of fucking nowhere. What else is there to know?

OK, Tom, OK, take a breath. I know this isn't easy for you. Let's take a moment to recap, shall we? Joel and I are only interested in the truth. We are only interested in as much of that as we need to fill in the blanks of our report. Anything extraneous to that does not need to leave this room. Are you with me so far?

Briar-Gold was taking rapid notes, left-handed. Biel deflated back into his chair, looked at the table.

Yes.

Thank you. Good. You have told us that you love Holly. You have told us that you know that Holly would not kill herself, and that she did not kill herself. You have told us that you know that it was an accident. Have I got all that right?

Yes.

How do you know all that, Tom?

Because I know my wife, and because the facts speak for themselves.

And Holly? Who's going to speak for her? You said you love Holly. Show her, show us, what that means. Sometimes we make a mess of things and we just have to face up to it and accept the consequences or we can never move on. Look at me, Tom.

Biel did, with as wracked a face as Porter had ever seen.

Holly wasn't alone when she died, was she?

Briar-Gold gave his chair a violent shove as he stood up and stuffed his legal pad into his briefcase.

All right, we're out of here. Come on, Tom.

Biel began to stand unsteadily. Briar-Gold took him by the elbow. It was time to talk fast, but not so fast as to appear desperate. Biel did not need any more of that. Porter kept his voice low to match the control he needed.

Listen Tom, leave now and your situation can only get worse. Won't you at least let me finish? Just sit down and listen, that's all. I think I can help you if you'll let me.

Biel was dead weight in Briar-Gold's grip. He slipped free. Briar-Gold remained standing in a frozen plea for mobility as Biel fell back into his chair, releasing the smell of sweated leather.

Help me? You can't help me.

Maybe you're looking at this the wrong way. I want you to focus on the love you say you have for Holly. I believe you. Now I want you to forget about yourself for a moment and concentrate on what's best for her. She isn't here to speak for herself. She's gone. It may be hard to accept but you have to try. There's nothing you can do that is going to bring her back. But she can do one thing for you with that same love, and that is convince you to honor her memory by it, by owning up to your responsibility to her. Because no one can do that one thing for her except you. I want you to picture her standing here, now, right in front of you. Isn't that what she would want?

Biel stared blankly, somewhere internal, at a memory, or a projection of her ghost. His posture was subdued but Porter could feel the heat coming off him from clear across the table. Briar-Gold lowered his voice to a whisper, tried to talk him off the ledge.

Come on, Tom. Let's go get some air.

Biel spoke to his hands.

What would be the point of that? It's the same air she's not breathing.

Mister Porter—Listen to me, Tom, this is not in your best interest—I need a moment with my client.

Porter ignored him.

Just remember, Tom. It isn't about you anymore. It's about Holly.

Biel was either unwilling or unable to obey his attorney's efforts to get him up and out of the room, but Briar-Gold got Biel turned in his chair enough to put Biel's back to Porter. He squatted for a face-to-face with his client, spewing sibilant urgency. Biel was tired and insistent. Beyond that all Porter got was pieces:

Bob...enough...I know what to do.

When Biel turned back around he squared up to the table. Briar-Gold took his chair again, but seemed to have forgotten his briefcase in his lap. Biel spoke first.

I know it was an accident because I was there.

Porter had his whys and hows but this was not the time to ask. Biel was moving on with or without him anyway.

Holly was spending a lot of time with Harry, but it wasn't what everyone wants to think. She was working on a story. Harry was supposed to be helping her. You think I didn't know that? I think she was a little naïve about how much she could expect from him, but that's all there was. It's my fault. She wanted my help too, but I could only give her so much, same as Harry. I thought, I think we both thought she would look around and conclude that the sky was blue and that would be the end of it. But she wouldn't leave it alone and let me make it work. She wanted things simpler. That's what I was worried about, not about her and Harry. You see, unlike a lot of people, my wife and I trust each other, and I really don't give a damn what other people think about that. What matters to me, because it would matter to her, is that she isn't remembered as the woman who killed herself, and not just because she is Catholic. She is so much more than that. What happened was...

Porter waited. They all waited, but Biel was off somewhere to the side, drawing a curtain down the left side of his face with his eyes, then he raised it back up.

You see, I knew she was going up the coast that night to see Harry, so there couldn't have been much going on, now could there?

There was no way Porter was going to respond to that, and he did not have to glance over at Joel to know he did not have to worry about him, either.

What happened was, I finished some district business up in Crescent City and I thought I would drive down and surprise her, spend our weekend together on the coast. It was also convenient, since I was thinking that it was time to have a heart to heart with her about what her work was costing me. Besides, the rumors about her and the governor were becoming disruptive, and I wanted her to know it was particularly bad judgment to agree to meet him in some hideaway. My joining her there would stifle conjecture about that. I called her just as I got to the turnoff and she told me she had just left. She sounded upset, but she wouldn't say what was wrong. The service was bad. We kept getting cut off. Finally, I asked her to just pull over and wait. I wasn't sure if she heard me, but I found her parked at a pullout a few minutes later. I walked over to her window and I could tell right away something was really wrong. She wouldn't look at me. She didn't want to talk, she said she was tired and she just wanted to go home; we could talk there.

To this day I can't figure for the life of me why she pulled over and waited for me then. If she didn't want to talk to me, why didn't she just keep driving? I would never have known the difference. Maybe she had something she wanted to tell me, too, but changed her mind when I got there. What I saw was she was distraught, and I didn't want her driving in that condition. I started to walk around the car to get in so we could talk, but she said no, we could talk when we got home. She started to drive away and said she just wanted to be alone for a while. I started running along beside her trying to get her to stop so we could talk, and then I saw the edge of the cliff and I yelled stop, stop. She had her head out the window, yelling at me to just leave her alone. She went a little faster, and I kept running and yelling stop. I even tried to reach in and turn off the key, and then she turned around and saw.

Porter found himself looking at the top of Biel's head, and wondered when it was he had lost eye contact.

Couldn't she—? Did she do or say anything?

Biel drew a shuddering breath.

She said Tom. Just, Tom. And then she was gone.

Porter sat listening, waiting for a sound that was never coming. There was only the plummeting silence, then some clearing of throats, both his and Joel's.

What happened then, Tom?

Biel had to push against the table just to get his head up and looked around as if the answer might be written on the walls somewhere other than Porter's face.

Nothing. There was nothing I could do. I heard crashing and tumbling and then a big splash, but I couldn't see. I couldn't even get down the cliff to see if—I couldn't see anything, just black ocean. I yelled for her but there was just the wind. I tried to call for help but I couldn't get a signal. I got in my car and started driving, hoping to get to a place where I could call for help, but it was all dead, and I kept going and going. At some point I guess I just kept going.

Joel's blank look overflowed with dubious: Oh, please.

Briar-Gold came in, too loud.

What my client is trying to say is that it was an accident that he was powerless to prevent, although he tried. You did contact the authorities though, didn't you, Tom?

Biel nodded.

I called 9-1-1 from a pay phone in Braxton.

Joel interjected: Did you identify yourself?

Biel shook his head. Briar-Gold placed a hand on his shoulder.

Gentlemen, you have to appreciate my client's mental state. Tom had just experienced the traumatic loss of his wife, a loss he felt responsible for even though it was entirely accidental, and in the midst of his grief and anguish he made a poor decision. That's all.

Biel had more.

You have to understand, I thought I was protecting her, from just—just this type of speculation. Maybe what happened was bound to happen, but it wasn't what either of us intended. It was just an accident. That's all it was. The rest is nobody's business.

Porter could see how it might have happened like that. He could also see how he might have been handed an extra helping of self-serving. Joel's glance said he was full of it, too.

Thank you, Tom. I appreciate that. However, you have to see that your actions have resulted in just the sort of attention you hoped to avoid. I know this is painful, but I have a few things I still need to clear up. Are you sure you were alone when you met your wife?

Biel turned to Briar-Gold—

I'm sorry, Bob. Maybe you were right.

—and then he turned back to Porter.

You're pretending to hear, but you haven't been listening. You want to turn this into some kind of conspiracy you can tie up with a neat bow.

I just want to get at the truth.

No you don't. You want my life to conform to your myopic list of culpabilities. That there has to be a bad guy here. There is nothing in the world harder than trying to make someone see what you see when they don't want to, which is why my wife is dead. All I'm guilty of is loving my wife too much to protect her from herself.

As you say, but put yourself in my shoes. How can I know this for sure? Have you any proof?

What, that I love my wife or that I'm not responsible for her death? I can't prove either. Why don't you try putting yourself in *my* shoes?

To Porter, Biel's shoes were looking like abandonment at best. He was not prepared to venture into that, personally or professionally.

I'd like nothing better, but when you won't answer a question, I'm left to wonder. Again, were you alone? Is there anything else you haven't told me that will help clear this up?

Porter could see that Biel was agitated now, furiously scrubbing the tabletop back and forth with his palms as though he would push the table away, then pull it back. Now he had his thumbs over the edge with his fingers drumming on top, thinking. His eyes came up on Porter, decided.

Have it your way.

Biel was reaching inside his coat as he spoke, for what Porter supposed might be his cell, a letter, a pack of cigarettes, but what came out was a chrome, small-frame Smith revolver, which Biel jostled in his hand in the guise of a man guessing its weight, unmindful that it was pointed right at Porter, propelling Porter past shock at its sudden, other-worldly appearance, and past his internal plea bargain: *This can't be happening—Surely he intends some unexpected explanation, a confession, a twisted joke.*

Joel yelled: *Gun.*

The table was too wide for a lunge. There was no time to duck under it, which would have been a trap anyway. The nearest door was behind Biel. Porter had to do it right if he wanted any chance—a good grip. He was half standing, regretting immediately his enlarged target as his chair hit the wall behind him with the backward slam of his knees. His off hand grabbed the edge of the table for leverage while his gun hand found his lapel, followed it down and swept his coat tail back away from his hip. He could already see his first rounds scattering papers and ripping the polished mahogany in his haste, which was pretty standard for cops starting last, and then a round would catch Biel somewhere at the belt line as he worked his way up.

And then he closed his fist around air and he saw his gun laying inert, implacable, entombed in its little mailbox locked downstairs. And he is sinking, slipping down a muddy slope, weak and sick, losing his grasp on code red as he slides toward the edge, into the code-black hole of the barrel that is opening up in front of him, wide enough to meet the walls that are closing in on either side, squeezing together at the back, tighter than the inside of the car he is strapped into beside Holly Morris, skidding down that funnel to a black precipice, hurtling toward the edge of the blacker black while he fumbles at the latch. But he can barely move his shoulders in the tiny car, especially with Anita and the Osario boy crowded in back, shoving hysterically against his seatback. Too late. Nothing to grab but the dashboard because they are going over. Now they are sliding sideways as the gun barrel begins to heave in an excruciating arc. He grabs for the wheel, pulls and pulls to keep that turn, but they are still sliding, sliding. Then a tire explodes with the slam of a thick law book on the table. It makes him jump, makes Biel cough a red mist and recoil into his chair where his expression disposes itself inward. His head begins an inexorable drift back behind a blue haze, there to face a terminal engagement with the ceiling as roses bloom on the smoking ruin of his shirtfront.

Porter's wrist hurt. He saw his fingers vising the table edge, marveled at the bright wine pinprick constellations that had flown across the table from Biel, across the scattered papers and up the back of his hand. Joel was yelling: *Dammit, Dammit.* Briar-Gold was pressed against the wall, hugging his briefcase with the desperate face of a small boy who won a panda on the midway only to be told he had to give it back. Porter pawed for a handkerchief to wipe his hand. Failed at that, too. Vomited.

CHAPTER XX

A CURE FOR ABSOLUTION

The capitol guards all came rushing in, fetched by the gun's report or the alacritous Bill. Of course they all had *their* guns. Had them out and pointed, too, which Joel was quite vocal about, especially when they insisted on proning out the three men still breathing and patting them down, which only jacked Joel up even more, to the point they threatened to leave his cuffs on. Porter had to listen to all this with his face on the floor within inches of his own vomit, and told them to shut up and use their goddamn eyes instead of the rookie manual. The guards were nothing if not too careful. They dutifully donned their rubber gloves to check Biel's carotid, bending over carefully so as not to sully their tan and blues. No one ventured to suggest mouth to mouth, their sense of duty ending at Biel's countenance, which the capitol's finest were only too eager to accept at face value.

Then the parade of paramedics, CHP brass, forensic techs, coroner, district attorney investigators and DOJ suits, none of whom Porter knew, which hit him with a mixture of estrangement and gratitude that no one he knew would see him, and he would not have to see them, engaged in this surreal pantomime. Nobody was taking anything for granted now. Butt covering was on all their faces as they took the three of them downstairs into separate rooms and presumably asked them all the same questions three or four times by various self-importants over the next however many hours. An eon or two later, memorable if only for the uncommonly drinkable coffee, Warren walked in, handed him his gun and asked him if he wanted to call his wife.

Porter only accepted because Warren was handing him his own cell phone, the suits having wandered off with Porter's. It would have been rude to decline the gesture. Anita sounded pro-forma sympathetic.

I'm sorry, Michael. So you're OK? You didn't shoot anyone?

Was she missing the point or was he? Had she no imagination whatsoever or was he imagining that she was not past bothering to try? What would it take? More than he had left to offer, apparently. Short of him shorting out, having a breakdown of some sort right there on the phone in front of Warren, she was signing his release papers before he had even been admitted, as if ambulatory met her standard of care.

No, I'm fine.

Well, OK. Good. Thanks for letting me know before I heard it on the news. That poor man. His poor wife. Do you need a ride home or anything? I'm in the middle of a parent teacher conference right now, but I could be downtown in about an hour and a half.

No, he did not. He was not a piece of dry cleaning waiting for pickup. He gave Warren back his phone. Joel met them in the hall, did a lazy Heil Hitler, wanting to slap him a high five, then saw his face and dropped his hand.

Come on, Mike, you were awesome. Where'd that come from?

What?

That bit with Biel. That was some performance. It was like you were right inside his head looking out. How'd you know?

I didn't. (What had Joel seen?) It just felt like there was a scab, so I was picking.

Well, you sure knew where to pick. Did you think he was going to do you?

Yes. Can we get out of here?

Warren steered them away from the front doors and took them downstairs to the basement garage, having been granted use of a members-only elevator that made it belatedly obvious how Biel had bypassed security with his revolver. After they got in the car and hit the top of the ramp he could see why the members privilege had been extended to them; the street out front was lined with white trucks and vans sporting satellite dishes on boom antennas spiraled with black techno-chic cable like a monochromatic dry run for Christmas streetlight decorations of tinsel boas and candy canes. The support crews by the vans paused in their cable stringing and scrutinized their passage out into traffic. Warren stayed on script.

Tell me you left me out of it.

Porter almost felt sorry for him.

I just told them it was an official investigation, and I was acting on orders. You and Maddie can get your story up and tell them whatever you want.

Warren hmmphed: Speak of the devil, and flipped open his phone.

Hello, Madeline, we were just talking about you. Yes, they're both OK. Me? That's up to you. For me, you were short-handed and wanted somebody good on auto fraud to tag some bases. That's as far as I'm going unless I have to, but I'm not falling on any swords. Yeah, they're both with me. Here.

Warren handed his phone over to Porter. Maddie's: *How are you doing?* sounded so sincere he could not tell if it was just worry about her own position, or if some of this splatter had rattled her dedication to tossing staff around like so many spurious warrants.

Terrific. You?

And she was off, breathlessly apologetic, conciliatory, and probing for nuggets to offer in her own defense. It really was not his problem, and he gave her only the half-listen of a man on the phone to a neurotic mother as they made the corner and he could see the west steps lit like a stage, reporters with their cameramen in scattered knots against the columned backdrop.

Maddie was all about the great job he had done, and how she wanted to get together after the holidays and see what could be done to improve his situation. What Biel said now made sense.

My situation? What the hell would you know about that, Maddie? You get that I could be dead right now? That we helped destroy a man? And we still don't really know squat.

Now she was overtly her old self.

He built his own box, Michael. You want to own that, that's your business. My advice is let it go. Go home. Get some rest.

And the governor? He gets a pass on this? Vaneros is involved. I just don't know if it was his personal relationship with Morris that sent Biel after her or if she was chasing down one of their schemes, maybe both. Either way it undercuts Biel's story that it was an accident. And no, I'm not saying I think he killed his wife. I'm saying we can't prove he did or didn't unless we make some other people squirm. At minimum we need to know who the governor called just before midnight that night.

Let it go, Michael. It's as good as a confession. Vaneros is a non-issue anyway. Didn't you hear? They certified the recount this afternoon. Vaneros is out, Gorman is in, and things over here are changing as we speak. Go home to your wife. Have some turkey. I'll call you next week.

His wife. He was beyond any more explaining for one day. He told Maddie he thought Warren had something he wanted to say and handed the phone back to Warren, who did in fact look like a man with second and third thoughts, and so took the opportunity that was handed him with no sign that he saw the subterfuge, or the funk of the man sitting next to him pondering the never-mind winterscape that Maddie would whitewash over the dead man's portrait as backdrop for a holiday greeting card scene of pristine make believe. He could see it in soft focus: the country farmhouse with snow on the roof, a smoking chimney and a light in the kitchen welcoming the family arriving at grandma's house by horse-drawn sleigh. Joel's hand came over the back seat and landed on his shoulder.

Think about it. He armed himself before the interview. It wasn't a spur of the moment thing.

It was our interview. We never should have agreed to that setup.

So, what, you're upset because we didn't control the interview better or because we can't control the world? Biel could have just as easily dumped us both. Fuck him. I'm happy to be breathing.

Profoundly relieved was more like it, that Biel had been in a position to give them both what he made it clear they profusely deserved, and then passed on the opportunity as irrelevant to his flight of self-distraction. He had not absolved them of anything. Just weighed his commitment, taken his time, simply dismissed the two functionaries as having discharged their tedious conceit of duty. All Porter had accomplished was to pull down the mask on a profoundly spent man who was way past his lease on self-regard. If he found himself in Biel's shoes would he be any more willing to face the truth about himself, or would he prefer to keep painting over his facade? Biel's orderly boxes of old coins could not possibly be any more of a sanctuary than Porter's own scrapbook of his museum and art gallery trysts—those cheap and tawdry substitutes for genuine engagement, not the least of it with himself—his myriad forms. And, indirectly or not, intended or not, Biel had his wife's blood on his hands. Blood he had tried to hide. So perhaps Biel could be excused if not forgiven for executing his escape clause. His perspective might have changed given time, but the meantime would have been a tortuous gamble; no hobby, new wardrobe or hairstyle could unchain Biel from the bumper of that tumbling car any more than Porter's suit and tie would severe him from the betrayal on Alejandro Osario's face as it met the pavement, or Anita's in the aftermath. So if it got to where he felt he needed to tear off his canvas and stretch a new one or, more precisely in Biel's case, skip his confederate coin across the Styx, who could blame him? A personal deceit was one thing; a public sham unveiled would be a whole other purgatory. But it was a fatal misstep not to see the inadvertent opening Biel offered up with his challenge to switch shoes. Biel was reflecting Porter's suggestion, even if the intent was to rebuff him. If he had absorbed that instead of being so quick to reject Biel's retort, he might have responded: *It sounds like we are both saying the same thing. So it would seem we should be in agreement—Neither one of us may like the fit, but sometimes you have to accept what's given, put one foot in front of the other and you will find yourself moving forward again.* And taken his own advice.

Joel must have heard his silence as concurrence and left Porter alone. Warren drove on, in his shiny black town car full of well-meaning coats and ties.

Around the car the fog had almost lifted as they drove west along Capitol Mall, and then the day lost resolve, the retrograde marked with frozen halos adhering around the street lights. Warren dropped them at their car on a side street of abandoned office buildings as flocks of crows wheeled with hoarse cries, flaring in restless clouds among the stark branches blackening against a smeared sunset. Porter and Joel declined Warren's offer to meet at Heywood's for a drink, and then immediately agreed that was just what they needed as they watched the steam sputtering away with Warren's tailpipe.

It was a mistake. Heywood's was just a lunch and happy-hour hideout that encouraged drinkers to fling peanut shells on the floor in an overworked presumption of ambience as thin as the flat-screen sportscasters' attempts to make their run-ups to the next day's football games sound as compelling as the contests themselves. Joel's offhand toast was as apt in capturing the accumulation of the day's events.

Here's to dodging a bullet, even if we didn't exactly close the case.

Porter gave his glass a half-hearted clink.

It's probably as closed as it's likely to get, even if some other people ought to get their noses rubbed in it. Hol—Morris deserved better, but, yeah, we're through.

Well, I'm good. Whether he killed her or not is beside the point. Either way he screwed himself.

Porter thought what he could not say: Perhaps Biel deserved better, too.

I don't think we are ever going to know, Joel, but down deep I really don't think he did. Otherwise, all he had to do was keep his mouth shut and say he talked to her on the phone but never saw her. Even if we had let him think we found his tire tracks and footprints at the pullout with hers he could have claimed it was just coincidence. It was the logical place for anyone to pull over if they were trying to get cell reception, and we have no real proof they were there at the same time. So why kill yourself? He could only be blaming himself or thinking he was still protecting her, her and her perfectible world view. We'll never know unless we know why she was up there. But Maddie isn't about to OK issuing subpoenas to lame-duck governors, not with what amounts to a dying declaration. How convenient. That should satisfy the courts and, most likely, her family.

I don't get you, Mike. Why are you still having heartburn about this?

Because, without all the facts, there is still too much rumor and innuendo floating around for everyone involved. There could be some people looking for scapegoats, dead or alive. I wouldn't be surprised to wake up tomorrow and read that she was a round-heeled, headline-happy parasite, or we are a couple of renegade bureau dicks who hounded a politician to death about his wife's suicide. It could be weeks or never before the papers figure out Morris and Biel might have gotten in the way of each other's dope crusade. In the meantime, there's these two dumb investigators to fry. Anyway, I hope we're out of it, but

I'm keeping my notes.

Joel waived the bartender back over.

Well, here's to renegade-free tomorrows then.

Porter did not feel much like raising a glass to that. Perhaps he could lose himself momentarily in Joel's.

Any big plans?

Tomorrow? Just dinner with my folks, some in-laws. You?

(Great.)

My parents are both gone. Anita will be heading up to the snow to join the kids at her parents.

Joel fiddled with his glass, had something to say.

You should go see her. She shouldn't be alone tonight. Neither should you.

She didn't give me that impression. Anyway, it's not happening.

Joel still would not look at him, was talking to the mirror behind the cash register.

Are you absolutely sure about that?

Absolutely. Let's get out of here.

They gulped their second round as they stood up, as though they did this all the time and were used to being in a hurry, even if it was just to put the day behind them. They split up back at the office, shook hands and wished each other a happy Thanksgiving in the parking lot. Joel was still standing there watching him as Porter turned and walked to his car. Just what he needed, Joel acting concerned for him. He could not wait to be free of that, got in his car and drove off, and then was disappointed with his success.

CHAPTER XXI

PRESS HARD

On the way out of town someone honked and blew around him using the oncoming lane. Shit or get off. He pulled to the curb, seeing finally that his driving had been unconscious, tentative, and he realized he had been fighting to keep his car from drifting to the side for blocks.

What did he know? Not much, apparently. What did he care? Too much, or not enough? The luxury of the working class; the things that could be said to take precedence were infinite. No, he was not some librarian fretting about leaving a cart of books unshelved, a baker at home in bed wondering if he had remembered to turn off the oven, but was he any different than a sheet rocker regretting a hole left unpatched at some Section 8 remodel while ignoring the steaming crater of his very own bachelor apartment? Time to admit it, Anita was a cold case he had C-filed for years, dusting off the box every once and awhile but not really doing much to follow up on any clues. They had so much in common. They had nothing in common, and probably never did except for their fantasies. She wanted a champion. She got stuck with him. He wanted a fairy-tale bride. He mistook one for her. They were still in love. They had no clue what that was, unless blame was how they spelled it. How would they ever know, especially if Anita was no better than he was, just reviewing her notes in a half-hearted manner, like the way he had been driving, letting a more recent case hijack his attention?

He needed a phone booth, which was what he now realized that he had been looking for. They were hard to find these days. There was a nice bank of mahogany confessionals outside the committee rooms upstairs back at the capitol. Glass-doored, complete with bench seats. That would have been perfect, nice and private and quiet today, although it would help to have a host of lobbyists scurrying by to blend in with, but he could not go back there. Then he looked across the street. There was an actual full-sized relic booth still standing sentry at one of the older gas stations. He would not have to shout in the wind at one of the newer waist-high kiosks that were themselves disappearing before the cell phone onslaught. The door had the familiar screech swinging closed, the reek of urine and the auditory nod to privacy that was as much as a folding piece of transparency provided. He put the phone to his ear for the benefit of the few passing cars, listened to his own breathing while he stared at the button array as if it were a code to be deciphered, felt the wind on his ankles through the gap at the bottom of the glass. Even drug dealers did not do business like this anymore. After a while he felt ridiculous just standing there and cuddled the sticky earpiece to his shoulder while he read the card in one hand, poked with the other. There was a shoombling and swishing, voices in the background, laughter, then an introductory cough.

Dylan Frank.

I suppose you heard Assemblyman Biel checked out. You need to know you can probably quit looking over your shoulder.

Hang on.

More shooshing. The background celebration receded as Frank withdrew down some hall or into a closet.

Who is this? Is this Michael Porter?

Sorry to disappoint you.

If it is, you should know I protect my sources.

How do you know I'm not the one protecting you?

I thought you said I could stop looking over my shoulder.

Let's just say this will help make sure I'm never the guy you have to watch out for. Got a pencil?

Sure, but I also have some standards.

Porter savored the boozy plastic cigarette smell coming back at him from the handset.

Save it. You and I both know you're not going to hang up until you've heard what I have to say. You can check it out later. That is, if you have standards.

The tinny party noise became his laugh track.

Funny. OK, what have you got?

The story you were working on with Morris. Here are a few people you might want to talk to.

He came out of the booth wanting to wash his hands. He was the loosest of cannons now, indiscriminate, recoiling on this stranger who had to be obsessed to employ such tactics. Like the sky darkening over this day, knowing it needed doing was small comfort. The crows had settled down for the night, the street now deserted. He could hear the click of the signal lights trip inside the control box at the corner, following its hardwired instructions. His feet stalled at the curb even though the light was his. There was a soft freeway rush skipping to him along the canyon of empty buildings. People were picking up their turkeys and pies, hurrying to relatives, breaking their water a week before their due date, fixing flats, working late, passing a joint, getting in their desperate flirts, buying lottery tickets before the seven p.m. cutoff, buying a bottle, picking off drunk drivers, picking up their kids at preschool, up in the attic dragging down boxes to get a jump on the neighbors' outdoor displays, playing with the dog, setting out a centerpiece of dried squash and flowers, walking hand in hand, visiting the coroner to identify the remains, huddling around a trash fire. The cold was getting into his bones. He should get moving. Move along. Get home if he had one. In that respect, too, he was as shiftless as the bums at Discovery Park. When his light turned red, he walked.

CHAPTER XXII

CASE SUMMARY

He was an altar boy, a hit man, a triathlete. She was a high diver, a travel agent, a ballroom dance teacher. Every day he swept the sanctuary, pulled his tights, and sprinted with his pistol from mark to mark. She corrected posture and demoed steps at her third floor studio, dove out the window into the courtyard fountain below promptly at three on Tuesdays and Thursdays, then spun an imaginary partner across the street to the travel agency to paint itineraries for tourists and idlers drawn to her plunging neckline. One day her splashdown caught him on the footrace leg, squelched his censer, soaked his tights, fouled his pistol. How could he blend in now? Sneak up unawares? Do the whack? Perfect his escape? But she too was drenched, standing there slippery as a smuggler flicking finger paints in his face. He had to admit she had a good turnout. A good half gainer, now that he thought back. He could use her for cover, just two lost vacationers out for a dip. First he had to lose the tights. Go for the trunks. Hey, hey, she wanted to know, what's in it for me? Was he thinking out loud? He told her she could pick the color. She laughed black in his face, saying it would match his pretty pistol. He was astound-ed. It shows? She coughed a small cough. Oh, right. The tights. What say the back pew? Midnight. I'll even light some candles. She took his hand. Placed it on her waist. Not good enough. You know the agency would not approve. First you must dance with me. This is easy. One just goes so. And so. And she was right. They were elated, over the crowd. Hovered above tele-phone pole crossbars, shimmering wires. Drifted on the breeze to her third floor window. She floated in. He stumbled across the sill, blinded by bliss. Anyone could do this. Except him. The room had been painted over, but he had been here before. It was a trap. He flew, or rather fled, having remembered he had forgotten. The dancing. The how. Sweet harmony. How they sprung arrested breath, their spurtive exhalations gusting the pages of their class schedules and hymnals off her day bed and out the window to mingle and burst on the wind. Would he see her again? After the class, after the splash, after her phone shift, depending. What did she know about dependent? He, too, was contingent, on the advent calendar, on finding a cold throw-down gun, blisters. He was late for mass, for the mark, for the set-go. She watched his flit. Blew him a kiss as he plummeted to the fountain. He wanted her anything but up there. She wanted him nothing but. Now she was some-where within. He was somewhere without. Flailing. They were in love, in synch, perpetually in a stasis of transient orbits on thousand-year intersects. Call this year a near miss. He missed the fountain. Smashed into a news rack. The secret was out. They would never see each other again, at least not the same. He risked a peek. Saw her hanging out of her blouse and the window, fanning herself with his performance review, looking disappointed. He could see himself looking back at himself tiny in her ocean eyes. Too much. He grew dizzy. Sank. Re-surfaced to a gathering sky, with paramedic exertions raining in his face. They had the wrong victim. She had dropped her paintbrush. He grabbed it, sprang up and ran across the street to the agency to find her. It would only take a minute.

CHAPTER XXIII

ICE OUT

In concert with a failed marriage it was sleep in name only, and after what seemed hours of wandering through empty corridors and vacant capitol committee rooms he swung his feet over the side and rubbed his face. It was still dark, but in November that meant nothing; it could be seven o'clock. He turned on the light and looked at the bedside clock. Not even close, which matched his failed attempt to gather enough votes in time, or whatever he had been after. He knew from long bouts with this that he might as well get up. Hot coffee might be the counterintuitive flood to send his boat back to sea. It had worked before.

No luck there either. He found himself leaning against the kitchen counter with an empty cup, cold toes on the linoleum, his head too full for his apartment's barren walls of white sheetrock. The light on his answering machine was blinking.

—Porter, this is Toby Sim. I heard. Tough break. Did you change your shorts yet? Listen, I got a call from Howard Zephur. He didn't have your number and figured you wouldn't be back in the office until Monday, so he called me. Wanted you to know sooner rather than later because he didn't want it hanging over him. Biel had a falling out with Vaneros because he found out Vaneros was stifling his drive for a referendum to legalize pot. Seems one of the Mexican cartels was funneling money into Vaneros' re-election and so Vaneros was happy with the status quo. Biel wasn't too picky about his backers either, drug companies and tobacco, but at least they were arguably domestic, and legalization would have put a crimp in dope imports, especially if more states picked it up. So Vaneros was screwing them both, Biel and Morris. Morris didn't like any of it and was about to blow them both up in the press. That's why Biel wanted to track her down that night—to talk her out of it. Oh, and it seems Maddie was freelancing with you. Thought she was doing Gorman a favor without needing to be asked. As governor-elect he was not happy to find out about it. Maddie doesn't know it yet, but she is history. Looks like I will be taking her place and I need a team I can trust. You interested? You've got Maddie shit all over you, but I know you're a good soldier and you were just doing your job. I can probably get you hosed off if you want to come back to DOJ. Let me know—

—Wednesday, five thirty-seven p.m.

A team he could trust. And if the players could not be trusted to stay in character? Porter stood looking at the machine for a moment, then hit the erase button. Dissolution seemed to be more the order of the day. The inevitable diaspora of people wandering in flight from, or in pursuit of, their own nature. Anita would call it constructive abandonment, whether or not it met the legal definition. The feeling was mutual. It remained to be seen if he had built himself a monk's cell or been released from one. One thing was sure, Joel was right; he should go see Anita, even if it was just to say good-bye. Biel never had the chance, if what he said was true. Celeste never had the chance. He would be the bigger fool if he kept waiting for something he could do something about. With the kids gone he wouldn't have to maneuver Anita aside to settle what they both already knew.

He got dressed by habit and realized he was staring at his front door, patting himself down for his keys. He could be a man going anywhere: for milk and eggs, for vacation, for good.

The streets were on holiday, that much was clear. Slumbering under a dark blanket of asphalt, the world was swept free of humanity in what could have been an everlasting display of gratitude for having endured and survived mankind's gifts. Yet here he was sullying the scene, his passing rumble a brash echo of the aggregate snoring behind the stucco-sided bedroom walls along his old street. His upstart breath fogging his windshield the only warmth visible in a world otherwise frozen in its natural state. The papers were not even out yet. So much for his plan to walk in behind the folds of get-out-of-town presidential fowl pardons, holiday recipes and Black Friday ads. What was he thinking? And he could not very well sit in his car waiting in front of his own house for his own wife to wake up. Awkward would not begin to describe it, especially—

He pulled over to the curb, ignoring the urge to double check the house number.

—especially with Joel's car parked in his driveway.

He ticked off the immediate observations that went with the most obvious one while his engine alternately raced and purred. House dark. Joel's trunk lid and rear window sparkling with frosted dew.

What was the evening news drill for a man in his position? Simply absurd: Gun too close at hand. Rounds: eleven plus one. Joel probably armed, too, but asleep in a strange house. There would be fumbling. He could walk it blindfolded.

His horror-tinged shudder merged with a tremor of self-mirth. He could hear Tina saying: *As if, Dad.* To go with that, he would have to be a mental bankrupt just drunk enough to convince himself he was too loaded to know right from wrong. He was neither. He was just a man on a street that was not his anymore. Besides, where would that leave the kids? Maybe they already knew; it would explain a few things. So make it official. Might make visitation simpler without their mother lurking nearby, hanging crepe. Hadn't he come here to green light her life anyway, with his implicit acquiescence to a scenario just such as this? She knew he drove by, especially mornings. Either Joel convinced her he was taking the day off, or she had grown tired of the game and decided it was time for his wake-up. Maybe Joel just came by to fill in for his absent partner. Yeah, sure. Or to get some consolation of his own, more likely. Wine thing led to another and they overslept. What difference did it make? Joel might be a better fit anyway. Anita could use a jogging partner. One who still thought a day chasing deliberate falsehoods was engaging enough. Was its own reward: a surrogate truth. It might even be healthier in some respects.

He caught himself watching himself in his rearview mirror. Joel. Anita. You never saw your own nose unless you were looking in the mirror.

So what to do with it? It seemed he had the wrong subject. Also the wrong form. The one he had would be of marginal use even if it could be altered—

<table>
<tr><td colspan="2">State of California
DEPARTMENT OF CORRECTIONS AND REHABILITATION

RELEASE FROM CUSTODY / PAROLE

Parole Board Decision: <u>2010A-2378</u>
Date: <u>11/23/2009</u></td><td>Release Date
____

Institution:

CALIFORNIA ~~WOMEN'S~~ MEN'S COLONY</td></tr>
<tr><td>Inmate</td><td colspan="2">~~Porter, Anita, Ann~~
Porter, Michael, Glen</td></tr>
<tr><td>Aliases</td><td colspan="2">1) Husband; 2) Father</td></tr>
<tr><td>Scars / Tattoos</td><td colspan="2">None visible</td></tr>
<tr><td>Criminal ~~Her~~History</td><td colspan="2">1) Corruption:
Vision, Devotions, Aesthetic.

2) False Personation:
All the world is not a stage.</td></tr>
<tr><td>Parole Officer</td><td colspan="2">TBD—None currently available</td></tr>
<tr><td>Substance Abuse Cure</td><td colspan="2">Cold Turkey</td></tr>
<tr><td>Halfway House</td><td colspan="2">Riverside Townhouses
3214 River Ave., Unit # 2511
Roseville, CA 95661</td></tr>
<tr><td>Skills/Education</td><td>M.F.A.
(Gen Ed)</td><td>Peripatetic School</td></tr>
<tr><td>Gainful Employment Offer</td><td colspan="2">Define gainful.</td></tr>
<tr><td>Demonstrated Commitment</td><td colspan="2">Time Served.</td></tr>
<tr><td>Support Resources</td><td colspan="2">Minimal*: Annual Pass: Artesian Museum of Modern Art.
*Waiver Required</td></tr>
<tr><td>Warden</td><td>Signature</td><td>Date</td></tr>
</table>

DOC Form 1199 (REV 11/2007)

—but it was the only form he had thought to bring. All he had besides was his car still in drive with his foot on the brake, which he released, and the car embarked on a forward glide as though of its own volition, unmoored, carried forward with the flow on a black river at ice out. He was going to need a new partner all right. Or two. For now he would survey the riverbanks of sidewalk unfolding alongside, paperless. The other driveways, all empty. The other homes, dark, asleep, innocent. An imitation of perfection no form could equal.

CHAPTER XXIV

PAINTING BLINDFOLDED

She stood on her deck with her coffee cup, waking up, squinting at the rumpled comforter of blinding white, at the fluffy pillows of fog that rendered the foreground out to her horizon as obliterated as the bland canvas she had waiting inside. Both held a seascape submerged somewhere beneath, her painting an abandoned mess of scale or proportion she could not reconcile, and so she had whitewashed the whole thing for a fresh start. But now what? Even her telescope was not going to penetrate the clouds poured to a level halfway up the ridge. It was alluringly wrong to sit here warming in the sun while her work was somewhere down there in the mist, beyond wishes or artifice. There was nothing to do but pack her stuff in the truck and drive down into it or she was going to waste the whole morning waiting for the fog to dissolve, if it even would.

She had to start getting used to it anyway. Ruth and Al were throwing in the towel, were going to put the land up for sale and get a small place closer to Redding, paved roads, and doctors. And now that it was happening she could see it was just a pattern that repeated in a design not of her choosing, at least not at the frayed edges: people moving in with their ideas and energy just exploding, digging and hammering and making love to create something, even if it was just their own replication before the tiredness set in, or the world moved on. The world was moving on without her, but she had not grown tired of it enough to move to Redding. She would find a place in town and make do, and in a way she was a bit more than resigned, relieved to realize—OK, admit—she had been holding her breath, living underwater ever since Owen was gone, knowing that today was really only a broken hip or another of Ruth's heart episodes away despite what Ruth or Al or any of them wanted.

So it was pack up the easel, the tubes of paint, some rags and brushes, crank up the truck and dive into the fog. Through the towering second growth with tops lost in mist, past ghostly stumps of their forebears the size of squat, limbless water tanks covered in moss and pan-sized brackets of fungi, down to the T of the coast highway, which always took too long to get to and was always a bit of surprise when she did. Time to come to after the interminable curves.

There were more cars than usual in that there were any at all—two headed south and one headed north—what constituted the pre-holiday rush of people headed to their second homes on the coast, or perhaps to relatives, which were more likely the ones going south. Part of the trade-off of moving here was enduring a flood of visitors when they first heard, which quickly dwindled to a trickle after a few years when friends and relatives figured out the getaway visits came at a price: hours in the car on bad roads. Older relatives were not up to the trip in the first place, so if you wanted a family sit-down it meant driving to the city. She told them this year was out since Ruth and Al needed help, and she was family to them anyway, but that was tomorrow. Today she had to decide up or down coast. She was free to toss a coin if she wanted, but then she might as well paint blindfolded. She sat there idling at the edge of the blacktop, waiting for a sense of pull one direction or the other.

The pull ended up south, or more a rejection of up coast toward Breakwater, whose beaches and coves were getting so familiar she could not see them anymore. They had become photos of cousins passed in the hall so many times the walls may as well have been bare. Still, it would have been nice to have some destination in mind. Otherwise she was just driving, aimless. There was not much in the way of beaches down this way, just cliffs and rocks, and she had too much stuff to hike very far. She needed a vantage point with some interest, but not too far from the road. The fog was lifting, too, just when she was getting its mood, so the morning was slipping away with some expensive gas which gradually made the search more urgent, made inspiration elusive behind her increasing sense of frustrated purpose. At the next corner she simply pulled over on the shoulder and got out.

When she looked over the edge there was nothing but black water far below the straggle of brush at the road edge, unfurling a northwest swell circling the bend of coast as the waves curled inland around the point she stood on. The road behind her slanted down across the face and disappeared around curve after curve, baring a shoulder here and there as it crossed each spur ridge, then was gone in the trees again as it fell to the momentary resolve of bridge across the creek the cape was named for, spanning the graveyard of a millworks that had long since been reduced to the jagged headstones of a few ghostly pilings in the willow- and alder-choked channel.

Most people, even a lot of locals, did not know and would hardly believe there had once been a town at the creek's mouth even if they had heard about the mill. The tendency was to see a thing as confined to, and dimensioned by, the corporeal, visible only within sight of the immediate and tangible, as unknowable as the hereafter absent any sort of monument to a foregone context. Yet, industrious, maybe foolish people had survived down there for a time, until they figured out that the creek was too small and the flows too irregular to float logs down to the mill with any reliability. Next they tried splash dams of giant pilings that they cabled together to trap the water along with a raft of logs before they dynamited the dams in succession to create a timber-crested flood. The logs jackstrawed in the narrow canyon, making tumblestick dams of their profits that had to be dynamited in turn. The canyon walls were too steep to push a practical and affordable railroad very far inland either, and after the easy trees in the front lands were gone the town drifted away too, the mill torn down for other mills, for fences, barns and squatter shacks.

The cars driving now up the opposite canyon wall on a feat of common modern engineering hubris, ascending to the view at Hell's Corner, were most likely carrying people who thought Hallelujah was what the road engineer thought when he finally crossed the ridge, but it was really a cartographer's nod to a venture that was anything but triumphant, that briefly drew breath as a fleeting and sanguine prophecy far removed from any consummate fulfillment.

Above the road cut was another thousand feet to the cape's invisible yet inevitable crest punched clear through the overcast ceiling, dropping its vertical axis straight to the water like the edge of the earth tipped on end. How many people from a teeming world full to overflowing had been jostled off that brink while the sea removed a few more inches of the cape every year? The water had to be full of lost souls, and if that was true, it meant Owen was not really alone, which meant she did not have to carry this all alone either. Here was her spot.

She set up her easel but despaired at the prospect of paint tubes, brushes and mixing. It was a direct connection she wanted, and if she could have reached across the distance and traced the cape's profile with her finger to imprint its outline, touch its mass and form so that she could see it with her eyes closed, she would have done it. She did the next best thing, took up a charcoal pencil, looked and looked until the spine of land burned white when she crushed her eyes shut, and launched.

Later she could recall the swish of tires rounding the curve behind her, the rumble of trucks struggling up the grade, someone even honked at her, but as she sketched she heard nothing at all except the surf shushing far below and the wind kissing her ears, sounds and smells coming back to her after one of those warm afternoons when Owen would come up behind her and gather her, slide his hands underneath her arms, encircle her waist, then seek her hands, his fingers smooth and cool along the insides of her wrists. It was not Owen, but Porter who had been the first man to make her feel like that, and he did not even know it. He had been way too self-conscious. But he could be distracted, pulled away from himself for a moment to just let go, and then he could bring her—to a place like this.

But they were both just sightseeing. The rest of the time Porter did not seem to really know who he was or what he wanted. He looked to be just trying on hats, and she sensed she was a bad fit, or he was. Porter also did not know he had made her suspect that her work was shallow, even as he told her he liked it. His compliments only made her question his taste and judgment both as he claimed to see depths in her work she had not imagined or attempted. The constant effort to deflect his praise only made her start to doubt herself, too. She did not need a mistaken acolyte. It was exhausting, and got to be a bore. She had been so easily bored. And while the younger Porter continued to waste his flattery, she came to see her painting back then really was facile, superficial, clumsy profiles of means to ends, impatient outlines of places to get to, not places to be. It took coming up here to slow down enough, to look close enough, to see the feeling in order to paint it. See also that her mistake had been thinking she could pull another box off a shelf, only to wonder if new and improved was a figment, until she met Owen, and then Owen was gone, too.

But along came Porter again, anything but new, or much improved, but at least resigned enough about life or himself to see her more clearly. He could certainly do that. It made her shiver.

And now here she was, sketching portraits of permanent impermanence, the top of the cape unquestionably somewhere up there in the clouds, but the top had to be both presumed and imagined, accepted as enduring by all that there was to see or in memory. She had just the outlines of a foundation but the proportions felt right, only—only it was still too remote. She needed something in the foreground to bring it closer, force the eye, give it some balance, some focus. It needed a human scale that was missing entirely, a grounding to keep the cape from floating off the paper. There was a tiny scrap of sand snuggled up at the bottom, inaccessible except by the waves, a tiny splash of light that might anchor the looming monolith, make it approachable, make it less threatening.

She dug through a wad of lighter pencils wrapped in a faded remnant of one of Owen's plaid flannel shirts. That helped, but reduced to paper it was still a landscape photograph taken with a lens that did not do it justice, the scene rendered as tiny and insignificant as a picture of a place she had never been. She needed to make it her own, but she was not ready to carve her initials into it. A suggestion would have to do. She found a warmer pencil and made the marks tentatively, the way you would touch up a wedding cake with frosting that was almost perfect, but just needed an extra dash of promise, or hope. She stepped back to look. At one end of the beach, almost lost against the rocks, were two stick-like smudges that emerged as a couple if she stood back a ways. They would be easy to overlook, but the fall of rock would take you there, if you bothered.

And now here was the sun, warming the land and the water, and she could enjoy it because she had what she came for without its help. Almost immediately the hillside below took notice, and a breeze gathered a bit of mint and sage from the damp earth smell and offered it upslope to play in her hair as she admired the emerge of blue water from black with shreds of clouds reflected. Last came a hint of brine, from way up here. She had forgotten how good the ocean smelled.

CHAPTER XXV

FREEFORM

Returning to his apartment now was out of the question, and the valley fog congealed around the emergent day impelled him while he took comfort, if not exactly exaltation, in an admitted pretense of escape, of whim, of change. Not since the invention of the automobile was there a man so willing to let his car take him where it would, even if it took perverse joy in trading the valley submerged in white for his nemesis of mountain curves. To do it right, real caprice had to be unplanned, unscripted, outside of any policy internal or external, trusting that there could be agreeable consequences as well as not. He was not very good at this. He had the outlines of a design, but as a Plan B it was pretty weak.

But who was there to call for advice? It was too early and everyone would have other engagements. Besides, the CHP still had his cell phone and all its phone numbers.

Then the interior of the car brightened and he surfaced up out of the fog, warming slowly in the cold winter sunlight as the road wound over a ridge. He had left something else behind, too. Maybe it was the back and forth over the past few days, or maybe it was having no place particular to go. He got into a sort of rhythm bleeding off speed on the approaches, letting the springs settle into the turns, then rolling on the throttle pulling out. After a while it was even a little relaxing. About the time he realized his stomach was going to be all right he smelled the salty sting of the coast, able now to really appreciate gliding along the bluffs above the white lines of surf without his insides crashing. His equilibrium was, if not ebullient, now a little better than neutral. He meant to put his toes in actual sand, actual ocean, even if they froze.

But he was a bit deflated when he hit Breakwater. He did not know what he was expecting, but the streets seemed to have constricted, folded inward as families gathered elsewhere. Everything would be closed, of course, at least until the afternoon when he could see whatever the one-show theater had to offer, but there was the tiny *Open* script in bright green neon at the café. Someone must have left it on in their hurry to close the day before. But the knob turned, and with a bit of extra shove the door unstuck and gave with a tinkle. There was only one person at the counter, leaning desultorily over a spread paper. She looked up and the room overflowed with her smile. He could think of only the stupid and obvious:

What are you doing here on Thanksgiving?

Me? Tuesdays and Thursdays, remember? But only until noon today. What's your excuse?

Excuses he had none, until just that instant. But he was not ready to come right out with it.

I hear the coffee here sucks.

She roused herself and stretched over the counter to grab the pot and got him a mug. He took the stool next to hers while she watched him raptly, this odd forest creature that had wandered into her yard. It brought his head out of his cup, the creature now on alert.

What?

Footloose, huh?

He made for the nearest shrub, went back to his cup with a feint toward the headlines.

Fancy free. What's in the paper?

She pushed it across, pointed out the headline with a slender finger, but the finger with the band of pale was where his eye landed. Perhaps he was not giving her coffee enough credit.

Ruth and Al, mostly. It's been on the radio but the paper is only a weekly so the whole story is just coming out. The letters to the editor are a mix of there-goes-the-neighborhood and the same tired testimonials pushing the medical benefits of marijuana. They caught one of the guys who robbed them. They think the other fled the state.

He had nothing to say to that. They were yesterday's news. If she knew them she was not saying, and he did not want to know. What he wanted went beyond discussions of people who were more into easy withdrawals than risky investments. She had to know that, too. Knew they were just making talk, congealing in the side-by-side inertia of an old married couple with nothing to talk about when there was too much to know where to start. He had to make one, even if he had to dress it in a beige, leafy print.

And how are you?

She said nothing. Then took a breath.

We're all fine, except Al's jaw is wired so he will have to have a turkey and gravy milkshake—

So she was deferring to his camouflage.

—I'm having dinner with them after I close up here. Why don't you come join us? If you won't take it the wrong way, that is, and don't tell me you have business.

So much for camouflage. He deserved it. He could hardly say he just happened to find himself a couple hundred miles from some excuse of a home on today of all days, in this of all places. Where he stood was as threadbare as the second-hand pea coat he froze in those undergraduate winters in San Francisco thinking it stylish, his dissembled ensemble unraveled, rendered transparent. Then as now he need not have bothered. There was not going to be a run through before, and no one was on script anyway; everyone was pushed from the wings cold, blinking in the lights, never quite sure if it was dance or sing, dizzied by the cost of passions more shaded than the twin burdens of black hat or white. The only way through was to improvise. People did what they did, and if you were lucky there might be the occasional duet, or pas de deux. But for a chance at a real engagement, even for a run that was always anybody's guess but where the good nights still made the off nights worthwhile—that amounted to more than a half-hearted attempt at getting in step, in tune—expression was part of the bargain. Exposure. That is, if he wanted a shot at more than a moaning monologue to an empty house. So, was he all in or not? She was not waiting for a bus.

I think I'd like that, more than you can imagine, but—he pointed at himself—like this?

Her look said, *Are you kidding?*

You're fine. If you haven't noticed, it's come-as-you-are around here. Even on Thanksgiving. And you look more comfortable in jeans and a sweatshirt.

He had not given any thought to how he was dressed until now. She was right, though. He felt less constricted, his chest uncramped.

I had this idea about seeing some waves up close. It's been a while. Would there be time for a walk on the beach first?

She gathered the paper and set it aside.

Well, one of the many benefits of being the cook, waitress and dishwasher on Thanksgiving is deciding when it's slow enough to call it noon. Why don't you go window shopping or something and I'll close up.

He held out his hand.

Mind if I take the want-ads with me?

She was incredulous.

You're looking for *work*?

Maybe.

What kind?

I'm not sure, exactly. Busboy? Odd jobs? House painter? What was it you said the other day? *Something else.*

She handed it over, and told him to take his ceramic mug

with him, which was a touching bit of small town VIP treatment. She knew he was coming back, but still it was a tiny but genuine thing he held in his hands, giving outsized warmth in inverse proportion to her offhand, spontaneous benevolence.

Back on the sidewalk, he would never have guessed it from the outside. The café and hotel could use some paint to better suggest the potential of a decent cup of coffee and a bed to do justice to the spectacular surroundings. A lot of the other shabby storefronts could, too, their crumbling aspirations showing more tired pride than recent perspicacity. Dilapidated was just a couple of loose nails past quaint; once that got started it was hard to see a place any differently. But it would not take much to improve things if the town put its mind to it. A little commitment and some fundraising and they could fix up that sagging pier at the end of the street and give tourists a promenade above the waves. It could be a focal point for a travel brochure. And the gallery. It looked pretty dismal with overnight mist still blurring the window. He could hardly make out anything inside. They should shuffle their stock if someone was not going to buy her pastel in the front display. Oh, they had. The style was the same, with a similar theme, but, whereas the other was despairing, this one was, if not exactly hopeful, allowed for the possibility. As an interesting companion piece to the other it was— He looked closer. It was the same picture, but— He palmed the glass. It was the same picture. Where the one dancer had been in the throes of falling, grasping collapse or prostration, he could see now that the other dancer might be in the act of arresting the fall, or inviting an embrace that the first was in the midst of offering, or receiving. Perhaps it was just one figure dancing with its own shadow all along.

And then the dancers were gone, the picture shrouded again, obscured behind a surgent veil. There was just the warmth in his hands, the blood coursing in his ears, the shush of surf somewhere behind him in an arrangement that had fallen out of style, one that slowly tempered the urgent pulsing with a more measured serenity lavished beneath. After a time, there was movement: passing clouds fleeing seaward on the wet glass, chased by gulls wheeling their endless wheels. And a flash just beneath his vision. He looked down and saw his reflection wavering in his cup. Took a sip. There was a companion flicker at the side of his awareness. Two doors up, the café sign went dark, plunging the street back into desolation. He might have imagined the whole thing if not for this cup, which was in fact borrowed. He was asking too much of it to hold so much when what would come of it was anybody's guess—any tourist could stand here sipping.

Anita would say he was in a hurry again, or was just hedging his bets, when the truth was there was suddenly, finally, no rush at all. No, what he intended required as much promise to himself as faith. Might take a while getting used to. And if the gallery was closed? So what? It would surely be open tomorrow. He had no place to get to and he could come back. He had all the time in the world. He could wait a little longer. He had just the place for it.